CW00822910

That Boy's Facts of Life

DAVID ROSS

ISBN 1530137799
ISBN 13: 9781530137794

To Judith, Andrew and Abigail

Book One

↢ Chapter 1 ↣

I came out of nowhere and then I was there.

That's what I remember. Long Island.

I remember a rootless world of no friends and no family, except Mark. But there he was, my older brother, always there, while cold and absent Mom and Dad were busy being cold and absent.

It was Peggy and Mark, Mark and Peggy, isolated together on Long Endless Island.

Until I went off to college. Then it was me hundreds of miles away in New England with Mark back there in his dingy little room in Mom and Dad's sad little house in that lower-middle-class ghetto called home. I missed him and missed him, but he wouldn't answer my texts, emails or phone calls, ever.

No one came to my college graduation and I knew I had to get even farther away from the cretin parents. I didn't owe them anything because they didn't pay a dime for Tufts and they despised me for going to that fancy damned university. I had to get as far away as possible.

And maybe Mark was lost to me and I just had to get used to being completely on my own in the world.

So I came up with a plan and worked long hours for over a year in a restaurant in Boston, managing to save enough money for a train ticket. A sleeper across the country. I had a new job and a new city on my horizon. San Francisco.

First, I had an appointment.

It was September seventh at just after ten in the morning. I walked through a stretch of voices and shoes echoing in the public corridors of the Museum of Fine Arts in Boston. There were a few polished marble galleries before I got to a heavy oak door. Inside, quiet filled the air with soft white light coming from a huge bank of windows along one wall. I was in the Department of Prints, Drawings and Photographs.

I looked at the back half of the long room at three separate desks, each one surrounded by bookcases, making small, beautiful curatorial niches.

There she was with thin silvery hues of hair down past her shoulders, all brushed back. Margy Zorn, the person I left the drawing with the day before, was walking toward me wearing her badge that said she was, *Assistant Curator*. There was a man walking toward me too.

"Peggy, this is Eric Matheson. He's helped me with your drawing."

I didn't bother saying it wasn't mine, that it was my brother's, as I took in Eric Matheson's staff badge stating he was an, *Associate Curator*. So two big worthies were examining the drawing. I couldn't guess the hulking maleman's age, but he looked a few years younger than Margy Zorn.

"So Peggy, yeah, let's see what we know at this point." Margy Zorn was gesturing for me to come around to their side of the table, sticking me between them.

It looked so exposed out of its frame, still in its mat, but small and paper-thin on a big antique oak table.

"Okay. We see pen and brush and brown wash, heightened with white on paper with a dark brown preparation. About eight by ten inches. Um, there's no inscription and there are no collector's stamps and no signature anywhere.

But drawings were seldom signed, especially centuries ago. Anyway, uhh, the watermark . . . we'd have to . . ."

The phone in her left hand was vibrating. She glanced at it turning away, reading some sort of text, then looked directly at me. "Sorry. We have to look at that more closely in the lab on a light table to try to identify the watermark but the paper has very strong laid lines and seems to be what we refer to as, *antique Italian*."

She stopped herself, stepped back and stared at her phone again for a few seconds, her facial muscles tightening. Pointing herself at the drawing, she continued. She said the subject was from the Old Testament, the story of, "Absalom Being Counseled". Her voice was raspy. So was she getting nasty texts? Problems at home?

She went on, "We haven't definitely narrowed it down to any town or region, but we think it's mid to late sixteenth century Italian in style. We might be looking at Florence or Bologna around that time." She paused, looking at me and I looked back, startled.

She bent at the waist, pointing her face at the drawing. "Uh, it's very nicely drawn and not a sketch, but a fairly complete work. And also, the style's intriguing. We've got the elongated figures, the dramatic use of light at night. Star light. And the composition's crowded that way with the sort of otherworldly, but still naturalistic feeling of the work. So, yeah, a good drawing!"

The last bit of excitement was rushed, and she stood straight, coughing away into her fist.

I was stunned. Mark actually found a rare Italian Renaissance drawing? Margy was silent now and Eric was saying nothing, and we all bent down and stared into the little work of art.

A figure with a crown seated in a chair was leaning out toward the left foreground, and behind him there were a few other men gesturing emotionally. They were all in a classical building's portico. In the right background something was going on with a man opening a trap door in the ground and some figures emerging.

It was beautiful, I guessed. Right after Mark gave it to me, I did compare it with drawings in books at Tufts, but I never had a clue and just hid it under the bed in my dorm or later in my apartment.

Now what? It was an important old master drawing lying there and waiting. For what?

She was facing away again, reading some phone messages, and Eric and I stepped back from the table. He remained silent for some reason, just standing by and I glanced. He was tall, about six-two, with a weathered, ruddy face and a full head of light brown hair. His wide forehead stuck out a bit. He wasn't exactly standard handsome but great looking in some way, and he had a very elegant, understated look in that suit. It was a beautiful olive-green gabardine, with almost no shoulder pads suit.

"The condition seems very good, depending upon closer examination by our conservators." Margy turned to me, putting her phone in her skirt's deep pocket.

She was winding up and I needed more.

"Thank you. Wow, that's very exciting. Do you have any idea who the artist might be?"

From her pained expression and from the slow, deep intake of air from Eric, I knew I'd just asked a really stupid question. Margy winced and smiled, shaking her head at me condescendingly, and it looked like Eric wanted to laugh. I felt my whole body contract and I just stood, embarrassed about being embarrassed, like I was fifteen.

Facing the drawing, she said, "No Peggy, but that's the point. We can refer you to someone who specializes in this area, who does formal attributions. We were happy to look at it and get you started, especially because Professor Hemmling at Tufts is such a good friend and she asked us to." Moving only her eyes toward me, Margy laughed. "Good grief, you know how to put on the pressure."

"No." I was going to apologize but she interrupted me, grinning.

"No, sorry, I'm just kidding. I'm bowled over. We know you got it for forty-five dollars. That's amazing! Where? Mind me asking? Boston?"

"New York. My brother found it in a used furniture store, years ago and then at one point he gave it to me. I wanted to send it back to him before I left. I just had to get some information for him." I stopped, not knowing how to finish that story now.

She leaned over, scanning the drawing. "Umm, what a great find! Anyway, no, maybe you'll find it's by or after Guido Reni. Or by one of the many artists who followed Parmigianino, which is more likely." She stood up straight and turned to me again. "You know, an old master artist and worth a lot of money so you'd have to rush off and put it in a bank vault. Not that you'd necessarily want to get into any of that. But no, sorry, it has to be studied by someone who specializes in sixteenth century Italian art."

She stepped away from the drawing. Then, pale, her eyes hollow, she glanced down at the floor and said, "Of course you do know that we don't get into who should attribute things. You have to get some names of dealers and auction houses and you choose."

I nodded, twisting inside. I just needed some basic information and was being told it was somewhere out there out of reach. After a few stilted moments of silence, with all of us standing back gazing down at the little work of art, Eric finally seemed to want to say something as he moved forward and leaned into the drawing.

"Uhm, anyway, Peggy, after further looking and studying you could find it's a sixteenth century, or later, copy after a painting or another drawing or print. It could certainly be a preliminary study for a painting. We don't know much yet. But it's anonymous and may never get a specific artist attribution. You see what we're saying?" He was leaning on the table on his hands and moved his face back and forth from the drawing to me. He had a British accent.

I nodded. I knew he might be a lot of all right, especially according to him, but I really couldn't indulge in endless issues right then.

"Well, actually, I'm on my way." I looked at the clock on the wall for emphasis. "I have a train connection in New York tomorrow."

He nodded, murmuring to himself, "Uh-huh, that's what I was told."

He looked at Margy and she still had her head aimed at the drawing. We were all silent.

I'd get to my train ride.

Eric sighed just audibly, dragging his eyes from me to the table, then to me again. "There are some drawings you could compare it with here today and there are some great Italian drawings at the Harvard Art Museums."

The damned guy was pushy. I said nothing, but I must have looked like I wanted to grab the drawing and run because he said, "Okay. Margy, you said you were going to Matting and Framing anyway, right? Could you take it?"

❧ Chapter 2 ❧

Eric Matheson and I walked slowly and silently to the museum exit. I knew he had something he had to say to me, to explain to me, simple young tool that I was.

Standing near the large Huntington Avenue doors, he turned and faced me. "So anyway Peggy, you can call some of the larger museums in California and ask for their list of referrals for experts in Italian Renaissance art and maybe even more specifically, sixteenth century Italian art. You can tell them we looked at it, so they don't just refer you to some generalist. Okay? You just need someone whose area this is."

"What's your area?" It gushed out of me. His face flushed and his gray-blue eyes narrowed at me and I half wished I'd stayed quiet. But it was kind of funny.

"Uhm, well I studied nineteenth century British art in England and then came here to Yale to study Victorian art, to do research at the Center for British Art. Anyway."

He stopped and shook his head. "But so, you'll find the de Young Museum in San Francisco and south of there, the Getty and the LA County Museum and they should help point you to the right experts in California who can do an attribution like this."

He smiled crookedly and awkwardly at me, with his head back, raised, not seeming to know what to say next. I'd been waiting for over a year for my train ride out. Now this older guy was peering at me. He was some sort of official arbiter of high cools to high and low and he was peering at me. I turned away.

Nothing was said by either of us as we stood watching people walk by. Something like five minutes faded into a very long, agonizing, non-verbal blur before Margy Zorn began arriving in sporadic bits from a distance. She was aimed at us, appearing from behind a group, her beautiful, elegant silver hair weaving through people in the distant corridor, then slowing and disappearing behind another, very slow moving, shuffling, lost looking group. Finally, she was in front of us holding the package of corrugated board and bubble wrap with the framed drawing sandwiched inside.

She handed the package to me, saying, "Thanks for bringing it in, and best of luck." She handed me an information sheet from the Conservation Department. She walked away, weaving again.

That curator just dismissed me and my little work of art. I turned to the other one. "I want to thank you. I appreciate all your time and help. Thanks."

We were both backing up methodically, nodding and I felt relieved as he turned and walked away. But even if I was free to go, I wasn't free of the complicated little drawing.

❧ Chapter 3 ❧

Sweet circumstance, elude, elude
me not here or there
when facts of life intrude, intrude

The next day on the bus, me and the drawing to New York, my poem rode along in my brain. It kept repeating itself, rumbling along, my only poem, written by me when I was seventeen. Seventeen was when I applied to those colleges, all those mystical, liberal arts, top-ranked colleges. Brown, Amherst, Chicago, nope. When Tufts was a yes, with enough financial aid, I was amazed. The glow of Greater Boston was upon me and, maybe after four years there, I'd be a person of great merit.

Maybe I had enough merit to take a long train ride.

After schlepping to Penn Station, I finally made my way to my room. I closed the door and sat and straightened my back, looking around. As a matter of fact, everything I needed was there, perfectly designed for me. I pulled out the brochure from Amtrak that had diagrams and pictures and described my, *Viewliner Standard Bedroom…designed for one or two passengers, with comfortable reclining seats on either side of a sweeping picture window. At night, the seats convert to a bed, and an upper berth with its own picture window folds out from the upper wall.*

I'd ignore the upper berth. The rest was just like I hoped. There was a small niche with my sink and toilet and shower. There were warm lights on the blue walls and enough space to stand in or sit in or run in place in or lie down in and sleep in.

A transporting room of my own. I sat back to let my trip sink into my pores, waiting for the train to move. My laptop and phone were stuffed into my backpack, off for the whole trip. The drawing was stuffed in there too.

Half an hour of everything remaining stationary and it was eight-ten with the train moving in the station, then into the dark, pulling steadily, slowly, out from under the city. The trip would take three and a half days to get to San Francisco, a long time to be suspended that way, somewhere between passive and active.

After the tunnel and the city were behind me, I put on one small light and pulled out an apple, some crackers and some water. There was just the hum and rattle of train movement and the lights from cars and buildings flickering by, sometimes more, sometimes less.

I ate, drank, read and slept. I woke up and sat and gazed. I ran in place and took a shower.

By early the next afternoon we were out of Chicago on a new train and I had another private room, almost the same as before, and even though I slept a lot the night before, it was in odd spurts, turning and glancing out the window, more intoxicated than asleep. So I got a couple of hours sleep in the daylight. Then, sitting in my new chair in my room that had beautiful orange and red striped upholstery and white walls, I saw a big, harsh strip of spread out, ramshackle buildings and bits of rotting pressed board exposed around some windows. If I looked past the plastic billboards and the wires and utility poles, there was the train's reflection in some panes of glass.

I watched knowing I had to write a letter to Mark. He wouldn't answer emails and wouldn't join any social media or text anyone, so a handwritten letter and an envelope stamped, *San Francisco*, was probably the only way to finally, formally say goodbye.

I just had no idea what to write. I was too stuffed with memories.

My favorite memory, probably by far, was Mark standing at my door with a book in his hand, thumb holding a section open, and asking me if I could talk for a minute. It was a really ceremonious question coming from fifteen-year-old Mark, me only twelve years old and all arms and legs.

He found a book online on Classical Greek philosophy or something, and it wasn't like he read many books. But somehow, he could find things.

We were sitting across the room from each other as he read aloud from the philosopher, Empedocles, who wrote something that I only half remember about sexual reproduction being the essential form of love that proves the basic power of love in human lives. Something like that.

Mark moved on to his main point.

"The Greeks divided love into seven aspects." He read slowly and deliberately. "Sexual passion, love of parents, love of children, love of siblings, love of friends, love of country and love of wisdom."

He put the book down and after a second, still speaking slowly, said to me, "I wanted you to hear that. Okay? Seven kinds of love. I mean there's more to the facts of life than sex and so somehow all together those are probably the facts of life. But you'll never hear that from Mom and Dad. You probably won't hear anything, and I don't know why the hell that is. But I'm getting more and more sure it's because they don't know the facts of life."

⟞ Chapter 4 ⟝

More and more time passed with nothing much happening but more train movement and light shimmering through my big window. The passing towns, pastures, strips, suburban sprawl and the sounds of train movement formed an endless show.

But it was time to get to it. I pulled out some paper and a pen, leaned against my window table and wrote.

Dear Mark,

I'm on a train, writing to you with some-where in the Midwest outside my window. I'm moving away to the West Coast, Mark. Of course, Boston is great, but to be honest, just like New York, I don't want it to become my entire world before I get a chance to see the world. And Mark I hope you'll find some way to get away too.

Mom and Dad. Mom and Dad. Mom and Dad. Mom and Dad. (Read that, Mark, to the rhythm of a train taking you away).

I haven't told them I'm doing this yet, but do you know what's on my mind most of all? Not them being upset because they don't give a damn anyway, but I keep getting the sensation of leaving my childhood home for good and you're stuck there for good.

Are you?

You and I always knew our hearts and souls were somewhere else. Mom and Dad knew it too. They ignored us and we ignored them. They were away working or if they were at home, they were off in the kitchen eating, or in bed watching television. We were some-where else.

Mark, you were the one who said, "We need more substance in our lives." Remember? What a kid. You actually said that. More than once.

You were the one who told me how much you loved old Italian movies. I think I was only fourteen years old when you found, The Bicycle Thief *and,* Roma *on your computer and showed them to me, and I had no idea what I was watching. You were the monk who closed your door and sat on the floor listening to a couple of early blues CD's and that one Philip Glass CD, again and again from that little, really old, cheap boom box. You sitting on your floor in a room stripped of everything but a bed and that old black boom box with its black wire poking into the blank white wall.*

I stopped writing, put my pen down, sat back and took in a breath. The sunlight was very strong and right on me, so I had to pull the long shade halfway down.

I'd get back to the letter later, but now I was shaking my head at all the drama. Mark would do fine on his own, even-tually. He was the one who took the first independent steps for us so maybe I should relax and not lose faith in him. My half-shaded room soothed me. It was just enough cover to allow the soft bronze sunlight to flicker on the white walls around me.

After five minutes of taking that in, I stood up and stretched, raised the shade and then walked to my far wall, leaned back and looked out the window.

There were all those journeys with Mark. They were our teen trips out into the world, just us alone, setting off on a commuter train, away from our gigantic, sometimes Irish or Italian or African-American or Hispanic or Middle Eastern or Asian, and yet, still always deadly boring neighborhood, Chauncy Park. It was one of the least distinguished suburban spreads in the middle of what a local disc jockey always squealed was, "flat-as-an-old-roadkill, Long Island".

Actually, the trips started that day we found ourselves at Uncle Ethan's house in Brooklyn. It was lucky because extremely old Uncle Ethan was really Mom's uncle and our parents only took us that one time when Mark and I were still kids. Mark was thirteen and I was ten. That was our first look at the nineteenth century tree-lined cityscape. Suddenly, all around us were beautiful three story, bow front, row houses. Most seemed to be sandstone, some brick. Bay Ridge had been the old family neighborhood, but like so many people back then, our relatives drove away to somewhere new, like suburban Philadelphia or Florida or Long Cretin Island.

Mom and Dad never visited anyone and, except for that time, never went back to Brooklyn. At eighty-one, Uncle Ethan was the only relative still living there.

"He's a relative relic," Mark whispered to me in the car before we got there.

We left the parents and our ancient white haired uncle in the front parlor and I got caught-up in Mark's wide-eyed trance, walking up and down stairs and in and around tall handsome rooms with dark, dry, cracking, creaking floors and floor length, thin white lace curtains blowing just barely in the breeze and very old light fixtures sticking out of walls of the almost totally unrenovated, three story Victorian red brick town house. We walked slowly, looking at the faded nineteenth century wallpaper with beautiful vines everywhere, except one bedroom on the third floor where the wallpaper was a weird, sensual knock-out. It had an orange-pumpkin background with large silver stars stenciled all over the walls. The stars were over two inches tall and they glowed with a cool metallic sheen while the background color looked dry and dull and gorgeous in the opposite way. It was the most beautiful room I had ever seen, by far.

A long-lost year went by with Mom telling us Uncle Ethan was too old for any more visits. One long, cold, socked-in winter afternoon of nothing but Mark and me alone in the dull little brown Long Island box for hours, Mark just phoned Uncle Ethan. Something told him to just do it, and it worked. We got a yes for that Saturday, for a visit from Mark and me.

❧ Chapter 5 ❧

The dry air suddenly turned very wet. It was raining outside my train room window and getting dark, so I turned on the small overhead light and stretched and ran in place for ten minutes, just to limber up. I sat down and watched the window show. I liked the rain streaking against the glass, me moving along sheltered and free.

I snapped open the latch of my metal door and walked down a few cars to get something to drink.

Vibrating back into my room, cardboard tea in hand, I sat down, thinking again, back to the commuter train rides with Mark to Bay Ridge. It was a middle-class area, not very gentrified so it had local shops and old Italian and Irish families. It had genuine charm. We went there every chance we could, seeking the special care and attention of our newfound relative. And we began to learn that old Uncle Ethan was accomplished and well-read and we were very impressed he was a lawyer, the only professional in our family. He came to the United States back when he was twenty-one, after graduating from the National University, Dublin. He went to New York University a few years later, nights, and didn't become a lawyer until he was in his early thirties. All those years later, when he was in our lives, he still ran his own small practice out of an office on the first floor of his Brooklyn house. He couldn't have done much business in his eighties, but it kept him engaged in the world. In fact, his practice was probably never much of a moneymaker because he always worked alone.

But he wasn't alone all his long life waiting for Mark and me, even if we thought otherwise at first. Somewhere buried in his own story was his wife, Mom's Aunt Margaret, who died at least ten years before our first visit, and they had one son who died in a car accident in his late teens.

It only took a few months for Mark and me to learn all those things, nosy little things that we were.

Old fashioned Uncle Ethan told us to not stay out past nine when we started to spend weekends and that was soon after we started going. I managed to get the room with the orange walls and the silver stars, after Mark said he hated that wallpaper.

And the parents seemed to give up on us more and more, first walking away as Mark and I told them how good a time we had and how exciting it was and how nice Uncle Ethan was. They stayed away more and more.

We were gone. We began going to Brooklyn a couple of times a month at least. We'd get to 72nd Street in Bay Ridge around four on Friday, then hang around in our rooms doing homework or reading, aiming to go downstairs to meet up with our uncle when he was finished with work for the day, around six. Then we'd start getting dinner ready while Uncle Ethan washed up and changed his clothes, and we'd all eat and spend Friday night sitting around talking.

Uncle Ethan died at the end of my senior year in high school. Mark had just dropped out of community college for the second time.

❧ Chapter 6 ❧

I was standing, leaning my shoulder against the window, looking through smooth, hard, cold glass. The track seemed even flatter and straighter and the landscape was starting to get gargantuan. The fields the train was crossing were filled with wheat or oats or something and went on forever just like schoolbooks said. Writing and thinking stopped for the day and I felt the quick, lighter rattling, gliding along.

I went down four cars to dinner.

There was only one seat available, across a table from a fifty something couple from Illinois. "Glendale, outside Chicago," they said together, shaking my hand. They looked like dull, dull twins. Both had brown, dyed hair two inches out from their gray scalps. Both had on cheap cotton sweatshirts and some sort of equivalent below. What was it, years of erosion?

There were all sorts of seemingly well developed, interesting looking people around us. I was stuck.

Sharon and Kevin Schmidt. They loved trains and were going to their timeshare in Santa Cruz. They had a lot to say and said it right away. Kevin let me know he had made enough money in his dental supply business to send four kids to college. Two went to Northwestern, then Loyola and some other place were mumbled. Northwestern was broadcast a few times. I had an image of them driving around in a huge SUV with that university's sticker on the rear window.

"What's that, the family jewels?" Kevin pointed his nose and squinted at the odd-looking package in my backpack. I only opened the backpack to get out a sweater. It was colder in the dining car.

"No just a picture," I said.

They both gazed, seeing nothing but bubble wrap, with me just zipping up my backpack again.

"A photograph or painting?" he asked.

"No. Just a drawing."

"Oh-yeah? Is it old or something?"

"No. Yeah, it's old." I tried to think of something else to talk about.

"Yeah? Who did it?"

"No idea. Sorry, I don't know. I'll have to find out."

He sat back, looking at me, old triangular eyes trying to breach the young, smooth, slippery female fortifications, despite having no chance in this world.

"Are you a young collector?" His wife was adjusting herself on her seat, trying to stay excited but with such heavy, sagging, wined and dined eyes.

"No. No, I majored in art history but . . ."

"Art history? Where?" she asked, her whole face straining upward.

"Tufts. Uhh, but I don't know what that thing is." I found myself pointing with my thumb and shrugging like an oaf.

She asked me where I was from. I wanted to just eat and get out of there, but as I said, "Long Island", they nodded, four eyebrows arched, raised for the young East Coast socialite. Jesus Christ.

I washed the cardboard apple pie dessert down with my old ice water and excused myself a few minutes later after a short, rare, silent gap.

DAVID ROSS

The guy who said the mass of men lead lives of, *quiet* desperation was not from the twenty-first century. I was walking fast down rattling, drafty train corridors with my backpack strapped on as usual.

Chest filled with air, back in my room, door locked, I turned off the lights and undressed as quickly as I could, shedding frustration about some of those people out there.

I kicked my backpack and clothes into the corner and stood in the middle of the room, stripped bare, shaking a bit in the cool twilight air. Naked was what I wanted, and I stood still for a few minutes.

Crawling slowly onto the bed, next to the cold hard glass, it was easy to feel raw next to all of creation's endless space. Moving through it, on my hands and knees, then on my back, it was me, present and aware of just me, moving along in my very own secluded nest, just moving along.

There had to be some inspiration to direct the sexual build-up in my brain and the cool air did make me so nicely aware of being so naked.

I saw myself spread out into my very own private orgasm.

But not now.

I pulled the covers over me.

I slept until the early morning sunlight, increasingly warm, cooked me. I managed to raise my head, slowly lifting my body from the dampness below. Face, breasts, thighs, lifting, and moist strands of hair stuck to my face, neck and shoulders, and it was the third day of the train ride and my room. I rolled over, feeling the blankets slide across my flesh and I looked out the window, thinking about nothing but some buried, distant sex.

My eyes were slits, so I only slowly began to take in what was around me. There was light everywhere, not a shadow left.

28

The train was probably somewhere in northern Nevada. There were no people or human things, just flat, hard desert forever. Gray-ochre under the palest hint of infinite air. And we never passed by anything.

About ten minutes into mindlessly staring, I got myself to stand up and get dressed. Food might ease my aching head.

I was starving and dizzy by the time I got back and closed the door, but it was good when the whole grain toast, scrambled eggs and coffee began to fill me. With my table in front and my legs extended, I sat and ate and tried to take in the abstract procession of desert and sky very slowly decomposing and reconstituting next to me. It was as austere and stunning as anything I could ever even imagine.

I watched for half an hour or so but knew I needed to finish the letter. I lifted my shoulders, got myself up, checked that the door was locked, made my bit of air cooler and pulled out what I had already written and read it. Picking up my pen, I continued.

Mark, I'm going to miss you, but I am going to stay out here for a while. A few years maybe. Maybe forever. Come and visit. Please. This trip has brought back all the teen trips we charted. All those journeys to Brooklyn and then, when we got older and braver, on into Manhattan. I was right there with you, Mark. So was Uncle Ethan while we had him. No one else was.

Of course, Mom and Dad never understood what we saw in Uncle Ethan and that was convenient for them and us. But we really had no friends, Mark. Everyone else from our neighborhood was at the mall or being decrepit online or at parties. Not you and me. We were unhinged but then we were lost at sea or some damned, mixed-metaphor thing.

Anyway, I just want to establish myself, somewhere. I only have a nebulous job in San Francisco in an insurance company, but the pays not bad and I need some money to cobble together a life, Mark.

I'll tell you about my life after I've been at it for a while. But one thing I do know at my still unknowing, ripening age, is that move-ment leads to things happening, even if it's only falling off the tree (into the sea, hingeless, cobbling).

Love, Peggy

P.S. - I took the drawing, your drawing, to the Boston Museum of Fine Arts. They said it was really beautiful and probably even sixteenth century Italian! I'll take it to an art dealer in California to get an official attribution - find out who did it. Then I'm sending it back to you. You can start an old master art collection.

Time passed and the train kept rolling along and along. The empty, melancholy feeling at the end of writing the letter grew smaller and more distant as the train moved west and time passed.

The letter would be mailed in San Francisco and that fact was starting to form itself around me as we pushed through hot, dry eastern California toward the cool ocean. I put on my sunglasses. The broad, light blue cloudless sky baked the flat, wide stretches of farms and suburbs and more and more suburbs. I kept thinking I was almost there, but the train just lugged on through the blank light.

A few hours of end-of-the-trip blankness and it was dark as the train pulled itself to a stop, breaks squeaking for some interminable stretch of time, into San Francisco. I had to drag the weight of myself out of my room, from my three and a half days of solitude and repose, out, me dragging three huge, heavy bags and my drawing in its backpack toward an escalator, to manage to get outside, somewhere.

The glaring city lights flooded Mission Street and I breathed in some damp, cold San Francisco night air.

◆ Chapter 7 ◆

For the next few months, I seemed to do nothing but walk and sit. I walked to work and sat there for eight hours and then walked back home and sat. On weekends I just walked and walked for the sake of not sitting. San Francisco offered me beautiful sights and smells, with Pacific air flowing all around me and around long stretches of hills of fetching Victorian and twentieth century and contemporary buildings.

Then I sat inside my itsy bitsy, one-room-with-a-bathroom apartment. It was all I could find online when I was planning my life back in Boston. It was midway up Union Street on Telegraph Hill, one of the best known and most central, attractive areas of town. My tiny studio space was, they claimed, two hundred and seventy-five square feet, and I could never spend a dime on anything but rent and food. But it was only a fifteen-minute walk downhill to work and a thirty-minute haul back up. I had myself a prime location.

The formless, mediocre apartment building was nothing more than aging, graying nineteen seventies white stucco, even inside. Up two floors and inside my place, a chair and a table lamp on the light green wall to wall carpeted floor filled up the living room that was across from the kitchenette. My single bed on the same light green wall to wall carpet filled up the other end of the room.

I went to a consignment store many blocks away and found an old rust colored leather chair for only two hundred dollars. It was fairly dirty and torn and cracked but I figured I'd clean and tape the leather and it didn't smell of mold or mildew.

I was alone a lot, but I was away and that was enough for me. The drawing was between the wall and my bed, stashed safely. It was easy to ignore it. It was easy to ignore all the impossible cautionary notes printed on the art conservation instruction sheet attached to it by those museum people in Boston. They warned me about the ways works of art on paper deteriorate. There was the threat from heat, from cold, from fluctuations of temperature and humidity, and most of all from light.

What a pain in the bewtocks. Maybe Eric Matheson and Margy Zorn, all the way back in Boston, thought I'd go to some dealer out in California to get an attribution for the drawing. Maybe they'd forgotten all about it. They were long gone now.

And I still never heard anything from Mark. There was no response to my letter. The possibility of never hearing from him again loomed somewhere out there in the vast continental divide.

Anyway, I liked my solitary walks up and down hills, crisscrossing my new beautiful city. I'd walk down my pebbled, white stucco hall to the elevator. Some crazy old mechanisms made a lot of noise coming up to me on the third floor. Then I'd clank and shake and creep down to the small lobby, smelling the outside ocean air, more and more.

The strong light would hit me. Down Union Street, the smog mixed with the fog in the morning and the light was almost amber in places. But by mid-morning, the ocean breezes pushed and pulled that away and a crystalline light hit any white walls and contrasted with any colored walls, making the green or blue or sienna stand out sharply. It was fantastic.

Walking was great but sitting at work was just expedient. Days on the job just followed each other, each one with the same amount of certainty that nothing much would happen, and I worked hard so that I was tired at the end of the day, feeling good and worn out. My management trainee salary wasn't at all bad for a twenty-three-year-old, me scrutinizing what seemed like archaic, endless, endless small print kinds of insurance jargon on a computer for the first week. They called them, *simple contracts.* Then I was off to more basic clerical computer work for the rest of time.

I co-mingled at lunch with this person or that, but no one seemed inspiring enough to see after hours. Everyone knows dullness breeds like a brain virus under cheap lighting in big workspaces.

❧ Chapter 8 ❧

The train ride was fading, and I found myself looking for it. I'd probably been looking for it for a while, but one late afternoon, sitting in my room in my chair with the lights out, coffee cup in my lap, I became almost totally enervated. It was a Saturday, almost the end of November, after a tiring work week, me sipping coffee and looking out the window at a five o'clock, half dark, light absorbent sky. No scenes flickered by outside, no rumble inside, just stillness, apart from the occasional hum of the little refrigerator. The sound of unseen cars going by every so often meshed with the thinnest gray chiaroscuro shapes on my ugly old hung ceiling.

I was there for a few months, three thousand miles west and it was very easy for me to be independent. I just couldn't turn down the heat in my miniature apartment and had only one window. So it was the opposite of cross ventilation.

I sat on, stuck to my cracked maroon leather chair and I tried to think of something to do, other than get lost in my computer that I spent two hours on earlier in the day, knowing I could get stuck in that tangled web forever and ever. I couldn't read a book. I just finished Hemingway's "A Farewell to Arms" the night before. I tried the radio a few times already, from news and interviews, to the petty hysteria of pop music stations.

The news was always more and more unnerving. The Chinese and Japanese and Russians and Americans were facing each other down once again, with weapons of mass destruction over islands in the South China Sea. Terrorists were killing anyone they could, anywhere. Rich politicians were running for office.

I began to pace around. Kurt came to mind, and, as usual, reimaging him easily replaced my boredom and fears. There was handsome Kurt at handsome Tufts my sophomore year. It was funny remembering how he thought being a pre-international law student gave him automatic clout that only the youngest undergraduates pretended to have. But I thought he was mighty fine as soon as I saw him. When we met at the Sigma Chi party and talked about hating fraternities and sororities for twenty minutes, it felt like we were bonded. Then we left and walked around the glittering Saturday night version of the beautiful campus on the hill, so excited by how cool we must be. That was our peak. We never reached that romantic height again, not drunk, not stoned. When the quiet recesses of the seductively beautiful library offered me more and more solitary contentment, after a year of having tall, muscular, lithesome, ambitious Kurt as my very own, I finally had to own up. It was awful telling him, watching him go from hurt to relieved in only an hour. But I think he actually hated the arts, and me blathering on about some movie or novel I liked. The sex was very nice. It was very, very nice. In fact, it was just about all I missed later. It was still so irritating when I saw him the end of junior year with that girl from my Modern European History class. They looked so right together. So maybe Kurt and I had only been teen lab rats for each other. I spent some time with interesting guys after Kurt, but I spent more and more time in that library alone, increasingly aware that I was going to graduate some day and move away from the fine university on the fine hill.

Now, I sat down to YouTube to play the old video of Kate Bush in a long white dress, singing and dancing her hypnotic interpretation of "Wuthering Heights". I always loved it. I leaned back and roared with pure glee and played it again. I got up and began to dance around replacing old Kurt with Heathcliff, only adding to the greedy sex and romance on my mind. I did that for about five minutes and finally got a bit worn out emotionally. Plus, I had to be careful not to bother the neighbors below. I debated if I should go out for a walk -- a nice hilly San Francisco schlep. But it was nighttime, and I didn't like walking alone at night.

❧ Chapter 9 ❧

More weeks went by. It was a Wednesday after work and after walking up my hill. I was breathing in short heaves, standing at the mailboxes in my lobby, seeing that I had something more than junk mail. For the first time there was an actual letter addressed to me. I got pretty excited, noting the return address was, *Eric Matheson, Museum of Fine Arts, Boston.*

I opened it carefully, trying to not tear the envelope, and started reading in the elevator. It was hand-written in blue gel ink. The handwriting was an old-fashioned cursive in upright vertical dashes, British style.

> *Dear Ms. Avakian,*
> *I hope you're well. I got your current postal address through Regina Hemmling at Tufts. I hope you don't mind.*

I stopped reading and waited for the rattling elevator doors to pull open, as the whole heavy metal contraption shook with old age.

I might mind. It might be a tad intrusive. Thank God he didn't have my email address or phone number. Or did he?

A minute later, reclined diagonally across my torn, crinkling, leather chair, my legs over one arm and my head on the other, I opened the letter again and read on.

First, let me say I hope we didn't discour-
age you when you were here. While we needed
to state that more consultation with the right
expert would be required for an attribution, I
don't want you to assume it would be an end-
less process. Once you connect with the right
person, whatever can be known about an
anonymous, undocumented drawing, should
be accomplished within a few weeks at most.

So if you would like to get a written attri-
bution for your own satisfaction or to insure
the drawing, I would be happy to send you
names of people I know in San Francisco, the
L.A. County Museum and at the Getty, who
would give you the names of any number of
reputable art experts on the West Coast.

Yours Sincerely,
Eric Matheson
Associate Curator

I stared at the ceiling, breathing in slowly. Maybe he thought I was pretty damned cool walking into the big old Museum of Fine Arts in my new gray flannel skirt and my only cashmere, crew-neck sweater, walking around with an Italian Renaissance drawing in its antique mat and antique frame.

And, since I wasn't actually that person, what was next? Nothing? Nothing would come of nothing, which was better than most things.

I looked out the window at the glossy baby blue sky. For some reason Eric Matheson wanted to push for expert examinations to start out west. They'd be expert examinations for Mark way back there, who wouldn't even talk to me and got rid of the drawing as soon as he could. I stood up.

I got in a shower and I ate some yogurt and a pear. Finally, most of my edgy prevarication exhausted itself and I sat myself down to channel my thoughts and emotions. I put my head back on my cool, then warm old leather chair and looked up at rectangle after rectangle of cheap old Styrofoam ceiling board.

The thing was, I always saw the drawing as Mark's. And the thing was, he seemed to treat the drawing like a hot potato. We were on one of our early Manhattan trips, staying with Uncle Ethan for the weekend and traipsing through a Tribeca junk shop with no goals in mind, and Mark picked up the thing off the floor in the back of the shop that was filled up to the ceiling with estate furniture or something. He began looking at it at angles and I noticed that and went over to him.

"Wow. Interesting," he grumbled, gripping the picture tightly, his head pointed at it.

He had that glazed-dazed expression he could get, barely moving or blinking. The picture really was strange looking. There were a lot of pictures in the place but that one had a multicolored paper border around it and an old frame that was partly broken. The glass was filthy but not broken. I looked out of the corner of my eye at the old guy who was bending his neck like a barn owl, leering at us from his chair in the corner. But Mark just stood holding the picture at arm's length and staring, seeming to sense he had a hold of something good.

A few minutes later we were out the door with the thing. "Forty-five buckaroos", were the only words ever uttered by the old barn owl, who never got up from his chair but was clearly happy when we paid in cash.

"It's great." Finally, Mark said something. He held it under his arm as we walked quickly toward the subway.

"What is it?" I was frustrated that we'd just spent so much money on the weird thing.

He just shook his head and began discussing our plans for the rest of the day. Forty-five dollars wasn't a disposable amount of money for us and I always resented the way Mark would pay no attention to how much money we had and be so impulsive. Once again, we were searching our pockets to see if we had enough money to take the subway. A few weeks before we had to panhandle for the two dollars we were short, begging next to the subway station for over two hours before we finally had enough. We got home after dinner, cold, hungry and filled with feeble excuses. Uncle Ethan sat us down and gave us a stern talking to about being mature and responsible.

This time I'd buried a few dollars in my coat pocket just in case. Mark didn't flinch as I uncovered them.

We were sitting on the subway to Brooklyn, the drawing on the floor behind Mark's feet and me seeing him in the rippling, shaking black window across from us. I just didn't want to ignore practical issues. He was so philosophical. He was doing that now.

"The East Village, Tribeca, and whatever, are not the places they're trumped-up to be. It's like, really, we'll turn into freaking goats if we keep going there. You know, eating up anything that's put in front of us. Yeah, like that great scene in that old Disney movie, Pinocchio where the kids get lured to Pleasure Island and turn into donkeys. Man! It's like, I had nightmares after seeing that because it was so, you know, all around us and shit, I mean, it is all around us. Pleasure Island."

I nodded, trying to not get totally lost in his thoughts. He'd even find depth in the really old kiddie movies Uncle Ethan bought us. Eighty-four-year-old Uncle Ethan, from Ireland, had no idea what was current or would appeal to American kids our age. Or maybe he did.

"What is it, Mark? You have any idea?"

"Yeah, it's like, a nice drawing or a reproduction of some great old thing. Shit, you know, there's definitely something beautiful about it." He was warding-off the responsibility question that was in the air between us.

He gave me his attempt at a dry look, his eyes calmer, both of us dancing gently in our seats to the shaking and loud metallic clankings of the train.

"I'll give it to Uncle Ethan." He was slouched, looking around. "I don't want anything like it in my life. Uhh, it's like, you know, just too old. I want to keep things simple right now and that thing's too, uhh, like, delicate, or . . ." He shrugged. "I think he'll like it since he has those big books on art in the living room." He turned away from me.

I got as reasonable as I could. "I don't know if we should give it to Uncle Ethan. It's nice. But, you know, for one thing the frame's all dirty and broken and the glass is scratched or something. We don't want him wondering what the hell we're doing. Right?"

Nothing was said for a minute. I began to laugh, just nervously at first, but then more in that way I knew would get me going. Mark turned to look at me. After watching me fight for control, he started to laugh a bit.

"Yeah, well . . ." I stopped myself from laughing barely enough to get some words out, "Maybe somebody on this train will give us a couple of bucks for it, or some food. Think anyone here has an apple on them?"

Mark liked that and got red and looked around the car with his head half down and his eyes looking up.

He said, "Leftover mac and cheese? Old meatloaf on rye?"

I howled and had to put my hand over my mouth.

So he said, "Let's stand on it and wipe our shoes on it."

Now we were both undone.

We were leaning, moaning, tears pouring from me after a minute and Mark groaning. People were watching.

At some point he was leaning forward, supporting his shaking upper body, covering his face with his hands. I was trying to not look at that but falling back and to the right side away from him, falling into convulsions, unable to stop. I'd get an image of the stupid looking frame with some weird picture in it, all seeming unbelievably absurd, just plain hysterical. My stomach hurt. The subway car was half filled, and we found our way earlier to the least crowded end, but just about everyone was looking at us now. The old woman with the large box in her lap, diagonally across from us made me gasp and shake every time I saw her. She got pinched looking and pursed her lips and that just sent me off. I tried to stop, breathing in and out, but even if I stopped for half a minute or a whole minute, something, usually Mark, would get me laughing again.

Ten minutes later we were standing up and struggling to get off at our stop, leaning on seats to support ourselves. Something about having to stand up and having those people look, like when the old woman with the big box on her lap moved her feet away and glared at us, undid any composure. We just made it out before the doors closed, stumbling into a new crowd of people. The cold air and strange faces sobered me up almost immediately, but Mark not for a couple of minutes, trudging up the steps.

That Christmas the picture was received by Uncle Ethan with accolades, as expected even if we'd given him a pair of socks.

Mark was excited and pretty soon on a roll.

"But I just like drawings, uhh, really more than paintings. There's something about them? You know? They're smaller and, you know, what's the word? You know what I mean? It's like you could just look at them closely and on your own. Like pictures in books, you sit alone in a chair. I don't know. You know what I mean? Uhh, what's the word?"

"Right. I know. Intimate?" Uncle Ethan said, and I was relieved because I only had a vague sense what Mark was getting at. I wished he'd be quiet.

Uncle Ethan was getting a concerned look on his face. He said, "It's beautiful. And I thank you both. The frame and the mat are really unusual. Umm, extremely attractive. Where did you get it? I'm sorry, I don't want to spoil any of the surprise, but the frame and the mat look antique and so special. The frame's actual tortoise shell." He sat up straighter.

"I think it's just a reproduction." I looked at Uncle Ethan and then Mark, as maturely and calmly as I could. I didn't want it to look like we'd spent a fortune on the crazy thing. "Mark just found it on the floor in a used furniture store in the city."

I didn't say we had to fix up the old frame. The guy in the frame shop in Brooklyn Heights seemed to really love the thing. The mat was an old French Mat, he said. He said it was gorgeous and would really be with a bit of brushing off. But he thought the mat and antique frame alone were worth a lot more than the price of his work. And then we were told it would cost two hundred and seventy dollars plus change to get the acid free materials put in and the frame glued.

I had a part time job at Panera Bread and Mark worked at Macy's warehouse and we barely managed to pay all of that bill and still buy a few other presents. But Uncle Ethan seemed to really like the picture and that was the important thing.

✧ Chapter 10 ✧

It was a brisk, damp, sunny day at work, a couple of weeks after getting Eric Matheson's letter, when I decided I should phone Margy Zorn. I'd avoid nasty, arcane old Eric Matheson.

I waited until lunchtime and flew instantly across time and space and culture right into the Department of Prints and Drawings in Boston. The department assistant's greeting echoed in my phone.

I was passed on to the raspy voice of Zorn.

"Hi Peggy. How's your drawing?"

"Fine, uh, I'm calling from San Francisco, but I wanted to get a bit of advice. First, I want to thank you once again for all your help this past September."

"Happy to help."

"I received a letter from Eric Matheson about two weeks ago, and he wanted to encourage me to get a formal attribution from an expert out here. He also said he could give me names of people in museums here who might give me names of dealers, I guess."

"Oh. I didn't know he wrote to you. I mean you can just call any major museum there and they'll have lists of independent people they know who give attributions."

I fumbled, wondering how much a formal attribution would cost. "No, I understand that. But really, I had a concern. I'm guessing the drawing's unusual enough, so I have to find

DAVID ROSS

the right specialist. So I probably can't just pick out someone randomly from a list. I mean, meanwhile I can't insure it until I know what it is, of course. And what it's worth."

"Umm. You know Peggy, I'm glad you phoned. You seem slightly reluctant to take the next step. But I do get that you're sort of on your own making a fairly complicated choice. After the people in museums give you some names, who do you pick? So maybe what you'd like to do is research the drawing yourself a bit. It wouldn't take an enormous amount of commitment. Then any information you've gathered might make you more comfortable or more prepared to get a formal, written attribution. You'd know more and maybe even hear names of experts. Right? Curatorial staff have to be careful and unbiased, but you'd get who they really recommend out there soon enough. And then, after finding an Italian Renaissance specialist, you'd get an attribution and things like insurance would be easily resolved." Her tone was somewhere between impatient and patronizing.

"No, I will take the drawing to a museum. I was just calling basically to say that." It was a stretch, but I was feeling annoyed because she seemed to be talking down to me. Meanwhile, I was feeling more reluctant if I had to do a lot of research, whatever that meant.

There was a pause.

"Sorry, Peggy. It's just that, obviously you can do nothing but just hang it on a wall. It's your drawing. Look, Peggy, you studied art history at Tufts, right?"

"Yes."

"Yeah, great. Well why not enjoy the research? Do you plan to go on to graduate school?"

I tried to catch a cogent thought. "I don't think I can afford to."

"Oh, well, let's hope money won't be a problem. Do you want to pursue a career in the arts?"

"Yes." I had to say yes to accomplished, established, rich and sophisticated Margy Zorn, or sound like a dud. I didn't want to work for insurance companies for the rest of my life, but I sure as hell didn't want to get into huge debt.

I had no idea where this conversation was heading. She grunted and was silent, putting some sort of thoughts about me together as I waited in darkness, very sorry I bothered calling.

"You know what? I know someone at Stanford who likes nothing more than Renaissance drawings. He'd love your mysterious one. I could send him a copy of the picture we took of it and tell him about you? Would you like that?"

"Uhh, sure." I was becoming stupefied, squeezing the phone.

"Yeah, Andy Zimmer. He's Chair of the Art History Department and we're old friends and he owes me. I'll tell you what. I know how hard it is to get into these graduate programs and get scholarship money these days. If you'd like we could feed his ego by asking for his help with the drawing and then I'll tell him about your interest in Stanford. If you are interested."

"Yeah, I am, very much," spewed right out of me.

I said nothing more as she talked about the Stanford art history department that she thought was one of the best. She ended it with, "So, obviously, you can find great art collections where you are now to get started researching." She took an audible breath, a long one.

She was sorry she lectured me about not following through with the drawing, so she was going to push for me to get into Stanford? With a scholarship of some kind?

I said, "No, I'd love to do research on it under someone's supervision."

"Okay, good. So I'll pursue Andy Zimmer."

I was too hyped to hear her last words or mine toward saying goodbye.

❧ Chapter 11 ❧

I got back into my work and home alone routine but with voices whispering somewhere outside my window about Stanford. It was there. It was almost impossible to get into, but it was out there, south of me somewhere, nearby, about an hour away. Could I get accepted the way she seemed to be suggesting? Margy Zorn might help me? Pictures online showed me tall dark palm trees all around brilliant California Spanish arcades, all around old baked sandstone buildings with rows of open stony arches and dark red tiled roofs everywhere. Libraries and galleries and lecture rooms were somewhere inside the shadows of all those stunning old arches. It all undulated so provocatively. I really wanted to undulate with it.

Meanwhile, I couldn't do any actual, serious research into the drawing before at least a few years of graduate school. No matter what, it would be years before I gave it back to Mark.

I just had to wait to hear from Margy Zorn or her contact at Stanford.

At least I was getting a heck of a lot of reading done, like Thomas Hardy for the first time. Cool late fall winds came in my window finally, and the heat never stopped churning from the radiator, mingling with the wind and blowing across my room. That was it for the next few weeks in my apartment, in my tiny nest on the sun blanched hill. I seldom went out after work, except to the small, expensive grocery store, "Foodstuffs", down the street – a few hundred square feet of wall to ceiling Italian tile and cool spotlights on expensive organic produce.

I became distracted one Saturday, too distracted to read. Thoughts of the drawing festered and I searched online for the Old Testament, "Story of Absalom". After sifting through extraneous texts, it appeared.

> *Absalom Being Counseled by Ahitopel and Hushai: Old Testament, chapters 14-18. Absalom rebels against his father, King David. Absalom is known for his great beauty, especially his long hair, a source of pride. David's adviser, Ahitopel, joins the rebellion. Hushai, another of King David's advisers, warns the king and plots with David. Hushai pretends to join the rebellion and gives Absalom bad advice. The rebellion fails and Absalom hangs, caught by his hair in a tree. He dies.*

Okay. I read it a few times. So parent-child relations can be good or get nasty and there's good advice and bad advice. And our pride and vanity can kill us.

I got up from my chair. The drawing was still hiding between my bed and the wall. The dust back there was disgusting. I leaned the drawing against the wall near my window, wiping the frame and glass with a sock from my laundry basket. I made myself a cup of coffee, swallowing a few gulps after I sat cross-legged on the floor. I planted my eyes, remembering the times I stared at the thing in my dorm or later in my Medford apartment near Tufts, trying to take it in, gripping the little thing, but not really ever seeing it.

Now I held the drawing in both hands, stayed sitting on the floor, and looked. My eyes followed the long strokes and short strokes of pen and ink and wash, of figures and some ground and some architecture. Definitely an Italian scene. My eyes did what they were supposed to do next. Extraneous or unconvincing pen strokes? No, none. It was beautiful and there was some sort of great compositional whole. I stared on for another few minutes.

I got the Boston museum's conservation sheet that had the address on its letterhead and knelt on the floor, leaned over and wrote on a post card.

> *Mr. Eric Matheson,*
> *Thanks for your advice. I will research the drawing on my own and will let you know if I need names of people out here. Once again, thank you.*
>
> *Sincerely,*
> *Peggy Avakian*

I wouldn't email him and be open to emails back. He'd be put off by the dismissive tone of the short note, especially since it took me over a month to answer him.

I stood and glanced out my living room window. The sun looked like it just hit the white painted stucco five story building across the street, denser and more strident than the thin white light in New England.

Walking outside, instead of sitting by myself, I was moving in a good steady rhythm. It would be one of those three-hour, extensive walks.

Along the way I had an inspiration. When I got back, I wrote on a postcard, vintage telegram style.

> *To Mark Avakian:*
> *Arrived Pacific Ocean. No more land. Please advise.*

❧ Chapter 12 ❧

Days and days and nights and nights on a dull hill with my mind stuck on nothing in particular. In the middle of that state a little card came from Mark. It had a reproduction of a Birket Foster wood engraving on it of evergreens and snow in black and white. I read it haltingly at my mailbox in the front hallway of my building. It was the first communication from Mark in almost four years.

> *Peggy, Merry Christmas.*
> *I don't get the idea of just moving around. If you don't have any more land maybe it means you have to stop the movement. Mom and Dad are getting older and that's not easy for anyone. So they're going through some rough stuff too. They need us now, so I guess it is time for us to be the adults.*
>
> *Mark*

Making my way by slow elevator up to my apartment and shaking my head in pain, I was unable to accept it. He was concerned about Mom and Dad? He would have loved a funny little telegram like that years ago. He used to send me emails with a few lines on them when we were kids. But the point was, he stopped a long time ago. Cry all I wanted, that was the point.

A little more than a week later I was sitting in my chair in that familiar diagonal position with a card in my hand that had just arrived from my parents. My Christmas card to them and theirs back was always the only contact there was.

Dear Peggy,

Dad and I were happy to hear you got a job after that expensive college. Better than waiting on tables. It sounds like it might pay a decent wage and train you for the future. Hold onto to it for as long as you can. Decent jobs are hard to find.

The weather has been awful and cold and shitty but it doesn't bother us as much because we're warm with our new pellet stove in the living room! Finally did it! Those workmen drove us nuts. We wanted it to lower the cost of heating.

Merry Christmas and happy New Year.

Love,
Mom and Dad

I got up and put the card down on the counter between the living room and kitchen area. I flicked at it with my finger and it flopped onto the kitchen floor.

I sat down to think about Uncle Ethan. There was that one time he followed through so incredibly well. It was an October and it was dark and cold out and I was mesmerized by his flickering old spirit fully materializing in front of us in that crowded public space, JT's restaurant, in the Village, near New York University. I was a senior in high school and Mark was in his second try at community college not far away from our house on Long Island. We were still close, and we had hung around the N.Y.U. campus many times and in a sense this was just one more Friday night of kids pretending to be cool. Except we were getting older and we were waiting for our very, especially old uncle.

I came up with the invitation to help Mark. I already knew he wasn't thrilled with his industrial park looking college. He complained about it being boring and he didn't seem to make any friends there. I was a squirt, but I already knew, basically, that education and money amounted to power in the world. But just then sitting there looking at Mark, any power issues felt threatening. I wasn't exactly sure why and it scared me.

We weren't talking. We were gazing around at the space and the people. The space was early twentieth century, with narrow dark green painted iron beams on the ceiling matched by heavier green iron posts throughout the open big room. The floor was a mosaic, geometric pattern throughout of blue and red small marble tiles that were worn and faded. The people there were all the epitome of sophisticated college students engrossed in each other and drinking and laughing and ignoring us.

I got up and went to the bathroom out of dire need, not wanting to miss Uncle Ethan arriving and sure enough, just as I sat back down at the table, Mark raised his hand to wave at the door and I turned and there he was. My heart filled with the sight of him, me sensing the wonder and envy of people around us. He loomed tall in his dark forest green, heavy wool overcoat and he seemed planted down into those heavy black leather shoes he wore, that I always figured he bought in some obscure store owned by Russian emigres or something. He always wore narrow stripped silk ties. They didn't make them like Uncle Ethan anymore.

His thin, combed back white hair accentuated his long sloping nose with pronounced nostrils and large, light blue eyes and rough gray skin.

He gave us both a one-armed hug and a warm kiss on the cheek, holding onto his overcoat and long scarf with his other hand.

"Yes, what a nice place, yes. This will be terrific. Much better than just eating at home tonight." He still had a quiet Irish lilt to his voice.

We all ate a version of salad and chatted. Mark and I described our long-lasting enthusiasm for JT's. And Uncle Ethan smiled and listened. After three cakes and coffees appeared for us, I began what was obviously my prepared speech.

"Yeah, so, Mark, I found some legal papers when I was cleaning up in the living room a few weeks ago and I didn't read them. Mom and Dad were at work, but I knew I shouldn't because, once I got started reading I could see right away that they were to do with Mom and Dad and Uncle Ethan and the sale of a house in Bay Ridge."

Mark was quiet so I went on, "Well, I decided I should ask Uncle Ethan about it. And I did."

"Mark," Uncle Ethan said. "I didn't want your sister to get the wrong impression, a negative impression about what went on with the house, your grandparent's house. It was left to me, but everyone expected that I would eventually pass it on to your mother and father. I'm sorry your grandparents passed away before you got to know them, but they were good to me and, yes, they had me write their will."

"Umm," I spoke up. "Yeah, Grandpa gave you the house, right, Uncle Ethan? I mean, he left the house to you, and then Mom and Dad asked you to sell it before you even had a chance to live in it, right?" All my blood pumped to my head because we never wanted to speak too bluntly or disrespectfully to Uncle Ethan.

"Uh, well I don't want you or Mark to think things were all that fixed. Your grandfather was clear enough in his long-term intentions and I just sped things up a bit."

"I could see what happened. Right, Mark?"

"Um, yeah," Mark mumbled.

"Mom and Dad -- well, you and I too -- we benefited from the sale of Uncle Ethan's house. Uncle Ethan didn't have to sell it. And rent a house a block away."

Uncle Ethan stepped in, "No, no, no. Well, see, I didn't want to move anyway. I get my house for a good rent with rent control. Your parents presented their case very effectively. They were living in that small house and your house now, in Chauncy Park, is larger I'm told and does have a nice yard. And your parents didn't force any issues or emotions and I decided with plenty of time that, yes, we could sell the house and split up the money gained. I don't want to preempt your point, Peggy, but I want to keep things in a certain perspective, that your mother and father needed to purchase a new house and raise a family and I only needed to maintain an already established law practice."

Mark looked at Uncle Ethan with blank eyes. I was surprised by his lack of reaction and waited.

He turned to me, saying quietly, "Uncle Ethan lost out. Yeah, his chance to live in that house."

"No." Uncle Ethan raised his head and studied Mark for a second, then turned to me. "You two understand I have no regrets here? I want no recriminations?"

"Okay." I was a mix of chastised and seething.

"Your parents always had your best interests at heart, and I am old school I guess because I think honoring one's parents is a cardinal rule. Anyway, there's much more to life than money or houses."

I nodded solemnly, having to acknowledge such noble values, but it all seemed to exhaust Mark, who sat dull-eyed and listless.

"Well . . ." I sat up, feeling the need to follow through with my mission. "But, okay, during our talk back a couple of weeks ago Uncle Ethan asked me what colleges I was applying to, and I mean, it was like, I began to ask him why he was asking and I began to get suspicious and finally, after being a pain for ten minutes and asking questions, I found out Uncle Ethan agreed to let Mom and Dad keep half the money from the sale of the house to buy their own house, but then, a few years ago he also gave them two hundred thousand dollars for a college fund for you and me. Can you believe it!? There's a fund, Mark, for college. For you and me."

I looked directly into Mark's face to see how he'd react. He didn't react much. His face wasn't even puffed up the way it got when he was upset. I got frustrated. "It's like, Uncle Ethan's been waiting for Mom and Dad to spend that money on college for us, for any college you'd want and could get into. But they never told us about the deal, that there was a college fund! With that much! I mean, it's weird enough that they'd even take Uncle Ethan's money for this, but to not tell us!?" My jaw was jutting forward as I finished enunciating this.

"No, no. Please!" Uncle Ethan wanted to stop me, but it was too late. And Mark stared at me and Uncle Ethan was staring at me too, but I watched Mark for a few seconds.

He blinked, ambling, bewildered, "They never told me, but, it's like, pathetic they'd just take the money, and I wish I'd been able to just thank you, but, how could I know?"

It wasn't a surprise that Uncle Ethan jumped in here, "Please, please. See, when you're my age you'll see, time has a way of rounding off the sharp, clear edges of things. Really, that money is there for a good purpose. And I was taking good care of myself and I love you two as much as anything I ever thought I could. You came into my life and you mean everything to me, and it was so simple to do something like this for you. Really, what better legacy could I have, and while I'm alive to enjoy the results?"

We all breathed heavily for a full minute and said nothing and didn't look at each other. I barely kept back the tears.

Mark jerked out, "Well, thanks, but I could never take money from you." He was looking down at the table.

I began to squirm in my seat. Uncle Ethan looked like he stopped breathing as he sat narrowing his eyes at Mark, probably as winnowed out as I was.

He said, "Well, Mark, just realize the money is already there for you for college. That's what it's there for. It won't pay for everything, but it might encourage some financial aid coming your way. Sort of water in the well style."

Mark nodded, wordless. He seemed to be holding onto to his refusal to take money from Uncle Ethan. I wanted to shake him. It was like he was stuck with some momentary feel-good principle, grasping it like some Goddamned syringe in his arm.

I managed to pay the check without saying anything more. Mark managed to pay his half in the cab, over the rugged old suspended bridge, then through elegant, expensive Brooklyn Heights. Sitting silently next to him in the back seat, I finally leaned over to whisper in his ear., "It's a special present, Mark. It's what he can do for us."

We chugged on quietly past Carroll Gardens, toward less elegant, less expensive Bay Ridge. Nothing more was said in the cab.

And it felt like time stopped when we got back to Uncle Ethan's. For the rest of the weekend urgent conversation was avoided and all our normal routines like going shopping for food, cooking, talking, cleaning, watching YouTube, felt insipid at best. The fact was it was two long days in Brooklyn of waiting for the coming confrontation with Mom and Dad. Anger peculated inside me, brewing to its fullest, most righteous density. I had no idea what Mark was thinking or feeling and that was a new sensation.

Somehow it was Sunday night on Long Island. Mark and I were upstairs unpacking. They were downstairs eating chips and dip, celebrating the next day being Columbus Day or whatever they called it.

It was after ten at night and I told Mark I was going down to talk to them. He followed. The whole downstairs was pretty much one big room. The parents always bragged about gutting the place before we moved in. They were in the kitchen area in the back.

They stared at us, both of them sitting on the wooden stools next to the off-white, sparkly granite covered island. Mark and I stayed ten feet back. Dad had on his weekend shorts and sweatshirt, making him look older and paunchier than he did in his sports jacket and chinos of the work week. He was at least fifty pounds overweight. Mom was always a skinny little thing. She had on her streaky blue and yellow tight running pants and matching top. They both had short dyed black hair. She had Irish pale skin and those bulging blue eyes, ready to pop out. Dad had the dark brown sunken Armenian eyes with the predator in a cave look.

"When were you going to tell us about the money that was supposed to be set aside for college, for Mark and me?" I was shaking a bit, voice and body.

"What money?" Mom was always ready for a fight.

I said nothing.

"Money for college? Have you gotten into college?" she said.

"Not yet. I'm just about to apply. Then Uncle Ethan told me about the money."

"Yeah? So? What's your problem? Shit Peggy, you get so fucking worked up over nothing. What are you worried you won't get to go to some expensive private college? We told you to apply to state ones."

"Right. And live at home?"

"Yeah! It's what we all did."

"But Uncle Ethan gave us money for this, and I want to go away to college. I've busted and I have straight A's for two years straight."

"Jesus H. Christ, Peggy. Look at you! So, you're too good for a local state college. Everyone else here's been fine with state colleges. What a freaken princess! Holy shit!" As Mom said this, standing with her fist on her hip, Dad stood up, shaking his head and laughing.

Mark said, "You know my college sucks. And you two never had a good thing to say about where you went."

Dad stopped shaking his head and growled, "I learned some useless shit in college. Then I learned a trade for a job. A job, Mark. You know what a real fucking job is? Your mother learned accounting and has a job. It's the real-world you guys." He gazed through glassy eyes, leaning his bulky form on the kitchen island with both hands.

I stayed as calm as I could. "Yeah, state universities are great. I'll apply to some and I'll go where I get the best financial aid deal. That's great. But see with the information from Uncle Ethan, I know I'll also apply to a bunch of private ones too."

Both parents stood staring, too disgusted by what I just said to find the words, yet. Mark and I waited.

Mark broke the impasse. "So when were you going to tell us Uncle Ethan gave you money for us for college? Never?"

Dad stood up straight.

Mom made one step forward. "It's not Uncle Ethan's money. It was handed down to us."

I said, "He told us about the sale of his house, Mom. His house, Mom. Then a college fund was set aside by him, Mom."

Dad gritted his teeth, then shouted, "We always said we'd pay for college! Fuck!"

Mom was sneering, furious. She looked at me. "We don't know what the hell he told you. Who knows what the stupid senile old man thinks? We have no idea what he's telling you two or what the hell's going on, why you two hang around some old guy, hang around each other all the time. Who the hell knows what you two are up to! Shit. You don't act like a normal brother and sister, going off all the time together. It's weird as hell. You act like freaken boyfriend and girlfriend."

She stopped herself, her eyes trying to focus.

The room emptied of all sound.

I think I sucked in a breath and maybe Mark moved. My father stood still, blinking and breathing.

Mark walked out. I walked out a few seconds later, quietly up the stairs and, as silently as possible, over the thick maroon, wall-to-wall carpet to the door to my room. Mark's door across the hallway was closed and there was no sound in there, just a light in the crack at the top.

I got inside my room, heart in my stomach, closed the door, sat on my bed, feet flat on the musty carpet, and leaned on my elbows, hands holding the sides of my neck. Time eked and I couldn't move.

At some point I turned off my light and got under the covers with my clothes on. I heard my parents coming up the stairs and then pass my door, then quietly mumble a thing or two in their room. Then there was silence. Not moving was exhausting and eventually I collapsed into sleep, but not before I resolved, I'd go away to college, anywhere I could, and stay away.

Book Two

✦ Chapter 1 ✦

I was in bed staring down at my floor in my long-ago Long Island room. The stale air might pilfer the life out of me. I couldn't sleep wondering if Eric Matheson could help me sell the drawing. Margy Zorn wouldn't. It was March, three months since I spoke to her and I never heard from her again or from her contact at Stanford. Nothing. It was four-thirty in the morning, and I was awake. I leaned over and opened the vent, making the dry, hot air blow, pumping dust through my childhood room. The damned vent either stayed all the way open or closed.

The pillow smelled like a combination of mildew and sweet perfumed detergent. My sweating was awful under those two polyesters, angora blankets on that box spring and mattress purporting to be a bed. A disc jockey once said an orgasm was like laughing and sneezing at the same time. Funny when I heard it at twelve or fourteen. Now it just sat on my brain. Grubby, absurdist crap everywhere, and I was feeling the gnawing, petty downward spiral in the pit of my stomach at four-thirty in the morning.

I'd get to my new *Temp* job on Thursday. Tomorrow was Tuesday. I had to go see the psychologist tomorrow. I had to be up at six-thirty, walk to the bus in the Long Island cold, thick humidity and smog. It was awful, but I had to. Mark was beyond thinking, just caught up in crazy episodes in whatever private hell that was. He stayed in his room and smoked, alone, staring, doing nothing as a preoccupation, alone. I had to plan or we'd both be stuck in the little vinyl hellhole forever. He had, "an episode, some kind of episode", Mom said on the phone to me. Me back there in San Francisco, suddenly no longer feeling quite so distant and independent.

Two weeks later I was back on Long Island standing in long hallways, sitting in designated waiting areas, talking about Mark with an adroit, frightened stare at Mark's psychologist. And that short, polite conversation got me no information, except that I had an appointment for the following week.

The week felt like forever and now I just had to sleep, or I'd be a wreck when I talked to the psychologist in the morning.

The lack of fresh air did knock me out and, late getting up, I shuffled along, eating the two health bars I stashed in my handbag. I shuffled along until I was somewhere. The psychiatric ward of Saint Luke's was huge, and the long halls reverberated with creepy and depressing institutional ambiguity. I shuffled along feeling trapped in those lost, meandering hallways and then, finally after reading one more wall directory, I was in a hushed office with warm, plush armchairs and soft, colorful throw rugs and anti-hysterical, pallid landscape photographs on the walls. Mark picked out his psychotherapist. I was looking at him, middle-aged Dr. Frederick Tuck, not too put-off by his large horn-rimmed glasses, blotchy complexion and large, white, worn out Reeboks, and longish brown hair that needed cleaning and some shape.

But thank God Mark signed a release form allowing me access to his doctor. It was already clear that Mom and Dad couldn't or wouldn't figure out what to do and so it gave me some serious leverage with them and I had to get Mark out somehow and first I had to ask questions. First, I had to try to relax.

"Dr. Tuck, could you tell me what you meant when you said something about an episode?" I was stuttering a bit, ready to cry.

"Oh. Yeah, you know I don't want to overemphasize the idea of an episode. For instance, I don't think Mark had a severe psychotic break suddenly . . . not from I can gather at this point. But it's just that he's shown fairly clear symptoms of schizophrenia."

I didn't move and he didn't. I was in shock. The doctor was giving me a direct gaze and appeal. Schizophrenia. Mark used that word describing himself when I first got back, but I didn't let it sink in. Now the word was being uttered as some kind of fact, the beginning of a medical diagnosis. It was unavoidable.

I wanted to leave, run away. He was saying things and I wasn't listening, "Yeah, Peggy, there can be different degrees of severity with schizophrenia."

"I'm sorry but I just have this bug in me. Was there something that happened a month ago? I just haven't been able to understand what my parents are saying."

"Um, right. Well, Mark's told me to tell you whatever he's told me. You two are close. But I have to maintain some confidentiality. Let me describe, basically, what Mark told me when he first came here. He described finding himself at the local gas station or, convenient store and gas station, and was disorientated. He couldn't remember if he paid for his gas and I guess he wasn't sure how long he'd been there. He found himself watching the television they had on. He didn't know how long. And feeling lost in it. He stressed that he felt lost in the television show."

That sounded fairly bad, but I didn't want to interrupt the flow. Tuck was speaking hesitantly, censoring what to pass on to me.

"Apparently the people at the store couldn't deal with Mark and they asked him to leave finally. Mark seemed very upset by that, so upset he came here asking to see a psychologist. And Peggy, the thing I want to say is that Mark still seemed a bit disoriented when I saw him later that morning. So it must have been quite an effort for him to get himself here."

No thoughts occurred to me. My brain was sore, and I could easily shut down. He was still talking, "And see, Peggy, he isn't describing audio or visual hallucinations."

"Okay." My God. Should I have seen signs of something wrong years ago? I'd let him speak on. He was watching me, probably thinking I was crazy too. But I still had a bug in me.

"What about Mark being stuck in the house all day? I mean, you know, he's kind of old to be living there, with my parents and wouldn't he be better off out and away?"

"Well, but he doesn't have a job. You think there are problems at home?"

"Yeah, I mean, without spending years describing it. It's just not great. I mean, frankly, my parents both work and are out most of the time, but . . ." I came to a worn out stop.

"Umm, yeah. Yeah, of course, Mark has talked about your family. I can't violate that trust except to say, at this point it seems fairly clear that you and your Uncle Ethan who died were very important to Mark and still are. Maybe the way he gets along with your parents is more complicated. He has to figure some things out."

If I said much of anything, I was going to get sucked into this endlessly vague, disturbing analysis. Did Mark say anything to this guy about what Mom accused us of? I just sat. We both sat quietly for a few seconds, looking around.

He breathed in. "Anyway, can I tell you my basic take on things at this point? I mean, Mark's only been to see me half a dozen times. I have to tell you Peggy, from what he's describing it sounds to me like Mark might have been under some pressures in the past. Right?"

I didn't respond. I just shrugged slightly, not sure.

"Didn't Mark struggle throughout high school and have very few friends?"

"That just about describes me too."

"But you did very well in high school, so well academically you got into Tufts University and you went there and did well and graduated and went to California and got a job."

I looked into his eyes. "How do you know all that?"

"Mark."

Tears started to steam down my face. He handed me the box of tissues and waited.

"Yeah, I got away but I'm back now."

"Um, to help Mark. Right? But you can take care of yourself. I mean, can't you?"

I shifted in my chair. "Yeah."

He sat back, ready to make a point. "Okay. I really think it's tough for Mark. Enough anyway to mean he has a much steeper, up-hill climb than maybe you or I do. We all have our problems. All of us."

I wanted to get the hell out of there. I put my head back on the chair and closed my eyes just to get away from his eyes.

He was letting me stew, typical freaking psychologist. It took a few minutes, but at least sightless I could breathe calmly.

Without changing my position and with my eyes still closed, I said, "I'm hating this idea of some biological cause of Mark's mental condition, when I want to rant about our Goddamned parents, or the nasty, tacky, consumer world that surrounds Mark."

"Okay. I get that, Peggy. I don't think there's a simple bio-logical cause of Mark's condition. The world around him is really always a major factor, just like it is for everyone."

"And the world around him is still just Mommy and Daddy."

Dr. Tuck was stopped by my sudden, combative out-burst. He said nothing and let my words bounce off the walls for half a minute.

I had to add something of course. "And there I was three thousand miles away, so I'm the other extreme."

"Well, but you came back."

Back I was. Doing what? Uncle Ethan told Mark and me a few times, "There's no human life without family." I assumed he meant that in the reproductive sense when I was fifteen. I had to listen. Doctor Tuck was saying something.

"So he was upset enough to drive himself here. Do you understand that he was disoriented but he still seemed to feel the need to get here? Not everyone is ready to sign themselves into a psych ward in a hospital?"

I slowly raised my head, eyes open, and nodded but no thoughts came to me.

"Okay. Look, Peggy, since you've come all this way to help your brother, I'm trying to help you by getting to what-ever I can at this point. The person I met and talked to that first morning was fairly confused. He looked very calm and chatted about things, like about what courses he took in col-lege, as though being here wasn't upsetting to him. But his words were a bit garbled and he seemed distracted. Do you get what I'm saying?

"Uh-huh, yeah? I think. Why? Sorry, no, what are you saying?"

"Do me a favor and describe what I just said. About Mark. Maybe with just a few words."

"That he was upset and made a big effort to get here and was trying to calm down."

"Uh, that's not really quite what I was saying, I don't think."

I waved my head blindly, "I don't know." I tried to think. "Uh, he was too calm and not getting at what was happening. It was inappropriate or he was incoherent."

"Uh-huh. Not as extreme as incoherent. But, yeah, having a bit of a problem making sense. He seemed lost in his own thoughts and maybe even lost in thinking in distorted thought patterns. But, yeah, he's been better since, but still needs some time. And, by the way, we should all be aware that his problems can come and go a bit and he's not going to think or talk or behave the same way here as with you at home, or out at a restaurant. And our time is about up so let me finish by saying that we have to encourage Mark to stay on his medication. The vital thing is for him to stay on his meds and come to see me regularly. Once a week for now."

❧ Chapter 2 ❧

Mark's room was looking and smelling all around me just the way I expected it to, even though it was many years, over five years, since I sat down in it. It was very scary how being in that room made me feel invisible to my adult self. There it was, the ten by ten feet of flimsy, graying white drywall with two small windows on adjacent walls with beige, cheap shades, down. They were always down. There was never anything on Mark's walls. Instead, he always put his few things on the floor around himself.

He sat in his same old spot, leaning against the same wall next to the same single mattress and box spring bed. Same as six years ago.

On his right was a large, heavy five-inch square glass ashtray, an attractive one potentially, except it was never cleaned. He found it in the East Village once, years before, and ever since it was filled with butts and ashes and one burning cigarette, almost always one burning cigarette.

"Let's talk. Okay?" I whispered.

"Um. Yeah. It's just, close the door, please," he whispered too, but with a dark exasperation as he shook his head, indicating he didn't have to say a thing about the extreme need to stay away from the parents.

"Mom and Dad are at work. And why are we whispering?" I asked, leaning over to give the door a shove.

"Fear."

I laughed, and I shook off the reversal. He told me in his note at Christmas to try to connect with the parents.

"Okay. We're safe, Mark. They're never around. We have no idea why they had kids. Remember?" I sat cross-legged on his old maroon wall to wall carpet. There were drifting lines of smoke in the beige light all around us, getting pulled down into maroon dust.

"Umm, I mean, Mom and Dad are paying for this. And I'm not working. I hear the complaining all the time. They're, like, pissed that I'm ruining their lives. They won't be able to go to Florida."

I took that in.

He added, "They want to move there you know."

"Really? When? I guess I knew they liked it down there."

"Yeah. They want to sit there for years. What, twenty years? And wait to die. A slow, like, radiation meltdown of little old raisin people." He blew out remnants of deep lung smoke.

I forced a smile, trying to not wince at the grim humor and grimmer environment.

I said, "Mark what are the meds you take supposed to do for you?"

"I don't know, calm me down, speed me up and make me one with the universe. But I'm going to stop taking it. Don't tell Tuck."

"What about trying another prescription?" I said while thinking I knew almost nothing about the drug he was taking, except what the confusing hospital printouts told me.

"No. I don't want any drugs. I hate drugs. Smoking is good. Nicotine is good for the brain, at least for schizophrenics. I read that somewhere."

"But yeah, Mark, that's why I wanted to talk. Because I didn't just come back here to visit you or see if you were all right. I figured you needed to get out of here. You know?"

He didn't move or blink or say a thing.

I went on, "So, but, really, what about us finding an apartment? You know where I'd like to live? Brooklyn. You know? It really appeals to me in a big way. It's what we talked about as kids."

He still didn't say anything. He just looked at me, eyes tired but bugging.

"I don't want to persuade you in any way, though, to do something right now. You can, really you should, take your time. You've been through something here."

He leaned his head back, then said, "It's really just the same old crap. I have to go away to college."

"Go to some college?"

"Yeah. You liked it, right?"

I shrugged and nodded.

He said, "I need the experience. I never got that. I was going to ask you about Boston, or Up-State New York. Almost all of the greatest colleges are there. I mean, even if I didn't get into say, Tufts or Cornell. Isn't that . . . didn't you say that's, where?"

"Cornell? Yeah, it's in the middle of Up-State New York. Uh, yeah."

"Yeah," he said in a low voice. "It's like, in a great town, or village, right? All those small college towns. Small movie theaters and bookstores and restaurants and local bars. I need to have that kind of experience."

❧ Chapter 3 ❧

It was the first week of April. I'd been back for over a month and maybe I could see a bit of a way out for Mark. I had almost four thousand dollars saved from my San Francisco job and my temporary Long Island jobs. Maybe that was enough to get us started. I wanted to wait to sell the drawing, after getting to Brooklyn, where I could actually ask Eric Matheson, or Margy Zorn if they knew someone in New York who could attribute it. That would be all right after I got Mark and me settled in Brooklyn.

It was four in the morning. These were usually middle of the night obsessions, the kind that kept me from sleeping and made my skin break out. Because now I was really in trouble because life threatened to expose me, me no longer an escapee, but just a tiny, shrinking jerk from Cretinville Long Island.

I sat up and ran my fingers slowly through my hair, massaging my temples.

So just like Mark, when I was at home I hid in my room, even when everyone was awake. It was the only way to avoid the tense lack of conversation between me and Mom and Dad, who as usual were always together and always avoiding being in the same room as me. They were co-independents or something. They almost never had meals at home, claiming they had to work late all the time.

Meanwhile, Mom and Dad relished thinking whatever relationship Mark and I had was wrecked by them.

So much for the love of parents and children in our family. Envy made them despise me and Uncle Ethan, and half of humanity.

I had to stop dwelling on them. I had to stop dwelling in their house. I put my head down.

We needed money to get out of the stupid vinyl box. There was nothing to do most of the time but gape at my calculator and add up what I had. I could just barely keep myself from doing it at that moment, at four-something in the morning, gaping at the ceiling. I gaped at money constantly on my phone's little calculator, on the bus to work, at work, back home on the bus. I needed money. Too bad I could only get weird, hodgepodge temporary jobs, tapping at other people's computers, or answering the phone for them while they were on vacation.

Brooklyn was expensive. I already searched online for weeks. Greenpoint was one of the few areas of Brooklyn that still had some affordable places and was close enough to Manhattan.

I finally fell asleep.

The next day I just did it. I set up appointments with an agency for Mark and me to look at three places. Two days later, the weekend came, and it was our first trip out of the house together in so many years, and it was over in a flash. It was a fairly short train ride there, and Mark said he loved the first place. We didn't bother looking at anything else. Mark seemed too tired to even talk about it on the train ride back. He liked the apartment and he loved Brooklyn and he always had, he said.

I had to wait, but just for a few days. I planned to run around the parents with our done deal. That was my plan.

I was getting insanely good at waiting, even if I did toss and turn at night.

Mark and I both walked into the parents' kitchen on the following morning, Sunday. There they were, facing us.

I lurched into it, "Mark and I have been looking for an apartment and we found one." I was a little nervous but also ready to fight.

"What?!" Mom looked at me but then stared at Mark Dad had his elbows of the counter, with the twenty-inch television on next to him, the same station on the huge, flat screen set in the, open-plan living area, twenty feet away. Flickering voices and anxious smiles from CNN rebounded everywhere. Anger spread across Dad's face instantly. There were the dark, sunken, Armenian eyes and the squat, thick physique that, thanks be to God, I didn't get. I got the attenuated Irish Famine bones, with just enough flesh and muscle to walk and sit comfortably.

He glared at me, shoulders wide and, without moving anything but his eyes, still leaning forward, stared at my brother.

My mother did the talking for now. "You can't. What do you mean? Mark's in no condition to do something like that yet. What are you talking about?"

"No, Mark's okay for doing this. And I talked to Dr. Tuck and he thought it was a good idea, in fact." My voice was becoming bizarrely steady and slow and entirely resolved.

"A good idea to do what?" Mom asked. "Live in an apartment? Are you going to work, Mark?"

"Yeah, I start next week. It's like, I'm going to work like Peggy has as a temp for a while and then try to get a permanent one when something comes up."

"How much money can you make, and how reliable are these temporary jobs?"

"Very," I said.

"Peggy, cut the shit!" She was always knee-jerk.

I didn't move or speak. I was never even remotely close to the Queens, gum chewing, hard little woman. Even the mass of freckles across the bridge of her nose never could have made her cute. She was the skinny, brittle result of cheap suburban streets. Marginal New York anger. Pissed-off and proud of it. Never said she loved her kids because no one she knew ever said that to anyone. She was shaking her head now and had a metal nail file between her thumb and index finger, stopped for now.

"Okay, Mom." I was ready. "I have some money saved. I plan on looking for full time jobs, but not out here. The jobs are in the city. I can't even look for them here."

"Yeah. That's you. What about Mark?" Her staccato voice.

"What about Mark? Mark needs his own life," I said, fairly aware they might think it was weird, Mark and me living together. And I was ready to just walk away if they even hinted at anything like that.

Mom was livid and all her muscles tightened, especially in her little neck.

Mark jumped in, "Mom! Goddamn-it, I'm fine. It's like, I have to move out. I'm twenty-six!"

"Oh my God! I mean, what do I have to say? It's like, you're not fine, Mark! I mean, so what have we been going through here then?" She had her back to Dad, but he was right there for her and he remained very still. You never knew if he might strike. He wouldn't hit his kids, although he smacked Mark a few times years earlier, but he used his bulk and aggression to threaten, often, whenever he got angry, often.

"Yeah, well . . ." Dad stretched, shook his head and with his low, slow, molten voice, said, "Go, ahead. You'll be back here in three months. Yeah, if that long. And Peggy, you act like you have all the answers, when we're the ones who've been here, day-in, day-out. Fuck. And I don't give a fuck what that Dr. Tuck at Saint Luke's says because he hasn't said anything worth shit yet as far as we're concerned."

Mom's turn. "What if you can't get a job, Mark? Are you going to rely on these temp jobs? How's that going to pay for anything? You can't live off your sister."

Mark marched out, yelling he wouldn't talk anymore, that he'd do what he wanted to do, which was a very good idea, walking away. But his yelling sounded fairly shrill and unconvincing. I stood stuck on the plastic coated, engineered wood floor I landed on when I first walked in six weeks before. Mom fidgeted with the string tie of her blue and gold pajamas she wore on weekends, that she probably bought herself at Macy's. Her job in the mall as an assistant accountant got her discounts. Dad worked at the same mall selling furniture at Nory's. He had his back to us, putting his heavy coffee mug in the sink and looking out the window. He had on his weekend paunchy shorts and paunchy sweatshirt.

Then I told them we were moving to Brooklyn and they ranted in disgust, walking in circles, not even looking at me. Brooklyn was filled with gangs or rich people and nothing in between, they said. Dad left the room, shaking his head, walking upstairs.

It would actually happen. They didn't really want us around anyway and that was the point. I could smell it as I waited. The meeting came to an unnatural close, as nothing was said by Mom for half a minute. She sabotaged my relationship with Mark five years earlier, and now I was taking him back. We both knew it.

I turned and left the room, saying I'd let them know what day we'd be moving.

✿ Chapter 4 ✿

It was April twentieth when we moved away. Greenpoint would be our new Brooklyn home. I was resolved even though a sudden, demented heat wave feeling like August was surrounding us. It hovered in the eighties. All the sultry, dripping moisture calling itself air massed in hot, shapeless gray clouds. The sun burned through every now and then. Fortunately, that was all outside the air-conditioned cab window for a while and then outside the commuter train window. Out of the train, Mark and I sweated over five suitcases, dragging ourselves to a cab that took us to the apartment building on Poland Avenue.

Lugging the five suitcases up four flights of stairs just about did us in. We sat still on windowsills, just breathing for ten minutes. No air conditioning for the summer here, I was thinking, but not saying. We walked through the railroad layout, everything off a long hall, from the first room, the twelve by fourteen foot living room, down the hall past the two small bedrooms, the tiny kitchen, the bathroom and then the back door to the old fire escape. Decades of paint over plaster walls and ceilings wobbled into one monotonous dirty white hue, and thousands of tiny round speckles of the same paint mixed with many years of black grime on the battered narrow oak floors.

We were on the top floor, five stories up in a red brick building. It was stolid from its inception in about nineteen twenty something.

I got us walking, worried we wouldn't have anything to sleep on or eat on for that night. Mark was tall, around six-three, so I was sort of galloping next to him. He needed a better haircut. His was too long on the sides and short on the top. It was sandy blond, but darker and darker as he got older. And he was in those red and blue striped, *Nippon Jeans* teenagers all wore but he had become too pear shaped, and he wasn't a teenager. But I kept my mouth shut.

We got cheap stuff at Poland Street Used Furniture. In ten minutes, I picked out some necessary dishes with Mark saying it was all fine. He said, he really didn't care. I bought a little plastic garden table we'd squeeze into our kitchen. Mrs. Diaz, who seemed to own the store, suggested a place for box springs and mattresses, and phoned her friend, or cousin or something, and everything would be delivered that afternoon.

❧ Chapter 5 ❧

I had to balance looking for work with keeping an eye on Mark. The money we had would keep us going for about two months if we never added anything to it. Mark only owned two large suitcases of clothes and his ashtray and two hundred and fifty-six dollars. It turned out he didn't even have a checking account. He kept his cash in his wallet and some in a shirt pocket and some in a back pocket of his pants.

We both seemed to get into our routines three days later, the following Monday. Mark went to the Temp Technique office on Newell Avenue, a couple of blocks away. He thought it would be a good place to start, and I went into Manhattan on the subway to an employment office on West 39th street. I figured I'd wait, breathing normally, for him to contribute money to our mutual, living together, cause.

At least it cooled down to normal spring weather and the morning went fairly smoothly. I told my *Career Search Counselor*, Sondra Gotlieb, I'd do almost anything for a salary of thirty-five thousand to start with. She got a telling, slightly condescending twinkle in her eyes and said I could ask for forty thousand and go down from there, unless I was willing to settle for something less interesting because I needed the work immediately.

I left after telling her I could wait for two or three weeks at most. She had my resume. I'd call every day at least once. Now I just had to get myself back to the apartment in Brooklyn, eat something and look online for jobs.

The midday subway was filled with enough unhappy, unwashed, probably unemployed people to threaten anyone's outlook. We all faced away from each other and it looked like everyone was trying to not breathe in too much of the fetid air. Finally, I escaped up the stairs of our subway stop and walked the five blocks home.

Mark was there sitting on the floor of the living room and so he was the first thing I saw. We'd just spent the weekend sitting and talking and drinking coffee or tea, with him smoking and slowly rambling on about the old days in Brooklyn, the cost of food in convenient stores, global warming, college campuses having more student run movie theaters and bookstores in New England than Up-State New York. And I just listened most of the time.

Now, there we were. He was smoking and the place smelled of it.

I wasn't sure what I wanted. The easy, sometimes rote intimacy we could muster certainly seemed like a nauseatingly overripe possibility at that point. It was twenty minutes to two on a Monday afternoon. I had to change into some shorts, eat and there were some actual things that had to get done.

"How did it go for you?" I asked sitting on the floor, leaning against the opposite wall ten feet across from him.

"Okay. How about you?" He had a coffee cup next to him on the floor, next to his ashtray. He drank instant coffee and I liked to tease him about that, but not now.

I said, "Yeah, fine, I think."

"Yeah?" He waited for more, but I did too, because I wanted him to pay attention to tangible issues. He coughed. "I feel like, there will be something. It's like, it'll be dumb work, probably, but the woman I saw was nice in a way to talk to about things. And she said she'd have something for me before the end of the week. This week, I guess is what she meant."

"Great!" I was afraid of his gloom. I didn't want depression to add to his problems.

"So, but what sort of jobs are there? I mean, can you get something you might at least like a bit?" My eyes were starting to water from the smoke.

"Yeah, I hope. It'll be crap work." He spoke quietly and slowly, staring at the wall behind me. "The thing is, I just want the money anyway. Uhh, I mean, the more money I can save the better."

"Right."

He mumbled something.

"What? Sorry, I could hear you."

His mumbling was only a bit louder, "I just can't do everything at once. I hate it when Tuck starts asking me about how I'm thinking about my plans. I have to learn to reassess things. I don't know."

"Reassess?"

"Yeah, trying to think things through, clearly and then get something done, something or other done. I have to forget about worrying about it and concentrate on something I choose. Concentration is the main thing."

He shifted his blank stare from the wall to me, his voice stronger. "I don't know what I choose. I hate it when he says that shit. I think it's what I read about online a few weeks ago. *Cognitive Behavioral Therapy*. Or some happy horseshit like that. Might as well be, *The Power of Positive Thinking*, bullshit. You know? Fucking hell. He's all set in life. So, yeah, anyway, forget about Tuck and Mom and Dad. It wasn't that confusing and all I know is, I didn't get out of the freaking house and go away to college. It's obvious to anyone. The jobs were so stupid, and I hated them. Now, I'm looking at them again. Stupid, boring jobs. I hate them. I get so tired going around and around the same problems, like I have for years and years and years. Real problems. Tuck does nothing and has no problems. I want his job, sitting there watching people as they whine about everything and he says, you know, I should think something through and move on."

"Maybe he's moving on to charging his fee and making money." The sarcasm just fell out of me.

No reaction. Mark was back to not listening or even looking at me. It was my last desperate attempt at breaking into the darkness between us.

I stood up, having to go to the bathroom and telling him that as I walked away, glancing at him stuck staring at the wall.

At least my moving around worked in a way. He looked more content as I occupied myself for the next hour, cleaning the kitchen and mopping the floors everywhere but Mark's room and the living room.

"I'm retiring to my room," I announced, walking by. "I'm reading a new book, a biography of Yeats I found on sale."

"Great," he called out as I closed my door

And I did read for a few minutes.

But aggravation just led me to thoughts of Mark in the other room, aware he pretty much never read anything anymore and certainly not about Yeats. Maybe it was absurd to want him to but if we were ever going to be close the way we had been, he'd have to grow, read some books or blogs or magazines and go to some movies and listen to music. He only listened to the radio on his old boom box now. It was in his room. He didn't even bring his few CD's.

Was that all finished for him? Weary, I put the book down and drifted off to a short nap.

At four I went out, telling him I'd be right back, that I was just getting a few things for dinner. But he looked unable to move away from that spot, smoking, sipping coffee or tea, thinking whatever thoughts he lived with.

The next day went like that and the day after that. I found myself trying to stir Mark. Any talk from him about far-fetched plans to go away somewhere to college or complaining about the parents or the awful jobs he had years ago, got me up and moving around. I couldn't help myself, it just scared and irritated me, the sedentary state of Mark. He reminded me of old homeless people who couldn't lift themselves off the ground anymore. He sat there, I calculated this, at least ten hours a day. The only thing he did was sit, smoke and eat and drink beer, tea, sometimes coffee, and stare. When he would get up, after a few hours of staring, staring and staring, he might go into his room to listen to his little radio talk shows, or sleep. He must have been averaging twelve hours sleep a day.

I did take him shopping for food or once for his cigarettes, that he smoked at a rate of almost two packs a day. Almost forty burning, diseased cigarettes got sucked into his body every day. Even walking down the street, he smoked, sucking them in. That was one of his only self-generated activities now. No medication in him but he looked sedated most of the time. He stood back in stores and I ended up doing everything. If I prodded him, asked him to do something, like get some apples and any other fruit that looked good, he'd do it in the most perfunctory way possible, getting only apples and nothing else and then standing behind me or next to me. As soon as he could, he'd be back inside the apartment, sitting and staring into space.

I called the New York Employment Personnel Consulting, Inc. every morning. On Thursday, almost two weeks into the search, I was told about a job possibility. First Patriot Trust needed someone in their personnel department. It was thirty-eight thousand a year, which sounded pretty good, so I told Sondra Gotlieb I'd take it. But there was an obvious lack of response for a second or two on her end.

"Yeah, you know Margaret, uh, I don't want to prejudice you in any way." She hesitated, thinking. "But you might have some other choices in a few days. Can you wait?"

"Uh, I guess, why? You think this isn't a good job for me in some way?"

"It's a little dead end, even in salary. It's a small bank and, yeah, can you wait? Even just to tomorrow. This might not be filled for a few days anyway."

"Okay. Yeah, okay, thanks for the advice. I'll call you tomorrow." I hoped the woman's exuberant advice wasn't irrational.

✦ Chapter 6 ✦

Another week passed by idly, aiming somewhere toward deep spring. The weather was still in the sixties most days, but the light was getting softer and fuller. I did try to clean the apartment, but I didn't want to spend money on paint yet, so it still looked fairly bad. The money I saved was our safety net and, with Mark not looking very engaged in a job search, I was feeling very cautious. Still, the craven apartment was so ugly with the walls so desperate for paint and the worn old oak floors needing heavy duty refinishing. The lack of furniture seemed absurdly ironic to me, with the totally empty living room filled with Mark's daydreams.

On Friday afternoon I had something to tell him, a theme that needed a conversation, and so I made us both tea and sat on the floor.

"You know . . ." I said blithely . . . "tea is supposed to actually be fairly good for you. I've read that a lot recently."

I had on jeans and crisscrossed my legs a few feet in front of him.

"Sure. It's better than coffee. I drink coffee, but it's like, who cares? I get so sick of the coffee rituals of all the, you know, all those rich BMW driving people. And Mercedes."

I flinched. That was pretty fatuous. "Um. Yeah, well, at least at Tufts there were a few people who drove little cheap cars or old cars, even if they could afford expensive ones. The older the better. Old gray Buicks were very cool." I shifted my weight to get more comfortable and shake off the embarrassing banality of what I just said.

I tried to get more serious. "So, speaking of college, I heard a lecture when I was at Tufts that I really liked."

Mark's eyes were sort of on me, sort of not focused. I kept going. "Yeah, anyway, umm, this old guy from Harvard, I think, Howard Gardner, who keeps writing and lecturing on the different types of intelligence, uhh, eight or nine. I can't remember." I grunted a laugh at that but still, Mark was showing no sign of being with me.

I bludgeoned on, "You know, he talked about basketball players using visual-spatial intelligence and some people having social intelligence. That might be successful salespeople and teachers. But, you know, not just the narrow definition that could manage to dry up the whole universe with engineers and lawyers and their high SAT scores and powerful university degrees."

I paused to take a breath. Mark didn't respond. I needed to complete my lecture and move on to some more personal subjects. Mark spoke first.

"Yeah, well, it's like, fuck Harvard, anyway. I just want a quiet liberal arts college. And, it's why I want to go to a liberal arts college in New England. Any time now. Not some big university anywhere, but, yeah, maybe Cape Cod or Maine. I like that anti-materialistic thing."

God. I took in some smoky air, but there wasn't anything I could add.

What was I doing? I was trying to tell Mark he was smart and cool? I was trying to give him confidence like I was his mother?

Sitting there, me sucking on my teeth, was beyond boring. I didn't want us to start talking about him wanting to go to college again, both of us stuck in some sort of soul grinding inertia. He didn't have a job and he didn't have any money. I still hadn't contacted Eric Matheson or anyone else about selling the drawing, but that wouldn't amount to enough to pay for Mark, *having the college experience.*

"Mark, have you ever asked Mom and Dad if there's any money left from Uncle Ethan for you?"

He glowered at the far wall, his head back on the one behind him. "No."

I pushed my hair behind my ears. "I got them to give me more than half of it. I mean, I had to whine at them a few times to sign the financial aid forms. But you didn't get any of that money."

"Fuck, no-no-no. I'm twenty-six now. I lived at home and they paid for that. You got into Tufts and I couldn't get through community college."

I grumbled and looked down at the pockmarked floor. I took a sip of almost cold tea as Mark was lighting a cigarette. He blew out smoke and leaned his head against the wall behind him, banging it as he did, stopping both of us for a few embarrassed seconds.

"Anyway," I said. "Look, I just got a job from that place, that employment agency?"

"What job?"

"Uh, United Insurance. I think I got it because of what I was doing in San Francisco and I think it could be pretty good. Fifty-two thousand a year, Mark! Can you believe it?!"

A sinking feeling grew in me as I said this to Mark who was getting more still, eyes fixed on me suddenly.

"Yeah. You have a degree and I don't and there isn't a fucking thing I'm qualified to do. Jesus, my job experience adds up to shit. Working the dock in Reinhart Supplies, moving boxes of electrical equipment around or all those years working part-time in Nory's, moving furniture around in a warehouse again. I'm a warehouse expert, moving fucking boxes around."

Actually, I knew all that. It was wedged into my brain like a long, jagged splinter. Mark had a fairly horrendous work record. He quit three or four jobs after only a short time, and he was fired twice and then didn't work at all for two years. And now he was making no effort to find any job.

He stood. "Forget what they say in movies about nice people doing this stuff, uh, honest physical work. It's like it's nine-to-five hell again and again and again and you're surrounded by frustrated fucking psychos who hate everyone. And they'd shoot you in a second for no reason if they could."

I sat up and tightened inside as Mark's words fell out and that was it. He was finished speaking. This was my brother, Mark, who used to have insights and hope. We sat there in the empty room in the darkening light. It was about four in the afternoon and the sun was behind some buildings and some clouds. It was, Ashcan School light I thought, realizing exactly how demented it was to think up an art reference when Mark was sinking slowly into the damned floor.

He added, "It's like it doesn't make any difference what I do. I won't get a real job."

I arched my back and sat up to relieve my muscles from that awkward position on the floor. "What jobs did they say you might get at the temp agency?"

"No jobs, Peggy!" His jaw was sticking out suddenly and his eyes were bugging. "They don't have any jobs! They pretend they do! I could get the same jobs they post myself! Minimum wage, minimum wage, minimum, minimum, minimum, minimum!" Some spit came out of his mouth and a bit hit my forehead.

❧ Chapter 7 ❧

The following Monday I had a break at work and called Margy Zorn for some help. Maybe she could give me the name of a specialist in New York so I could finally get an attribution for the damned drawing and sell it and give the money to Mark.

I explained who I was to the department assistant.

"Sorry, Margy Zorn isn't here right now. But I remember your drawing and Eric Matheson's here. Would you like to speak with him?"

"Yeah, thanks." I had no choice, but I was feeling very queasy.

"Hold on. I'll see if he's busy."

Half a minute of holding on and I had cold water lapping at me, floating, lost at sea.

"Hello." It was the man himself.

"Hi, this is Peggy Avakian. I took in an Italian drawing you and Mrs. Zorn looked at."

"Yeah, hi, of course. How are you, Peggy? How's it going with your drawing?"

"Fine. I wondered, actually, if I could take you up on your offer to give me names I could call. I'm actually in New York."

"Okay. New York? Are you just there for a while?"

"Yeah, I'm from here."

"Do you want to get into a museum to do some research? I think Margy said you were applying to graduate school in art history and wanted to do some research on your drawing?"

"Yeah." My heart sank. Goddamned Margy. Both these worthies were constantly telling me how important it was to research it myself, as if I could. And I wasn't going to Goddamned graduate school! He couldn't see me shaking the phone in the air.

I had to fake a calm voice, "No, I know I can just call the obvious places, like the Met." I puffed up my cheeks in frustration.

"Right. Tell them you were here."

"Okay, great. I'll call them."

"We know people at other museums, but yeah, I'd imagine you'd do especially well in the Drawings and Prints Department there, at the Metropolitan Museum."

"Great. Thanks." I wanted the pointless conversation to end.

"Would you like me to email them? Christa Hiaphin is the Chief Curator."

"Oh, no. Thank you. I'm sorry to be such a pest. I can just phone them and make an appointment."

"No. That's fine. Yeah, they certainly have the collection."

"Good, thank you."

I was about to say good-bye.

"You know, I'm going there. Actually, I go there a fair amount now to visit my sister. Uh, if you'd like I could talk to Christa then, or really, we could show it to her together if you'd like. I mean, I don't know what you'd like to do."

I was surprised. "Oh, no. I wouldn't want you to go to that much trouble. No, yeah, I have to sell it. Uh, I hate to say that, but . . ." I was lost at sea again.

"No, that's fine. Actually, though, if you're in a hurry at all, I don't know, but I would think it might help if we did show it to someone." He was halting, thinking apparently. "Uh, yeah, what I'm trying to say is, Christa Hiaphin or one of her assistants could get you started and then you can look into finding an old master dealer."

My caution remained. "That would be a big help. Thank you."

"You can pick your own person for an attribution, of course."

"Oh, I know, but it would be great to get introduced to someone, to some expert in the field. I just hate putting you to so much trouble." I was shaking my head again at all the extra steps.

"Nope. Apart from visiting Amanda, my sister, I usually visit people in museums down there. Partly, it's a way to get some work done while I'm there."

I thanked him. Somehow, we said goodbye with an agreement to meet at the Metropolitan Museum on a tentative date, depending on Eric Matheson getting an appointment for me with the Met's curator. I wasn't sure how it happened, but it was an intimidating prospect looming over me. She was going to want me to do some sort of high level research on the damned drawing.

❧ Chapter 8 ❧

Rain scattered on dusty spring streets outside as I plodded along as a factotum once more at work. Why did I major in art history? Why? Meanwhile, while Mark seemed lost in everlasting introspection on the floor for more weeks, I said nothing to him about the drawing and, finally on a Monday in mid-May, during lunch break I took it with me, as always in my backpack, by taxi to the big, old fancy Metropolitan Museum. I told my boss who told her boss that I wanted a two-hour lunch break on that date, and I put in some extra hours before violating the office time frame. So I was all set and so was the weather. It was a sunny, crispy clear day.

I made my way to the front of the Met on Fifth Avenue. There were quite a few people, students and tourists probably, drifting up and down the broad granite steps. Some were sitting. Most of them were in casual, cheap, faddish clothes and I figured I probably didn't fit into any of those groups anymore. I bought a fairly conservative Brooks Brothers dress for the occasion. Narrow, midnight blue cotton. I found the dress in a secondhand shop in Brooklyn for eighty-five dollars.

And there was Eric Matheson inside the large, beautiful lobby of the museum near the doors so I wouldn't miss him. He looked the same, with his broad, strong-boned head. He had on the same sort of elegant, expensive clothes, this time in a sleek dark green silk suit. The guy seemed partial to green, and partial to himself.

He nodded when he saw me, not quite smiling, and when I got to him, we shook hands. We quickly made our way, parallel walking, to the elevator and stood, parallel again, exchanging the fewest pleasantries about the weather being nice and not too hot, and then made our way to the Print Department. I just needed to get through this and hoped it would help me just get an expert to attribute the drawing, soon.

The Study Room for Drawings and Prints we were walking through looked like a variation on the theme of the Boston Museum but there was something more urgent about the whole occurrence. They called him, "Eric" a lot and it was clear he was a major player and I was with him, with a drawing that first Christa Hiaphin ogled, then Geoffrey, her assistant, ogled. She had very short maroon dyed hair, wrinkled, powdery white skin and had to be at least sixty.

She was a very serious person, looking impatient.

"Are you in a graduate program somewhere?" she asked me.

"No."

Eric stepped in when I looked lost for words.

"Yes, well Peggy wants to get an attribution, partly because she's decided to sell the drawing, if I'm right. Is that right?" He looked at me and I blushed, not wanting them to see me as a money grub. But my brain lunged, and thoughts and words formed on their own.

"Yeah," I said. "I have to. It belongs to my brother and he gave it to me because I majored in art history and he needs the money right now, so I'm here with it." I took in a full breath.

"How did you come to own it?" Christa Hiaphin was standing across the large table. Her eyes were cold, not really wanting to see me.

"I used to come to the city with my brother, all the time when we were teenagers, uh, really just to hang around and get away from the grimmest wastelands. Of Long Island." It came out with classic comic timing, mostly because I spoke hesitantly, hesitant to make the standard cheap shot of putting down the burbs.

Christa smirked and her assistant laughed heartily. Eric seemed to step back.

"Probably SoHo and the East Village." she grumbled distractedly.

"We found this in Tribeca, in an antique store."

I smiled at her and shrugged slowly. She had one hand holding the back her head, looking at the drawing, not quite hearing me. Eric stayed back, and the assistant, Geoffrey, was reduced to a fixed smile on his face. He looked like a hanger-oner.

Christa suddenly began walking toward the door. "Well, all we can do is point you to some boxes of drawings. You can compare it. Just call and make an appointment." she said, walking rapidly away. Eric and I followed.

"I was wondering if Peter Cundy could see it," Eric said to her back.

We all stopped at the department door. "Yep, if he's here and the drawing is at the same time, that would be fine with us. Up to Peggy to work it all out. He comes here pretty often." She looked at me. "We don't offer the public attributions, of course. You know that?"

I nodded and she glared. Clearly, she was busy, and I was lucky to get any attention from such a major player. She said good-bye while doing an about-face and was gone.

Eric and I made our way out of the department door. I was put off. Why did I tell Margy Zorn and Eric Matheson I wanted to go to graduate school? These people were all convinced I was going to take a lot of time off from work and study the hell out of the drawing. The museum's public space was still noisy, clattering with tourists and groups of school kids. I was alone with Eric. I really wasn't in the mood to try to converse with him, and even though I owed him some recognition for all his trouble in going with me to the museum, I wasn't sure how to acknowledge it. I decided to wait, guided by the rush and noise of the place around us. We got to the main lobby, through it without an utterance, to the doors where he opened one for us, and out into the startling sunlight and wispier, unconditioned air. Halfway down the steps we stopped, and I was all set to say thank you and goodbye, when he asked me where I was headed.

I must have looked unwilling to answer because he added, "What direction?"

"Downtown."

"Okay. Well, we might share a taxi and save some money. Do you think? I have to go to the Village as a matter of fact."

I didn't want to, but what could I say? I mumbled in the affirmative and walked by his side. We made our way to the street and there were quite a few cabs there as always, dropping off people, so we got right into one. After a minute of sitting and cruising in silence I partially turned to him.

"Uh, I want to thank you for your help here."

"Great, I was glad to. I have to see my sister, Amanda, anyway and the museum's close enough."

"Your sister lives in New York?"

"She's just spending a year here. She does volunteer work at the Donnell Library. Do you know it? It's a library for children near the Museum of Modern Art. It's part of the New York Public Library."

I nodded even though I'd never heard of it. We were going fairly rapidly down Fifth Avenue with the midday direct May light making Central Park's foliage look new and eager. He didn't say anything else for half a minute, poking at his small leather suitcase and looking out his window.

Out of the blue, he said, "So, if I can ask, what are you doing for work?"

"Uhh, nothing much. I work for an insurance company."

"Oh. Do you like it?"

"Yeah, yes, I do, oddly enough. I might not for long, but I have to pay the rent. And it's not bad."

"Great."

The cab came to a halt at the end of the park. Eric and I both leaned forward, looking at a line of cars as far as the eye could see. The Plaza and a row of very expensive hotels lined the Park to our right, but inside the old cab the air smelled unremarkably like remnants of past passengers and getting back to my job and separating from the cultural anomaly next to me felt inexorable, traffic or not. I sat back and so did he. He stared straight ahead, silently. I had the drawing tucked away once again in my backpack on my lap.

He opened his suitcase and pulled out a dozen or so papers. Some had handwritten scribblings, some seemed to be documents, cheap black and white copies with faded images of works of art in the middle of text. I was looking past the driver now and watching the traffic not move. Too bad I didn't have something to read. And I refused to read my phone like a drudge.

The drawing might be gone in a few weeks. So it would be potential realized and capital spent in some way. Weird thought after all those years. And the time dragged as we didn't move, and the cab driver grumbled in some language and Eric studied his pages and I gaped out until five minutes must have passed.

"Have you applied to graduate programs?" he asked.

He didn't have to talk to me.

"Well." I cleared my throat a bit. "I'm waiting. It costs an arm and a leg, and to be honest I have a few other, more immediate, tangible issues in my life right now that I'd rather face up to."

The cab lurched forward a bit, stopped, and then did it a few more times as I said this. There was something comical to me about that and speaking to this extremely well-educated English guy about graduate school or jobs or anything approaching career ambitions since he was clearly pretty well set. What wasn't funny was how easy it is to have high standards when you're all set. Whatever his background, he had to be making more than decent money at his posh job. And he reeked of the self-assurance of people who base their standards on some old traditions from some old country somewhere else. He didn't even belong here, I was thinking.

We both sat back again after leaning forward to look out the windshield. There were sirens off in the distance and cars fuming everywhere in a nasty gridlock.

"Yeah, looks like it's jammed-up. Are you in a hurry?" He looked at me.

A thought raced through me. What if I said, no, I wasn't in a hurry and he wanted to go get a drink at the Plaza or something?

So I said, "Yes."

"Yeah, I am a bit too. I don't think it looks good, does it?"

"No." A bit of my petty conceit fell to dust. I wanted to laugh.

He was looking out the window next to him. When he spoke, he usually looked directly at a person and then away, then back again. I noticed that the first time I met him. His body language was like something from an ancient silent movie. We were both looking out now and the fact was sirens were getting closer and no one in front, behind or to the side was moving if they were in a stupid car. Two tons of burden. The happy souls who were walking, they were doing fine.

They were all over the sidewalks, looking bemused, it seemed to me. It would be about a twenty-minute walk if I got out.

"You said you're from England?"

He looked at me more open eyed than before.

"Well, sort of. My father was English and my mother's from Romania." He suddenly looked wistful, continuing, "My parents met when my father was stationed in Berlin. During the cold war Romania was out of bounds, of course. My mother's family escaped after the Second World War, but that was as far as they got and I went to school in Berlin growing up, because my father was stationed there with NATO Forces. So an army brat, yeah."

He did it again. He turned his head back and forth a couple of times.

"As far? Sorry? As far as they got?" I was surprised he said so much to me and I was in a researching mood.

"Hm? Uh, well, my mother's family didn't want to be in Berlin. Not then, during the Cold War. They wanted to head farther west but there were so many restrictions at first and they didn't have the right connections, I don't think."

I nodded at him and then said nothing, turning and looking out the windshield again.

After half a minute, he spoke again and this time I could see peripherally that he wasn't looking at me. He was faced forward too.

"I think it made them value the basic things in life, my mother's family. They weren't spoiled."

I looked at him wondering why he'd say that particular thing. No one at Tufts ever used old expressions like that. But then I wondered if he thought I might just be one more spoiled American brat.

He stretched forward and away, looking anxious for the cab to get moving. His haircut was sort of old fashioned. It was in between short and long and seemed to all aim for some midpoint at the back of his head.

I spoke up. "Yeah, I'll be honest. I'm not idealistic about survival, and I'd imagine it would make people careful about life. Maybe hold onto a sense of reverence." I stopped myself, my eyes looking out the windshield. Sure enough, he reacted.

"Sense of reverence," he was looking sideways at me.

"Um, otherwise life really does just become a rat race, I think." I glanced at him and got a quizzical look back and then I looked away.

"Hmm. Yeah, that's interesting. So, do you find the rat race in your work?"

That sounded pretty damned sad to me. *My work.*

"No. Yes, of course. Same as anywhere, I guess. There are tons of rats everywhere."

He chuckled, but not enthusiastically. As we both stared out the windshield, I wished the cab would move. We still hadn't gone more than a block since we hit Central Park South. Walkers were still cheerfully moving along.

"But so tell me. You do value practical things, like money, right?"

I looked at him after he said that. Was he eighty years old and enjoying this somehow, my youthful bantering?

I looked straight at him, saying, "Yeah. I'm aware only idiots don't value money. No, life's too short to be stupid and impractical." I turned toward the windshield and slowed myself down as much as I could, but my voice was tight, probably sounding angry. "I had an uncle, an immigrant from Ireland who had to survive on his own in Brooklyn for years, who lived very well all by himself with some money . . . enough so he could afford to have principles and afford to stay away from all the money grubbing or power grubbing types out there. I looked up to him. He was the only person

I've ever actually looked up to that way." I turned to Eric. "So, yeah, I think living well is the best revenge all right."

He looked irritated and I leaned forward and looked out the window, just to look away for a few seconds. But then he sat so stiffly and for so long, it communicated some reaction.

"Yeah, your uncle sounds like a rare, principled man. That's great. But, you know, it's funny. *Living well is the best revenge,* is an old English phrase. I think it was from George Herbert in the seventeenth century and had religious meaning and all that. But in the modern materialistic world, who's living well and who's it revenge against usually? Makes me wonder if it isn't more than a little bit of a beady-eyed excuse sometimes."

I said nothing. He was lecturing me about materialism? What was his problem? He knew some beady-eyed people he didn't like? He thought all Americans were beady-eyed? I was still leaning forward and just turned and looked at him. If this was now a debate, how could I state the obvious? I said nothing and he stared back.

My words escaped quietly, "It's revenge against the rats. The beady-eyed ones are the rats. And they're everywhere."

And he gave me a very odd, awkward, forced smile. I had to turn away. The cab was stopped again.

Grumbling to myself, looking out my side window, I turned to him.

"You know, I have to walk. It's only a ten- or fifteen-minute walk from here. This way it could take an hour."

"Okay." He wasn't going to try to stop me.

I got some money out of my backpack and handed him my share, moving quickly past the beginnings of him resisting that offer. He was just an arrogant, old fashioned snob. They gathered around art like rats to garbage.

✒ Chapter 9 ✒

Slick old Eric Matheson helped me though and I was excited to tell Mark. It was dinner time before I could sit down across from him with a plate of organic, whole grain spaghetti. He'd already eaten.

Mark looked confused while I recounted my Boston and New York museum trips.

He blew out some smoke. "I'm not sure I really get what an attribution is."

"Uhh, it's basically an art expert saying who the artist is and some other facts about a work. They might say it's, *from the studio of* someone." I made quotation marks in the air. "Or if they don't want to commit to that, sometimes they say a work is, *by a follower of* someone, or if they don't even know that, they might label it, *after Rembrandt*, or someone. So I'm not sure but I think that would basically mean it's in the style of Rembrandt but who knows who did it or when. That kind of thing."

He just glared at me and I laughed and then laughed harder. He smiled, watching and I leaned over onto the floor, balancing my plate of spaghetti. It was the best laugh I'd had in months.

He said, "Jesus, is it a good drawing or isn't it?"

I coughed and sputtered, laughing, and finally collected myself. "Yeah, I know, but it gets touchy. The more of a brand name attached to it, the better. Right? Life in the big stupid city."

"Anyway, too bad it isn't a Rembrandt."

"Yeah."

We both grumbled and I laughed a bit and I ate some more, sitting uncomfortably on the floor with my legs crossed and the fairly cold plate of spaghetti balanced half on my thighs, half on my lap.

I drank some water. "So, Mark, anyway, as I said, so far all we know is it's probably Italian, late sixteenth century. Okay? I'll look into it and eventually get it attributed and then you can sell the thing. I'll have to take a day off from work and go to their Study Room and all that. I mean, sorry, but they want me to research it myself and then choose some dealer they know. It sounds complicated but it isn't."

After watching me blankfaced, he thought out loud, "I just wonder what we could get for it."

"I don't know. No idea, but it's for you, Mark, not us."

Silence for a minute, me eating.

"But, I mean, like, around two thousand, or ten thousand?"

"Hm? I really have no idea. Sorry. We don't know enough about it yet."

Silence again as he stared at space.

"Yeah, anyway, it would be very nice for us to get as much as ten thousand."

"That would be nice, but it's yours Mark. Whatever it's worth, it's yours. Uh, but, yeah, it's just not anything I have a clue about. The museum people I took it to in Boston and at the Met only gave me the most basic information, but I was lucky to get that. They want me to research it myself because I majored in art history, for what that's worth. God. And I can't take a day off for a couple of weeks."

Mark rested his head back onto the wall, looking up. After half a minute he said, "I still wonder what good Italian Renaissance drawings go for. I know, you don't know, but you hear about paintings getting millions at auctions, right? Jesus."

"Paintings, right. Not drawings. And even then, those are the paintings done by major artists, certified in some way."

His face narrowed. "They said it was pretty good at the museum in Boston."

"But Mark, I'm sorry, but I don't want you getting your hopes up and then finding out it's only worth four hundred dollars. You know what I mean, right? Who knows what the heck it's worth? We have no idea, yet."

He finally got back to smoking and staring into space and I finished eating. He was pretty worked up in some distant way and I worried that, when his bubble burst, he'd crash back down onto the floor. It was why I hadn't mentioned the drawing since I moved back.

The college obsession came up in the puny kitchen as we cleaned the dishes. State universities were my main pitch since he wasn't going to ask the parents for any money. And I had to just listen without responding when he described wanting to go to Union or Clark or Syracuse or Skidmore. I couldn't see him getting into, or affording, any of those. I tried to reason with him. Maybe I could help him with applications to find some nice collegiate experience somewhere. Maybe he'd get some financial aid somewhere. It was exhausting wandering down these long, vague byways with Mark, though, and I finally got away and went to bed.

And so the days passed and the college conversation seldom varied. I sat down across from him less often to avoid reinforcing his unreal ambitions. I did ask him if he was looking for work a couple of times and got told nothing was offered beyond some warehouse jobs, sure enough.

My work seldom varied. It buzzed on a computer screen in front of me, feeling about as meaningful as pointless busy-work usually does.

Mark called me at work one day. He never did that. It was a week after I talked to him about the drawing.

I kept my voice low, not wanting Sonya, the department assistant to the director, to hear me. It was the middle of the morning.

He was hyped, breathing heavily. "Yeah, listen. I'm home. I was just at an art dealer with the drawing and I left it there, Peggy. I got a receipt and all that, but the guy said he really liked the drawing and could sell it for us."

I had a sudden claustrophobic feeling.

"No, Mark, what? What dealer?"

"Yeah, I found him. I found him in the West Village, from lists online. I chose him because his address is so good and, sure enough, he has a nice gallery and lots of great stuff. So he said he can sell it. He has connections all over the country and sells things like this. He liked it."

I couldn't stand it. Mark was desperate and finally left the apartment, wanting the money for whatever. I could barely speak. What stupid dealer was he talking about?

I just said, "Fine", as reasonably as I could so the conversation could end.

All I could do was move along and ignore whatever I couldn't control. I blocked it as well as I could and got back to busywork as well as I could.

❧ Chapter 10 ❧

It wasn't easy, but I never asked Mark about the drawing. I aimed any verbal excursions on the grimy floor in the living room toward anything else. He never mentioned the thing, so I assumed it was being examined by some art dealer out there. Time dribbled on.

Two weeks into the drawing's absence, I got a phone call from Margy Zorn. It was early June, around eleven on a Saturday morning and Mark was in his usual spot on the floor. I was in my room reading the Washington Post online. My first thought was Margy Zorn had some news, finally, about Stanford.

"Sorry, Mrs. Zorn, I couldn't really hear you."

"No, call me Margy," she said in a raised, slower voice. "I wanted to let you know some word reached us that a Mr. Daniel Loring has been trying to sell your drawing, sending letters to collectors." She let that attach itself to me. "Uh, and the thing is, that's fine, but it's a little unprofessional of him to be using our museum as a reference in a sense, claiming the drawing was basically attributed by us, and the Met too, as an anonymous late Renaissance, Italian Renaissance drawing."

"Oh, God." My heart began to race.

"No, I'm sure you have some explanation, Peggy. I'm not calling to complain or reprimand you. It's just, it can get messy if dealers misrepresent things in that way. I mean, you know, you have to be careful with people. Do you know much about this Daniel Loring?"

"No. I have no idea. Uh, my brother's the one who's taken it to him. I only knew my brother took it to somebody, uh . . ."

"Okay. Peggy, can I speak candidly with you? It's why I waited until the weekend. Sorry to bother you."

"No, that's fine. Thank you for telling me."

"Well, this dealer is probably not used to rare works of art. I've never heard of him. You say you didn't find him for your brother?"

"No."

"Okay. Well, I'm sure it will just straighten itself out. You might want to see if this dealer's at all legit, then maybe see if he'll retract any statements about the Boston Museum or the Met in his advertising. At least he has said the work's anonymous."

"Yeah, it's awful. I'm sorry. I'll talk to my brother and we'll straighten out the dealer. My brother wouldn't just do anything for the money. He'll be really upset, in fact, if he thinks the dealer's been misrepresenting things." I was pacing.

I noticed she was staying quiet. I had to calm down.

I stopped pacing and tried to slow my breathing. "So, but, Mrs. Zorn, how did you hear about the letters?"

"From a collector we know up in Ipswich, Massachusetts who got one in the mail. Yeah, there are dealers, of course, who can represent you and your brother in a way that'll avoid this sort of thing. Actually, there's probably a better chance of getting it sold. Okay, Peggy? No, I don't want to upset you. And the collector, by the way, who told us about the letter she got, doesn't collect Italian drawings. She collects French nineteenth century prints. So much for the dealer's mailing list. But, anyway, it is why you have to go about things a bit more methodically. Okay?"

"Yeah, I know. I should have gotten an expert attribution before I gave it to my brother. I didn't know he'd do this. But I'll have to talk to him." I was hesitant about making any promises. Mark might be too emotionally unstable for many promises.

"Thank you, Peggy. I'm relieved," she exhaled. "Spilt milk under the bridge, right?"

I barely answered, barely able to. The conversation fidgeted to its own dead end. I heard myself thanking her, no one saying anything about Stanford.

I walked right into the living room and sat on the floor across from Mark. I told him about the phone call from Margy Zorn.

He gave me that unblinking gaze of his.

With me done, he said, "But, what?" His voice was compacted, and his eyes got filled with confusion and anger. He was leaning back against the wall but with his head forward. "It's our drawing."

"No, see, that dealer hasn't attributed it, Mark, because he's not up to the task. The museums in Boston and New York haven't attributed it. They made that clear. No one has attributed the drawing yet. I was going to go back to the Met to get someone they recommended."

"The dealer looked at it and thought it was great."

"Mark, he said in a letter, that he sent around God knows where, that these museums said it was an Italian Renaissance drawing, like it was a seal of approval or something."

Mark didn't move. His mouth was now slack. I waited, trying to not completely lose patience.

He seemed to be looking at my chin. "They did say that, and the dealer said it was great and he thought it was an Italian Renaissance drawing and he sells drawings and paintings."

I sat with my back arched, as upright as I could and faced him. "Mark, sorry, but please listen to me. I can only tell you how it works according to the people I'm talking to and to me too. It's misrepresenting the thing the way it stands now. A run-of-the-mill dealer like this, who probably can't do an attribution on anything, sure as hell can't do one on sixteenth century Italian drawings, especially anonymous ones. Has he spent twenty or thirty years studying this particular area of art? He profits from saying these major museums studied the drawing and concluded it's late Italian Renaissance. They didn't ever really study it. They glanced at it as a favor. This dealer wants to use the big, prestigious museum names so he'll get more money for it. It's a conflict of interest, Mark."

I was disgusted and didn't do a lot to hide it with my precise formulation of words. Mark was sitting very still, his face a deep, sweaty red and still staring wide-eyed toward me, somewhere.

He shook his head. "Okay, shit. Yeah, I'll call him and ask him to get the museum names off his letters, or whatever." He blew out some smoky air, looking up at the ceiling, then at me. "It's hell. You can have the drawing Mark. No, you can't."

"No! I'm sorry. I wanted to find a dealer, an expert. What can I say? Yeah, just phone him, please."

He smirked, not looking at me at all now.

What step was missing? How should I communicate with Mark? It made me want to say more, to explain more, and I knew I couldn't or shouldn't. The truncated conversation meant I sat there, blood rushing to my head, feeling a crazy combination of fury at Mark and squelched by him. Since I said nothing and just looked out the window, clenching my teeth, he got up and walked into the kitchen.

I was so Goddamned sorry I gave him the drawing. Now what? He really wouldn't get a job because he'd get some quick cash to live on? For how long? He was delusional. And I was beyond delusional sitting in that dump of an apartment in the

grayest part of Brooklyn, for no good reason except a childhood dream of kinship.

I thought he'd get some beer, and that was what I heard,
the sound of a beer can pop open and fizz. I was unable to
move as I thought about what might happen next. Would he
come back to the living room? I listened to him being very
quiet in the kitchen. *He's drinking,* I thought. *I hope he stays in
there. I was hungry before. I will be. Maybe I should leave and
eat in a restaurant.*

❧ Chapter 11 ❧

The restaurant was fine. I ran most of the four blocks there in the rain, wanting to get away from the frustration, away from the depressing apartment. I was incapable of really helping Mark. He was incapable of being close to me anymore. So what were we both doing? I wasn't sure if I was lost in a black dungeon or just in a dark, wet paper bag. I'd have to go back to that dingy, barren apartment with no furniture in it and see Mark. I didn't want to do anything like that, but I had to. Tomorrow I'd phone Dr. Tuck. I'd go to work, happy to get out of the apartment and make that phone call when I could, as soon as I could. In the meantime, I had to go back, and hope Mark and I would be all right with each other.

After taking a cab back, I opened the apartment door slowly to see, Mark wasn't in his spot on the floor. I walked quietly down the hallway noting his door was closed, his light on and his radio talking. It was what people at Tufts called, *squawk radio.* I very quietly latched my door and went to bed and heard the radio grumbling through the wall for the next couple of hours as I drifted in and out of sleep.

A headache mixing with bubbling anxiety, I got to work the next day. I didn't see Mark in the morning, but I usually didn't see him in the morning because he slept in late every day, sometimes from what I saw on my days off, until eleven or twelve.

There was my appointment to see Dr. Tuck. I'd have to wait four days, until Saturday at ten, but I felt a little sense of relief at just seeing someone on the horizon I could talk to reasonably.

But the urge for going was growing dangerously strong in me. I knew more and more, I wanted to get away. I ached to get away from the place I'd supposedly already gotten away from. I couldn't think about it. And I couldn't say any of it to Dr. Tuck. Mark was the subject, not me.

It was the second time meeting with him. I sat in his comfortable stuffed armchair as he wheeled his desk chair around to face me, six or seven feet away, crossing his legs, exposing thin white socks. I looked away, knowing I'd have to do most of the talking in the beginning so I just waded in, telling him as much of what had been going on as I could. He nodded a few times and cleaned his glasses, but I thought I noticed some concern on his face.

"Yeah, you know Peggy I'll have to admit that there seems to be too little progress with Mark. His sitting and staring for hours on end, yeah, and not getting a job. I'm talking about progress with limitations. He does have a condition that won't just go away. I mean basically he'll have to deal with it all his life to some extent."

I waited after hearing that grim freaking prognosis. The psychologist leaned his head back for a few seconds, facing the white ceiling, thinking.

His eyes were back on me. "See, I think we have to admit he's not getting to the next stage in his thinking or his behavior. Working and making enough money to take care of yourself is essential if you want to function as an independent person. Right? I mean, you know that, and I know that. We don't know what the actual steps are for him, because he has to figure out somethings. He talks about this, uhh, college thing when he talks to me too. I don't know. He does sort of seem distracted and unfocused when he talks about it."

Once again, I could tell Dr. Tuck was wrestling with how much he should say to me, and I had the feeling he might have just said more than he normally might. I had to listen and wait.

"Uh, look." He sat forward, leaning his arms on the narrow, wooden arms of his chair. "Mark has to take care of himself, basically, like anyone else, or be taken care of. But see, the vicious circle can be that all this counseling means people give up a piece of themselves and that can make it much harder to learn to think for yourself and to function. Then, on the other hand there are some people who need help getting through life and the issue just ends up coming down to that."

"Yeah," I sighed. "I want to help him, but I do feel pretty unsure how to at times."

"And is he acting like he resents you for it? Like the business with the drawing?"

"Um, I don't know."

I was holding my chin in my hand, my elbow on the arm of the chair looking at him, feeling comfortable, in that chair and that office with someone speaking intelligently to me and with the best, sincere intentions. I couldn't get too comfortable, schmoozing.

Dr. Tuck sat like me, thinking. After a minute he just looked at me and shook his head, his brownish hair as dirty and greasy as ever. He took in a deep breath. "Yeah, so we're just dealing with limits on what we can do. All of us."

I blinked, considering that.

He leaned forward.

I must have been gawking and looking semiconscious because he raised his voice for the first time ever, just a bit. "Want to know what I think is crazy?"

I automatically nodded, minimally.

"Life." He concentrated, his face emphatic. "For so many thousands and thousands of years we lived in larger family groups, much larger because we needed that to survive. We're tribal, social animals, but now, suddenly, so many of us live in smaller and smaller families, stragglers, staring at each other, wondering what we're supposed to do next."

I groaned, "Sounds like a nightmare."

He said, "And we live longer."

He was trying to be funny and I wanted to laugh but couldn't.

"And it was just you and Mark most of the time."

Okay, the psychologist was making his point.

He sat back. "I guess all we can do is watch and wait. If you can hold on a bit longer. You took on more than most people would, at least these days, when you quit your job and came three thousand miles back here for your brother. But your love and generosity helped get him out of that house, out of his rut on Long Island."

I shook my head and looked away. It sounded much too complimentary now, when I knew I wanted to get away from Mark. I couldn't, but I wanted to. I left the psychologist's office a few minutes later, feeling afraid I created a nightmare of a rut for Mark and me in Brooklyn.

✿ Chapter 12 ✿

It was harder and harder to look up that bright sunny June. There were no guidelines in my life. Bumbling off to endless dull work, bumbling back to the strange apartment, sometimes entangled in long discussions with Mark about whatever we conjured up . . . me opening the windows to let out the cigarette smoke. Meanwhile, I spent all my money on rent, Mark's Dr. Tuck visits and a savings account for Mark for college, knowing I could only do that for so long before my life would collapse under its own dead weight.

But weeks pushed by and hot, thick summer happened. I got Mark out and took a cab to the nearest hardware store and bought a small window air conditioner that we put in the living room window.

Then the outlook for the future became a not very distant precipice when an email arrived on my computer inviting Mark and me home for Father's Day. It was only that, nothing else mentioned. It was nuts. Birthdays were universally ignored in our broken little family and I hadn't done anything for Mother's Day or Father's Day since high school, and then just a cheap card. It was one week away. I walked into the living room and stood across from Mark, feeling very calm and self-possessed for some reason, more than for as long as I could remember. Maybe I finally had both feet firmly on the bottom.

"Yeah, I'm not going to Long Island for Father's Day."

"No?"

His simple response irritated me, but I just moved on, not wanting to get bogged down on the damned living room floor. I stayed standing and outlined the obvious.

"Do what you want, but I don't have that kind of relationship with Mom and Dad right now. Maybe someday, but not yet. I had it with Uncle Ethan and you but not them. I'm going to keep my distance from them for now. But that's what I'm going to do. You do what's best for you. But let me ask you, since we haven't talked about it for a while, what your plans are?"

"Plans? What, you mean? College?"

"Sure, college, etcetera."

He flinched just a bit. "Uhh, I plan on going as soon as I can. I have that book I showed you and I've been reading about colleges in New England. Yeah, they seem great, a lot of them. But I was going to sit you down to tell you some news. The dealer sold the drawing and gave me a check yesterday. Thirty-two thousand dollars!" Mark's face got bloated and shiny and his eyes were suddenly focused on me. He was back on some sort of medication. I knew that.

Flinching myself, I got what he just said.

I grunted, "Thirty-two? What? Are you kidding?" I was a teetering mixture of doubt and curiosity.

"No. I didn't want to bring it up until the time was right. But, yeah, isn't that amazing? But I knew the guy was telling the truth when he said he could sell it. And he did take the museum names off his website, uhh, a week ago, I think."

Mark stared at me waiting for me or any other strange forces out there to come down on him. The most I could do was wait and remain positive, so I just nodded, smiling nervously, beginning to understand how much he said he got. Thirty-two thousand, after the dealers cut? It must have sold for something approaching as much as forty thousand dollars. My skin getting goosebumps, I sat on the floor. I didn't want to get involved with the drawing anymore, so I tried to not show my astonishment, but I sure as hell never would have guessed it was worth that much.

I lost any ability to smile as Mark talked about things for a minute.

"Uhh, yeah, the dealer told me . . ." He began to look for something in his pants pockets, stretching his long legs and searching in his two front pockets, then both his back pockets, then all of them again as he spoke. "Yeah, I don't know if I have it on me, but, uh, he took a commission, twenty percent, and I got, or we got, thirty-two thousand. You want to see the check?" He stood up.

My mouth was open, and I shook my head and shrugged off seeing the check.

"Uh, so, it's all yours. That's enough for a great start for college," I said.

"Yeah, well, I want you to have half."

I glared up at him. "Mark. Jesus, I love you. Please don't make me scream bloody murder and call the police, and I'll have to if we go down that path. It's yours, please," I groaned, mindlessly grinning now, like a drunk filled with stupid good will. He sniggered hesitantly, standing in the middle of the room, his eyes on the wall behind me.

"Yeah, well, we'll see. But, yeah . . ." he was muttering partly to himself. "Peggy, I think I got into Clark University for this coming fall term."

I stretched my neck and rolled my eyes.

"Yeah, I can't believe it," he said.

"What? What do you mean, you *think* you got in?"

"Well, uh, it's been mainly on the phone, you know, talking to admissions and a couple of letters back and forth. They got my transcript. But, Christ Peggy, you know what?"

"No, I don't know anything. What?"

"After I told them I saved sixteen thousand myself, they offered me a scholarship for most of the rest, as long as I fill out all the forms. I might need your help for that. Jesus, I hate forms."

I just sat trying to understand.

He said, "Most of the tuition and room and board for three years, Peggy. Shit, can you believe it? I mean, I have to work and there will be some loans."

He glared down at me, wanting me to be delighted.

I pulled myself back, holding onto one knee. "I saw some letters from colleges coming in. But my God, Mark, that's incredible. Clark, wow, amazing! And you saved thirty-two thousand, by the way, not sixteen . . . I mean, before taxes. And you'd better get that check in the bank. Wow. But, so they gave you credit for a year of community college?"

"Yeah, I had enough A's and B's. But, yeah, you know what? I played the older, mature student angle on the Skype interview and in my personal statement on the application, saying I know what I want to study now, and I've worked hard and saved money for this."

"Jesus. Unbelievable." I had no idea he could manage Skype on his old computer he never seemed to use. I came to. "Wow. What do you want to study?"

"Psychology. I've told you that. Psychology's a big deal at Clark."

My arms were wrapped around both my knees, sitting in a ball, thinking about how anxious I'd been, assuming Mark was conjuring up crazy false hopes about college. What complicated schemes was he conjuring while I thought he was only staring at dead space? I leaned back and looked up at the ceiling and laughed and groaned.

"Mark, Mark, Mark. You're unbelievable."

He joined in laughing, still standing, hovering. "It didn't hurt that I could write about schizophrenia in family members being one of the main reasons for my commitment to the cause."

My arms still wrapped around my legs, my head was turning in circles and he was just getting warmed up. This was the old Mark.

He smiled down at me broadly. "It's called the power of psychotic channeling."

I groaned again, laughing, wanting to roll around on the floor. I wanted go outside and dance in the street. For Mark's sake, I stayed as stationary as humanly possible, using words of support and encouragement, repeating how great his news was.

He sat, leaning against his usual wall.

"So I didn't tell them I'm on meds. I have been taking the meds for over a month now. But you know what?"

"No, I don't know what."

"Nuts like me fairly often do pretty well coming up with angles like this, left to our own devices, I guess. And psychology might be something I can really do. Right? Nuts like me like reading about all the different ways of being nuts."

I chortled with him over that. Then we sobered up a bit and drank some coffee and he answered my questions about Clark University. Basically, he only knew it was a seriously good university and had a beautiful campus in Worcester, Massachusetts and he'd be getting his acceptance letter in the next week or two. I noticed he began to withdraw and looked tired after telling me that. His emotions were spent. Not wanting to somehow trample on a good thing, I said good-night and left him there, smoking, head back against the wall, staring at something in midair.

❧ Chapter 13 ❧

Rag-snot, turtledove
Sea-breeze agrees
Frozen spaghetti
Lots of cheese, please

It was the middle of the night when Mark's poem came back to me. He wrote it on my birthday card when I was eleven.

It was one long sleepless night after he told me about the money for the drawing and Clark University.

It was great, but whatever flimsy hold I had on my relationship with him was going to stay flimsy. If he left and managed to get through college, we'd be separated for a long time. If he failed, I'd be burdened with how much endless, flimsy effort?

The next few days passed with no more talk about college. We avoided anything beyond weather and food chatter. I went to bed early each night and read, often drifting off to thinking, almost always the same delirious, half-sleeping thoughts. Maybe I had choices.

If he was actually going to Clark and going sometime soon, what was next for me? I'd be a free woman? A free, young woman? I hadn't felt young or free for a while now, not since leaving San Francisco. I got away and now I'd get away again? My life was appearing before me in fits and bits.

Less than a week later Mark got his acceptance letter and even got a work-study job in the student union, helping with lectures or something for fifteen hours a week. If he could handle that, he'd owe something around fifteen or twenty thousand when he graduated. He'd have to work full-time during the summer doing something else for the University. It was all stuff I had done at Tufts, all part of a financial aid package, except I owed nothing, thanks to Uncle Ethan and Tufts and my working odd hours the whole time. I wondered if Mark would be able to handle all the part time working and studying, but if he was apprehensive about things, he didn't show it, except maybe by not talking about it. The only thing he brought up a few times was his concern about living in a dorm with a bunch of what the university labeled, *mature undergraduates*. Mark called it, "Dregs Dorm".

He really was leaving.

I waved goodbye to him as he left to spend some time celebrating Father's Day on Long Freakin Cretin Island with the parents.

Mark and I had our own weird little celebration sitting on the floor at the end of June. He was leaving for Clark orientation and to start work in a few days. I bought him a hundred dollar gift certificate to Panera and a late nineteenth century leather bound copy of, "The Works of Ralph Waldo Emerson", and kept myself from crying as he told me about reading Emerson's essay called, "Self-Reliance", in high school.

Mark left, inevitably, driving away from a Brooklyn rental car company five blocks from our apartment. I watched him get into his large ugly white car with his striped jeans and flouncy old, vintage silk sports jacket, his hair uncombed. When I saw the back of his head moving down the street, I could only shudder at the loss of him. Mark was never on his own before. I walked back to the apartment, feeling displaced and alone myself and tried to think of what I should do to help if things got to be too much for him, wherever he was going. He'd never send me the pictures I asked him to send of the dorm and his new friends up there.

I stood alone in that ugly apartment that never felt like mine, or anyone's, and wagged my head in anguish. Whatever few things I had in my life were gone. Uncle Ethan was dead. Tufts was in my past. And Mark was gone. I walked back and forth until I was exhausted and went to lie down.

Short naps, often only fifteen or twenty minutes, were my form of meditation. All I had to do was lie back and close my eyes and breathe deeply, slowly, in and out. I always told myself I wasn't there to sleep, but to rest . . . just rest. I seldom dreamed of anything irritating or upsetting and instead so often managed to float into a dark, beautiful stream of physical and mental sedation. Sometimes there were wet, muscular, naked men.

I woke up in an altered state, rested and stronger.

Later that day, the tears I shed mostly dried, replaced by the dawning possibilities of my next move. I had to stop quitting jobs after only a few months. But San Francisco again? Boston? I had always liked the Cape Ann area, north of Boston. Yup, Gloucester. I was leaning way over toward that. It was close to the sea, but up high to avoid rising seas, with clean air, crispy, interesting people, a train, an actual train to Boston for museums and music, a job, maybe graduate school. What the hell, Gloucester had its own great art museum and stores and restaurants.

The next day, in the middle of humming along just so emphatically, I got the email. It was a showstopper.

Peggy - I don't know what you know about
the sale of your drawing, but I'm afraid things

got fairly messy. During our initial meeting I tried to be clear about the correct procedures for getting an attribution. We thought we made it plain to you that it was never attributed by us, or later, the Met. Unfortunately, trying to explain that to the very serious collector who brought it into our department was not easy -- because, he was told otherwise by your dealer.

That important collector did get rid of the drawing, but, unfortunately, by passing it on to another important collector. The unnecessary repercussions go on.

Marjorie Zorn

Book Three

❧ Chapter 1 ❧

Eric Matheson bought the drawing. I sat alone in a corner near the window of the Poland Street, Au Bon Pain, sipping occasionally on my small coffee on a frosty air-conditioned Saturday in steamy July. Obviously Margy Zorn was extremely frustrated and angry at me for not getting the drawing properly attributed before trying to sell it. And obviously, after reading her email a few times, I had to email her back to ask who the hell the important people were who bought the drawing. Her second email came back a day later.

> *Museum Trustee, Stephen Kensett sold it*
> *to Eric Matheson, and I have no idea why. I do*
> *know I'm finished with it.*

And everything suddenly shifted even more, and I had to ask myself constantly why Eric Matheson bought the drawing. Why would he do that? It unnerved me to no end.

Sitting and thinking, my solitary, sorry state was making me feel pathetic and substandard. Sitting and thinking couldn't be all I had in life, me sipping my coffee and staring out the window at people out there I didn't know at all and never would.

Mark got the money for college from Eric Matheson? That was one hell of a degrading thought. I hated that forced connection or obligation.

I grimaced, scanning the busy, searing, hot human street scene of cars driving by and people scurrying to get out of the sun. My jaw was clenched, and my head ached.

I was in a hurry to get home, ducking through the curdled outside air, to escape inside to concentrate on my computer. I had to take a shower first, to cool down and reduce the grime. I almost never looked at my atrophied Facebook stuff, with bare-bones information on it and damned few friends. Did Eric Matheson still have one? I looked at some information online back in San Francisco. It was standard professional profiling as I recalled -- inconsequential deets that stuffed the internet in general. There were a few pictures of him standing next to well-dressed old people at museum openings. Maybe I missed something.

With my single sputtering air conditioner, me almost naked and all shades down, I was online. Sure enough, it took twenty minutes to find anything much at all. There were pictures of him half smiling, sometimes frowning at the camera. He looked good in one picture, maybe because it caught him off guard, not looking straight into the lens. He didn't seem to be photogenic and, yeah, when he didn't know they were photographing him, he looked very distinguished.

Not a lot was written about him that I didn't already know. There sure as hell wasn't anything about him collecting old Italian drawings. He was a curator, who specialized in nineteenth century British art, especially Victorian illustrated books and apparently that was the heyday for beautiful engraved book illustrations. I searched. Sure enough, nothing was said about him being a collector of anything. I stared at the pictures and they never looked back at me. Pictures weren't close to being enough. I sat thinking, then stood and stretched, not able to remember what he really looked like in person. I thought of emailing or phoning him, but it would be much too feeble. I needed information before I could try to talk to him. It all seemed to be some sort of gnawing, morbid obsession, driving me crazy, like a blunt sword poking at a Gordian brain knot. All I was thinking about suddenly was strange and distant Eric Matheson.

Sunday was just as sun-filled and humid and I sat inside my empty, dank apartment and showered one more time and paced and centered on my obsession until, finally too exhausted to think, a plan began to form on its own.

Stephen Kensett. After creeping around various websites for an hour, I saw his email address on a list of museum trustees. I wrote to him.

After waiting another week, I was on my way to New Salem, Connecticut. The drive, in a red Ford rental that smelled like fermenting vinyl, would take me about three hours. Mr. Kensett politely agreed to meet with me on Saturday at one. The weather was the same long July sun-rays, with the addition now of simmering asphalt as far as I could see. I wore my sunglasses, with nothing in my way but potential shame and ignorance. Mark added to that potential a few days before, sending me a big postcard of Sigmund Freud and Carl Jung and a few other renowned psychologists posing on the Clark University campus in some old black and white photograph. Mark liked his dorm room and was starting classes, and everything was great. Nothing was said in his three sentences about him already dipping into his cash, Eric Matheson's cash, a money trough from a bank account whose source was purely abstract to Mark -- not a mercenary compromise for Mark.

So was Stephen Kensett going to just sneer at me for being a nasty little sleaze pot?

The asphalt simmered on. New Salem, Connecticut was as far north as you could go before being in Massachusetts.

Definitely the New England half of Connecticut. I thought for a while about how much I would love to keep driving up north, up to Maine or someplace cool and clean to the touch and free from my life's petty explanations. The three-paragraph article on the Internet, written in honor of Mr. Kensett's retirement from the board of the Museum of Fine Arts, summed up his background enough to give me a composite picture of the man. Mr. Kensett's great-grandfather was one of the architects who built the Museum of Fine Arts in Boston. His firm did. Then Mr. Kensett's grandfather and father were on the board there and collected a good portion of the Japanese screen and Chinese porcelain collections in Boston, Worcester, Hartford, New York, Philadelphia and Washington. They were donated by them. This Stephen Kensett collected rare books, prints and drawings and was connected to the same museums as his forebears.

I was passing the white church that was in the middle of the village, of course, and on a hill like God placed it, and looking about that old. It was plain to the point of distilled perfection with antique white, rippling clapboard and a steeple of the same. Its sign said, *First Congregational, est. 1671.* Bloxham Road was next to the church, so I turned left onto what was basically a dirt path looking for number nineteen. But there were no houses until, right behind the church, there was a small white clapboard farmhouse and that was it, nineteen.

I parked in the short driveway to the side of the rambling, with a few odd shapes from small additions, nineteenth century house. It was gorgeous but not big, maybe about two thousand square feet. Was this all the man wanted, or all he could afford? Had to be one of many houses. It was tucked into the side of a hill with back views of a valley below for miles, along with views in front of the old church and compact Puritan graveyard.

"Peggy Avakian?"

The voice and the arm opening the door welcomed me in. Why hadn't I thought I could be attacked by a strange man in his house on an isolated road in the country?

The Internet article on the guy told me his wife died.

With me seated in the living room, in an antique wooden side-chair with spindly, hand carved arms, he went downstairs to the kitchen. The room around me was about twenty by twenty-five feet, with many paned windows on three sides and a gorgeous, rudimentary old brick fireplace with a maroon painted mantle in the center of the fourth wall. I noted the stunner of a seascape hanging over the mantle, heightened by blues and slashes of aqua-marine, looking like a Winslow Homer. That was the only work of art in sight. The rows of windows drew in nature from the rolling acres outside, into the room, contrasting that green with the white plaster walls and complimenting the reddish-brown, wide planked, old pine floor. Yeah, it was one of the most beautiful rooms I had ever seen, but that thought, any thought, was agitating me. The damned room was distilled perfection too. And quiet. My skin was tingling from the contrasts of hot and damp outside and cool and dry inside.

It was very private of course. Why would a man like this, with so much power, invite a complete stranger into his house?

Back upstairs he quietly placed the tray on a small table and walked mine over to me. He sat on the only new piece of furniture, a gorgeous small light green silk uphol-stered sofa, ten feet away. The tea was a bit soothing, warm and settling. Taking that in, not wanting to be diverted, I still had to take in my host. He was a treat for the eyes in his light blue button-down collared shirt -- an age-honed guy with cropped white tufts of hair on each side of his head, combed back, and tawny cheeks. Yup, sinewy, he was, and around six feet tall, with a fine coating of gray cilia on his long, strong forearms.

Fortunately, in a steady-low, resonant voice, he got to the point. "Good. So, Peggy, what did you want to say? You said in your email you were concerned the Italian drawing was misrepresented."

"Right, Mr. Kensett, I feel at least partly responsible for this. Uh, I wanted to get it fully studied and get an attribution from a reputable expert, but I gave it to my brother sooner than I should have."

He was leaning back a bit. "No, I don't think you have to worry about that as far as I'm concerned. But you said on the phone you know Eric Matheson bought the drawing?"

"Yes. I feel bad about not getting the drawing attributed when I could have, and I wondered if you knew why he bought it?"

He gaped at me and sat forward, the sofa rumbling softly. "No idea. I wasn't taking it into the museum to show it to him. I was showing it to the other people there, like the curator, Ann Vander and her assistant, Margy Zorn. It's a very nice drawing and in an area I felt made it very desirable. So, if the dealer's price was a bit high, I knew I could give it to a museum, Peggy. Do you see what I'm saying? The valuation of art varies according to who wants it and how badly."

I nodded. He had an on-going, rich-person, back-up plan. The drawing would have been just one more museum gift, a tax write-off, valued at whatever price he paid for it.

He went on since I didn't. "So don't worry about me. I never felt anything was being really misrepresented. I mean, the dealer didn't have anything in writing from a major art historian. I knew that. And I certainly knew that dealer wasn't a sixteenth century Italian expert."

He stopped and gazed at me. I continued to just gaze back, waiting for more. It wasn't him I was worried about. It was Eric Matheson.

He added, "I'm a good friend of the Boston Museum, so all I can say is, don't worry about it. The dealer stating the Boston and New York museums studied the drawing was not an issue for me."

He was protesting a little too much. It seemed pretty clear to me he never would have even looked at the drawing without the MFA and the Met connections.

I didn't know what to say and my blushing seemed to make him blush.

"Anyway," he said. "Really, I wanted to ask you though if you knew why Eric bought the drawing?"

I shook my head. He invited me there to ask me that? It was all I could do to not show my frustration.

"I have no idea. That's what I wanted to ask you." I took a breath. "I don't know him very well. He helped me with it a few times, but I certainly didn't want, or expect him to end up buying it. But, Mr. Kensett, why did you decide you didn't want it? Did he suddenly want it? Sorry to be so nosy, but what happened?"

He shrugged and spoke slowly, "Well, he came here and asked me if he could buy it. I was surprised but said yes. He's a good guy, Eric and I didn't mind. And please call me Stephen."

I sat more upright. "But he told me Italian drawings weren't his actual interest. I mean, I'm happy to hear you weren't very bothered by the dealer's hyped-up attribution claims, but I'm sure Margy Zorn and Eric Matheson were irritated by that."

"Yeah, actually that's what we can assume, I guess."

I didn't want to hear that and leaned down on the arms of the antique chair. I wanted to ask him if Eric Matheson was wealthy enough to casually throw forty thousand dollars at a drawing. This old guy was obviously rich enough to do that.

He was giving me a wan, maybe avuncular smile, probably to smooth over any possible controversies. They'd be minor controversies for him. He stood up and walked ten feet away to the mantle, where, with a dry voice, he said, "I thought Eric might have been a close friend of yours and that would explain him wanting to buy the drawing. He came here and sat right where you are now and pushed pretty hard for it. And I know Eric fairly well, and he's never done anything like that before. Apart from curators not normally asking trustees for works of art for themselves, it isn't in his field of interest, as you said."

Eyes on me, he leaned his elbow on the mantle. I wondered what the next move was in this two-person straw-grasping game. He looked like he wanted to grasp me. He was probably lonely out in the country, empty nesting on his own.

Distracted, I mumbled. "Anyway, as I said, I barely know Eric Matheson."

"I do as an associate. But he seemed to want the drawing, and, yeah, we don't seem to know why."

I murmured, "And it was too expensive. It was overpriced."

Mr. Kensett's face became paler gray and he moved away from the mantle at this. The flirtation with the young female ended after I expressed doubt about his art buying skills.

He rumpled back into the sofa and took his time, politely. "That might be true, or it might not. Remember, it's always hard to know what art's worth and especially anonymous pieces. Let's just hope Eric's happy with the drawing, because it's over. Not much we can do about it now."

Wanting a lot more substance than that and wanting to yell that at the kindly old gent across from me, I barely managed to keep a lid on. This major collector and museum trustee wanted an end to this muddled little interaction and his deep blue eyes were far removed from me, out the window, over gorgeous fields below.

And I didn't want to hang around any longer and stood up.

"Thank you, Mr. Kensett. Stephen." I aimed us toward the door. "I appreciate your openness and taking the time."

Outside, I was only half listening to his departure pleasantries about the nice weather. It was just too bright and hurting my eyes. I stood by my little dark red Ford rental car in his gravel driveway, reaching out my hand.

"Thanks. It doesn't make sense that Eric Matheson bought the drawing, uhh, but thanks."

"Right, no, I know. And we'll all miss him."

"Miss him?" I stood glaring into Stephen Kensett's eyes.

"Yeah. I assumed you knew. Sorry. He left for Dublin. Just left, I think. Uhh, he said he took a position at the Trevor Cobery Museum, there. Director. I don't know much about that museum, but it's too bad Boston's lost him."

❧ Chapter 2 ❧

For days I saw Eric Matheson walking around with the drawing, three thousand miles away. There was no sound to the vision. I tried to shake it off, but the haunting silent movie would just reappear in front of me, him carrying the drawing around, way far away.

He grabbed the drawing, left his job and went to Ireland?

I'd never heard of the Trevor Cobery Museum and looked up its website. It looked like an attractive, small art museum. I searched again for pictures of him in Boston. Maybe if I stared at pictures of him and read whatever the Boston Globe said about him at some Special Exhibition opening, I'd absorb some kind of information about the apparition, Eric Matheson. Not close.

At one point, on lunch hour at busywork, sitting in my boss's momentarily quiet office, I decided I had to talk to someone and phoned Christa Hiaphin. She was in but came to the phone ten minutes after I was told to please wait. I barely introduced the topic when she interrupted, "No, I know most of the details and yeah, it's too bad. I understand you didn't get what we were all trying to say, but it really is kind of a shame. I don't know what I can add at this point." Her voice was constrained.

I had to plow through. "Sorry, I won't keep you, but the thing is I've heard Eric Matheson bought the drawing and is now in Dublin. Do you have any idea why he's done either of those things?"

"Oh, I'm not comfortable talking about Eric this way. Sorry, but I know him and don't really know you."

"Sorry. It just surprised me."

"Yes, well I'm a bit perplexed myself. But really, I'm busy right now and I'm just not sure anything more can be done. Margy Zorn seemed to have a conniption over the drawing getting an attribution. You think it's your fault. Eric apparently thought he had to raise the bar of ethical standards in museums or something, and so he actually bought it. I think we're all overreacting just a bit. Anyway, it's water under the bridge at this point." She wanted to put me off with the sternness of her voice and she did. She hung up, barely uttering goodbye.

That rudeness, and her saying Eric Matheson felt forced to raise ethical standards, made me smolder even more.

Sometime later I remembered Margy Zorn using that hybrid expression, *spilt milk under the bridge*, during one of those phone conversations I had with her about the drawing. What Goddamned bridge were these people on?

ᴥ Chapter 3 ᴥ

I didn't care what Christa Hiaphin cared about, but what did Eric Matheson care about? He wasn't a friend of mine. He wasn't a colleague. He was somewhere far away and my morbid, distant connection with him wasn't going away. July was almost over but the hot streets of New York looked like they'd stew forever. I managed to move the window air conditioner to my bedroom so I could sleep at night. Still, I found myself escaping the confines of that small room during the day only as far as the rest of the desolate, clammy apartment. I walked in circles inside the mean old rooms. I wasn't going to bother buying curtains for the place, but the canvas shades were so bleak when they were down and the view of the poor, ragged city outside gave me nothing to look at, so I put on fans and tried to not look, out or in.

One more Saturday night, I was fused to my computer for an hour before I jerked my head away and turned it off. I sat, crouched, hugging my knees, wanting to scream. Lost in frustration forever, I suddenly came up with a plan. I got off the floor and walked around the living room. It was desperate, but so was I and I began to feel more and more sure of my aim as the plan at least pointed me in some direction. Eric said he had a sister living in New York volunteering with children at the Donnell Library. She lived in the Village somewhere. That was where he was heading in the cab that day, that day

I acted like an obnoxious little jerk with him, trying to hide my insecurities by treating him like it was his problem. Me, the same jerk who just dragged him into the Metropolitan Museum and was about to not follow through a second time!

I'd have to try to remember her name. He did mention it. Going through the alphabet, I stopped right away. "A" sounded right. Amelia. Amanda. He said the name, Amanda, to me. I already knew where she worked. I had to do nothing -- one more time -- for the rest of the weekend.

Eleven o'clock on Monday I pressed the numbers and got a female voice.

"Donnell Library, hello."

"Yes, hi, I'm trying to reach Amanda Matheson. Is she there today?"

"Can I ask who's calling?"

"My name's Peggy Avakian. I'm a friend of her brother, Eric."

"Sorry, Amanda doesn't work here on Mondays. She's due in, let's see. Wednesday morning. Can I take a phone number so she can get back to you?"

"Yes, thanks."

I gave her my number and spelled my name twice and emphasized once more that I was a friend of Amanda's brother, Eric.

Nothing for three days. At work Thursday at around four in the afternoon my cell phone rang.

"Peggy Avakian?"

"Yes."

"This is Eric's sister. I got a message you phoned?"

Her voice lurched backward into a remote, dark silence.

"Yes. Amanda? Yeah, I wondered if I could speak with you. It's just something to do with your brother and I wanted to see if you could help me with something."

More dark quiet.

I tried to hold onto her by speaking steadily, reasonably. "I don't want to sound overly mysterious or anything but, could I meet you somewhere?"

Nothing back.

"Maybe we could meet at a place near you? He said you live in the West Village. Could I buy you dinner? I know it must sound crazy, but I can explain it fairly well in person." I was not doing this well.

"Sorry, did you say you were a friend of Eric's?"

She had more of a polished English accent than he did, her brother. Maybe his sounded half German or something. I forced myself to speak more clearly and slowly.

"Yes, I met him at the Boston museum. Not a close friend but I got to know him a bit and, well, I wanted to tell you about something. Sorry, I'm sounding like a weirdo and I'm avoiding getting to the point and I hate to, but what I wanted to talk about would be too weirdly complicated on the phone. If I could meet you at JT's? Is it still there?"

"JT's? Yes, it's a place near Washington Square."

"Can I meet you there sometime? Tonight, even? We could just sit and have some coffee or a drink or something to eat. Whatever you'd like." I was pleading way too much. I just wanted to get her to say yes, and I could tell she was still holding back.

This time when she stayed quiet, I stayed quiet. It worked. She quietly agreed to meet with me and so I let her pick the day and time and clicked the red stop button feeling the muscle in my hand release its grip on my little phone.

It was the next day, Friday, and it was half raining, sometimes just spitting when my taxi pulled up to the door of the very familiar old haunt. The iron beams were still green. I saw that through JT's large, dark, old metal framed windows.

I entered and pushed all distraction aside when I saw a young girl sitting alone at a table and, since it was only five-thirty and not picking up with a dinner crowd yet, she stood out. What was immediately notable was that she looked so young, pretty and related to her brother. It was a bit odd to see the resemblance since I hadn't anticipated it, for no good reason, but also because she looked young and so feminine, and he looked older and the opposite of feminine.

She blushed when I approached, dewy soft round cheeks and light blue eyes and brownish blonde hair, not dark brown like her brother's. She wore narrow blue jeans, a heavy knit sweater and ankle boots, looking very good and I couldn't miss her broad forehead that reminded me of Eric.

We made awkward attempts at conversation. Ten minutes of that and my glass of red wine came, the same wine she had. I was bent on befriending this stranger, me so used to not making the effort.

"Well, I should tell you why I phoned."

"Um, I think I might guess. My brother asked you to." She looked studiously at me, her eyes narrowing, and her face twisted in a sardonic leer. My sudden inclusion with her brother shocked me.

"No. He didn't. Why? What?" I barely smiled, very embarrassed and she narrowed her eyes again, showing disbelief.

"I've already heard from three people. My brother really is hopeless."

My smile was still rigid, but I was beginning to like what she was thinking. Maybe I wouldn't have to get into endless crap right away about the drawing and my need to get at her older brother.

"I really decided to phone you on my own."

"Umm, well, as you can see, I'm in one piece and really just fine. You're pretty young, aren't you? He usually sends old people like him around."

"He didn't." I gave her a pointed stare and raised my shoulders. "You know what? I just came up with the idea on my own, and I'm afraid I can't prove it."

Now her expression lost its careful wrinkles and she seemed to relax. She leaned one elbow on the table.

Suddenly she smiled from ear to ear. "Um, I think I remember your name. Yes, Peggy something. I didn't remember your last name, Avakian. You and Eric dated?"

"No, we didn't, ever." I felt mortified, my face red hot. My God, what a nightmare if he thought I was saying we were involved that way.

Her smile didn't leave her. She sat back and took a sip of wine, studying me with the personal satisfaction of conquering intimacy.

"I'm pretty sure he said he was dating someone named Margaret," she said breezily.

"Okay. Well I hope they're very happy together." I drank some more wine to relax a little, more titillated than seemed smart. "So, tell me. How does he like his new job in Dublin?" I spoke as slowly as I could.

"Oh, I think he will. It's so new for him. But Dublin's lovely, isn't it? I mean, it really is such a wonderful place to be. . . uhm, great people, a nice size, plenty to do, beautiful to look at. Kind of like Boston."

"Do you have any friends in New York? What about roommates?"

"A few friends. Two roommates. But I never see them. No, I haven't ventured out much in that way. I wanted to come here for a year with a bit of savings to see what it was like and meet some Americans, but I haven't met many, have I?

I've been here for six months and keep bumping into Brits or Italian tourists." She raised one eyebrow and tilted her head.

"Your roommates must be American."

"No! One's Dutch and the other's English. They're fine. They're nice, but that's not why I'm here. So it's quite good to meet an American and have a drink and some conversation."

"How did you get two non-American roommates? Sorry, I'm interrogating you."

She grinned. "No, not at all. I found them through a British site online, which made all this much easier. It's a find and I can afford it even though it's in the middle of the West Village and safe enough and central and very pretty all around here."

"Yeah, it's murder to find an apartment that isn't extremely expensive in an area like this. So that's great, right?"

"Hmm? Yeah. No, I'm very happy. But that was why I . . ." She stopped. "Eric was in Boston and he's upset that I'm here and he's gone so far away now."

I seriously didn't like hearing that. But it did sound a little overbearing possibly. She seemed sweet and maybe even sort of innocent, but not childlike, not at all. I sat still, trying to relax, but my thoughts must have been obvious.

"I'm not being thoroughly honest. I was very comfortable with the arrangement too. I visited him all the time by train and he came here, but we had our own worlds too."

"Sounds like you and your brother are close."

"Um, we are."

I took that in. The arbiter of high cools was a loving brother? She took in a deep breath and smiled gently at me. Apparently, I met her approval, so far. She had the gentlest, most elegant way of being dramatic and emphatic at the same time. She was my second English person.

She leaned her head to one side and quietly elaborated, "Yes, well, it's the three of us. My mother lives in Cirencester.

It's in the middle of the country. She's very neatly woven into the fabric of small town, English life there. At least that's what she wants, being from Romania. But, in some ways she does seem more English than anyone I know. My father died years ago when I was only six. He died of cancer. He smoked cigarettes all his life. But see, Eric and I don't have many relatives because my mother was foreign, and my father's side all seemed to disappear into cheap pubs in areas of Essex somewhere. And, so, my brother, mother and I are all we have, it seems. And Eric thinks he has to look after me, like I'm still six."

Amanda took a sip of wine, not focused on me at that moment, not making any eye contact. I drank some more too and was feeling tipsy.

She sat straighter. "Tell me about you and feel free to include stuff about Eric."

I centered my thoughts and told her the story of the drawing in pure, bland outline form, omitting her brother's latest role in the drama. It was about me needing to follow through with things, I told her. I asked her to not say anything to him about meeting me and she agreed, looking at me with adoring pity. She just thought I was in love with the guy. The whole get-together was so much more insane than I'd anticipated in that way. We just talked like old friends for an hour. It was getting crowded and noisy and we were getting very impatient looks from the wait staff since people were lining up for tables. I knew from experience what that meant in tips. Amanda didn't want to spend money on eating she said, and I decided to not push it, wanting to leave well enough alone, especially with the sister of Anomaly Man, Eric Matheson.

❧ Chapter 4 ❧

I phoned Amanda a number of times and she phoned me and over the next month we actually got fairly genuinely close. Still, there weren't even brief moments when I forgot whose sister she was, and when I constantly asked her not to mention my name to Eric, she continued to promise she wouldn't. I had to keep asking because she seemed to text him and email him and phone him and their mother, constantly.

More and more I lived with the growing knowledge of this close, brother, sister relationship, dementedly symmetrical to Mark and me. And I could see and feel the harsh contrast with my brother. Mark was back to not answering my emails or texts. Given the way he was currently benefiting from the sale of the drawing to Amanda's brother, I hated the idea of telling her anything about that fiasco. Someday I'd have to tell her, just not before I got to know her and Eric a bit more.

She and I went to a play at beautiful Brooklyn College. We went to a bar one night near Gramercy Park. We went to an antiquarian bookstore near her apartment in the Village where she showed me the sorts of Victorian illustrated books her brother loved. And I began to look more closely at those books. I couldn't afford them, but the bookstore manager didn't know that as he pulled the elaborately embossed volumes out of the glass cases and watched me as I handled them if they were the main link to humankind's past.

When we went to the Metropolitan Art Museum, Amanda laughed as I told her I was learning to love some Victorian Art. It didn't take much to reinforce her view that I was in love with her brother and I saw less and less reason to keep telling her I didn't know him. I wanted to get any information about her brother I could, any way I could.

It was frustrating though. Getting to know Amanda was great but it was not getting me the kind of access to her brother I needed. Who was he and why the hell did he buy the drawing?

Walking through the Brooklyn Museum one rainy August Sunday my curiosity about Amanda's views on Eric rose to a peak. We'd been looking at paintings by Pennsylvania Impressionists for a while, about an hour, and were ambling on.

Out of the blue she said, "You know, Peggy, my brother isn't just a career fiend or workaholic."

"Yeah? I never really guessed he was. Why?" I couldn't think of anything we'd said near that topic, ever.

"Well, I think he gives that appearance sometimes, doesn't he? Very serious and austere."

Nothing came out of me as we continued our slow meandering through galleries.

"He's very talented, if I can say so as his sister. And he didn't have to work all that hard at university. He never admits that, but I have mutual friends who were with him there. He found it easy enough to get the high marks and work at a job to pay for it all. He started out being fascinated with film. Did you know that?"

I didn't know anything but had given up arguing that point. I shook my head and listened.

"Uhm, he still is, I think. But in school he headed a film club, you know as an activity. No, I think he's really working at something he's good at and loves, which is pretty remarkable, isn't it? I hope he can continue."

"Why? Why wouldn't he continue?"

"Hm? No, he probably will. But let's face it, there's not a lot of money to be made in art museums. I'm sure you know that. The few jobs that actually pay anything are so few and far between and the competition is something awful."

"Uhh, yeah. Now you're depressing me." I looked away from her. "People in museums live off their salaries somehow. Unless they're rich."

"No-no, I know. Eric and I were never rich. No, it's just he was making a really good salary in Boston and had a great job, and now, I don't know. From what he's indicating, he's making less."

I swallowed that reluctantly and just walked.

A gallery later I asked, "But, so why did he leave Boston?"

"I'm not really sure. I was hoping you could tell me." She smiled at me and I stopped walking.

"Amanda." I frowned at her.

She laughed. "Okay, okay. I accept that you two were not involved but I am going to have to say something to him at some point, aren't I?"

"Fine. I know. Just not yet. I have to save a bit more money and get a flight to Dublin and ask him a couple of questions. You're no good at all. I thought you'd tell me why he moved to Ireland."

"No idea, Toots. Yeah, you're going to have go ask him. Stare him down, face to face."

We were walking again.

"Um, yeah, anyway, you know, it's cobbling things together. Money's important but not everything. I told your brother that once in a taxi in as haughty a way as I could, and he said he was going to tattoo it on his chest. He thought it was that profound."

She laughed. "Did he now? Did you know he spent what little money we had on me going to Dean Close while he worked his way through odd bits of schooling? I mean, it was a tough row to hoe for Eric after my father died, but he managed to do everything he could for my mother and me."

I looked into her eyes. She was lost in thoughts and emotions and I felt myself getting swept along. It unnerved me. I wanted to point the conversation to something less adoring of her brother. We walked along.

"You've mentioned that name, Dean something, before," I said.

"Yeah, sorry, it was my high school. But I loved it. Eric took me there when I was thirteen. He took me around to a few schools he said he thought would be good for me, but I chose that one. My mother had no idea about the endless machinations of English education."

"So you liked it. Was it a boarding school?" I stopped looking at an Albrecht Durer woodcut and looked at her.

"I did like it a lot. It was boarding and day and I was a day pupil and took a stupid bus and hated that but seemed to live through it. No, I loved the school and made great friends and even read some books and all that. But Eric didn't get a chance to do that. He went to a lousy comprehensive and then put together a patchwork of A level colleges and things. He could have gone to a good high school. Fact was he really wanted to go to a good school but didn't. I did." Her eyes sank away.

"But he got into a good university. He got into Yale."

She took a deep breath, waited and then blew out the words, slowly. "Eventually. His English university was okay.

It wasn't Oxbridge or University of London. He worked at it. I took the green and pleasant route. He didn't and he's much more of a student than I am." She gave me a fast, penetrating look and I stood still, forced to accept her high appraisal of her brother, that apparently contained a fair share of guilt.

Neither of us had anything to add and we shuffled on, but I knew I had some profound information about Eric, exhausting as all this was, all this far-out circling around him. He seemed to be exceptionally good to his mother and his sister and apparently, he had some serious scruples.

❧ Chapter 5 ❧

What I was discovering was I seriously liked the Matheson family. It was the kind of family I always wanted to have, and did for a while, a few years. Then Uncle Ethan died, and Mark fell away, and I left home. Or I left home, and Mark fell away?

Mark was back to his solitary self. I hadn't heard a word apart from the one exchange in early September when I phoned him and he actually answered, saying, practically in monosyllables, he was, fine, okay, doing great, loved the college, loved his dorm, loved the courses he was taking, had lots of friends.

I sent him an email a week later.

> *Mark – How about a visit from me in a few weeks? The third week in September? Would that be okay? Let me know, though.*

He sent an email back a few days later.

> *Yeah come visit. I might be busy with studying and my job, but it should be a good time to show you around.*

I emailed him for last minute directions three days before the scheduled date. He emailed back right away.

Peggy, sorry I have to call it off. Maybe another time. I just have too much work with my classes just starting. Sorry.

Apparently, he wasn't as sorry as I was. Apparently, the same day, I had to be sorry again, teased by fate in a new and bizarre way. After a dinner of salad from the nearby convenience store, I was so bored and desperate for any substance in my life I drifted off toward my past, to the Tufts Art History site online, where I read an internship post.

The Ashmolean Museum, Oxford, UK is looking for a post-undergraduate student in History, Art or Art History for an internship in Museum Studies. Duties will include mounting of works on paper and assisting Department of Western Art, Paper Conservator, Mary Felsted. Intern will be generally supervised by Ian O'Connor, Assistant Keeper. Stipend of 20,000 pounds per annum, with the internship terminating at the end of two years. Interested candidates should send an email with a one-page curriculum vitae and two letters of reference, to the address listed below not later than 1 May. Internship starting date is 7 September.

The address was Bowdoin College, care of Ms. Eleanor Payne, Curator Emeritus of the Bowdoin College Museum of Art. It took a few minutes for me to even notice it was over three months too late for me to apply. It was September ninth now and Tufts left the stupid post on way past the due date. I also knew the competition would have been crazy. But, wow, what a freaking voluptuous internship. It got me up and doing something, anything, to stretch some muscles and not wallow in Neverland. I took a shower and ate some yogurt. There must have been thousands of extremely qualified candidates, but it was so irritating that I didn't see it sooner. Was it aimed at Americans? I did some sit-ups and read my Washington Post online in fits and bits, sitting in my white cotton T shirt, ready for a slow, creeping decent into sleep. I sat and stared into space for ten minutes half thinking, half letting images bounce around in me, making me more and more agitated. God. Oxford. England. Camelot. Albion. It was insane, but I walked to the new, ultra-thin laptop I bought a few weeks earlier. It was ten-thirty at night and the email might just be buried by morning, but what the hell.

Subject – Oxford Museum Internship

Dear Professor Payne.

I just saw the notice for the Ashmolean Internship posted online last spring. I would be extremely interested if anything like that is available in the future. I do have experience in collections management issues from a museum course I took at Tufts University that was then related to a summer job. The job was in a non-profit firm affiliated with Tufts, called, The Collections Care Resource Center, located in the middle of Back Bay, Boston. The people there who taught me conservation matting and framing, packing and shipping techniques and handling works of art, were all trained at the Museum of Fine Arts, Boston, or the Harvard Art Museums. Unfortunately, it closed its doors

a year ago from lack of funding. I was very
lucky to work there.

 I have attached my letter of recommenda-
tion from the Director, Michael Morris. Please
also see my list of art history courses and grades
at Tufts. Thank you very much.

Respectfully,
Margaret Avakian

Less than a week later at home right after work, I had to remind myself who Eleanor Payne was. I almost deleted her email.

Dear Ms. Avakian:

 Thank you for your email and interest
in the Ashmolean Museum Internship. I took
the liberty of phoning Professor Hemmling at
Tufts and got a fine informal recommendation
for you and, if you are interested, the posi-
tion is open. There was a young woman from
Bowdoin all set for it, but she had to back out
last minute. Since the actual starting date for
this internship was September, and that has
already passed, I think we should move towards
the next stages expeditiously. Please respond to
this email ASAP. You can also phone me to dis-
cuss the internship. Thank you.

Regards,
Eleanor Payne
Professor Emeritus, Art History

I read it ploddingly twice. Halfway through the third time my mind danced and I actually got up on my toes in some form in the middle of the living room until, at some point later, I arrived back on the floor and ran to the computer to respond to her email. Yes, I answered. I was very interested. I'd phone her the next day during lunch break at work.

I was numb during the phone call. Any planned pitches to win the Ashmolean Museum, Oxford, England two-year paid internship, were so far overreaching I barely got a word out. Dazzled, my mind zigzagged around the issue well after I hung up and I didn't get much work done that afternoon, trying to make sense out of the phantasmagorical phenomenon. Maybe Professor Payne's ego was on the line there, up in Maine, since she concocted the internship and provided the funding for it. Her few cautious words were something about not all Americans fitting in or feeling that they do over there. But she actually did say it was mine if I wanted it, and if I could get all the application materials to her promptly.

Wow. Goddamned right, I'd be prompt.

As fate would have it. She said that. I remembered her saying, "As fate would have it, I know the man who was Director of the Collections Care Resource Center, Michael Morris, and know about its programs at Tufts."

It occurred to me, getting blood flowing to my brain on the walk to the subway after work, I was getting such an amazing prize because I applied so late. She needed someone to replace the egocentric, shithead student who suddenly dropped out and maybe I popped up precisely-conveniently. She said the dropout got into a PHD program at Penn or something and Eleanor Payne clearly didn't want to talk about it. All I actually knew was, weird luck was even better than great luck sometimes.

At home I shifted into high alert. I'd have to get myself to England November ninth, less than three weeks away. When I calculated how much money I'd have to take over, how I'd sublet my Greenpoint apartment, how much a flight would cost there, what internet sites on Oxford were best for that city and the colleges, I was already halfway there, spiritually. But the next step was seeing Amanda on Saturday. Amanda was the next step.

I took a cab, mumbling to myself that the expense was for a special cause, and I got to Amanda's building at nine. It was a bit early for a Saturday, even though I told her the previous night on the phone I had to see her early to tell her something. The street was classic, beautiful West Village, with billowing trees, narrow bending streets and almost entirely complementary, elegant nineteenth century buildings with a few beautiful twentieth century ones. Amanda was renting a condo unit that was only a little over five hundred square feet. She had to pull out a sofa-bed in the living room every night. Her two roommates were tucked into two other corners of the place, one in what might as well have been described as a large closet, the other in the kitchen, but with a makeshift wall of tall Ikea bookshelves separating her from the stove, refrigerator and sink.

Amanda didn't say much as I entered. She looked like she'd suddenly been roused by the door buzzer. I waited impatiently, pacing as she made us both coffees very quietly, next to a sleeping body on the other side of those bookcases. She had organic donuts and I teased her about that in a whisper as we sat down in the living room, but I ate one because I'd only had an apple for breakfast. She sat on her still open sleeper couch in her robe with the blankets spread across the open bed and her nestled, cross-legged in the middle. I sat on a sagging, cheap canvas beach chair.

I whispered about Oxford. She began to wake up a bit.

"Wow," she gurgled in a quiet, low morning voice. "That's amazing! When do you go?"

"In around three weeks, if I go."

"Why wouldn't you?!"

"Because, that's why I'm here. I have to tell you something." I pulled my neck and shoulders back to get more aligned. Whispering hoarsely, "I've told you about the drawing escapade, but I didn't tell you your brother's the one who bought the drawing."

"He is? Why?" She yawned and was still fighting back sleep.

"Yeah, I don't know."

"What are you saying?" She looked bewildered and just barely managed a shy smile.

"I have something I want to do. I want you to go over to Oxford with me. We could live there together. You'd be close to your brother and your mother and could get some work."

"Work there? Um, it might be hard in Oxford. I'd guess the competition's intense, and it's expensive, because it's just so popular with people, not just university types. Uhm, but wait, now. Eric bought your drawing? Why didn't you say something sooner? Peggy? What's this about?"

I licked my dry lips. "I wanted to get to know you and thought telling you too soon would get in the way."

She was trying to put a couple of pieces together, carefully. Her speech was a slow grumble, half to herself. "I'm not sure what the connection is between me, uhh, and the drawing and my brother, sorry. It's early, but you'll have to explain. I mean, you want me to share a place in Oxford. Okay."

"Yeah, no, I'm sorry. I know it might be hard to understand but apart from considering you a good friend and, of course, wanting to go to Oxford, I want to do something to at least partially repay your brother. What he did was, well, sorry, it's just that I didn't know anything. I had no idea you were going to become a good friend, or this opportunity would come up to move to England for a couple of years. I just wanted to pursue things, blindly, and then, this." I waved both hands up and raised my eyebrows like I was in a trance.

"Umm, you almost sound rational there, but I'm not sure what you're really saying."

"It's dense but we're not. It could be terrific. You'd be a healthy couple of hundred miles away from your brother, an hour's drive from your mother and I'd have a roommate, and your brother would feel better about you. You know, not being left for dead in a back alley in New York." I rested for a second. "But please think about it. Uh, but, Amanda, please. There are two things I'd have to have from you. Two promises."

"I had no idea about you, did I? I thought I did. What promises, pray tell?"

"Really, please, I'm very serious. I'd pay for rent and food for the first six months. And you'd wait to tell your brother about me. Let me talk to him first."

"You're drunk or drugged."

"Amanda, I love you dearly. I really, sincerely do, like the sister I never had. So this offer is so important to me, okay? You don't understand, and you probably never will because no one's bought some personal thing from you -- a thing you've been carrying around all your life -- and some stranger suddenly buys it for a ridiculous price and then suddenly disappears with it, off to a distant land."

Amanda was probably as surprised as I was by my intense emote. She took her time, then said, moderately, "He may have had a reason, apart from the drawing possibly being something he really liked."

I stood up and tightened my fists, a fierce frustration peaking. She had no reason to give a damn about things that were vital to me.

"Amanda, I don't know why he moved three thousand miles away. You don't even know, and he spent forty thousand dollars on some odd thing that probably really wasn't worth that much, and he certainly never claimed to know what it was. Nobody knows what the thing even is!"

Probably didn't have to raise my voice an octave because, sure enough, the dollar amount hit the target.

"Shit! He spent that much?! I don't believe it!" We both looked over at the sound of the groaning roommate.

"Yes," I whispered harshly. Really not wanting to carp at her, I forced myself to whisper calmly, "He did. I don't know why, but he must have felt obligated in some damned way."

"How did he have that much to just spend on one drawing?" Amanda was looking fully awake now, and ashen, worried about her brother. That got my adrenaline pumping even more.

Again, I forced myself to speak moderately. "I have no idea."

"He might have saved some money. He probably did. But that is so much." She was thinking out loud.

"Yeah."

She lowered her head, her index finger across her upper lip, thumb under her chin, looking at her bedspread.

"Amanda, do this if you have any desire to go to Oxford and share an apartment and find a job. You were going back in four months anyway."

"Um. So much for getting to know New York." She sighed and then wrinkled her face in frustration, still trying to cope with the sudden rush of issues. "What if I do find a job? What's this thing about not sharing the rent?"

"Or costs for food, utilities, everything. I am going to be able to pay for it all for six months because I'm going to get five thousand dollars back from my brother for this, for you.

That's the least I can do." I wasn't at all sure I'd get that money from my brother, but I wanted to lasso Amanda.

"My God, you're sick, aren't you?! There really is something wrong with you. It's like some sort of weird, personal, payback vendetta."

I hunched my shoulders, standing very still as she gazed at me, then down at the floor. After a minute of silence, I was walking away saying goodbye quietly.

❧ Chapter 6 ❧

Amanda phoned me on Wednesday night to talk about Oxford and within ten seconds I could tell she wanted to go. She said the library job was ending anyway and she was less than crazy about her roommates. They already had a replacement for her.

She'd have to go online fast and try to get a flight for the same day I was going, and we'd meet at London Heathrow, Terminal 5. At least tourist season was over. I told her I found a flight for myself on Icelandic Airlines for a good price, but it stopped in Iceland on the way.

I would have gone to Oxford without her, but it was much, much better to go with her. The conversation ended in five minutes after a mutually excited verbal jig around the central fact that we'd both be going to Oxford in just over two weeks. I still hadn't phoned Mark on his new phone, but now, I had to.

Mark didn't answer the first few times and I didn't want to leave a message, so I had to keep trying for two hours that Thursday night. I sat on my bed and called again and again, about half an hour apart worrying that the persuasive points I had in my mind were dulling away. Then he answered.

"Mark, hi. You won't believe this, but I've been accepted to an internship at Oxford University's Ashmolean Museum. I'm going there in about two weeks." I was jumpy.

"What? What the hell? For how long? Oxford, England?"

"No. Not England. Oxford, Oklahoma."

Silence. Then he said, "Yeah, very funny. Sorry, but holy fuck, that's amazing."

I grumbled, "Yeah. I will need to hit you up for a few thousand dollars, though."

"Yeah?"

"You doing all right up there?"

"I'm doing fine. Don't worry about me. My courses are pretty good. I mean, you know, they want me to take two semesters of statistics and that's not fun. But I really like the science courses and the psych courses are great."

"The dorm's still okay?"

"It's okay. I can't do anything in my room here because, even though most of these students are older, you'd think they were ten, some of them, and they make a lot of noise in the hallway at night after dinner. I just go to the library. Yeah, man, the library's so gorgeous and it's so big, I go and get a desk in a corner and it's quiet and there's nothing to do there but read, so I get a lot of work done."

"Yeah? I love libraries."

"Yeah."

"So, what about the money? You have enough left to give me five thousand?"

"What? Oh, you need money? Yeah, of course. I can give you more than five thousand."

"No, Mark. That's enough. Thanks. How are you doing in that area? How's your part-time job at the student union?"

"Sucks. Yeah, I hate the guy who's running the place and who screws off and then blames the rest of us when there are problems."

"Can you keep doing it or get another job? What is it again, power point presentations or something?"

"Yeah, no it's just setting things up for conferences, like chairs and tables and, yeah, I might try to get a job in the admissions office."

"Great."

I paused and so did he.

"Well, anyway, I can have the five thousand?"

"Yeah. I told you, you can have it. Of course. I wanted to give you some of the money before and you said no."

"So Mark, how's it going with money?"

"Fine. My bank has most of it in a savings account. It's fine. I'll send you a check."

"Okay. Thanks, Mark. I'll be in touch. You have to stay in touch!"

"I do."

"No, you're lazy or something about emails. You always have been."

"Emails? Hell, I never turn on my computer. Computers are cultural cesspools, with that internet stuff. They're only good for typing papers. Phones are for talking."

I laughed. "And looking up stuff on the internet."

"No. I use books most of the time."

"Okay. What century are you in? Were you born ninety years old?"

"Yup."

We said goodbye.

Two days later a letter arrived from a Mr. O'Connor at the Ashmolean Museum officially inviting me to work there for two years and offering the use of a, *bedsit,* a one room efficiency apartment. Housing was extremely tight in Oxford according to Mr. O'Connor and Amanda too.

The check arrived in the mail and I tore it up. Mark would probably never even know I hadn't cashed it. Anyway, Mark would have to pay tax on the proceeds from the drawing, so he'd need that five thousand and more. There was just something about that pile of money from the drawing that made my skin crawl. I had enough of my own money saved to take care of Amanda and me. It was barely enough, but enough.

⮞ Chapter 7 ⮜

The hum of the engines and the air pressure hissing constantly mixed with all the human sounds and my anxieties were subsumed for most of the long trip. Ultimately, I got to Heathrow and waited for Amanda in a coffee shop that overlooked the international passenger exit. She appeared, a familiar face, an hour after me and we slogged our way to the train to central London and then the train to Oxford. My head and my body ached from fatigue as the whole endless trip whirred around me.

I got a second or fifth wind when the train pulled into Oxford. Somewhere close was my own studio apartment or bedsit, I could call Amanda's and mine. 129 Leckford Road was waiting for us somewhere in town. It was my first time abroad and the medieval character around me had entirely aroused. Long, tall hunky old stone walls were everywhere.

Our taxi churned through the midday crowded streets, everybody looking especially zesty and engaged. It was the middle of their fall term and students were everywhere, a bunch on bicycles. I wanted to do more than look out the taxi window. I wanted to get out into it all, into all the medieval buildings. And there were luscious Georgian buildings and Greek Revival, and a few modernist accents.

We turned left and hurried up St. Giles, scooting now more than driving. We were leaving the town center behind as we went farther north, past Victorian brick houses, reminding me of the Gothic Revival styles of Eric Matheson's book bindings. We must have gone less than a mile when we turned left again and were on Leckford Road, then 129.

It wasn't the most beautiful house on the road and the road looked like one of the duller roads in the area, and yet it was still attractive.

There was a smell of mold inside as soon as our noses crossed the threshold of the main door. The old chipped black and white tiled floor of the foyer was damp. On the left, 1*a*, was ours. After fumbling with suitcases and me finally getting the key to work, we entered our double bedsit, and it wasn't bad. It was good. It had been a large living room, or smallish ballroom or something. The ceiling was way up there, over twelve feet was my guess. Seven huge sash windows ran along two walls. They must have been over seven feet high. One bed was in the left corner backing against those windows, and the other bed was perpendicular to that in the right corner, parallel to some windows. We put our bags down and wandered around the room and gaped, mostly at the big empty space in the center.

"It's about twice the size of the studio I had in San Francisco."

Amanda pointed. "That's the kitchen." Her finger was aimed at the corner closest to the door, where there was a small sink, a smaller electric stove, and a mini refrigerator.

"Yeah, it's fine," I said walking to it. "Looks like it'll do. Looks like it's for a cheap hotel suite."

She chuckled a little and sat down across the room, on the bed in the farthest corner, about twenty-five feet away.

"Umm." Amanda yawned. "The room's huge and there isn't much in the way of radiators, is there? There's one over there and, yeah, that's it. We'll have to wear overcoats and pray for a warm winter."

I looked at the flat white radiator against the wall next to the kitchen area. It was about two and a half feet tall and a bit more in width.

"That's it?"

"Um, maybe that's why this place was available." She yawned again and sank back onto the bed. "Sorry. I'm done in."

Curled up under a shiny, mostly red tartan bedcover, made from some synthetic material that had a God-awful shine to it, Amanda was departing. I glanced at my own shiny green tartan bedcover, rationalizing that, ugly as it was, it would seal in body heat.

I walked over to a few big beautiful windows, careful to be quiet. Pulling at the long, heavy curtains gingerly, I slowly let in more of light, looking over at Amanda who was already in a deep sleep, her cheeks red from the cool, moist inside air. More and more silvery green light entered the room. The gentle, filmy noon glow and the dense trees and bushes were all a part of our space. It was how Pre-Raphaelites got their extra-delineated greens and browns and it was overwhelming how much I felt entwined in it. I sat on my bed and stared for ten minutes, then fell back, with barely enough energy to get under my shiny cover.

It was going on three when I opened my eyes. Muffled sounds surrounded the room. I raised my head, still in my clothes, too warm under the cover, a bit grimy but very content with the three hours of sleep I had.

The sounds from the room above and down the hall and then actually in the hall became louder, largely because I was more awake. I got up quickly, excited about going for a walk. Amanda didn't seem to be stirring, and I wanted to get out there, on my own. Amanda was seeming standoffish recently and I wondered why. I half wondered. Maybe like her, I wanted to define some distance from my roommate.

Outside, the sun raked low across hedges and gardens and onto tan and sometimes red gravel paths and driveways, all damp from the light rain. It must have been almost sixty degrees, perfect for walking. I walked up Woodstock Road for fifteen minutes and stopped when I came to a school. A sign read, *St. Edwards, Oxford, founded 1863. An independent day and boarding school.* There were open, flat, deep green playing fields for a hundred or so acres on my left, and orange and red brick school buildings to compliment them on my right.

I stopped. It was easy to be impressed. The theme was Romantic Victorian Gothic like most of gorgeous Romantic North Oxford. I watched a group of boys playing what looked like field hockey, mud on their knees and elbows. Beyond them in another field was a group of girls playing the same thing. Was this part of the tradition of Amanda and Eric's childhoods?

The shouting and laughing thinned after I turned away and crossed busy Woodstock Road, wandering down narrow Oakthorpe Road, away from teenagers and traffic and into the thick of the lush residential area.

I walked and walked on cultivated road after road, past buildings blending with rose bushes and vines and ivy and trees and dense green grass. I was in a terrarium of perfect human scale and I was lost in it. But I had to go back. I could blissfully walk around, in and through for hours but Amanda would wake up and wonder where I was.

❧ Chapter 8 ❧

The next two days were about digging in, for me anyway. I was excited even if it was just sipping coffee or tea with Amanda, who had definitely changed. She was edgy. I hadn't really thought of her as edgy until I saw her there, where she seemed to get into an automatic mode of operation. She was up early Monday morning, briskly, going down the hall to the shared bathroom, showering, humming as she came back into our room, fixing breakfast, for me too, until I made an effort to help.

Purposeful.

I teased her about it as I ate a bowl of muesli quickly, anxious to get to the first day at the Ashmolean.

Amanda stopped in the middle of our large floor, trying to understand.

I said, "Yeah, it's probably a British trait. If you're not purposeful, you're a sad sack. 'Let us now be up and doing.'" I made quotation marks in the air.

"Who said that smut?" she asked.

I roared laughing, a bit too much. "Uhh, Longfellow, actually, and he was American. I know, and with that name."

She pretended to spit at the floor. "So much for that."

I smiled at her but then stopped. I was edgy too, wanting to get to that museum, see if I could manage things there. So I stopped the sprightly chatter and aimed myself out the door for a rousing Oxford walk, feeling more than thinking, knowing something beyond the Ashmolean Museum was making me nervous, and it was Eric. Obviously, he'd visit Amanda at some point. I'd see him and then what? I didn't know. I just had to face the guy and try to find out what happened.

A bit more than a twenty-minute walk. The imposing neoclassical Ashmolean Museum on Beaumont Street was across the street from the Oxford Playhouse. I scouted-out the area and the museum for a couple of hours over the weekend. I'd introduced myself to most of the Ashmolean galleries, stunned by the gorgeous building and collections. But now I was on my way in officially, between the tall perfect stone columns, through the tall doorway and inside. The hard stone floor felt so smooth under my feet, my thin, elegant leather flats, allowing me to feel it all, like I was gripping each tactile moment.

Two museum receptionists were stationed in the central atrium. A young woman, with Jenny Zubri on her identity badge, and a man named, Richard Cummings. She was busy typing into a computer and he smiled and said hello. He was a big old man with statuesque posture, busy gray eyebrows and lightening blue eyes that concentrated when he spoke to me. He raised his phone, contacting the Department of Western Art Print Room, asking for Ian O'Connor, then saying, "Yes. Um-hm, yes, yes".

I watched Ian O'Connor walking toward me quickly, swinging his arms distractedly, walking in one way a few steps then altering it, careening and leaning a bit to the side, shuffling his feet, all sort of lopsided. It looked like he had the backbone and maybe the muscle but not quite enough need to walk.

"Yes, how do you do, uhm, Margaret Avakian? Good to see you. Right." He stood and looked at me and then down at his black rubber ankle boots. His suit was clamored with broad white stripes over dark blue. He wore a long light blue silk scarf around his neck, draped to his waist and that was over a black sweater. "Uhm, and so you had a good flight, I hope? And your bedsit? Is it all right? You like it, I hope?" His pitch went up and down theatrically.

"Yes, it's very nice. Thank you." My flat, easy American voice ended the hesitant introduction and I shuffled to the side a bit, wanting to feel more floor beneath my feet.

He arched himself backward and swiveled on his heals. He was something between thirty-five and fifty. Who knew? He was average height, bony more than thin and as pale as the mist on the moors. Grayish-black puffs of hair, cowlicks, stood up in two spots at the top, back of his bald head.

When he stopped himself from swiveling, facing the main staircase, we started walking. Just steady enough, step by step up the stairs by my side, he said in a baritone, "So you no doubt already know this is the oldest university museum in the country, but it's been restored fairly recently and done nicely, I'd say." We wandered into galleries, pausing haphazardly, from what I could see, in front of works of art or standing still at the end of one of Ian O'Connor's thoughts or the beginning of another. We stopped in front of, "Rive des Esclavons", by Turner, both of us saying it was wonderful.

He swiveled to face me. "Feel free to look around the museum when you can. It's fair to say, it is one of the world's greatest collections of everything comprehensive museums have, from fifteenth century Italian paintings to Asian art."

The museum was closed to the public on Mondays, but a few lights were on and along with large skylights, infused the gallery air with the softest, finest effervescence possible – blue walls or orange walls setting the tone.

We went down a back flight of stairs to a door, propped open, down a few steps and into a large, handsome Print Room with stacks of archival boxes of prints and drawings in glassed cases in the walls. Now, white plaster walls and the large windows looking out onto Beaumont Street brightened the space, setting off the warm wooden design of the floor and large tables and chairs. It seemed to all be the same wood -- oak?

I tried to relax during introductions, which came as we stood in the Print Room and people walked through. Eva Gilmore, an older woman, at least in her sixties, with a very pointy, twisting nose and narrow, odd looking face, that I found very attractive, spoke with a classic upper class resonance, with a few throaty, dry yes's snapped back at Ian O'Connor as he spoke about my internship. Like him, she was an Assistant Keeper. Walking away Ian mumbled, "Eva's speciality is eighteenth century watches."

Standing tall was Hugh Thorald, a middle-aged man who was well-built and even handsome, maybe. I had on a very professional, conservative, charcoal gray wool dress, below the knees. It could be that was why Hugh Thorald, with his trim and perfectly graying hair was lusting after me. Modesty does it for some men. It could be it was my toe cleavage in those Italian flats. It wasn't something I was conjuring up, when Hugh and Ian stood and stammered yes's and puffed up around me.

All I could do was stand still and wait for them to get a mental grip on their libidos.

Ian pointed at the wall of boxes as he walked me back across the room. "Feel free to look at any of the drawings or prints whenever you can."

Hugh looked on from his distance and I glanced and regretted it. He was some kind of rancid, with that hint of a leer smeared on his smooth face. His speciality was Italian seventeenth century prints. When we moved on and I could ask, Ian admitted these, *specialities* sounded narrow but referred to books published and doctoral theses written and were more descriptive of the nucleus of the person's interests.

I was finally taken to Stephanie Roberts, the Keeper's, office. I was relieved to see the small, slightly overweight, substantial woman. She had a very healthy shock of white hair, a square jaw and an open, kind face. She smiled, stood up politely and asked me to please take a chair. She asked me the requisite, polite questions about my trip, my accommodations, then she got to a point of concern for her.

"Now, I'm afraid the stipend isn't a lot. It's very expensive here, you know, and I hope you can afford to live. I mean, we do have to eat, don't we?" She was smiling but squinting, concerned.

"No, I know it's expensive. Uhh, but I do have some of my own money that I've saved to do this." I didn't want them to worry about me, but the stipend was enough to pay room and board, so why did she say that? I also didn't want them to think I was a rich American. She gave me a warm smile, bobbing her head.

"So you wanted to do this then, come to Oxford, or the Ashmolean?"

"Uh, yeah. I would have come here for half the stipend and no money saved at all."

She and Ian O'Connor laughed and shook their heads. I was a funny, earnest young American.

"Well hold onto your money and please feel free to let me know if you need anything, please, Margaret."

I'd almost always been called by my nickname but was happy to become one step more formal. Ian and I made a formal retreat, bobbing our heads, walking out sideways.

I was enjoying the attention of all these academic stars, but it was starting to feel a little strained. Mary Felsted was less formal. She was in her, Paper Laboratory, sitting at a workbench when we knocked and entered. She was at least fifty pounds overweight. Her hair was an inch short of her shoulders and a natural blend of gray and black. She had a large face with a protruding jaw and a solid set of white, slightly bucked teeth and dark shinny eyes behind black horn-rimmed glasses. She wore a white lab coat over a fairly plain wool, from what I saw, dress.

She smiled a lot, wanting a female friend and there I was for a couple of years. Ian O'Connor politely swiveled out of the room, an attractive laboratory space about twenty by fifteen with a large window facing out into a back street. It was the equipment I liked. There was a soapstone counter running the length of one wall, with a sink at one end, then a light table built in. There were flattening beds or drying tables for works of art on paper that had just been washed in some way or treated with a chemical and needing to either just lie still and dry for a while, or dry under enough weight to dry flat and then get matted and put back in the collection. A binocular microscope was attached to a small table in the corner and a large stainless-steel sink, probably four by six feet, was against the wall in the last available corner. A couple of high-tech looking lamps were poised here and there and two very handsome blue cloth and polished chrome stools with comfortable backs, sat ready for Mary and me.

I asked her to call me Peggy as we sat and talked. I'd start at 8:30 and work on matting prints from the collection in the old storage room down the hall. She'd show me that room in a few minutes, but said it was just a very small room with no windows and had once stored office supplies. She apologized for what she described was the, "mad dog attitude toward space in the Ashmolean," as she smiled reflectively at me, probably thinking I was fairly alien. She was clearly local from another British locality, originally, with an accent and speech mannerisms that said small town -- probably remote small town.

She showed me my workspace, which was a compact ex-storage room about ten feet long and seven feet wide, with, in fact, no windows. And she apologized for it again as I told her it was fine. I didn't say I'd grab any room to stake a claim in that building, and it seemed, in that small city, in that country.

After setting-up things, with some help from Mary and Ian, I settled into cutting a few mats for some knock-out, gorgeous seventeenth century Dutch prints. Shortly after noon Mary and I had lunch in a pub nearby, something she seldom did she said, since she took in a sandwich and some carrots or celery sticks normally. Novice that I was, I still figured it wasn't a particularly great choice for a pub – filled with American and Chinese tourists -- but let her make it as the host and it was fun eating a salad and trying to explain America. I'd find the really good pubs on my own.

❧ Chapter 9 ❧

The people, the buildings, the parks, the art, my odd, flexible job, were all seriously attaching themselves to me as weeks went by. It worried me at times because I'd have to leave. I couldn't pretend I belonged there, no matter how much I might want to. It was just that the walks down the streets would arouse urges, maybe just for a walk through the park, maybe an ale in a fifteenth century pub, maybe a romp with one of the many rosy-robust looking males I saw. There were a lot of very attractive, elegant men all over the place, but that wasn't all that was getting under my skin. It was the ease of getting through it all, politely left to my own devices as a foreigner in the ripe hunk of sumptuous green land in the North Sea. I knew I could knock-off a bunch of mats in a few hours on any morning, listening to BBC radio in my own space, then go upstairs and stare at whatever art I chose for an hour a day. They had one of the world's best collections of Italian Renaissance drawings, among other things. At lunch, I'd weave my way inside some snugly antique architectural warren in Oxford, tuck myself into a craggy corner with a book and have coffee, some soup or salad -- a bit awkward and nervous at first, being alone, but I adjusted rapidly. British people didn't invade my private space even in public.

The fact was I felt like I had a carnal attraction to the whole place. It wasn't entirely new. Tufts did that for me and so did Boston and San Francisco at times. Oxford was just doing it for me more profoundly all the time.

It fit. I was enveloped if I went to the Nosebag for lunch, for the best soup ever and great bread, or the Kings Arms for a pub lunch. Half the time I ate something homemade in the museum with Mary or in my workroom, or in the Universities Park, alone, reading and reading, tucked in.

I worked in the Paper Lab with Mary after lunch every day. She always had some fascinating works of art out that needed minor work done to them, like, *dry cleaning*, which meant sprinkling an inert rosin, or eraser crumbs, as I called them in my mind, and very gently rubbing them into the paper in a rotating, circular motion. There was me watching her do some meticulous, *spot bleaching* a few times. There were repairs made with very narrow, hand shredded strips of Japanese paper and wheat starch paste on the strips, painstakingly applied with tweezers to tears in a drawing or print. I watched and then practiced on plain scraps of paper. But I already knew how to do some of that from the Resource Center job in Boston.

I went to the Oxford Playhouse for plays and concerts, not paying much, sitting alone, contentedly. Amanda only went with me once. We let each other go, out the door alone, no explanations. As Amanda bustled along in her own world, I also worried at times I'd dragged her to a place that was great for me but might not fit her as well. She did say once, after some ale, that she'd never get into a graduate program there, in any of the Oxford University colleges. Whatever amount of accomplishment there was for me in just being there, she might feel she didn't belong to a university town she couldn't actually join. She said it was great, but I wasn't entirely convinced, especially when she admitted she hadn't dated in a long time. At least a year. And she continuously claimed she hated being kept by me and I simply nodded and wished her luck in finding a job eventually.

The bedsit was fine and as November evolved it got colder and damper in the morning and at night. We opened the drapes during sunny days, with that one thin radiator barely warming itself in its corner of our voluminous drafty room. We wore a lot of layers.

❧ Chapter 10 ❧

Most nights Amanda and I ate frugal meals in our bedsit, usually sitting on the floor. In the early stages of eating one night she suddenly remembered she got a phone call that day and her brother was coming to visit in a week and a half. I shrugged, not convincing myself. I'd been living blissfully in my English terrarium, but I was aware the whole time it didn't belong to me. Eric Matheson was coming for a visit. This was his country and I'd finally see him and talk to him, if he'd let me. I couldn't remember what he looked like.

"Great. I'm glad your new phone works." I tried to gauge her expectations about her brother and me by looking her in the eye. There was no doubt she'd become more distant since I told her about Eric buying my drawing for so much money, and she seemed withdrawn now. That added to my anxieties.

She turned her eyes to her tofu stir fry. "Yeah. But that will be good, right? Do you want to all go out to a pub dinner or maybe something good like, Chez Jean?"

It sounded too intense.

I said, "Okay. But you'll want to be alone with him too."

Facing her plate, she soured slightly, without even a glance at me. "Whatever you want to do, Peggy. He'll be here overnight. But, so, what will we say when he sees you?"

I sat, reduced to mulling alone on the floor. "Nothing. No, Amanda, I'll talk to him. I guess we could have told him I was here. I don't know. I thought he'd avoid me. It's all right."

We ate, washed up and said nothing more about it.

❧ Chapter 11 ❧

The day was coming for a while, day by day, and then it was December second. The only plan I definitely had was to simply explain I was confused about a couple of things and wanted to just ask him about them. I came to Oxford for other reasons too, mainly for other reasons. I'd have to stress that and just try to keep it simple. I wasn't stalking the guy. Amanda was a friend. I wanted to be in Oxford and thought it would be good, maybe good for her. It was all a bit of a coincidence. I wouldn't be boring, but I needed to know some things.

Five minutes after the phone call from inside the taxi, the car sounds and lights arrived in front of our house. Amanda walked quickly out to the front door of our building. I was a bit numb and stood waiting.

Noises of hello, how are you, how have you been filled the hallway, closer and then the bedsit door opened, and they were in, side by side, flushed, looking at me. I looked back.

"Hello, Peggy. How are you?" He spoke in a formal, polite way. He wasn't looking very surprised.

"Yeah, Eric, you know Peggy Avakian, from the States." Amanda sounded like an old matron just then, but I couldn't even manage a forced smile

"Hi," I said.

His travel wearied face was changing rapidly into something much more restrained.

182

Since the two siblings were being careful, formal, I reached out my hand and shook his.

Amanda said, "Peggy's been my roommate here."

He and I faced each other, silenced by something false in the air, everyone mindlessly transfixed. Amanda must have told him about me. Obviously. The silence pervaded for a few more seconds until he turned awkwardly and walked to the sink and asked Amanda for a glass of water. It was a ridiculous two-person pantomime with me as their audience.

"I met your sister in New York, and we became friends," I got out, struck by how disingenuous my words were.

"Uhm," He said, turning halfway toward me. "Yeah, well, I know. Sorry, I pried it out of Amanda. I mean, thank you for dragging her back here, by the way."

Amanda was at the sink, resorting to washing a couple of glasses. I just stood, limply.

Amanda turned just her head. "Sorry, Peggy. I just have a hard time keeping secrets from people and especially Eric. He can tell when I'm hiding something."

Eric smiled at that shyly, looking down at the floor. "It's a good quality in a person, Amanda, a sign of integrity. Plus, we talk on the phone all the time and I did wonder why you were going to art museums suddenly."

He glanced over at Amanda's back and then at me, clearly wanting to loosen things up. "No, Peggy, really it's brilliant that you got that Ashmolean internship and could manage to get Amanda to settle down here for a while."

"For a while," Amanda said, turning her head. "London still awaits."

He looked toward her but turned to me with a reassuring, slightly labored smile. All I was doing was standing, watching them.

He looked concerned.

"Would you like to go out for dinner. The three of us?"

God, I didn't want to at all. I'd be some sort of grotesque third wheel.

He tried to fill the void. "Uhm, or whatever you'd like. Want to order some pizza or Chinese food, pretend we're in Boston or New York?"

Amanda stepped in.

"We could go out and eat and meet you somewhere later?"

"Okay. No. I'll just grab something," I said ambiguously.

Amanda paused before saying, "Okay."

There was some shuffling around by them as she found her jacket and he waited, watching her. As they made their way out the door, he twisted his head back.

"Bye."

They were gone. I stood, staggered by how stupid I was.

After a few minutes of fidgeting and wondering what to think, I grabbed my jacket and headed for the door.

I walked fast, fueled by self-disgust. A mile or two of that and I was winded enough to relax a bit, slowly. I began to look around me. I thought I was going to ask him some questions and that happened? Why hadn't I anticipated that? I was pushing myself into the middle of their family. Amanda wasn't going to keep secrets of mine from her brother. So did Amanda tell him I got five thousand dollars out of the sale of the drawing for this Oxford escapade? I didn't, but they don't know that. So I was gloating or something?

I was on Beaumont Street, breathing in and out in a steady rhythm, finally. I had to avoid Broad Street or any of the center of town. My eyes were searching, afraid I'd bump into them, no longer knowing how to talk to either of them. They'd be out together eating dinner and then maybe going to the Kings Arms for a drink. And he didn't seem upset at all. He was so polite. Why?

I just headed north, back toward the bedsit.

By the time I walked in the door it was nine-thirty. I was light-headed from not eating and tried to think what I might find in the tiny refrigerator. Milk. I drank half a glass.

My phone buzzed.

"Hello."

"Peggy, Eric was wondering if you'd like to join us for a drink at the Turf." She lowered her voice. "Actually, Peggy?"

"Yeah?"

"I'm outside the loo at Chez Jean. He wants to speak with you but wanted me to get you there without freaking you out. Do you want to just be alone with him? I mean, you wanted to ask him about the drawing and why he left Boston, right?"

What a stupid farce.

"Yeah, Amanda, thanks. Sorry."

"Nope. No problem. I'll see him tomorrow and I'm back in England now. We'll see lots of each other."

I thanked her and headed out, walking quickly, hungry and dizzy, telling myself to focus and just ask my questions and then, leave him the hell alone.

Ironically, the Turf was my favorite pub. It was thirteenth century or something and filled with a series of unimaginably intimate medieval rooms. Thick hoary beams where everywhere with mounds of plaster between them.

I had to wind my way through students, twisting my way through the first room, then the second, then the third. There they were, sitting at a minute, dark wooden table in the last ancient, rustic corner.

"We got a table a minute ago," Amanda said. "There is a God."

She was more filled with enthusiasm than I'd ever seen from her. Compensating for something? I wasn't able to smile and they both looked away from me.

"Actually, Amanda got the table." Eric stood up. "Take my chair. I need to stretch anyway."

As I was shaking my head, Amanda was wagging hers. "I did. I feel empowered as an individual human person and I haven't even finished my beer. Actually, Peggy, do you want the rest of it? You know I can never drink a whole pint."

Amanda was still compensating, and it wasn't putting me at ease. I knew it was aimed at helping her brother with this awful, pushy, grasping girl. He was standing away from his little wooden stool and so I thanked him as I sat down, knowing Amanda would be leaving at some point. I said nothing, so Amanda did.

"I had a glass of wine with dinner and that's all I can handle. I'd like to go home and go to sleep now. Too much excitement in one day for me."

Eric hovered over us and chuckled, wrinkling his brow, and I tried to smile.

"So, you're okay, leaving?" he asked Amanda.

"Oh yes. If you don't mind, I'd just like to sleep. Ummm, delicious sleeeeeep."

There was one more conversational gap. He smiled but looked like a man ready to move on to the next task. I drank some ale and it was smooth and bitter all at once.

Amanda stood up and kissed him on the cheek and waved, walking away after thanking him for a great dinner. She was gone.

He sat down, looking into at the crowded room around us.

I only waited five seconds. "I have to ask you a couple of things."

He sat very still with one hand holding his mostly empty pint.

"I really wanted to grab this opportunity to come to Oxford. But since Amanda couldn't answer any of my questions, I also wanted to ask you face-to-face why you ended up buying the drawing."

"Right, I know. To be honest, Amanda told me you were bothered by things. No, Peggy, it's fine. I just wanted to talk to you to tell you that. I wanted to buy the drawing and I wanted to come over closer to my mother and Amanda. This is where I'm from, sort of."

"But you don't collect Italian drawings, do you?"

"Maybe it's the start of that. I have bought a few things over the years."

"Okay, well, I'm just sorry I didn't get the thing attributed when I could have."

"You really don't have to be so sorry. I'll get it attributed at some point. These things take time."

I didn't know how else to say I was sorry or to explain myself. For some reason he wasn't bothered by whatever happened. Maybe forty thousand dollars wasn't a lot of money for him? Seemed unlikely.

He asked me a few standard questions about what I was doing at the Ashmolean and what I liked about Tuft's University and I said some vaguely polite things and then stopped. The noise and the crush of students around us filled our space, squeezing us out and I was aware of losing any focus. He was finished with the subject of the drawing? That was it? He planned to speak to me but leave it at that?

He was letting me off easy. He was going out of his way to meet with me to try to make me feel better and I could feel my skin start to bristle with some sort of raw, uncontrollable frustration. I drank some more of Amanda's ale.

He watched me do that. "Can I buy you something to eat? Did you get anything to eat tonight?"

I shook my head and turned the subject to him. I'd get him to talk.

"The Trevor Cobery Gallery's looks great. I've only seen pictures online."

"It is. I was lucky to get the job. I wanted to be in England, closer to my family, but I like Ireland a lot and I'm closer than before."

"That's good." We both had to shout over the partying pub mates.

"Yeah, I sort of painted myself into a corner in Boston. Uhm, I mean, I wanted to work with a fantastic collection and all that, but more and more realized it was a lot of dry academic work and, to be honest, I'm not that academic."

"No? What do you mean?" Now, it was a shock hearing him open up so much.

"Well, I love the works of art and I love the issues to do with exhibiting them and conserving them and collecting them and even loaning them or not loaning them. You know, I even like the issues of raising money for museums." His accent was lyrical and clear, like a formally trained singer.

"Really?"

He smiled. "Do you think you would?"

The beer and the surprisingly personal conversation were making me even more lightheaded. "I don't know. I never thought about it. Actually, I don't think I'd be good at that at all. What, asking people for money?"

"Yup. It's not money for us. It's for a good cause and some of those people have too much money, Peggy."

He laughed and I tried to join in. He really wasn't anything like I thought he'd be.

"Anyway, there are all sorts of jobs in museums and it's good to have one where your strengths lie. I sound like an old guy, but I've had a few drinks. But, anyway, writing art historical tracts is not my strength. I did it for a few years and I figured that out. I think administrative work is more my thing. I hope I'm right, because I just quit a really good job and came all the way over here for an administrative job. But, yeah, a lot of people in the major museum world look down their noses at the less intellectual art trades, which is to be expected I guess, in the real world. Anyway . . ."

He finished his ale and looked at his watch, then at me.

"Actually, I have to get going. I have a crazy early start tomorrow."

I was feeling panicky. I was losing my chance. We got up and wound our way out of the gorgeous pub, me beyond dizzy, in a twitchy haze from the beer and lack of food.

We walked through narrow, dark medieval streets for a few minutes without saying anything, then stopped at the intersection of Broad Street and Cornmarket.

"Nice night for a long walk. I'm headed to my bed and breakfast, the opposite direction you're going. So, it was good talking with you. Best of luck with your job. It sounds about as good as an internship could possibly be. I certainly wish I did that years ago. Bye."

We both nodded. He was dismissing me. We walked away from each other, me sort of grinding along St. Giles. After ten seconds I looked back seeing bands of students and nothing of him. After a minute, walking more and more quickly, alone, I was waving my head back and forth. I was so frustrated and angry at myself. I didn't feel like I asked any questions or understood anything.

He just went to some trouble to take the high road? He wasn't a nasty snob? But there was no way he spent forty thousand dollars on that drawing so nonchalantly. Meanwhile, he was being nice to me at the pub. Why? But he was actually that way with me before, wasn't he? I was the one who was less than nice, much less, each time he tried to help me. God, it all made me feel like such a little pushy jerk. Yeah, as Eric said, Amanda had enough integrity to even compensate for me.

Somehow, I got home and fell into bed, because there was Amanda already asleep. It was a few minutes before ten-thirty and I knew she wanted to avoid me, now that no one could pretend I wasn't a problem. It took a while, but I finally fell asleep.

The next morning was pitiful. Amanda slept in while I waited for her. I took an aspirin trying to make my head stop throbbing, maybe from a lack of integrity. Should I go to see him? When was he leaving? He said he was leaving early. Three endless hours went by, from after six to nine o'clock before she stirred. I looked over at her one more time.

"Amanda."

"Um."

"Can I ask you a question?"

She waited a few seconds, then turned toward me and stretched. She slowly got up.

"Amanda."

"What?" She walked past me, expressionless.

"Let me just ask you something before you go to the bathroom." I only hesitated a second after she stopped and turned. "Should I try to talk to your brother? Is he still there or coming over here?"

"No, he's gone. I thought you talked to him last night." She was totally flat, tepid, with very tired eyes.

"Um." I tried to not beg.

"Let me just go. I'll be back." Her voice had more than a touch of irritation in it.

I stood there for the few minutes it took her to go down the hall to the toilet, which was a shared, small room next to the shared room with the bath tub that had a shower rigged with an insubstantial set of metal tubes and pipes and a moldy plastic curtain.

Amanda came back in the room.

I didn't wait. "Sorry I made things so awkward last night, for you too."

She walked by me, said nothing and was looking at me as she pulled on some jeans. "Yeah, no, Peggy, it's fine. It was just a bit weird to not tell Eric you and I were hanging out in New York. And, Peggy, it's okay. You don't have to bother about all sorts of things, please. I mean, really, you became my friend and I'm happy for that, but he's my brother. I owe him a lot." She terminated her remarks by sliding into a heavy sweater, then turning away.

I hated her turning her back on me. It was my turn to go mute and that seemed to forge a resolve in both of us, as she made herself busy putting things away in her chest of drawers.

When she was standing at the sink getting a bowl of cereal and making a cup of coffee with our French glass coffee plunger, she still had her back to me.

❧ Chapter 12 ❧

Walking always changed my state of mind and got me into the rhythm I needed. I was trying. But my walks on my new island had already changed me. I'd fallen in love with everything around me and that wasn't good.

It was one more day, over a week after Eric's visit, with me trekking up Woodstock Road, across North Parade to Banbury Road, down to the University Parks. I was in the otherworldly amber glow of the earth and air around me. The light was as low and as soft as raking light could be, and only in the middle of England in late fall. I knew that now. I wanted it forever and walked through it, along the path in the park, then along the little bubbling tributary to the River Cherwell. I had to leave in a year and a half.

The sound of the water flowing stopped me and I leaned on a tree and looked down at the cold grass of the creek bank. A few quiet middle-aged people passed.

The fact was, I kept thinking about Eric. I kept seeing him more clearly in my mind. It hit me again and again, that ton of bricks. I wasn't seeing him before. There he was, the elegant, polite, handsome, ton of bricks. He was so insanely beyond me, in his stage in life, in where he lived, where he came from, where he was going. It was freakish and absurd, but I was exhilarated and drowning and had to fight for my life.

I'd been fighting very, very hard for the past week and I was getting worn out. But, hell, after seeing him there in intrepid, high-minded Oxford, it was dead easy to see how pathetic it was to grasp at unreal goals in life and I forced myself to think about my actual situation. What was I going to do after the internship? It was an ugly question that had to be answered, so I'd been trying all week.

I had to walk some more but stayed there, leaning on the young oak tree. I didn't want to go back to the bedsit. I couldn't be around Amanda at all now. I'd lost her.

There was nowhere to go.

I was crying, groaning like a sick animal, right next to the little tributary of the Cherwell. No one was around. It was cold and damp out and most people were in libraries or pubs or were shopping because it was a week before Christmas. After ten minutes I was able to calm down a bit. The air was so wet, droplets floated here and there. My hair was wet, and my boots were. Everything around me was wet. The cool air never dried my cheeks and I watched the creek ripple by, flashing bits of gray-blue and umber in the black water filled with old leaves and evergreen needles. Everything mixed into floating protoplasm and I wanted to laugh because it was so obviously pornographic.

So, yeah, I was a goner and as greedy as can be, wanting everything. I was the jerk of the world.

After standing there for an hour or so, sitting part of the time, some people walked by and I finally left.

Keeping as busy as possible meant I didn't think constantly about Eric, not all the time. As the weeks went on, when I did think of him, I told myself immediately I had to grow up.

I still walked to work each day, taking twenty minutes out of being still. The weather was colder and black leaves flew everywhere in drafts. The long purple slants of a darker, odd mercurial light were just enough to make everything perfectly warm inside and hard and sensual outside in the cold, damp Oxford winter. But everything I loved was just out of reach. Mark, Eric and Britain. The better my island seemed, the more painful the time limit on staying. It felt like invisible, sadistic forces were playing with me.

One day Mary asked me if I was liking my, *stay so far*. I hated the question. It was all I could do not to groan and walk out the door.

"I am." A bit of grit in my voice. "I might be liking it too much. I may not want to go back, so I'll have to leave every six months for a while. Go back to New England or somewhere, then reenter with a new visa. They'd only let me do that a few times."

"Ah, well it's in your blood is it? Yes, they probably don't like foreigners overstaying their visa time. I don't know much about that."

"Umm." I bit my lip, then said, "Yeah, so I'm a foreigner."

She blushed deeply. "Oh, well, not very."

"Just an amorphous American."

Still blushing, she kept her head down, poking a scalpel at an old work of art. "I expect amorphous might describe a lot the modern world."

She said that to console me. She always lived within easy reach of her birthplace. She worked on contentedly, apparently glowing in the security of never leaving her homeland. In the past that kind of tight connection might have caused suffocation jitters in me, but now was I was feeling envious, or was I just, plain losing my mind?

It was always the same thing when I'd show up to look at prints and drawings in the Print room. Ian O'Connor, who actually asked me to call him Ian after two weeks, was always on hand to help and so was the biggest twit in Oxford, Hugh Thorald, who it turned out was some sort of rare English, Catholic aristocrat. He always found some way to stare at me and seem distant. I continued to call him Mr. Thorald and he was too special to alter that. Mrs. Gilmore, Eva, was distant but gave me warm, knowing smiles. If I spoke to her, she'd be very obliging but seemed to prefer watching, seeming to find the aristocratic enthusiasm for me amusing. She sat in the Print Room at times for hours, typing into her small computer, looking up over her reading glasses, the sole female intellectual spy, right out of a Le Carre novel.

I looked at the prints I was matting. They were the best examples, in mint condition, of artists I hadn't heard of but was getting to love: Jan and Esaias Van De Velde, Claes Jansz Visscher, Willem Buytewech, Hendrik Goudt, Hendrik Goltzius, and on and on.

☙ Chapter 13 ❧

By Christmas Amanda overcame her embarrassment for me and was relaxed and cool and collected again. At times, the temptation way inside me to talk about her brother was insanely strong, but I managed to discipline myself and go for long walks alone. As long as I didn't say a thing about him, she didn't.

But Christmas arrived awkwardly. No one at the Ashmolean invited me to his or her house because I passed around to everyone I could that I was getting together with some friends in London. That was a complete fabrication to avoid spending such an intimate family holiday with those people I admired and even really liked. But shared intimacy, no.

Amanda went off to Cirencester eagerly to spend Christmas with her mother and her brother. I don't think she half believed I had a friend in London. It was me, alone, somewhere between love starved and afraid, which was new. Something was new. My resilience was dying and being alone would never be the same.

The streets got quieter and I just automatically holed-up, sleeping, reading, running in place. Time passed and then Christmas was over, and I was still there.

January was cold and damp in every corner. The little radiator was an indolent insult to our wellbeing. Amanda and

I wore layers on top of layers and when either of us took a bath we had to heat up the bathroom with steam from the hot water, wait ten minutes back in our room, then run and jump in trying to not scald ourselves. The water stayed hot for twenty minutes. After getting out of the tub, we'd feel warm enough to calmly walk around in a mere two or three layers, for as long as an hour. The air coming in the huge windows always won.

Mary liked that silly tourist pub near the museum, and I hated spending the money, but did once a month. The food was expensive and tasteless, but she was always very easy to chatter on with about anything superficial. I had lunch with Mrs. Roberts one day and she was wonderful, laughing about me knowing more about real, local ales than she did and asking me about my interests and about Tufts and Boston. I met a guy named Chris in the King's Arms with Amanda one night. He was very nice to look at but had a grabby approach to the opposite sex and was sort of rude as he drank more. He tried to kiss me at the pub and then again as he walked Amanda and me home. It might have been the alcohol, but I really did want to be on the receiving end of his lust. For a while there, I really did want that.

Amanda had been with a guy too and actually planned on seeing him again, but she left him behind and walked alone. She was ahead of Chris and me after ten minutes. After standing outside our house and wrestling with him, I managed to get sober enough to get rid of Chris. Then, at lunch on the following Tuesday I found him to be as immature and smug as he had probably been the Saturday night before. That was the end of that. Amanda began to see the guy she met that night at the pub. She began to look much happier and I was relieved by that at least.

↦ Chapter 14 ↤

Fighting depression wasn't something I'd ever experienced. I walked and walked. I didn't want to be, "The Lady of Shalott", cursed to remain in a castle tower and only look at reflections of the beautiful life out my window. Eric, well, he must have phoned and emailed and sent texts to Amanda, but I'd very likely never see him in Oxford again. I wondered on and off if he managed to attribute the drawing. Was it by a major artist and worth a lot more than he paid for it? Or was it a piece of second-rate trivia and a constant reminder of the stupid Avakian jackasses who foisted it on him?

On a sunny, surprisingly warm mid-January day, I chanced an invitation to Amanda for lunch and got a careful yes. The conversation over broccoli and rice soup led to more chit-chat. Chit-chat was all we had left apparently, Amanda and me, and that frustrated me. I was almost finished with my soup and didn't feel like talking seriously next to a noisy teenage couple at the table near us.

"Uhh, let me tell you something." I studied her face and she seemed to resist me by showing no emotion at all. "Can we go to the Kings Arms and I'll tell you something?"

She gave me the most minimal, wary nod.

The five-minute familiar walk down Broad Street meant no conversation. I tried to look at the shops on our right and all the bikes and cars in the middle and the medieval walls of Trinity College. Everything seemed to point to the Kings Arms. We sat and sipped our ales separated by a tiny, low pub table of cast iron and marble, one foot in diameter and two and a half feet tall. As usual, students crowded around noisily jostling for drinks and conversation.

"I don't want to get into too much, but I just want you to know I'm going to Dublin. I haven't said anything to your brother yet and you can, of course, if you like, but, yeah, I have to ask him a question one last time. You can feel free to tell me I'm an idiot and an annoying little gnat. I would completely understand."

Her head was in profile with her eyes looking sideways at me. "No, I don't know what you want to do and, no, Eric can manage his own life without me playing at being some guardian at the gate, or whatever."

I just looked at her.

Seemingly forced to face me, she said, "Look, Peggy, I don't know a lot about what happened between you and Eric with that drawing. I do know he couldn't afford it and probably wishes he'd never bought it. But, no . . ."

"He couldn't afford it?"

"Shit Peggy. Talk to him about it, once and for all. Keep me out of it. Please."

I jerked back. Amanda was just so filled with contempt for me. I hadn't realized how much. I could feel rigor mortis taking over both of us and I just barely managed to excuse myself and walk to the loo. When I got back, she was gone.

Amanda was entirely gone. She stopped speaking to me, even in our bedsit.

I had an abbreviated itinerary: a train to Bristol, where I'd stay overnight, then a plane to Ireland. I told myself I always wanted to see Dublin.

❧ Chapter 15 ❧

I tried to sleep on the train, but it was a public space, so I had to think about anything but my goals on the horizon. Thoughts of Uncle Ethan came and went and fiddled with the turning in my stomach. Dublin belonged to him. So why didn't he stay? I groaned inwardly, wishing my brain would shut up. It was raining against the window, silently, making the normally burnished English landscapes just dull and slow.

Later, when the train wore on some more, I thought about how difficult it was to hold onto relationships when everyone's moving all over the map. Mark had a theory once. What was it? After fighting heavy moods for hours, I was getting tired and fey.

I leaned my head against the train window, waiting for one of Mark's sage theories to reoccur.

He said he thought people became adults in their twenties. Before that we're all just simps, kids. It was during your twenties that you became an adult by being independent and then expanding your horizons. Then, after thirty something happens, some sort of plateau. For the rest of your life you act out in that world, the one you've mapped out for yourself in your twenties. Meanwhile, Mark was only sixteen or seventeen when he was telling me that theory.

I suddenly remembered something. He talked about the film, "Swiss Family Robinson". He always used the last movie he'd seen as an example for his theories. I laughed suddenly, half smothering a deep belly laugh for a while. An old man sitting across the aisle from me grinned shyly at me, blushing, probably wondering what was so funny out the window or in the Economist magazine I clutched. I managed to stop, tears in my eyes. God! Good old Mark. He loved some motheaten, classic movies Uncle Ethan gave us. Yeah, Mark started using it as an example and then realized the people were probably too old. The parents were probably in their forties. I had to take in a breath. I was only fourteen or something when he and I watched that movie. The nineteenth century family gets shipwrecked and some of them spend the rest of their lives on the island, even when they don't have to anymore. One son goes back to England.

I tried to remember more of the story, like the great things they made in that huge tree house. Separate rooms on different limbs. The ultimate roost.

The thoughts and sensations of my brother coming up with that theory at that age still had its grip on me and I laughed some more, moaning about Mark. The old man was looking a bit nervous, maybe wondering if I was border-line and tripping over the border, which, naturally, made me laugh longer and harder. I forced myself to think about the old movie to calm myself down. They stayed alone on that island? The movie ends and we're supposed to assume they stay that isolated, that way? That was Mom and Dad.

I stopped laughing.

The train moved on to Bristol, me calming down out of raw fatigue. It was a beautiful midsized city. But it was late afternoon and I took a taxi to my small, cheap hotel. There were the wonderful collections at the City Museum, the really handsome Victorian looking University of Bristol in the middle of town. There was the Clifton section of town, an old, tony Georgian suburb. I read about them all but just stayed in my little hotel room and took a nap.

❧ Chapter 16 ❧

The plane to Dublin rolled up and over clouds, shaking on and on, the way, apparently, small planes do, over and over a flip-flopping sea that came in view at times. It all made me sick. It was part of the journey. Not quite everyone else was sick, but from what I heard, some people were. I had my bag to gag into and tried to not think about the hot sweat pouring over my face.

To my left Dublin was framed in minute bits by the small, square, thick window. It was a small mass of gray dots. I had to just keep on.

The land of Uncle Ethan, I thought, still keeping on with my suitcase, getting a taxi to my hotel, and in order to regain my strength by lying down, I stared up, needing to end the day and get to the next. I absorbed the smooth white plaster ceiling of the reasonably priced, generic hotel room, prostrate on the generic hotel bed.

I wanted to think about Uncle Ethan. I never stopped missing him.

My mother found the drawing on the front parlor wall that day, the day after Uncle Ethan's funeral. I was always so pleased to see the drawing there, looking so good on that wall in that house. The frame had our original Christmas card taped to the back. Mark and I were standing there supposedly taking in the house for the last time. Mark seemed eternally speechless. We weren't moving beyond the front hall-way. A large part of us was dying in pieces as the impossible realization of Uncle Ethan's death slashed away at us. Mom approached and handed me the drawing.

"I was just about to throw this picture out or give it to Goodwill. It has your card on the back of it. You want it?"

I nodded, blurred, barely seeing the drawing.

She smirked. "Okay? There's tons of stuff here that you kids can have. Don't be shy. Whatever you can manage to cart away."

Cart away whatever we want? Her attempt at being flip wasn't just her being inappropriate. She actually seemed to feel no respect for much of anything, including us or Uncle Ethan.

So there was a sudden tug of war between Mark, me and Mom, a rigid silence pulling us even farther apart and I didn't give an inch as Mom watched me frowning at her, saying nothing. She walked away with a frigid, angry shrug.

I turned to Mark. "It's yours. You found it."

He glanced at me and I could see he was trying to not weep and moan and groan uncontrollably and it was all I could do to not fall back into that tormented, cascading hell I lived in for three days after hearing the awful news.

"No. It's yours. I don't want it." Mark was still too thick tongued to speak much. We were walking out to the street together, unable to look at the house. The fresh air cooled us down.

"You're the one going away to college," he added, not looking at me.

We weren't going to take the subway together. We were going to drive back to Long Island in the Honda Accord with Mom and Dad. And so, I didn't reply and sat and pointed my head at nothing out the car window, hearing the rote, feckless tone of Mark's last statement, again and again.

Now, in Dublin, I needed to rest, maybe even sleep. A couple of hours would be good. I just wanted to aim at going out for food in a couple of hours. I fell asleep.

The small hotel was right in the middle of the tourist section of town, and at around four I wandered out. The architecture around me ranged from beautiful Georgian eighteenth century to twentieth, to some beautiful contemporary buildings. But the overall effect was beautiful, and the winter sun was present just enough to light a pedestrian's way, meekly.

He was out there somewhere. At least he was closer to his family now.

I shook my head and took in a deep breath. Ireland.

I couldn't absorb the fact that Uncle Ethan ever lived in the place around me. Uncle Ethan as a young man? He did though, until his parents, my great-grandparents, felt the need to leave for America and the possibility, as Uncle Ethan told me, of making a living. An amazing phrase, *making a living*. Yeah, Ireland was poor then and probably felt like it always had been. It was struggling with debt, but richer now.

I walked, looked and remained steady and it was a terrific walking city, so much to look at and relate to and no hills. Uncle Ethan once told me he would never visit Ireland. He left it and it closed up behind him. I wondered if America closed up behind me.

There were sleek and funky and traditional and even some dangerously expensive bars, pubs and restaurants everywhere, but I knew I couldn't eat. My whole self, body and soul, was in a knot, a new Gordian knot. I bought some yogurt, an apple and some almonds and headed back to the hotel. I had to aim toward the Cobery Museum for the next day and that was no problem in one way. Sleep. I was so tired from lack of food and frayed nerves that I was comatose.

Long, featureless hours later I lay in bed, just made awake very suddenly by remembering where I was. It was a few minutes after seven, bright and damp and cool out with people and car noises on the street. According to my calculations, after a shower, getting dressed, eating breakfast, I should reach the Cobery Museum around ten when it opened. That would be if I walked slowly. I was awake too early, but I got up and began my shower.

I poked at some cereal and juice, then some coffee and read news bits on my phone, and at ten to nine I was off. Dame Street was fascinating, but I was in no mood to even look at the exterior of City Hall or Dublin Castle. But I had to kill some time.

Since I was at the main entrance and had half an hour until the Cobery Museum opened, I wandered into Trinity College. My stomach was starting to burn but I walked slowly. It was a warm, muggy morning now, with creamy drops of sun falling here and there, through deep mounds of white clouds, onto spots of stone or gravel. I was sweaty because I was nervous but also because I had on a long dark blue herringbone overcoat covering a dark blue woolen dress.

I spent twenty minutes wandering around and around the beautiful Trinity College grounds, and, yeah, yeah, it was all gorgeous.

I didn't want to think, begging myself to stop. I walked along Nassau Street at a clip, then right toward Fitzwilliam Square. It was about one minute after ten when I arrived at the main entrance and made my way in. I barely took in the building. It was probably fine looking, gorgeous. The woman behind one desk pointed me toward another desk to get someone to phone the Director and tell him someone was there to see him.

"A Peggy Avakian?"

I waited as the young, peaches and cream girl with the gentle Irish accent that rolled over and through words, spoke with two different people at the other end of the line. I leaned forward and rocked a bit on my toes in those thin shoes and held my hands tightly together behind my back. My Italian flats were so incredibly scuffed. I shouldn't have worn them.

"Um, yes, yes, at the front entrance, um." She was speaking with his secretary. Then suddenly she put the receiver down.

"Mr. Matheson will be right here. Thank you."

I thanked her and stepped back. I licked my parched lips and waited. I wondered where the drawing was at that moment.

Five minutes later, there he was, walking toward me. Eric. He had a serious, rigorous energy about him, alert possibly, anxious to see what the damned issue was this time. I only knew I had no ideas in particular. He bent himself slightly forward, not assertive as much as avoiding my stare -- I thought suddenly, so I looked down too. In a dark suit, he stopped five feet in front of me and nodded a bit formally.

My eyes were woozy.

"Hi, Peggy, how are you?"

"Hi, I wondered if I could speak with you. Not necessarily now, but anytime it would work for you. I'm sure you're busy." I could have phoned or emailed, but I had my pushy immediate needs.

"Uh, I guess right now would work. I do have some appointments, but uhm . . ." He twisted halfway to the side and then back to me, then to the very pretty receptionist. Then back.

Looking forced, he said, "Okay, yeah, will ten minutes be okay?"

"Yes. Thanks." Obviously, Amanda told him I'd do this.

He looked drained of blood, probably wondering if I'd ever stop chasing him around the globe and he escorted me to a small cafe somewhere in the middle of the small museum, next to a courtyard. It was probably all beautiful. I just wondered why he hadn't taken me to his office or someplace private. But, since it was so early, there were only a few people in the museum, and we were alone in the cafe. We sat on a bench.

He said, "So, how's everything at the Ashmolean, Peggy?"

"Great. But I'm sorry I just keep popping up this way. I realize it has to seem very odd, but . . ."

I stopped. He was looking cautious while I spoke, before he swallowed and turned away, then looked down at his shoes. He must have liked smooth, thick, black leather shoes, Oxfords.

Facing me, he asked, "Is it something about the drawing? Because you don't seem to understand. All I can say is it was the right thing for me to do. For me. I hope it's worked out for you."

"I don't understand. I came here to ask you to not be so polite when you tell me why you bought the drawing."

"So polite?" Both of us were sitting rigidly alert. He leaned his whole body back and away from me and said, "Whatever happened with the drawing wasn't really a problem for me. I'm fine with it. You have to just believe me and move on. Really."

I was repetitive.

"But even though you want to reassure me that no harm was done, something happened. Sorry, Eric, but it doesn't make sense."

He looked at me, then away.

I bit my cracking lips. "Has it been attributed yet?"

He shook his head at me, still reluctant to say more.

"I feel like a rat."

"No, Peggy. Look, please. Okay. No, I haven't found the right person to attribute it, yet. I will. Forget about all this. Please?"

"So, you're going to get rid of it? Sell it?"

He looked worried. "Yes, well, I think so. I'll see."

Now I knew enough to know I was finished.

He said, "It's okay. I wanted to come back here and the drawing was just one last thing to tidy up."

I shook my head. "Yeah, I hate that. You didn't buy it because you wanted it."

He looked down at his shoes, out of words for me. I wanted to explain what happened with Mark, but that wouldn't help. I had to stop harassing Eric. I was finished only five minutes into the meager meeting.

I stood up, brittle and weak.

"Well . . ." I didn't want to cry. "Sorry. I came to say how sorry I am that you spent all that money on whatever it actually is, for whatever reasons you had. There's nothing I can do about it. If I could buy it back from you, I would. But I can't."

He stood up, looking truly sorry and embarrassed for me, and I walked on as fast as I could without running and didn't look back.

❧ Chapter 17 ❧

Mark sent a present. It was a small, probably very expensive
Navaho rug. It was really handsome, and I sat and stared at it,
lost somewhere for an hour, fighting tears and losing. It was
the damned letter he sent with the rug.

> *Dear Peggy,*
>
> *Sorry I'm sending this present so late.
> Hope you're ok over there. Is it really greener on
> that side of the fence? Looks like it in pictures. I
> have some news. I had to quit my job. The guy
> who was my supervisor in the Events Office
> kept screwing up every decision I made. I quit
> the other day. Ellen, my therapist, keeps telling
> me I have problems with work, and I guess I
> can't argue with that. But I've been doing really
> well in most of my courses. But, here's the thing.
> Mom and Dad are moving to Florida. I think
> I might go down there and live with them at
> the end of this semester. I hate to bail on Clark
> because I love it here and they've been so good
> to me, but I just don't know how to hold it all
> together financially if I don't work. The dorm
> situation is not great for me either. Maybe I can*

go to a college down there, live with Mom and
Dad and not worry about working too.
Hope you had a Merry Christmas.

Mark

I wrote a card back to Mark, offering my own belated Classical reckoning. Angry reckoning.

Wisdom may come from suffering, but
the rest of the seven kinds of love don't.

I tore it up and just sent an email wishing him the best. I was never sure if he read his emails, ever.

It didn't look good for Mark actually growing up, but it wasn't looking great for me either. Life was about to cave in on me. I had to fight it, but first I had to admit I wasn't much better off than Mark.

Amanda, my friend, my almost sister, moved to London. I only heard from her once. She sent me an email soon after getting there.

"Peggy - the drawing's finally been attributed. Mathew Andrews from Scotland looked at it. I guess he was a curator at the National Gallery at one point and taught at the University of Edinburgh and now he's an art dealer. His speciality is Parmigianino. I'm told. Anyway, he studied it for days and only came up with -- Anonymous, follower of Parmigianino, mid-to-late sixteenth century."

Book Four

✌ Chapter 1 ✌

Why was I thinking about England? Maybe it was the early spring, cool spongy ground out there and the spongy light coming through my living room window. Standing there in my condo in Boston, I wanted to remind myself I was English. I had a passport that said I was.

Maybe it was because I grew up in Germany and only spent a few years in England.

But I loved Boston and my South End condo. I made it mine.

Anyway, I didn't have to stand there, staring out the window, waiting for Amanda. I was liking what I saw through my tall, broad, curved window, out into a spring scene of winter-composted raw greens and browns and greys around old red brick everywhere. There were the buildings of nineteenth century urban New England all around me, as attractive as any time or place on earth.

Amanda had a key. I listened to her sounds, opening this nineteenth century building's main door, coming up one flight of stairs.

"You moved your sofa," she said, breathing the words out after her walk from the subway station. I stood holding her suitcase and pointed to the sofa and she sank into it, the way she always did.

"Mmm, oh my God. I was looking forward to this. It's heaven. This is what heaven must feel like." She shifted herself back and forth a few times. It was small, about sixty inches across and its dark brown velvet upholstery was fitted over soft old down and I just watched her, not saying anything. I didn't want Amanda to know I paid almost four thousand dollars for it.

"I like looking out the window from it," I said, walking to the kitchen to start some coffee.

"So don't I know!" She loved doing her hokey New Yorkisms.

"Yeah, so you're an embarrassment to the whole East Coast," I shouted from the kitchen.

"Hey dude, get some real work so you can afford some real good, solid furniture. Fill this place up."

It was that old joke, that I was obsessed with my interiors and exteriors. I wondered about her being too unsettled and immature to care about fixed things. For years she talked about this kind of traveling and living cheaply somewhere interesting. Her plan was to work and save money between trips. Then she'd go off again to someplace else like Rome or Tokyo.

So far, she worked in a restaurant in tame and tony little Cheltenham for a year and a half to save enough for this US trip, her first trip abroad.

"I really like my sofa." I was back, gazing down at it and there was no irony in my voice.

"I know. This place is a stunner." It became her Cheltenham voice. "God, you are going to make some American woman so happy someday, aren't you? How will you know if it's the flat she loves?"

I smirked and moved on into the kitchen again, leaving Amanda on the old crinkly sofa, head back, resting with her eyes staring at the ceiling, reminding me of a Milton Avery painting at the Museum of Fine Arts.

My kitchen was through the heavy Arts and Crafts oak door, a few steps down the hallway. It was a long narrow room with a large window at the end, with a Moravian tiled table hinged to the windowsill. It might have been the kitchen that sold me on the condo. It was designed by an inspired, and maybe crazy, previous owner who used the cabinets from some old boat, along with the old boat's antique dark cherry boards for the counters and walls. Even the lights and the sink were from some old boat.

The rest of the place was actually standard issue for the South End, which was pretty high standard. There were the high ceilings, thick plaster walls, original long narrow oak floors in the living room and bedrooms, with long narrow old maple floors in the hall. I sanded and left the floors fairly rough, with just a thin coating of tung oil varnish. I left everything plain and just lime washed the plaster. It was a celebration of the beauty of plainness, of America.

I walked back to the living room and handed Amanda a cup of coffee and a plate of seriously good oatmeal cookies from a local bakery. I sat across from her.

"God, Eric how can you spoil me so much? You know it'll make going back harder."

"Then move to Boston." My standard appeal.

"Um, well I might, and have my own bedroom in this huge, two bedroom flat." She chewed. "But I like New York. Even if it is too big and too noisy."

"And smells too much like too much trash rotting too slowly. Unless you're one of the few way up in a penthouse with too much money. That's why all the buildings are too tall."

"Okay." I got a laugh out of her. "That's nasty. It smells a little in Boston too, doesn't it? All cities do."

I let that float.

"Actually, I'm thinking of applying to a master's programme." The switch was done quietly by Amanda.

"Really? What sort of master's programme? Where? Here?"

"No, not here. Hell, I can't afford here. No, I don't know, some British University. I'm thinking of some version of child psychology."

"Fantastic. You've said things about that. Wow. You can get scholarship money over here you know. A lot of these private universities here have fat endowments, not like the government funded ones over there, and your being foreign might help you get in here."

Amanda recoiled just a bit, the slightest tightening of muscles around her eyes. She was the one who got Dad's light blue eyes and they could pierce lead.

I said, "Sorry, my habit of playing angles is hard to suppress and I just sounded like some awful, pushy relative, didn't I?"

"Um, Royal Holloway has a fantastic psychology department." She looked at her coffee.

And I tried to remember the pictures I saw of Royal Holloway when I was applying fifteen years before as an undergraduate. There was an enormous French Renaissance styled chateau with two big lush quadrangles in the middle. It was gorgeous. I didn't get in and the sinking feeling in my gut was that Amanda might not and knew it.

"Well that's a great choice."

"I know I didn't get the best marks at East Anglia. But I thought I'd take some courses first, somewhere." She folded her arms and leaned forward, looking a bit uncomfortable with having to pass those facts by me.

I kept a neutral face. I'd been avoiding thinking about her going back to the UK.

"What about you," she said. "With your fancy green card, your endless options. Where are you going to stay put? You're an American, aren't you?"

"Nope. I'm a man of the world."

"Um, right. You look pretty well set up here to me in this swank little palace." She swung her head, scanning the room.

"Except for a huge, huge mortgage."

She wrinkled her forehead and reached for her coffee. Suddenly she looked serious. "Are you American?"

"I don't know, yet, I guess. I mean, I'm only thirty-three and I've been here for seven years."

She seemed to contemplate that.

I continued, "Does it bother you? Not just me being over here, but do you wonder where you'll end up?"

"Me? No. I'll wander for a while, but I'm a Brit, through and throughout. Not so sure about you though."

I leaned back with my hands behind my head. "Yeah, well, I'm not the only one who wonders where he's from. I meet them out there in bars or parties, at work, even once on the subway."

Her eyes widened.

I laughed. "Not you. And not Edith. You come from the land of cool misty air mixed with low-lying northern sunlight, so gentle and distant you could swear it's the objects around you that are glowing."

"Shit! Who said that?"

"Me. It's me, here."

"Fucking hell, you are spooky weird there brother."

I grunted and got up with the dishes and headed for the kitchen. After an hour sitting in my living room and chatting on about nothing much, we headed out for a long walk to a restaurant, Choo-Choos, on Charles Street, at the bottom of Beacon Hill. It was an effort to keep Amanda walking, not stopping in the Public Garden to look at all the lush flower beds or the pond with its stone bridge or the exotic twisting trees. Everything was glistening in the clear high-pressure air of a vivid early May day, and it took us an hour to get to the restaurant.

I took Amanda to, Choo-Choos two visits before and now, it was her first choice. She always loved trains. The food was okay, and it wasn't too expensive, and the theme was old rail lines in America, with wallpaper of old photos of late nineteenth and early to mid-twentieth century trains. That dim, unfocused grey and white apparition spread around us, along with a model train on a track chugging along the wall of the wide room. The inevitable music was all train themes.

It got Amanda going as we sat and waited for our orders of crab cakes, beans and coleslaw. "Yup, it's as if trains are some cute thing of the past."

I sipped my beer and waited for the rest that I'd heard many times before.

She moved her head around the room the way she often did, reminding me of an egret or something, with long, fluffy sandy hair. "How can one of the world's most developed countries be so far behind in passenger rail service? It's as if people just get used to what's available. Some version of, *out of sight, out of mind.*" She stopped herself, suddenly aware that she could be overheard.

"You should be a conductor, on the Eurail."

"Very funny. Okay, I'll stop."

"No, I'm serious actually. Start with some job to pay your way through some post graduate program. Then, yeah, be a child psychologist on trains, or next to a station."

She smirked and drank some water. I saw people looking at us. They tended to stare a bit, Americans, or maybe they liked Brits. If they heard the accent, they wanted more. Our voices were sirens for them or something. Some part, way down inside them, heard a sound from the past, like their mother's heartbeat, and it drew them in. I mentioned this to Amanda in a whisper and she pulled herself up stiffly, folded her arms and lowered her head. Then, even more florid than usual, she glanced around in quick movements of only her eyes.

She leaned towards me to whisper, "I'm too young to be a mother."

The food came.

⚜ Chapter 2 ⚜

It was the middle of the week on a cool windy afternoon, an overcast day in May. It was almost two in the afternoon. I was sitting dry and comfortable on my plush sofa looking out my window, waiting a few more minutes to phone my mother in England. This was my lunch break and I'd go back to the museum and work into the night, until nine at least. That was the way to concentrate, get writing done for the catalogue entries. First, I'd call my mother.

"Hi Edith. It's Eric."

"Oh, yes, Eric!" She always sounded slightly surprised. After years, once a week at least.

"How are you?"

"Well. And how are *you!*"

I told her in a few ways how well I was, and she said, "ahh" and, "oohh", at every turn.

"How is Amanda?" Every syllable was enunciated, and the end of the question stressed.

"She's very well. She was just here."

"Oh, that's good." We both knew it was a routine conversation but Edith worried. The distance between us was pretty great and she had an aversion to traveling, to moving at all. This was a woman who wanted to be ensconced. This was a woman whose grandparents and their extended families were very nearly obliterated by different armies during the

Second World War. A few of them made it to Berlin and were surrounded by damned armies. As a little girl, a foreign little girl in Berlin in the eighties, her parents were always in flux. Would they be forced to run and hide again if the Russians attacked?

"I'm going down to see Amanda in two weeks."

"Oh, that's good. I hope she's okay in that place."

"She really is fine. How's medieval town life in England?"

"What is it? Oh, yes, it is such a pretty village. All the stone and the moss. Just like a fairy tale."

Cirencester really was a large town of almost twenty thousand people and most of its buildings weren't quite as old as medieval, but I wanted Edith to like it, to be enchanted, to be happy.

Edith and I talked on about the weather here and there and the rising cost of food and fuel. She had a wood burning stove in her reception room I bought her five years before and it could easily heat her tiny house, but she always worried about getting the wood and the cost of it and the pollution. Now I could only urge her to use it, and so she indulged me by responding. "Yes, I will."

"Money's all right?"

"Money? Oh yes, I have plenty. You? What about you?" She tried one-upping me.

"Uh, no, I'm fine. I'm rich. So I can send you more."

"No! You do not. If you have lots of money, good. Keep it. You are not so rich. I know it. But you are so successful. You need to save for your future, now. While you make some. Money comes and goes."

"Okay. Edith?"

"Yes?"

"Remember. We're in this together. I'm far away for now but not so far away I can't fly home if you need me to.

And you have to tell me if you need anything. Anything at all." I had to pull at her. I was afraid she'd suffer in silence in some way.

"Oh you sweet boy. You can come home during the summer sometime?"

"Absolutely."

Now I was feeling morose, half ready to weep. No one could do this to me like Edith.

"Okay. Thank you so much for telephoning me. I look forward to the next time."

"Okay. Lots of love."

"Oh yes and I love you. Please Eric, don't work too hard."

"Okay. Bye."

I was emotionally spent and put my head back on the sofa. I texted her all the time and we Skyped, but Edith was shy and preferred the phone calls without us glaring into each other's faces. I sent her emails between phone calls and so did Amanda. It was our tiny family version of the world-wide web.

Later, phoning from the museum, my conversation with Amanda was brief. I could hear her roommates acting up in the background and it was annoying. It was like they were tweenies at a sleepover. It embarrassed me to think one was from Amsterdam and the other from England. Sad representatives. The apartment they were all jammed into was a little dump.

The modest hotels I stayed in down there were pristine and deluxe in comparison.

Amanda and I agreed that I'd go down in a week and a half and we said goodbye.

❦ Chapter 3 ❧

The next day was May tenth. Noise filled the air with phones beeping, computers tapping and people talking. I knew it was quiet compared with most workspaces, but it could be hard to concentrate on writing. The catalogue entries for the eighty-six prints I picked out for the exhibition were almost finished and they were late. Catalogues for ongoing exhibitions were often late but I'd never been late. The exhibition was already half up.

Margy was in the, Special Exhibitions Galleries supervising Toby from the maintenance crew, who was busy attaching framed works of art to the walls with security screws.

I walked to her. "By the way, I heard from that girl with the Italian drawing."

She looked vacantly at me, waiting for more.

"Yeah, I forgot to mention it earlier. She phoned when you were away one day. You know, the girl from Tufts?"

"No, I know. She wanted help?" Margy's eyes were on the framed etching Toby was attaching to the wall.

"Yeah, she said she was living in New York and I offered to introduce her to Christa and encouraged her to do some research there."

Margy was still watching Toby but looking distracted now.

I added, "Peter will pop in at some point and get his hands on the drawing."

She swung her head to me. "Yeah, good luck with that. Anything else we can do for that girl?"

I laughed. "No, I think we're finished with it."

Margy frowned. "Maybe. It's a lot of effort. Christa doesn't mind?"

"No, she was interested to see it and she got that we wanted to get the girl to follow through."

We continued laying out the exhibition. The title on the catalogue would be, "America's Etching Revival: 1880 to 1917". It would be coauthored by Ann and me, but Ann was going away on a trip, so I was on my own.

I had lunch alone, eating an avocado, tuna, lettuce and red pepper sandwich from the Museum Cafe and sitting in a far corner of the Courtyard, almost in the bushes. I read through some of my exhibition entries.

Later that afternoon I took a taxi across the river to Harvard, carrying a photograph of the drawing.

Natalie Ziegler closed the door to her office. She was intrigued, she said, looking at the picture.

I stood watching her. "Sorry it's only a photograph, but the thing itself has some quality. I just want someone who knows this type of thing to help the girl who owns it understand it is, in fact, anonymous and unattributed. We don't want her just assuming it's a major work."

She looked up at me. "Uhh, why?"

"Well, Regina got us going on it and it's not my area exactly."

Natalie waited, hand on her hip.

I said, "Yeah, Ann was on a holiday trip and Ustaad was too."

"So you were no help at all, Mr. Victorian?"

"Not much. Margy was, but she only had a day to look at it and then, well . . ."

"Jesus, what? The girl has parents and grandparents on the Museum Board?"

"No, not at all. We just sort of hinted the drawing might be worth some money and, you know . . ."

"Oh, well, no I don't. I'm in control of my faculties, at least during the workday."

"We were off our game. Somehow, it just slipped out. And I just want the girl to get a few more opinions, you know, and also get more involved herself with what it actually is before she takes it to some auction house."

"Pour cold water on the darling little pit bull so she won't go litigation berserk if she doesn't get a million dollars for what she was promised was a lost drawing by Leonardo?"

I laughed. "Damn. Nothing that extreme, I hope."

"Okay. Is the girl actually a shithead by any chance? Or the loveliest creature you've ever seen? You're not related to her, are you?"

"Nope, nope. None of those things. But she's in her early twenties and not a hundred percent in focus. You know."

Natalie groaned and raised her head. "Dear God, I deal with the darling, entitled pit bull puppies all the time here. I think they're going to gang up and kill me soon."

It was almost scary how open and undisguised Natalie was, while also being brilliant. She was around forty, short and bony and had chin length, very thick wheat coloured hair and very sleek creamy coffee skin. She never seemed to have her shoes on and was standing there in a long, plain azure satin spring dress and white socks. She wrote major books on major subjects like nobody I knew.

She looked at the photograph again, then back at me, one eyebrow raised. "Okay, she's going to take it to New York?"

"She's down there in New York with it. No, I'll see if the Met has time for this. I emailed Christa and gave her the low-down. I just thought you might help them?"

"Help them? I mean, she should take it to Peter Cundy in Brooklyn, especially since he's a dealer and gets paid to do this stuff. I mean, I like to think I know something about that Florentine time and place. Yeah, from first glance, it looks like it might actually be late sixteenth century, maybe. But . . ." She swiveled around on her heals for a few seconds holding the photograph. In a murmur, "I mean, you want me to tell this girl to take it to someone. You don't want anyone else at your museum getting involved. So, I look at it for two seconds and write an email telling the girl to take it to Peter. Or Margaret Desmond in Chicago, who goes to New York fairly often."

"Perfect."

"Yeah. Weird is what it is. I won't ask again why you think this is necessary. I guess I can do it without getting too involved." Natalie laughed quietly to herself and shivered the way she did sometimes when she was enthralled or something. Her whole little body suddenly vibrated like she was suddenly cold. It was seriously erotic. But Natalie was married.

I walked to the door. "It's hard to explain. I wrote the girl's name and email address on the back of the photograph."

She followed. "Okay. So I'll wait a week and email this girl my advice?"

"Please. Thanks, Natalie." I shook her hand formally to seal my gratitude.

"You'll owe me, Mr. Victorian. I'm running around with a few interns." She feigned exhaustion, half folding at her knees and pretending to wipe her forehead. "New puppies need house training every year and I doubt more and more every year that they listen to a thing we say."

We said our goodbyes in the gallery outside her office.

Back across the river in Boston, the rest of the day was occupied with gallery hangings which I always loved and time slid passed because the gorgeous assortment of old frames and old prints on robin's egg blue felt walls made my heart sing, even if Margy was more sullen than usual.

It felt good to be home by five-thirty. I just had to finish the catalogue, at least a few entries that night. Christ, it was hard to write eighty-six entries and an introduction and manage to get the suspicious public excited. The attempt at intellectual hype felt so damned phony.

I could write some entries later and exercise now. There was a six by eight-foot rag rug on the floor in my bedroom and I liked to do my push-ups on that. I stood still in the middle of my living room, listening. There were scrapping noises above me from the couple up there arriving home from work, and now, there was mumbling. They were back from work and daycare. The two-year old twins, Todd and Cecile were paddling around. Really cute kids. Too bad I couldn't adopt them. Too bad I couldn't create with Barbara a couple of years ago in a family way and be happy, or run away with Natalie tonight, without her husband, and create with her. Umm, life's too bad.

I stripped down to my boxers and stretched, then, face down on the rug, I got to it. Seventy push-ups. The last ones were slow strains and took all I could manage and, after crumpling to the rug, I managed to slowly get myself up. I didn't have to pay for a gym somewhere because the half hour to the museum and back every day was a start and the push-ups and sit-ups were the finish.

I wandered slowly into the living room after a shower. I was shaved, dressed, had a bite to eat and was ready to read or listen to the radio or some music. Later, I'd watch some TV on my computer, then I'd do some entries. Sitting back on the sofa felt good. Spare moments of relief in solitude by getting away from the crush of people and events at the museum were great. It felt spectacular most of the time, my condo. But I wanted a woman there, both of us home. I hated breaking up with Barbara.

I thought about her a lot. Dusk was coming in my living room bay windows and the kitchen light was coming around the corner, radiating fuchsia. Pale as a sheet streetlights were roving up and down with shadows of tree limbs. It wasn't good. I'd never lived with a woman before, not past a few haphazard months and Barbara seemed like just the woman to do that with, join together, have babies. Except I wanted the babies more than I wanted Barbara. After a couple of years of practicing coupling, it was just wrong. She seemed just a bit boring. And now, I didn't miss her so much as I missed not reliving the guilt whenever I thought of coupling. It was scary to live with the shock when I told her we weren't working as far as I was concerned and the crumpling ego and hurt and then anger and then, day after day, all of those emotions from her again. And she was the most reasonable, cool, calm and collected person before the break-up and definitely the nicest.

I'd go to bed. I'd watch some TV on my computer.

❧ Chapter 4 ❧

I saw Amanda in New York over the weekend. I'd see Christa a few days later at the Met, with that Peggy Avakian, but was excited to accept Christa's invitation to her place for dinner first, for Saturday night. I took Amanda along thinking she'd find the old art historian interesting. After all, Christa lived in a plush old condo in Gramercy Park, filled, Victorian clutter style, with gorgeous antique furniture and Rembrandt etchings, and drawings by French and British and Italian and Dutch and German old masters. I'd been there once before but just for drinks and with Ann, my boss in Boston, who went to Harvard graduate school with Christa. This was a special invitation for dinner, ready-made at Whole Foods.

It was fun for me. Christa was in the same old condo for forty-plus years and it wrapped itself around us, especially the old gold Chinese tea chest paper on the walls in her living room. The candles reflected gentle, entrancing flickers from the uneven golden metal-leaf that tarnished over the centuries.

Amanda did not have fun. She seemed moody and bored the whole night and a bit rude.

I brought it up on the phone the next day. She disagreed.

"I wasn't rude Eric. Good God, these people matter so much to you!"

"Uhm. A normal amount."

"I don't know what's so normal about doing nothing but work! I mean, Eric, you come down here, and it's not like we never see each other, but you admit to working endlessly long hours and weekends and all that. I'm starting to think you've become possessed. I mean, good God."

"Steady please. I don't, or I rarely, talk about museum sorts of things with you."

"Uhm…?"

"Stop. We talk about all sorts of things."

"Less Eric. Really, you have to admit that woman was full of herself."

"That woman's brilliant. You? You aren't turning into a reverse snob, are you? Do you have any friends who are half-way developed socially or morally or intellectually?"

Amanda groaned, "Of course, I do. Or did."

"Anyway, Christa's husband died last year."

"But she still ignored me for hours. And I mean, she might be some sort of genius but really, she had nothing to say to me and her flat actually had no actual air, and Eric, last month you made me have lunch in that ugly Chinese restaurant with that little round pretentious couple. And that time it was because she worked at the Frick Collection or something."

"Amy and Bernie are great, sorry. I like them and I really like Christa, and, by the way, you and your degenerate flat-mates live in filth, anytime I'm brave enough to go into that place."

"I try to get them to clean, don't I? But Eric?"

"What?"

"I was almost asphyxiated. I was going to die. There was no air in that old flat and no air in the endless, in-depth conversation about the destruction of the old Museum of Modern Art, the meaning of art museums in the twenty-first century.

How can you stand it? That jammed place of hers and you, the bare bones man."

Amanda seemed disgruntled and argumentative lately, in a way she'd never been before.

"Okay. All right. Sorry. No meetings or dinners with other adult people and you."

"Thank you. And I'm sorry my flatmates are filthy human scum, but alas, I had no other choice."

I still didn't think Christa Hiaphin had to apologize for being genuinely well educated and talented. And if Columbia professors, Amy and Bernie, were overly intellectual at times, so what? It was for one dinner.

There were a few more minutes of repressed chatting about the weather and about Edith, about how she seemed to be sounding well and how we missed her. We said goodbye.

I wandered outside, around the neighborhood of my Airbnb room in the upper East Side. I had dinner at a restaurant called, East Side Dive. It looked like a Seinfeld diner, which drew me in, but the food was mediocre and expensive. I wandered back to my room and went to sleep early.

The next day was Monday.

It was about nine months after first seeing the drawing, when I walked up the stairs of the New York, Metropolitan Museum of Art to look at it again. New York can be very cold from the dampness blowing through and over and around all the concrete, glass and steel. Not a lot of room for the sun to break through, except at the Metropolitan Museum, where the immense building lies low and has the broad open park behind it. The sun felt good walking up the broad steps and did again coming through the glass of the entrance doors. It was about noon and noisy with people. I was waiting, wondering if I'd recognize the girl with the drawing or if she'd recognize me. The crowds were dense enough in their clusters, so

I had to search through the groups, even though she'd probably be on her own. And she was there, getting out of a cab. It was the form of the young female who presented herself in Boston nine months earlier, but now in a fairly formal long dark blue dress, and still with that small black backpack she had with her that day in Boston. The drawing had to be in the backpack. Up the steps past students, she looked a bit older.

As I pushed open the door, she saw me and waved and then we shook hands. There was the familiar form of her small frame, dark penetrating eyes, pale skin and dark hair in that classic, very elegant New York style, parted on one side and straight down an inch past her shoulders. Her shyness was odd in the way it was direct. She just smiled a bit, nothing broad and toothy, and said the polite, requisite things and then waited and watched me intensely. I imagined people around her age would find that off-putting. Boys might, especially because she was well above average in beauty.

As we made our way through the cavernous crowded lobby and through the guards to the elevator, I noticed she had on small, narrow leather shoes, very attractive ones that must have been expensive. I wondered if she might be making a lot of money at some fancy job or just came from money. I was just glad she was going to sort out the drawing and I was actually interested to look at it again.

The elevator was slow, but we got there, and Christa was her usual alert, professional self and got to it right away. It was an interesting drawing that had to be researched. She was standing across the table from Peggy, not even looking at the drawing anymore.

When Peggy said nothing, Christa asked her if she was studying in a graduate program somewhere.

"No."

That was all Peggy said.

I stepped in, not wanting Christa to lose patience.

"Yes, well, Peggy wants to get an attribution, partly because she's decided to sell the drawing. If I'm right. Is that right?"

Peggy's serious hazel eyes flashed at me and her face darkened. I wanted to laugh. Then she looked at Christa with the same penetration. "Yeah. I have to. It belongs to my brother and he gave it to me because I majored in art history and he wants the money right now, so I'm here with it."

Christa didn't seem impressed with Peggy's profit motive and just stared back steely-eyed, appearing obliged to ask, "How did you come to own it?"

Eyes directly into Christa's face, never blinking, Peggy said, "I used to come to the city with my brother all the time when we were teenagers, really just to hang around and get away from, you know, the boredom of the grimmest wastelands . . . of Long Island."

Christa smiled as Geoffrey laughed. He was a late twenties assistant to the department who seemed to cling to Christa. He always wore jeans and Columbia sweatshirts with ties hanging down in front of them.

"Probably in SoHo or the East Village?" Christa said, studying the drawing, momentarily.

"We found this in Tribeca, in an antique store."

"Well, all we can do is point you to some boxes of drawings. You can compare it. Just call and make an appointment." Christa, knowing how to steer Peggy, was walking towards the door.

"I was wondering if Peter Cundy could see it," I said to Christa's back.

She never lost a step. "Yep. If he's here and the drawing is at the same time, that would be fine with us. Up to Peggy to work it all out. He comes here pretty often." Reaching the department door, she stopped, and we all did. "We don't offer attributions to the public, of course. You know that?" Christa stared at Peggy like a stern schoolmistress and Peggy nodded. They shook hands and we were gone. I was impressed and owed Christa.

Everything sparkled outside in that very familiar, new air, spring way. There probably wouldn't be many more days like it before summer humidity weighed down. I didn't like New York in the summer.

Peggy was walking down the large, wide museum steps to Fifth Avenue and I felt obliged to ask her if she'd like to share a taxi. I worried she might have just been browbeaten a bit by Christa and me. We got in a taxi and headed down along the Park.

There were a few standard pleasantries in conversation before I decided to ease the awkwardness.

"So, if I can ask, what are you doing for work?"

"Um, nothing much. I work for an insurance company."

"Do you like it?"

"Yeah, I do, oddly enough. I might not for long, but I have to pay the rent and it's not bad."

The taxi got stopped in what looked like a long traffic jam and I waded through things in my briefcase. I had to approve the final entries for the ridiculously late exhibition catalogue. The entries seemed fine and I wanted to do anything but gape at them again, so I looked over at Peggy who looked bored with nothing to do.

"Have you applied to graduate programmes?" I asked.

"Well. I'm waiting. It cost an arm and a leg and to be honest, I have a few other more immediate, tangible issues in my life now that I'd rather face up to."

The cab jerked forward and stopped. I wasn't sure what to say to her. Maybe she had some relationship problems or something. I wanted to tell her to just go for it, if she wanted to go to graduate school. If I'd hesitated, I never would have been accepted to Yale with a full tuition scholarship and stipend. But I sensed some insecurity in this Peggy. It's rough being twenty-two or whatever she was. I changed the subject and we talked about where we were headed, looking at the traffic jam. She seemed anxious to get moving, glaring at the cars out the window, anxiously watching us not move.

We complained about the traffic and sat back.

"You said you're from England?" Those eyes were fixed on me.

"Well, sort of. My father was English and my mother's from Romania. My parents met when my father was stationed in Berlin. During the Cold War, Romania was out of bounds, of course. My mother's family had escaped after the Second World War. But that was as far as they got. I went to school in Berlin growing up because my father was stationed there with British forces. So an army brat, yeah."

Her stare seemed intrusive, so I looked away.

"As far as they got?" came out of her.

God, these New Yorkers. Get right in your face, whenever, wherever.

"Uhm, well, my mother's family, my grandparents, didn't want to be in Berlin. Not then, during the Cold War, especially. They wanted to head farther west but there were so many restrictions then and they didn't have the right connections, I don't think." I wanted to stop talking about my mother and father with this stranger. I never trivialized them.

But it seemed necessary to add something. "I think it made them value the basic things in life, my mother's family. They weren't spoiled."

She said, "Yeah, I'll be honest, I'm not idealistic about survival, and I'd imagine it would make people careful about life, maybe hold onto a sense of reverence." She was looking at me with even more ferocity than usual.

"Sense of reverence . . ." drifted out of me.

"Um, otherwise life really does just become a rat race, I think."

She was obviously bothered about something.

"Hm, that's interesting. Do you find the rat race in your work?"

"No. Yes, of course, same as anywhere. There are tons of rats everywhere."

I couldn't resist pushing back. "But, so tell me. You do value practical things, like money, right?"

"Yeah, I'm aware only idiots don't value money. No, life's too short to be stupid and impractical." She paused, thinking. "I had an uncle, an immigrant from Ireland who had to survive on his own in Brooklyn for years, who lived very well all by himself with some money, enough so he could afford to have principles and afford to stay away from all the money grubbing or power grubbing types out there. I looked up to him. He was the only person I've ever looked up to in that way. So yeah, I think living well is the best revenge all right."

This Peggy didn't do polite chit-chat and that phrase about living well grated, coming from this pretty, young, raised to be self-assertive, American.

"Yeah, your uncle sounds like a rare, principled man. That's great. But you know it's funny, *living well is the best revenge*, is an old British phrase. I think it was from George Herbert in the seventeenth century and had religious meaning and all that. But in the modern materialistic world, who's living well and who's it revenge against usually? Makes me wonder if it isn't more than a little bit of a beady-eyed excuse sometimes."

I wasn't surprised she was looking annoyed. She said, "It's revenge against the rats." She added, "The beady-eyed ones are the rats."

As I took that in, she began to get out some money. She handed me her share and got out of the taxi.

I only wanted to get to Amanda, say good-bye, get to the airport and get back to Boston.

Chapter 5

I made a mistake. I shouldn't have become that involved with the drawing. I did it for Margy. And I was also trying to do that Peggy a favour and she seemed to have some sort of nit attack. I'd have nothing more to do with her or the drawing. There were finishing touches to do on the catalogue layout, and I was plenty busy. It wasn't to be. A couple of weeks after the irritating taxi ride, Margy approached me.

"Ever heard of Daniel Loring? A dealer in New York City?" She was in my space and I was busy and in no mood.

"No ... sorry Margy ..."

"Lizzy Preston just called and read me a letter he sent to her describing a drawing for sale that's been attributed by this museum and the Met as, anonymous sixteenth century Italian."

I sat still and wrestled with conflicting interests inside me. There was my extremely late catalogue Ann had asked me about just that morning, and now this little bit of what?

Margy said, "Lizzy collects French nineteenth century prints. The Degas? Remember the monotypes she gave us two years ago?"

"Yeah? Yes, right. Your friend from school."

"Yeah, she got this letter from a guy I've never heard of. Have you? A Daniel Loring?"

"No. You think it's the same Italian drawing?"

"Yeah, the girl from Tufts. The letter's claiming it's been attributed by us, and the Met." Margy's voice was impatient.

I had to pay attention as the niggling, petty involvement pulled at me. Margy just looked plain angry. She went to her desk to call Christa to ask if Peggy ever turned up again with her drawing. She was back at my desk in about two minutes.

"Nope."

"Well, we've done our best for the girl. That's it. It's out of our hands." I wanted Margy to drop it.

"My God. That little snip must be playing us."

"Have you seen this letter?"

"No, not yet. But this guy must have a museum mailing list, because, God, if Lizzy up in Ipswich got one and she said it was a form letter with a faded picture of the drawing. Hell."

Margy was getting more and more agitated. It was too bad she worried about the small conflicts so much. There she stood, beaming red, her eyes brilliant grey-blue, her lustrous grey hair streaming down, dressed perfectly as always in an ankle length striped linen dress and elegant leather sandals. She had all the charm and smarts needed. She was model material for the major art museum world, but she seemed to make an enemy of Ann, and Ann was Senior Curator of the department.

And then Ustaad and Jean went along with Ann on anything. That seemed unfair to me, but I got it. Ann brought them along. Ustaad and her husband got out of Afghanistan in the nineteen nineties. They met at Yale where he was studying medicine and she was getting a PHD in Fine Arts. She made beautiful etchings and lithographs. They moved to Boston and met Ann at a dinner party and twenty-five years later Ustaad was still working with Ann, offering her expertise in modern and contemporary art on paper. Jean met Ann at a photography opening. We were all personal projects for Ann.

Margy wasn't. She was hired by Malcolm Frome, the same curator who hired Ann, but he hired Margy not long before he retired.

I was sitting, half listening, feeling guilty about the missing, inattentive half. Margy mumbled about disreputable dealers. She asked me about the trip to the Met. She said she was going to phone Peggy Avakian that Saturday. Christa sounded angry, she said. Yeah, I thought, but probably because we both kept bugging her with this one weird little issue.

I'd probably have to do something, but I didn't know what. Something away from Margy.

During lunch with Ustaad and Ann I described the situation. We were treating ourselves to an expensive lunch in the museum restaurant, which was one of my favourite places to eat. A big glass wall looked down at a large, gorgeously vegetated courtyard and up at whatever the sky was that moment. The light inside was always different because of the huge glass wall and the mix with the low yellowy table lights inside. Today it was almost June, with bright, thick puffs of white cloudy light from above.

The treat was for us finishing the catalogue. I did most of the work, along with some research assistance from Ustaad and Margy, as Ann did none of it. She never did. She must have done some work when she was younger, but not for years, according to Margy. We had a pact, Margy and I did, and we kept to it -- to not talk about it. It was a downward spiral and Ann was going to retire in a few years. So what was the point? Ann was so easy for me to get along with, so easy going and polite and revered by people outside the department and the museum. She had the basic pedigree academically, a BA from University of Massachusetts at Amherst, then a doctorate from Harvard. She grew up in an Irish family in Brockton,

Massachusetts, a pretty much blue-collar town and was the only college graduate in her family.

She never married and spent all her adulthood in the museum, amounting to almost forty years. She was one of the early female curators in the building. My guess was she worked hard for years, before she got lazy and burned out. She promoted me, so what if I had to share the authorship of the catalogue?

At lunch it was Ann who looked like and presided as the leader there in her dark green, long, crushed velvet v-necked dress with her charcoal grey hair straight to her shoulders held back with an invisible hair band. It looked to me like Ann tried to copy Margy in that way.

I grumbled, after eating for a while. "I can speak with Christa, after lunch. Maybe we can ask this dealer to change his wording if he's insinuating we actually studied the drawing."

Ann seemed less than interested.

"Happens, though, doesn't it?" Ustaad said.

"No, it does," Ann breathed out nonchalantly, almost whispering. She drank some red wine. "There are much worse cases than this. So don't worry about it. Really. And Eric, why drag Christa into it? Why did you go to so much trouble in New York?"

I blanched. "No, I was going to the Met anyway."

Ann studied me. She had questions she wasn't going to bother asking.

❧ Chapter 6 ❧

As solid and smart as the rows of brick or brownstone nineteenth century townhouses were, they'd seem half done without the heavy black outlines of wrought iron fences and stair railings. A few seamless weeks passed, and it was a beautiful Monday morning and summer was officially on the calendar for a few days. I was acutely aware I was leaving my stunning hunk of a condo behind to go to my stunning hunk of a job, to art, to fascinating little illusive fragments of people's cultures. For me they were actually fragile little old slips of paper with intense or serene scribbles and they wound me up with their beauty and their messages from the past. I didn't know how I fell into my nest of paper art. I just knew it was essential to not fall asleep on the job.

I also knew I liked taking my walk to work. It was just after eight and I was getting a second wind as I reached Huntington Avenue, a broad swath of straight east-west pavement with the Green Line trolley in the middle, squealing and braying like a line of robotic donkeys. The dense tree-lined streets of my South End were behind and now the hefty morning sun already dried the night's rain on the more open avenue ahead. Trolley wires protruded and tall, mediocre examples of twentieth century minimal architecture mixed with some beautiful new buildings of mostly glass. It was mostly Northeastern

University. Between some buildings were lawns and trees and some scruffy summer school students cavorting.

I walked for fifteen minutes next to the traffic and noise, but it would get me straight to the grand, stone monolith where I worked. I loved my job, even if I thought sometimes, I loved the idea of my job. Working in a big art museum, a major collection, seemed to mean I had a major career. Amanda teased me, calling me, "Mr. Aesthete", but she made it pretty clear how impressed she was. Edith was way too proud. No one in her family did anything beyond high school. Mostly factory workers or, back a bit, small plot farmers, truth be told. But we left Edith's past to Edith. She earned that.

The second wind felt good inside me, pushing me through the harsh street scene around me.

Amanda would be getting up late, locking the door behind her and taking the taxi to South Station. I left her with two twenty-dollar bills for the taxi and maybe a lunch on the train. I imagined her back there in my guest room asleep. It felt good to offer her my condo in Boston and a trip to New York she might never have taken if I hadn't been nearby. She had almost no money and no career and not even a job. I didn't know what to root for, some career moves from her soon, or experiencing Tokyo and Rome.

I was hyped. The sweat on me wasn't usual, and as I got near the city block the museum owned, there was something urging me on and I couldn't figure out what.

Barely taking in the wide, low, far reaching expanse of grey granite that bestrode Huntington Avenue, I aimed at a small, innocuous door.

Through the staff entrance, I morning-greeted the first guard, Marty Rosa, who was supposed to check for badges of staff going in. Other guards sat behind him next to computers, surrounded by flat screens on walls showing images of various corridors and galleries throughout the vast building.

"Tide's in Marty."

"It's in early today Mr. Matheson."

Couldn't get him to call me Eric, even though he had to be at least fifty and I'd just turned thirty-four. I guessed early-on it was him deferring to my being formal English, like it was a game.

Then it was hello to streams of staff in all directions in the basement corridors until we all parted to the stairs or elevators to one of three basic locations: Buildings and Grounds, Administration, and Curators/Conservation. The last one was me.

The Print Room was filled with its standard human hum. Margy was at her desk in the back and I could see and just hear Ustaad on her phone twenty feet back from the front of the room where I was checking my mail at the front desk. Jean had her own office now, behind Ann's. It was very small, but I envied her privacy. Anyway, I could calmly, easily interact with Jamie, who maintained the front desk as Department Assistant, but really as an office manager. He was good at being easy and calm as an example for the rest of us. Too bad he only had a few more months before he went to Saint Louis to start his doctorate in art history at Washington University. His job was only meant to last two years and he'd get some letters of recommendation for the future and all that. He joked with us a few times that he was going from a black neighborhood in Dorchester a few miles away to a black neighborhood in the Midwest because he hated diversity.

He'd always been fun to *up-chat,* a little made-up Britishism Jamie came up with for me.

"Thanks for the lousy mail, Jamie."

"Cheery-bye, old codswallop."

I laughed even though I'd heard that demented one from him before. I sat at my desk partially concealed from everyone and straightened the John Everett Millais drawing in the antique gold beaded frame hanging from my bookshelf. I hadn't had time to find out what book it illustrated. It was a beauty. I started reading all my neglected emails.

Right about eleven Jamie buzzed my phone to tell me Stephen Kensett was coming in.

"Why? I asked.

"A trustee, who used to be, whilst remaining a young boy at the Met."

I laughed. "You saying he's dead? I know who he is."

"No, not anymore," he said.

Something told me I had to try to retain some coherence, so I asked why Stephen Kensett was coming in."

"He's bringing in something that was here last September."

"What? What is it?"

"Uh, a drawing. Let's see..."

I looked around my bookcase and saw Jamie tapping at his computer, staring at the screen next to his phone.

"An Italian sixteenth century drawing."

"My God. No, I can't believe it," I grumbled.

"What?"

"Nothing. Sorry." I bit my lip and gazed around. Margy was out of the room somewhere. Ann was in her office.

"Jamie," I was still murmuring. "Do me a favour, please, and pass it on to Ustaad and Margy but let me tell Ann, if that's all right."

"Sure."

Ann was behind her grand Birdseye maple desk, glasses on, with some books lying flat next to a Lucas Van Leyden print in its mat. I told her what Jamie told me.

"Oh, I forgot to mention he emailed me a couple of days ago and wanted to come in. Sorry, I should have told you since he's so wrapped up in Victorian art, among other things."

"No, that's fine. It's just he's bringing in that sixteenth century Italian drawing Margy and I looked at."

"What? Oh." She sat still, eyes darting around. She took off her glasses. "You sure? Why?"

"No idea. He lives in New York most of the time. Maybe he got one of those letters, if it's the same drawing. But, yeah, I'll bet it is."

"Well, we'll see. It might not be. But, okay, if it is, that's fine. We can explain that it was only glanced at here."

"Okay. Good. Strange."

"It's okay, Eric. Don't worry. He brings in all sorts of things. He comes in less now that he's no longer an active board member here. The thing is, he may be bringing it in to offer it to us, instead of New York or Washington. That would be nice for a change."

"Yeah, I hate to mess around with a major donor. But, Ann, as I told you, we didn't tell the girl with the drawing we were giving her an attribution."

"No, I know. You told me. It's okay. I'm not used to you getting this bothered. Relax. I wish I'd been here or Ustaad had been. I mean, Eric, sorry, you know I totally trust your judgment in these things, but really, Margy . . ." Ann made a point of not finishing her words by raising her eyebrows.

"Italian sixteenth century's a lot more her expertise than mine."

"Yeah, well, maybe, but I have to say, she does have a way at times. God, she wants Regina to like her, so maybe she can teach some courses at Tufts or something. You have to tell me Eric, did she mislead the girl with the drawing in some way? Was anything said that exaggerated its importance?"

"We did say it might be valuable but stressed that it had to be formally attributed." I had to say something. I was leaning back on my heels, biting my lip.

"Um. Yeah, right. Who said that? You? That it might be valuable?"

I stood silent, feeling like a simpering kid.

"Yeah, that's my point. And I'm getting nervous that you, in your inimitable British way, are covering for her. She probably said she thought it was a rare old master drawing that needed to be insured. Or something. Yeah, and that's why you were getting the Met involved. You were worried something like this would happen and it has. And even Christa and company didn't coax a proper attribution out of the smarmy little creature with the drawing. Anyway, anyway, okay. Not a big deal. I'll try to not get too angry at Margy. She means well. Let's see if Stephen just wants to give *us* whatever drawing it is, and not the Met!" She rolled her eyes and forced a thin, tight-lipped smile, trying to relieve both of us.

I was riled when I went back to my desk. Somehow, that exchange with Ann resulted in me turning on Margy to protect myself?

Ten minutes later he arrived. Jamie buzzed me even though he knew I was aware. I paused a second waiting for Ann to come out of her office. Ustaad was already there shaking his hand as Ann and I walked forward to greet Mr. Kensett, the white haired, with black remnants, tall, thin, very fit looking man in his mid-sixties. He had on a classic, expensive, blue silk suit.

The chatter between Ann and him postponed any revelations about the package he was carrying. Five minutes of that, and he peeled off some tape and removed some cardboard and there it was, sure enough, in its frame. Altogether, the drawing surrounded by a gorgeous French mat and equally gorgeous nineteenth century, or earlier, tortoise shell frame, looked seriously good.

Ann looked at me and I nodded. She leaned over it. "Well, I'm sorry I wasn't here to see this."

"I thought it looked interesting. The photograph the dealer sent was very poor quality, but I looked him up when I was in New York and, yeah, bought it."

"Yes, well it's very handsome, but Stephen, we do have one concern, that this dealer, whatever his name is, is claiming we studied it or something."

"Right, I got that someone here and at the Met looked at it."

"Uh, well, I wasn't here. I'll let Eric explain."

I nodded and started to explain that the girl who owned it took it away after we only looked at it for one day and the Met only glanced at it. The door opened and Margy walked in, her eyes first focusing on Mr. Kensett, a man she'd seen many times over the years. She began to smile but quickly saw the drawing. She reddened.

Ann put her hand on my arm to stop me speaking, although I already had.

"Stephen, you know Margy Zorn," Ann said.

"Yes, of course." He shook her hand and smiled warmly. He knew Margy as well as any of us. In fact, he always seemed to especially like Margy.

But Margy, still red-faced, stood rigidly and squinted at the drawing lying on the table.

Mr. Kensett turned back to me. "So you were saying, Eric, that the owner brought it here, briefly and then to the Met. Right?"

"Yeah, I met with the person who owned the drawing at the Met with Christa Hiaphin. But it was made very clear that we weren't attributing the drawing in any way."

"Not in any way," Margy said, pointedly.

"Okay." Stephen Kensett looked at Margy.

Margy went on, "No, I don't know what's been discussed here, but we're fairly upset. I don't know if you've purchased this…"

"Yeah, I have."

"Oh." Margy's face turned moister and even redder. Her eyes engorged.

"No, I just brought it in to see what you think." There was a conciliatory questing in his voice.

"Um, good." Ann got in.

Margy said, "But, it hasn't actually been studied by us. I can't speak for Christa and company, but this girl seems to be claiming we said it's an anonymous sixteenth century something or other."

Margy looked down when she was upset, and now she was facing the floor.

Ann looked as caught in Margy's melodrama as the rest of us. "No, well it can be studied here or somewhere else if you like, Stephen," she said.

"Um, well, yes, that would be good. I didn't mean to upset anyone."

"Oh, good grief, you haven't, of course," Ann said loudly.

"Well, I'll have to admit Stephen that I'm upset." The veins in Margy's neck were sticking out. "I feel responsible and, well, Ann wasn't here, and it really is something we always try to avoid. I try to. I mean, the girl has misrepresented us here. Eric, you tried to persuade her to seek an actual attribution a number of times. And then, you even got Christa to encourage her."

"No. Margy." Ann took a step back.

I wanted to say something but Margy was still spinning in her own circle.

"No, just so you know, we do not stand behind that dealer the owner found. Really, it's just not right and I hate to think of someone like you, Stephen, getting pulled into that confusion."

"Oh, well, I just found it on my own," he said slowly and quietly.

"But, really, did you? This girl . . . no, sorry what I find so disturbing is that this girl has manipulated us all fairly callously."

"It's all right Margy. Stephan can do what he wants at this point." Ann was getting visibly angry and it took a lot for that to happen.

Margy looked down at the floor, with her arms folded. "Okay."

"Okay. Let's move on." Ann was mortified, not even trying to smile.

The seconds dragged. Margy was still looking at the floor and I wondered what to say.

"Look, I should say to Margy that we were just told half an hour ago about this meeting."

"Um." Margy looked up at me, eyes flashing, furious. "Right. I was in Conservation. I have a phone."

I glanced at Jamie and he stared back flinching, his shoulders hunched as if to say, *sorry, I forgot to call her.*

"But we should move on," Ann said. "I mean, if you like the drawing, there's no problem, Stephen. It looks very good to me. We'd all love to look at it more carefully. Let's go back to my office."

❦ Chapter 7 ❧

Two days after Margy's scene in the Print Room, I was still in a very uneasy mood. Margy stayed home both days and I saw almost nothing of Ann. She walked by quickly and stayed in her office. Ustaad looked at me a few times and smiled nervously and even shrugged once. Something was up and we didn't know what. I was afraid Margy was going to be dismissed. It took a hell of a lot to be bounced from a museum job, but it could happen.

On Wednesday night at around eight my phone rang and vibrated. I saw Ann's name and number and that was a shock. She rarely phoned, especially after hours.

"Hi. Ann."

"Eric, how are you? I'm sorry to call so late. Is this a good time for you? Tell me if it isn't, please."

"Yes, it's fine."

"Sure? Not being polite?"

"No, I'm not. I've finished eating and I'm sitting comfortably on my sofa with nothing to do."

"Good. I want to discuss some serious things and not in my office with interruptions."

"Okay. You're making me nervous."

"No, don't be. It's just I think the time has come to talk about the future. Yours, mine and maybe a couple of other people. I mean, clearly, you've known I'd be leaving eventually, and you know you've been groomed to take the position of Prints and Drawings Curator. Right?"

I swallowed hard. My heart was banging, and I stood up and began to pace. "Well, I thought I had a shot at it, but I didn't assume it was all wrapped up."

"Really? That's sort of sweet and noble. After we made you Associate Curator, along with Jean becoming Curator of Photography, it seemed sort of obvious I would have thought. Ustaad was the only person in the department who might have rivaled you, but she wants to retire in a few years. Anyway, really, Eric, the scene in the Print Room the other day just drove me nuts and I realized I had to act. It's been coming for a while and I talked it over with the Director and Monica in HR. We have to let Margy go. Uh, it's too bad, but she's just over her head."

"Oh, God. Really? My God."

"Yeah. I think it's been brewing for a while."

"I really hate hearing that. How soon are we talking about?"

"Well, not next week for me. For Margy, I'd say in the next few weeks. We'll let her stay at home for a few more days. I'm not sure when, but I am sure she has to go. Uh, no, I'm thinking in six months to a year for me. The Director's told me that sounds about right but that I should rest on it for a few weeks. But, so, Eric. How do you feel about taking over?"

I was still pacing. I stammered, with a heavy, concentrated weight in my chest. "Hmm, wow. Well, I'm a little surprised. I mean, I realized it was a possibility, but I guess I assumed it would be in a couple of years or maybe even five years."

"No, not even close to that long."

"Was it the scene with the drawing, you said?"

"Not just that. But let's not talk too much about Margy. No, I'm sixty-eight and have to leave at some point. No, the scene as you put it, was kind of the final straw for me with Margy. It was so inappropriate of her to say those things to Stephen Kennset. You know how important he is to the museum. If the trustees heard that he was harassed and embarrassed like that, wow. I mean you should have seen him in my office, Eric. He just plopped the drawing down and said he didn't want to bother leaving it to be examined. He practically apologized for ever buying it. According to what Margy said, clearly, he had been duped into buying some bogus piece of crap by some shady dealer who saw a rich idiot coming. My God, he was obviously depressed he ever came into our department. I hope he does come in again. You may have to mend that fence. He likes you."

I waited in silence for a few seconds, having a hard time swallowing. "Yeah, Ann, uhh, can I say something, something I've wanted to say for a while?"

"Sure."

"Well, first of all, I'm extremely complimented by your offer. Thank you very much. And I hope you're ready to leave. But, yeah, I've been fairly uncomfortable in a way. I bypassed Margy so swiftly. I mean, I waltz into the museum. I'm less experienced, and I'm the only guy, except for Jamie. He's practically a kid, and after only two years I get promoted above Margy. Now, I'd be Curator. You see how that might seem?"

"Like I did it because you're male? That doesn't jive at all with my promotions of Jean and Ustaad. No, Eric, it's a bunch of things. You came in with the right background at the right time. And you've done a great job. Please forget about Margy. She's done fine. There are hordes of art history majors who'd kill to be Assistant Curator in a major collection for so long."

I stopped pacing and stood. My thinking froze and I just tried to end the conversation as quickly as I could without making her think I was crazy. I thanked her a couple of times and we'd talk again soon. We both said that a few times. Finally, it was over, and I tossed the phone onto the sofa, grinding my teeth.

Goddamned Ann hated Margy and that was what this was all about.

I paced again, clenching my fists. And I hated Ann just then. She was offering me a major, major promotion and she could hear my crazy disgust and anger in that conversation. Why did it make me so damned angry? What the hell was with me? I'd never get back to England. Edith and Amanda would be there, and I'd be trying to be an art curator three thousand miles away forever.

The pacing wasn't helping, but I kept doing it for a minute.

Rattled, I sat and closed my eyes. I opened them and leaned forward.

Obviously, most people love getting more prestige and power, and more money. My God, it was one of the five largest art museums in America and one of the best prints and drawings collections anywhere. And I'd be one of the big fish in the big cool sea. And I'd never get back to England.

I stood again. Unlike Ann, Margy worked extremely hard for years for the job she had and was about to lose. Maybe her husband and two kids would help her feel the loss less. But, shit, Margy was being left to rot all because she lost her cool once? I'd never seen her do that before, but she didn't have to. She made Ann feel bad about herself. Margy went to private schools, then Brown as an undergrad and then got her doctorate in art history from Stanford, but that wasn't all Ann hated. Margy did Ann's job for her for decades and Ann loved having the power to promote me and Jean and Ustaad, and not Margy.

Obviously, Margy should be Senior Curator, not me.

And the cause of this sudden ugly crisis was that drawing. My God, I hated that damned thing and hated the way that damned Peggy Avakian abused our good will by selling it that way. Anything to get ahead, try to get a few extra bucks. And her singing her own praises about living well being the best revenge. What a little shit.

❧ Chapter 8 ❧

The rest of the week banged along with me knowing things were falling apart in Boston. Whenever and wherever I could, I did research online looking at jobs. I couldn't spread the word, go through the grapevine. Ann was going to have a fit as it was, and she could definitely sabotage my efforts with a negative letter of recommendation. Instead, I had to do it quietly with internet stealth, but I had to do it quickly somehow.

At least I found myself pointed towards England and getting closer to Edith and Amanda.

So I needed a job. The problem was that so often when things got posted online, it was just a front while someone was already being groomed and chosen from the inside. Back in England I was on the outside now. If I could get something, then I could get inside.

The slow days at my desk at the museum filled me with dread and I avoided Ustaad and Jamie and Jean, wondering if they knew anything about Margy. Rejected, abandoned Margy. I couldn't think of any way to console her without telling her I was planning to leave, and how much consolation would that offer her? I was the one offered the job of Curator? When would she get that news?

Meanwhile, how long would Ann wait before bringing up the content of our phone conversation? She seemed preoccupied and I avoided her.

When Saturday dawned, I was oddly exhilarated to get in my rental car and drive; nerve racked, but oddly exhilarated. The drive to New Salem, Connecticut would take about an hour and fifteen minutes. It was early afternoon, and July first and hot and humid enough to be entrenched in deep New England summer. I might have found a potential job, amazingly. The Trevor Cobery Museum near the National Gallery in Dublin wanted a Director. It was a small, but good collection and the day before at home in the early morning I had a very good conversation on Zoom with two people on their hiring committee. It seemed like a crazy rush, but maybe they'd say yes to me and me to them in the next week or two. I might be going home.

Now I had to drive to a place where I might be able to patch up a wound in Boston before I left.

I was lucky Stephen was available. He had a few houses and this one was a retreat in the country. The Massachusetts turnpike stared back at me for half the trip, and then narrower country highways, all more and more attractive, told me it must be nice to be rich.

New Salem, Connecticut was a hamlet of about fifty houses, all clapboard and old and inexplicably substantial looking. It never made total sense to me that East Coast America had so many two or three-hundred-year-old wooden houses still standing. And there was the white Puritan church steeple on the hill right next to the hamlet's common and also right next to Bloxham Road, a dirt road that curved behind the church, right to the door of Stephen Kensett. The setting was so perfectly pastoral I could see why he'd chosen it for an occasional getaway. It was a small white clapboard house with a couple of small additions, and it sat on a hill looking back onto miles of farmland and sky. There was a vintage, very nicely restored light green Mercedes in the short, wide gravel driveway.

He wanted to talk about England and then about Ireland when he heard my news. I didn't tell him Dublin was very tentative for me. I didn't tell him much and I could tell he wouldn't ask much. All I asked for was silence from him until I made my announcements. He agreed but looked concerned, probably wondering why I was there asking for that. He went downstairs to pour us some iced tea.

It was hard not to want what I saw around me. There was a plain old room with old sash windows, six on six antique panes of glass and there was more glass than walls, looking out on three sides. I resisted getting carried away by the charm. I even resisted asking him about the amazing Winslow Homer painting over the mantle, the plain old wooden mantle, as he handed me my tea. I sat down and he sat in his sofa across from me.

"Stephen, I came here to ask you about the drawing." I paused to let him breathe that in. "I don't know how attached you are to it or what you plan on doing with it."

"Uh, well, to be honest I don't know. The normal thing, the thing I usually do, of course, is pass something by people, get other views, then decide. That's especially what I do if the object's unattributed, mysterious." He raised his eyebrows with the last words and we both laughed mildly, mildly embarrassed.

I liked Stephen. Most people in his position would feign greater expertise. Him the great collector and connoisseur, deciding who might benefit from a few little gifts he might throw out. This guy had all the right stuff, Groton School and Harvard, the same as his father, grandfather and great-grandfather, and he grew up with art collections in houses spread around the world. Rumor had it a lot of his family's great wealth was spent. And he was still a multimillionaire who sat on boards of corporations and museums. Now his wife was dead, and he looked like he wasn't trying to prove anything.

Sitting back slowly, I wanted to give him time and space, to not appear to force any issues.

I also wanted to be straight forward. "I'm here to see if by some chance you might sell me the drawing. I know how odd and possibly awkward that might seem and so I wanted to come out with it and I also wanted to be here to explain."

He smiled and wrinkled his forehead, seeming to be curious.

I continued, "Uhm, see, I actually really like the drawing and wouldn't mind owning it. I wouldn't mind at all." We both shifted in our seats, both of us grinning Cheshire-like. "But please believe me I wouldn't suggest any such thing if I weren't leaving. I mean, Ann would kill me."

"Oh, well, Ann has never killed anyone as far as I know. Much too kind and professional." Again, some shifting, smiling.

That stopped me. He liked Ann and he liked Ustaad and he liked Margy. He liked me and he didn't know any of us and never would. He had his own circle of friends.

I had to move on.

"But please Stephen, if you want to keep the drawing, tell me. It's just, I got the impression . . ." I stopped.

"What impression?" He was pretending indignation, pulling his head back.

"Indifference maybe? No, please just say it if you want to keep it. I'm sorry I'm being so ridiculously squirrely."

"No-no. You're not and I know because I've seen squirrely when it comes to art. I've squirreled away a few things a few times myself. Uh, no, to be honest I wasn't sure what to do. One thing I did learn, in the middle of the minor fracas the other day, was the drawing needs to be looked at a fair amount more. And that's fine. But I have a few other things I'm looking at too. There are always other things to investigate."

I nodded. To him, the contaminated drawing had doubts cast upon it. It was suspect.

I sat forward. "Think it over, please. You can phone me. It was just a weird request, so I wanted to come here."

"When do you leave?"

"I'm really not sure, but soon, I'm afraid."

"Really? Well I'm sorry to see you go and I'm sure Ann and company will be too. The drawing's yours if you want it."

"Okay. Thank you." My heart pounded. I'd never tried to buy such a good, valuable work of art and it scared me, but it was also exciting. "Can I ask the price?"

"Forty thousand. That's what I paid."

He must have seen all the blood leave my face because he added, "Is that too much? That's what that dealer, the infamous dealer, charged. I should have asked to take it for a while before committing to it. Of course, I usually do that, but I was heading out of town, on my way up here for a while. Are you sure you still want it?"

He was sinking now, blushing, looking ashamed of paying too much and I was waving my head and hand to placate him. I was stuck with whatever the damned thing cost, and I was in a state of shock. I never dreamed it cost that much. I assumed twenty thousand, at most. I had no dignified option out. Christ.

"No, that's fine. Yes, I do want it. Uh, yeah, no, great." I got that out, trying to think fast, trying not to be a complete fool. "Uhm, I can get the money to you in a few days?" My mind was on the cheques in my jacket pocket that were useless for anything like that amount.

"Oh, please, don't worry. Send me the money, in segments. Take your time."

He was being really generous but there was that concern on his face, or was it pity? He'd been sort of studying me twitching after he told me the price.

I stood up and then he did and, as I reached out to shake his hand and leave, he asked me to wait. Two minutes later he arrived back in the living room and handed me the thing itself in all its wrappings and I was saying goodbye, leaving with the drawing. It was mine.

❧ Chapter 9 ❧

On Monday at eight-thirty at night, two days after my meeting with Stephen Kensett, I was in my condo trying to let my brain upload what my life was becoming. I kept the lights off because I wanted the dark, not to brood, but to concentrate, to desensitize myself, sitting on my beautiful sofa, that was heading for a storage unit soon. Everything was. I needed to think. Actually, I was trying not to think about the drawing the way I had for days, afraid it seriously damaged me financially. It was in my closet.

I stood and leaned on the window frame. From inside my shadows, it should have been tempting to look out at the gorgeous South End street scene, but instead I stared at the four large, curved, framed panes of glass.

I had to get back to England. This move would get me there, almost. It was over six hours since I told Beth Kelleher and Simon Cobery I wanted the job. What the hell, they were nice enough to offer it to me quickly, with very few references. Telling them I was refusing a promotion in Boston and had to wait to send more letters of recommendation was me either being smart or overreaching. I thought they'd balk at that, but they didn't.

And I'd be getting about twenty percent less money than I was making in Boston. Was I suffering from buyer's remorse after taking that job? It was impossible to know much with everything in an insane rush.

But money. What a disaster. I'd be lucky to break even on the condo, after paying off my mortgage. And, Jesus Christ, now I owed forty thousand dollars for that damned drawing. Was I nuts?

I walked around the room. I took off my shirt and launched myself into seventy push-ups. After getting some water to drink, I sat on the sofa again.

It should have felt ridiculously underhanded, emailing back and forth with those people in Dublin while no one in Boston had a clue I even intended to leave. It just felt necessary. Ann would be told in the morning and that was something to look forward to. I wanted to turn my back on her, not be one of Ann's minions.

I went to bed early, knowing I was tired but not sleepy. In fact, sure enough, I was walking around less than an hour later, eating a bowl of cereal, staring out my window at a stale still-life of parked cars and pavement and the flat shape of dark townhouses and trees waiting to be filled with the light of day. At one I slept for a couple of hours and was up again until four. It was hard to wake up at seven when the music started playing on my radio.

Walking and walking was easier.

I hated the, *tides-in* exchange with Marty at the staff door, me grumbling my way as politely as possible up the elevator and into the Print Room. I knew Ann would be in early because of the email I sent to her the evening before requesting a meeting, *as soon as she could manage it.* She answered that she'd see me at nine the next day.

Jamie and Ustaad looked as somber as I felt, as if they were smelling conflict in the air as I walked quickly by them, nodding, not uttering a sound.

There was no time to lose as I went straight to the back of the long room and knocked on the door with the old brass plaque stating, *Curator's Office.*

I sat forward stiffly on the Hepplewhite wing-back chair I normally leaned back into.

There was no reason to evade. "Ann. Thanks, yeah, I have to tell you, since our phone conversation I've thought things over and realize I can't take on the position of curator. I'm sorry. I know this might surprise you and maybe disappoint you, but I have thought it over very, very seriously and think I wouldn't be right for the job and the job wouldn't be right for me. Sorry."

I stopped and she just kept looking intently at me, getting increasingly pale. She shook her head and licked her upper lip.

"No, Eric, you can't what? You thought it over? But it's only been a few days. I don't get what you're saying."

Staying fixed on her, I measured my words. "I have thought about it for much longer, of course. It's just that the sudden offer and you saying you were leaving sooner than I thought . . ."

"Well, I don't know when I'll leave, though. I said that. It might be as much as a year from now. And, I'll be Curator Emeritus after I do retire. The Director's offered me an office upstairs. But, Eric, Eric, why do you think the job wouldn't suit you? I mean, I find that statement fairly disturbing."

My brain was reverberating from her being offered an office forever. I felt myself frowning. "Uhm, really, I've had to consider all this carefully. I just learned in the last couple of years that I prefer administrative work to strictly curatorial work."

Her eyes hardened as her mouth formed a circle as if she might whistle. She shook her head silently for a few seconds. She looked down at her desk and moved some books and papers around, clearly building up more and more anger. My sitting and watching her didn't reduce the tension.

"Well, what can I say to that? Really, Eric, I don't get what you're saying. Administrative work? What does that mean? I mean, when you took on the position of Associate Curator you knew what the job was, and you never complained. This is the first time I've had an inkling you didn't like your job."

"No, Ann, I've loved my job. I know how lucky I was to get it. Absolutely. I just have to move on, now if I'm going to."

"Now? When? What do you mean?"

"Well, I've accepted a position as Director of the Trevor Cobery Museum in Dublin."

"Oh my God. Starting when!?"

"They want me right away, but I told them I had to make sure things worked for you here."

"Oh, Eric, no, no, I can't believe it. I really cannot believe it. I mean, it's an awful blow and God, with Margy leaving how are we supposed to cope? It's awful."

Margy leaving? Margy was purged.

"Well, Ann, I know it's abrupt, but we have the exhibition up and August is a dead month." I was feeling a small triumph in my gut.

She sat back rigidly in her large, old Gothic Revival walnut chair with ornate carvings of angels on the tall, pointed head rest. I'd never seen her look so contemptuous, not even of Margy.

"Sounds like a fait accompli, Eric. Wow. There was never a discussion here at all."

"I didn't know I was going to get the job in Dublin. As I said, I will stay on for a couple of months."

She was biting her bottom lip in a fury, shaking her head rapidly in short jerks.

"I don't think so. I think you should leave as soon as possible. It would be extremely awkward. No."

I sat still. She said nothing and seemed to be refusing to even look at me. I stood up. She was looking down at her desk. I had planned telling her about the drawing, but maybe not.

I said goodbye and left the room. I tried to sit down at my desk but was too jumpy and got up and left the Print Room.

Lori the Chief Conservator for Works of Art on Paper passed me in the hallway and turned.

"Anything wrong, Eric? You look purple."

I stopped and faced her. She was my age and had thick auburn hair cut to her chin with just a few strands of fringe to her mid forehead. She knew she was seen by most of the curatorial staff as an underling with her lack of degrees and no outward sign of style, but she also seemed to know she was brittle and easily shrill. I mostly avoided her the way most people seemed to, and she kept to herself. Only Margy was her occasional pal at work. I always assumed Margy was being charitable.

"Lori, yeah, so you know, I'm leaving the museum. Probably in a couple of weeks."

Her tight, chalky white face suddenly went red and unfurled.

"No! You *and* Margy?"

How many people knew about Margy being fired? I said nothing.

She gave a throaty growl. "Ugh, that's awful. I'm so upset. God, it's awful."

"That's what Ann just said."

"Well, Ann wanted Margy out years ago. She wouldn't mind ejecting me too, if she could. But she can't. Did she eject you?"

I laughed, shaking my head, no. It took me a few seconds to compose myself and Lori laughed along with me. It was the best, by far, exchange I ever had with her.

"Don't tell me. It would be too American of you to spill your guts all over the floor here in front of me."

I started to walk on and turned, saying. "I'm taking a job in Dublin."

"Ireland? Not Texas?"

I laughed and shook my head and so did she. Why is it in times of terminal transition, the people you were close to are suddenly no longer there and fleeting stragglers appear?

↜ Chapter 10 ↝

My commotion slackened a little bit when I was airborne, sitting back catapulting ahead. In two days, I'd be at work in Dublin. In a few hours, I'd be landing there.

I'd never sleep on the plane, me jammed into the seat on the aisle, trying to stretch my legs whenever someone wasn't walking by. It was laughable to contemplate the luxury of first class, long, wide, obscenely expensive seating. Instead, I sat upright with both feet on the floor in front of me and closed my eyes. Then I put my head back.

Okay, how was I doing? Three groups of people looked at my condo and one was very interested right away. They were a newlywed couple in a romantic haze, but they sure as hell should have been interested because the asking price was ten percent lower than anything comparable in town. And it had that incredible kitchen. And they bought it. I wouldn't make anything, but I was in a big hurry. It sort of sickened me to think they'd own and live in my place. And, Christ, I hated having to put all my things in storage. I didn't have time to sell things and the little one room flat the Cobery Museum was putting me in was furnished. So I'd have to buy a flat when I could. I had to sell the drawing first.

I was turning into sweaty pulp from my sudden poverty.

Were letters of recommendation sent from Ann and Martin Shapiro, our Director? Sitting down in his big office that last day was awkward, him wishing me well. Mostly, he talked about his days, halcyon as hell apparently, at Oxford. I never interrupted him. I wanted to, but I never told him Oxford's in England, not Ireland, since he knew it. It was close enough and he didn't care. Then he had to take a call.

Ustaad, Jamie and Jean toasted me and my future with some red wine and cheese and crackers and overwrought attempts at polite conversation. Everyone was extremely aware I was being extremely abrupt in this life change and that Ann was pregnantly missing. Ann managed to never talk to me after that last session in her office and was busy in New York my last week. She must have spoken with Christa. I'd have to write to Christa, and Natalie. And Margy? Why did I feel reluctant to call Margy and have her say there was nothing I could do for her, and that I shouldn't have bought the drawing? That it didn't fix anything

After moving my meagre financial assets around, I sent the forty thousand to Stephen Kensett. That was my down payment on any potential place to live in Dublin. I'd have to save for years like I did before to buy a place of my own, wherever the hell that might be.

The drawing was in my briefcase under the seat, wrapped in bubble wrap as my carry-on. Only allowed one and that had to be it. They'd better not lose my bags because I'd have very little to wear even with what got boxed and shipped to my new Dublin address: 17 North Fitzwilliam Street, somewhere behind the Cobery Museum.

Edith was thrilled. We'd be neighbors, almost, for the first time in over seven years. Amanda was momentarily bent out of shape.

"You're kidding."

"Nope."

"You're really serious?"

"Yeah, I am. I'm set there, with a free flat from the job, furnished and all. I'll give you the address and phone number. I'll get a phone."

"I just came all the way over here and you're bailing on me?"

"No, I'm sorry. You can live in England whenever you want. I just had to grab this chance to get closer to home."

"Okay. Yeah, great. But is it as good a job? Is the museum there as good?"

"Oh, it's a great collection. It's a lot smaller, by a bit. But, I mean, it's running the place and I want to try that."

"Sure, whatever dude," said New York style.

"Hurry up and have some fun and then move to Dublin."

"No, not Dublin. I know it's very cool and I'll visit but it's too Northern European, not different enough."

So on it went and she adjusted to my bailing-out fairly instantly because she'd be going home in a few months. Actually, I was a bit worried she'd be angrier because she'd feel left behind.

Anyway, it wasn't Amanda I was leaving behind. It was America. It felt pretty awful. I'd done so much in seven years and those people, Margy and Ustaad and Jamie and Jean and Natalie, were great to me.

But Margy, yeah, it summed-up the sudden rupturing in my life that I never saw or heard from her before I left.

❦ Chapter 11 ❧

The wall facing me was a mix of small and mid-sized works of art on paper. Sure enough, there was one John Millais wood engraving that sort of looked like it had been cut out of a book. Not cool, but I said nothing, of course. Apparently, Trevor Cobery collected some engravings and etchings and lithographs from the mid nineteenth century into the early twentieth, along with paintings, sculpture and furniture.

He died in nineteen twenty-five when he was eighty-two. Simon Cobery just told me that, but I'd read biographical material online.

"Trevor was an upstart I guess you could say. He wasn't content with just staying in Cork and running the family business and he wasn't even a playboy wanting to spend his money on the high life in London or Paris. No, he wanted to spend it on modern Irish art. Very strange to the rest of the family. An odd duck."

We'd been standing and staring at the wall for twenty minutes at that point and I was weary. I'd only been on Irish land for a day and a half and didn't sleep well in my flat the night before.

"He seemed to know what to collect." I got that out.

"Oh yes. He also knew what dealers to rely on. He went to London and Paris often and I'm afraid he spent a bit more there than some family members thought prudent."

"Really? Yeah, I did read he was sort of the family rebel. So, but he obviously collected Irish art here. And in Paris and London he bought the rest of the collection?"

"Yes, that's it. No, he was just enough of a rebel, and with a fairly decent eye, to collect some French Impressionists and Post-Impressionists before everyone did."

"That's brilliant. Well, at least he saved some money there."

Simon chuckled, rocking back on his heals. "Yes, yes, and then spent that much more on his own private museum building, didn't he?"

Beth Kelleher walked to us with a middle-aged couple, both holding small white porcelain cups of coffee.

"Eric, I'd like you to meet Dorothy and Dennis Connors."

We all shook hands gently. They were on the board too. I had to try to remember all the names I was hearing. Mahogany-dyed long-haired Dorothy began to ask me questions about Boston and Beth thought it was time to move on. We all sat down at the large, early twentieth century maple table. I sat in the middle with Simon at one end and Beth at the other. Beth was Chairwoman of the Board along with heading Human Resources, which seemed odd to me. Simon didn't seem to have a title.

Beth stood. "Well, first let's thank Eric for coming all this way to help us run our wonderful museum, that we all love and cherish. We've all been very saddened by the long illness and death of Erin Rogers and are ready to begin a new chapter here. Since all of us have had a brief opportunity this morning to meet and speak with Eric, I thought it might be best if we let him ask us any questions he might have at this point. I'm sure you must have a few, Eric."

I'd been told this would happen and had planted a couple of questions inside me.

I stood. "Thank you, Beth and everyone. Yes, it's the first day and I only have the most basic sense of what this museum is all about, but, to start things going now, I'd like to ask in general, anyone, what they feel is the most pressing need of the museum. Beth and Simon spoke with me on Skype about the need for raising money. That isn't ever surprising for any museum. I know your endowment isn't what you'd like it to be. But what do you see as the goals for the museum as far as money goes?"

I sat down, looking around. They actually had a motley look to them. Simon was in an old suit that didn't fit him anymore. He was in his late seventies and scrawny, so it most likely fit half a generation ago. Beth was sort of formally dressed, in a plain dark blue cotton dress and low heels, but with no character or flair at all. She was twenty years younger than Simon and had chin length grey hair that was as neat and thin as the rest of her. Then, there were the plain looking fiftyish Connors and that sad looking, baggy-eyed young woman who seemed to always frown, that I'd tried to have an exchange with an hour earlier. Mary something. She was the first person to arrive, after me. There were only ten people on the board.

Sure enough, Mary raised her hand, looking like she was in school.

"We need money for building repairs. We can't really do anything before we take care of that."

I nodded. Beth jumped in, "No, that's a high priority. We do have a plan in place to try to repair slates on the roof next spring. We can talk in further meetings about other maintenance issues."

Mary raised her hand again and I had to bite my lip to keep from laughing.

"With Erin ill for most of two years, the Board hasn't been able to decide on a very workable plan for all the problems with the building. The roof is just the biggest problem because we have leaking in the third-floor galleries and the plaster's going to be damaged and we'll have to move the paintings and furniture out. But we have the flooding in the basement, and we have the broken windows in the Blue Room. We have toilets to be fixed and floors to be refinished and painting to do in the galleries."

"All in time, Mary. Eric will have to digest a number of issues and maintenance of the building is one of them."

❧ Chapter 12 ❧

Whatever the hell I got myself into, I'd find out soon enough. That little museum looked anemic and so did most of the staff. One day there shuffling around behind Beth Kelleher and listening to her describe the, *Museum Mission* that was written in stone apparently in the will left by Trevor Cobery and I was petrified. The mission was to stay a second-rate little museum.

All I could do was pack for the short weekend trip to see Edith. Monday was a bank holiday and the museum was closed. Not much was planned in the past few frenetic weeks, but I did aim to start work on a Friday right before a three-day holiday weekend. I did that one, tiny thing right.

It was Saturday morning. The August sun was brilliant but not too hot and the breezy air not too humid and my new phone rang in my pocket. It was Amanda. I'd emailed her my number and planned calling her at the airport. I sucked in some air and stood straight. No point passing on my anxieties.

"Hi. Something weird. Last night I had a drink with someone you know. Peggy Avakian?"

Twisting my head to one side, slightly horrified, I tried to think. "Really? How did you meet her?"

"She phoned me a couple of days ago and was very sort of secretive and asked me not to tell you and I don't know I sort of…"

"Wait. How did she know you, where you were?"

"Don't know. I thought you must have told her. Who is she?"

"Uhm, we met at the Boston Museum of Fine Arts. But why did she phone you?"

"To get together and have a drink, she said. So we did, a few streets from here, near New York University. And she was very sweet, and it was fine. I mean, did you date? She's kind of young."

"No. Why, did she say that!?"

"No. Sorry. Relax. I mean, I, of course, assumed you might be involved. I thought, overbearing old brother, you sent her to spy on me, now that you're so far away and I'm abandoned and might be brutalized by bad people, mightn't I?"

"No. I barely know her. It's really, seriously invasive." I had to stop the temptation to rant. I actually didn't know what to say or think.

"You helped her with her drawing, some drawing she took to the museum?"

"Yeah, right. Yeah, but that's over. God, I seriously don't get her looking you up. Did she say there was some big connection with the drawing, or some problem?" Talking about the drawing was way too complicated just then. That had to wait.

"No, just that you helped her. Okay. Well, I'm sure it's some big crush. You are the lady magnet."

"No. Stop. Stop. Please, seriously. I don't know her at all. We met twice and barely talked. She's very, very young and very much not my cup of tea, especially because she's so embarrassingly young and immature."

"Okay. Okay. I did get the joke."

"Really though, I'm actually serious. We don't know each other and so I don't know what the hell her problem is."

"I don't know. She may be okay. She seemed interesting. I won't encourage her if you don't want me to."

"Well, I don't see the point. It seems slightly insane as hell."

"Okay." Amanda's slow, steady voice seemed aimed at gently tamping down everyone's excess angst.

There was a dense pause. My sour mood about the first day at my new job had me by the throat.

Amanda said, "So, where are you as we speak?"

"In my flat. The Cobery Museum has a one bedroom flat for the Director. It's behind the main building."

"Right. You told me that before."

"Yeah, it's small and drab but I'll paint it or something. Listen, I'm leaving to see Edith in a few minutes. For the weekend."

"Oh, that's right, I forgot. Okay, I'll let you go."

"You don't have any other news? Everything's okay?"

"Yes, fine. We'll talk soon. Give Edith a hug for me. Lucky man."

I said goodbye and sat down on the flat's cheap, dark blue cotton slip-covered sofa.

Why would Peggy Avakian phone Amanda? And where did she even get her phone number? Why would she do that? I sort of remembered mentioning I had a sister in New York. But so what the hell was she doing looking her up? And she might actually know I bought the drawing? How? Again, why would she know or care, and what did Amanda have to do with the drawing? It sure as hell felt intrusive and off-putting.

I left for the airport and getting there was easy if I looked out the cab window and didn't think about my current life.

Waiting for my flight, I ruminated about where I was headed. Cirencester was my first experiment with lifestyle. It was a memory I recounted to myself at least once a week, for all my adult years since. I was only fifteen and did haphazard research on the Internet. Sitting there in Berlin, one site had what I was looking for, with pictures and descriptions of the most bucolic, ancient, tucked-away havens in England. The site was meant for tourists, but I only knew England was where I had to be and where I had to get my mother and sister. As I got older, I realized I was lucky to grow up in Berlin. It was such a beautiful, stimulating city in the heart of Europe. But it was foreign. I wanted my own place, and like a teenager, I wanted to get away from wherever I was. Those basic urges remained the theme in my memory.

Now I was shuffling around other shuffling people waiting for the announcement to queue and board. Memory dilutes the strength of emotions, so waiting in Dublin to fly to London and then take a train to Kemble and then get a taxi to Cirencester, I was trying to imagine those fluid fifteen-year-old emotions. Imagining made me feel ashamed. I saw Dad as a failure back then. He didn't go to university until he was an adult, and then it was part-time at night and no degree. All my friends' parents had degrees from major educational establishments. It was remarkable enough that Dad went into the army expecting to make it a career, maybe become an officer. It could have been enough accomplishment in his working-class northeast end of London that he finished high school, passed his exams. It was sort of impressive and disciplined of him to join the army, but more impressive and disciplined that he applied himself, did what he was told and went where he was told. That was Berlin.

The Wavell Barracks in Berlin was a strong memory, a three-bedroom terraced house as far back as I could remember. The faded, tepid-tan, long domestic structures built on concrete over ash and rubble were old scars from old European battles. All around our two storey buildings a chain-link fence kept out the foreign infections. The city surrounding us was filled with those damned Germans. There were crazy Americans over there and some weird French and whatever here and there, and then there were Russians about to kill us all. We were British and we were moral victors again and again, but we were getting tired of saving the world for democracy. What the hell was wrong with all those other damned people? Apparently, we had to constantly point weapons at them to keep the crazy, murdering bastards from our throats and everyone's throats. Basically, that was Dad's take. And Mom's.

Most of my friends' parents were a bit more nuanced.

"Never trust the Russians." Dad would say as Edith would nod solemnly.

My local British sector school offered a reasonable education. It was just that I watched as the officers with the right stuff sent their children back to Britain to go to *good* high schools. That was an undercurrent flowing through my early adolescence as kids would leave, float away, to Kings Canterbury or Sherbourne or St. Edwards, names that stuck with me. There was a book one boy had, Clive, a good friend, who left at age twelve to go where his parents met, something called Oundle School. There were pictures in that book of Romantic havens, dazzling schools with their Gothic towers and medieval thick stone walls next to long, green satin grounds. The title of the book was, "The Heart of Our Civilization".

I knew we couldn't afford that stuff, but I also knew most of the kids heading off to those schools had fathers who were Colonels or Brigadier Generals.

But Dad only vaguely aspired to being middle class and didn't ever figure out the route. He didn't know or care about education, and he didn't have the education himself, not the formal kind on paper, to advance beyond Major. He never said a thing around me about wanting more. He seemed very proud. Then he got sick. It was those damned cigarettes.

He fought it for over a year.

Selfish little shit that I was, I didn't even know he was brilliant for having a good life insurance policy. Five hundred thousand pounds. Maybe I panicked and maybe Edith did too. Actually, Edith did panic in some way, because she went along with fifteen-year-old me saying we had to live in England. I may have hinted it was farther away from the Russians.

There I was right away, online doing my fifteen-year-old version of research into the heartland, the homeland. We had to get back to the home of my ancestors.

Now I was a Director, trying to get to the homeland.

Is that why I grabbed the job? Director? I had to lean against a pillar after that thought. Would I have found a better job with less of a title if I'd searched a bit more? Was the Cobery Museum a sick joke? Was I a pretentious tool?

My stomach started to turn, and I had to calm down and wait. I just wanted to visit Edith and now I could do that more often.

We boarded.

Actual flying took very little time and I'd land in London soon and take a train and another train and then a taxi. It would all take hours and felt almost as long as from Boston. My mood was heavier and heavier.

Eventually, Cirencester was stunning. The edge of the Cotswolds.

The taxi took me to Barton Lane close to the middle of town. It was almost a year since I'd seen the serenely removed, stoney townscape. The rows of mostly joined, heavy stone cottages in the centre of town, parted just occasionally for a separate single property. Everything hugged everything, including the street and parks. There was just enough room for a side-walk in front of the houses, but often even that was narrow and sometimes only on one side of the street. The Cotswold stone was a golden grey or sometimes creamy gold and the harmony of the ancient buildings mesmerized me every time I saw them.

It rained the night before but was mostly clear now, with the sky shifting way up there. Edith's carriage house was back fifty feet to the right of one of the single properties, which was a large four-bedroom house that was built in the seventeenth century. Our stone carriage house was added a hundred years later or so and it was no bigger than a modern two car garage. It did have enough of a pitched roof though and when I read about it at fifteen, I thought it might do very well.

Transforming that little attic was my first construction project.

I paid the taxi, feeling lazy and stupid. I should have taken the bus. I had to watch money now.

But it was three-thirty with Edith at the door hugging me. She looked different.

"You cut your hair? What's changed?" I asked, stepping away inside. I had to stoop and stand between the beams that ran in two-foot intervals across the white plaster ceiling. I whitewashed those beams when I was eighteen.

"No, I have not changed my hair." She stood and blushed and looked even better than usual. Amanda and I always mar-veled over our naturally fit mother. She was in her mid-fifties and was thin with just a hint of wrinkles, mostly around her eyes. Her soft dark grey eyes were a powerful force, although her hair might have been her greatest physical feature. Edith kept it to her shoulders but never dyed it and it was stunning in its black and grey combinations. Still, it was her eyes that always intrigued me, with eyebrows that were straight and dark, so her eyes sort of hid but pulled you in with that softness and depth.

"You eat healthy food? You look thin. Too thin."

"Edith, I'm going to gain some weight soon, because I'm getting organized and I'll cook for myself again. It's moving."

"Oh, yes, moving. So difficult."

We moved into the kitchen where she'd made some tea, and a cake from scratch.

"A poppy-seed cake."

"God, Edith."

We sat next to the one window in the kitchen. It looked out past the small patio Edith planted a boxwood hedge around, then to the backyard of the family next door. I turned back and looked up. I whitewashed those beams, too. And I painted the old floors a pale grey. And I gave Edith a gift certificate for the kitchen table.

"Remember the gift certificate?" I asked as she sat down.

"For this? Yes, of course. To Berkeley Antiques." She still had an impossible time pronouncing that name. "You were very good with presents, all your life, you are."

"I was bad, Edith. I liked the stuff in that place. And it was your money. It was all your money, for this house, for schools and universities. I'd say I was fairly grabby with your money."

"I don't know how you can say this. I am your mother."

"Well, so we can go out for dinner."

"No, if you don't mind. Maybe tomorrow night. I have a pot of lentil soup and some of the oat bakery bread."

"Umm, I can smell it, even over this cake. Okay, tomorrow." I liked doing things for Edith, taking her out.

She sat back and we schmoozed. Half an hour went by. She told me about her job at the local library she'd had for almost fourteen years. A new man was hired part time for the front desk because Abigail something retired. Abigail was fulltime and everyone was hoping the library wouldn't have to reduce the staff. Some new neighbors from Wales, a young married couple, moved in down the road. He worked in the new restaurant on Castle Street as a waiter full time and she did part time. Very nice people. Edith babysat their four-year-old once or twice a month. "Nathan. Such a cute little boy." We washed up and then we went for a walk. It was dark but not as dark as it would get, and lights were still on in some shops. We made our way to St. John the Baptist church. It always made me speechless, but it was an astoundingly inspirational Gothic apparition in the twilight, of darkened stone jutting into the sky. As always, I gazed. It was fifteenth century and England had a bunch but this one belonged to me because I found it.

"You love buildings so much. Why not instead an architect?"

Was Edith worried about me in some way?

"I was not so good at maths? I don't know. I like other things too."

"That's good. Art. Paintings, etchings. Only some can really understand the beauty."

I wanted to hug her, but I'd already been hugging her so much and I didn't want her to think I was an emotional wreck or something. I was just acutely aware of being home. She stood with the winds rushing through her hair, the collar up on her dark green cotton shirt. Her eyes had disappeared inward now, and I only caught a glimmer when she smiled.

We walked through the Abbey Grounds and it really was getting dark, so I suggested we go back to her lentil soup and bread.

The next day I took Edith to a movie. We had to take a bus because she never owned a car and never had a license. It only took ten minutes. We were in a strip but it was subdued, just a parking lot with a couple of stores, a small movie theatre and a large grocery. It wasn't clear if it was an extension of a village or on its own. The movie was an action-packed extravaganza straight from the deluded minds and special effect machines of Hollywood. I groaned and Edith leaned over, whispering.

"We can leave."

"Do you mind?"

"No. They are not real people."

We waited at the bus stop, silently. Why is it that small suburban spreads around small cities or towns seem even less potent than their large city counterparts? It wasn't really that ugly, the rows of late twentieth century thin, cheaply built brick cottages. I tried to not see them.

Sitting on the bus, Edith saw my disgust.

"It is a very popular movie. For younger . . . for teenagers," she uttered, explaining life to her adult child.

I leaned closer to her ear to not be overheard, "Great, mould their little monkey minds into everything nasty we can imagine." I stopped myself and sat back. "No, I'm kidding. That was the perfect thing to do as quickly as that and now everything else we do will be brilliant in comparison." I folded my arms, gave her a gentle chuckle and she smiled back politely.

All I could do was try to shake off the half empty feeling. There didn't seem to be much to do. It wasn't Boston or Dublin. I couldn't show her a better time than a degenerate, violent movie?

I leaned towards her again. "And no big universities around here so you don't have the art house crowd. Lucky you." I tried to lighten the load.

"No, it is many more, uhm, older people like me. They have the parks to walk in and cafes and shops and they are all very good people."

"Good. If you ever want to move, tell me and I'll help." I knew I shouldn't be sarcastic.

She seemed to shiver, "No-no-no. Why would I move from such a lovely town? It suits me to a T."

Edith used whatever English phrases she could, whenever she could, with her German accent.

I remained still, waiting for our bus ride to end. I wondered sometimes if I landed her in the worst of pretentious horsey culture. There were some people with money in the grand countryside around the town who still hunted. They played polo in Cirencester Park, for Christ sake.

Anyway, not as bad as Nazis and Communists and, she wanted to feel safe and so maybe the centre of England represented that to her the way I thought it would when I chose it as a teenager. I didn't know about polo.

Our bus stop happened.

Walking home, she said, "Oxford University is not far." She imbued this hushed statement with the fullest possible respect, even awe.

I nodded. She said, "Maybe we can go there some day when you visit."

She seemed to think I was bored?

"Uhm, yeah, I think it might be . . ." I just nodded. I wanted to say it was at least an hour by rental car or by train and both would be very expensive. We'd have to take a bus that would stop a hundred and ten times along the way. I kept quiet and walked. The train could get us there.

We had what she called leftovers for dinner. She made potato pancakes and a salad of different greens from the refrigerator. Then we finished her soup. Edith was the world's best cook and always worked magic. Her lentil soup, with added fresh celery and onions and tomatoes was so delicious I moaned a lot, and her cake was ecstasy.

Later, upstairs in the attic, stooped over to protect my head, I stumbled around. Maybe I should take the rickety wall down that divided the long space in two, that I built at age fifteen. If Amanda and I were here at the same time now, I slept on a cot in the living room.

The next morning at eleven, I left Edith and Cirencester for my long day's journey to Dublin. I promised to see her again soon.

❧ Chapter 13 ❧

A vast, drafty Dublin sea-light filled up my little funky flat with a warm grey velvet fog. It was a late August morning and smelling of brine and sea mold and I opened all the windows I had to get more flow. Then I added an interior glow from a foot-tall midnight blue, cube shaped plastic lamp as the dim florescent bulb burned inside a long narrow, brown canvas shade. What an extravagance in nineteen eighties kitsch. It did add a pocket of dry warmth, though in my new bedroom with walls covered in pale blue paper with long shiny silver irises all over. It wasn't even remotely possible to convert into a cool flat. The greyish-blue wall to wall carpet was permanently smudged near the outside door and there was a narrow footpath of the same smudge straight through to where I was heading -- the table in the living room/dining room. Drinking coffee, eating cereal, I just chewed, swallowed and glazed over. Very soon I'd be on my way to work, two minutes away.

I had to recompose my agenda as I walked out my door, across thirty feet of concrete parking spaces with blue painted numbers in the middle. It was staff parking and one of them was for me, except I didn't have a car and doubted I could ever afford one. I had to raise my head and shoulders, stand up straight and not be negative.

It was Tuesday and the museum would open later, at ten, and I wanted to watch the public in the building using the museum. My keys worked on the back door and I walked through the empty Cobery Cafe. There were seven tables here and there and one counter facing the courtyard. A catering service brought in salads and soups and sandwiches and desserts and tea and coffee and various bottled drinks. The Museum Store was twice the size of the Cafe. Between them they squeezed about fifteen hundred square feet out of the back of the ground floor of the building.

My office was on the fourth floor and I took the small staff elevator up. And the view up there was beautiful. All the offices either looked down into the atrium and garden below, or out to Fitzwilliam Square. My corner office looked out to the square on one side and up North Fitzwilliam Street on the other. The Georgian windows were large, just not as large as in the galleries below. I had a huge mahogany desk with an old dark green leather writing pad as its centre and a mid-twentieth century striped silk sofa and two mid twentieth century cream coloured damask stuffed chairs and paintings all over my walls.

A second door led to my private loo. A third door adjacent to my desk led to a small, attractive room with a large oak desk and only one window. I poked my head in and said hello to Beatrice, my office assistant. She was looking smart with her short, curly brown hair behind both ears and her glasses on top of her head, ready to start something.

I asked her if she could set aside half an hour in the afternoon to sit down with me and review office procedures and ask any questions she might have. She typed that into her computer, and I closed her door as I left.

I sat down behind my desk and opened my office laptop. The Cobery website was slightly old fashioned but I found the financial data sent to me by Beth Kelleher.

The annual budget was slightly over four million Euros, not very high. And the endowment was only thirty-three million Euros. Annual attendance was listed as seventy-six thousand for the previous year. I knew all that when I took the job, back in Boston and I compared it with data for other similar museums in America and Europe. I did that again now. It was in the middle range, but that didn't account for the Cobery's prime location. There were small art museums in major cities that had four times those figures.

I went to the Sheridan mahogany sideboard and poured myself some tea and grabbed an oatmeal cookie from the pretty Chinese porcelain jar.

I sat on the sofa, sipped my tea, ate my cookie and tried to avoid the irritation building inside me. I opened my laptop and typed in some notes about concerns I had. I stood up and walked a few paces to the middle of my new, fancy office. It was bigger and grander in many ways than Ann's back in Boston. But I had to take a walk around the building.

Beatrice was at her desk as I told her what I was about to do and that it might take over an hour. I passed office doors on my way down the narrow, varnished, oak planked hallway. There was Human Resources after Beatrice's office and then the Finance/Development Office. At the end of the hallway, I looked to the right. The Library/Archives areas filled that wing. I kept going, down the stairs noting very old blue paint. At the ground floor I unlocked the door and entered the side of the lobby with the loos for the public, the cloakroom and reception booth farther along and the main corridor to the central courtyard. The public part of the building was shaped like a three-sided, incomplete rectangle, or a U. The fourth side was occupied by the cafe and store on the ground floor and by Maintenance and Conservation and storage on the two floors above.

So corridors around the courtyard led to galleries on the side. There were three galleries on the ground floor, and I made my way into the first one.

It was on my right through a six-foot-wide doorway. While the floors in all the corridors throughout the building were gorgeous black and brown marble, they varied in the galleries. I was walking on oak parquet now. There was an enormous Italian Renaissance dining table in the middle of the room with sixteen tall, matching, embroidered chairs around it in the middle of the room with a Louis the Fourteenth candelabra in the middle and antique china and silverware set out. There were two sidebars with various figurines and two settees and then paintings compiled here and there on the chartreuse silk wall covering.

Trevor Cobery radically transformed two huge Georgian townhouses into one building in the early twentieth century and I was in a dining room. There were five visitors walking through with me, all of us in different stages of gazing as we walked. A large doorway opened into the next gallery. It looked like a reception room and had a beautiful brown and light blue marble tiled floor with large Empire sofas at each end and four crystal chandeliers above in a row running down the center of the room. More Empire furniture filled the middle and sides of the room with early nineteenth century paintings above. There was a Turner above one shiny French polished table with two smaller works by Delacroix below. The lighting wasn't bright and there were no windows on the ground floor galleries and the placement of the pictures made visitors look up at odd angles, over furniture, sculpture and other pictures.

I walked on but had to retrace my route because of the dead ends of the U. That meant a lot of time was spent looking at the beautiful garden in the courtyard. A full-time gardener maintained the flowers and ferns and mosses and small trees. The glow that descended from the fifteen-foot-wide by thirty-foot-long skylight, four and a half stories above passed into the galleries. It was the nicest architectural feature of the whole building, by far. All public and official reviews agreed on that, and so did I.

The galleries continued in chronological order. Late nineteenth century on the floor above and early twentieth century on the top public floor. Somehow, at one stage, old Trevor lived above it all, where our administrative offices now were.

The light improved above the ground floor with some large Georgian windows, but the rooms remained cluttered, sort of in the style of the late nineteenth century. In fact, that seemed to be the whole point and the will said he didn't want anything moved.

My problem was that it wasn't an actual house. No one ever actually lived in the crazy place with one dining room, thirteen reception rooms and two bedrooms, all filled with various forms of art that mostly related to each other through Trevor's rich imagination.

I walked and walked and watched the visitors. It was a gorgeous August day, the peak of tourist time, with only a handful of people in most galleries. There were only a few places to sit and the labels were hard to match with the objects because so many of the objects were up too high and over something else.

People kept walking. They stopped and looked at the objects here and there, somewhat randomly, and moved on. They were strangers in a rich person's pretend house.

Yup, I was alienated. I said hello to a number of guards earlier but stopped back in the Irish nineteenth century gallery. There were some great paintings by James Arthur

O'Connor, John Lavery and Daniel Maclise and a sculpture by Mary Redmond, mixed with Victorian furniture and an old glassed-in case of antique dolls and another of Celtic brooches.

I approached the guard. We shook hands and he said his name was Brandon.

I told him I was a guard at the Fitzwilliam Museum in Cambridge years ago.

He looked surprised and nodded.

I said, "Now, I'm on Fitzwilliam Square, so some sort of karma."

He smiled awkwardly, so I added, "You see the public firsthand so I need to know anything you and the other guards might notice we could do better."

I stood at his side as I murmured this looking at a young family near across the room. The father held the hand of his toddler while the mother stood next to their seven or eight-year-old son looking up at a painting by Walter Osborne. They were speaking German quietly.

Brandon said, "No place to sit. Everyone complains about that. But there's no place to put in public seating, anyway."

"Right. Anything else?"

"No, I don't know. They think it's all beautiful."

"Yeah, good. It is. The building, the furniture?"

"Uh, yeah. No, the paintings mostly. Most people I see look at the paintings. They complain that it's hard to see things."

I blew out my cheeks as we watched a group of what looked like university students come into the gallery, gaze around, and ramble through bumping into each other. I thanked Brandon and left.

❧ Chapter 14 ❧

I tried to pace myself. If I flipped out no one would benefit. I just went through the motions at work. It seemed easy to conjure up enough directorial activities to get by, for now. No point in hating my job, yet. So it meant ignoring my instinct to build.

I sent the drawing off to Loraine Fitch in London to get an attribution and hoped it would be good news or good enough to leave it with her to sell, possibly leading to me paying off some of my debts.

It was another Sunday in the middle of September when I heard from Amanda. It was just after midnight and I was sliding down the slopes of deeper and deeper sleep. It was hard to pump my lungs, heart and brain back up to conscious, conversational level.

"Right, Eric, I'm thinking of going back in a few weeks, moving to Oxford. Yeah, sorry, but I haven't told you that I've seen Peggy Avakian a few times in the last month or so and she's moving there. Oxford."

"What?"

"She's got herself an internship at the Ashmolean, amazingly enough, and she wants me to room with her in Oxford for a while. I haven't said I would. What do you think?"

I sat up in bed and turned on the smaller version of the plastic kitsch lamp.

"Sorry, Eric. What, did I wake you up? Sorry."

"That's okay. Amanda, what the hell is going on?"

"I know. It's pretty weirdo stuff. I kept quiet about hanging out with Peggy a few times because it seemed to irritate you so much last month when I said something. But now this."

"Now what? Say it again?"

"I guess I wouldn't mind living in Oxford for half a year or whatever. I might get a job. She wants me to do this and she would pay the rent and utilities. She said she's getting some money from her brother from the drawing to pay for that. But, Eric, what in God's name did you pay for that drawing!? Forty thousand dollars!?"

I whimpered, "Christ, yeah, don't ask. I did. I'm going to try to sell the damned thing to get the money back. Don't ask, please. I lost my mind," I switched to alert mode. "No, no, no, speaking of losing your mind. What the hell is going on with this Peggy Avakian? It's so damned nuts. I mean, you thought I overreacted the last time but now she's doing what?"

"An internship. You mean it's crazy that she'd pay for me to stay there?"

"Sure as hell seems that way, doesn't it?"

"Yeah, I told her she was out of her mind and that it was some sort of crazy payback vendetta. She seems racked with guilt about the drawing or something and she kept asking me to not tell you we were hanging out."

"Why ask you to not tell me? And anyway, why are you hanging out? Christ, but you know what, Amanda? She could have just managed to get an actual attribution for the drawing. I mean, we did her a favour looking at it at all and then I even took her to the Met in New York and I wrote to her and kept telling her it had to go to an expert in the field and you know what she did instead?"

"What?"

"Precisely what we warned her against and just gave it to some two-bit shady dealer and they sent out letters exclaiming MFA and Met seals of approval. Smarmy stuff. I mean, what the hell, Amanda. Then they got an important trustee to spend forty thousand dollars for it. Jesus. I had to buy it from him."

"Oh. That's awful. So you mean, she lied to get more money or something?"

"Money or something. No, she enhanced the truth. And I just got caught up in it somehow. Like you are now!"

"Oh, God. That's so disturbing. I had no idea. You should have told me!"

"I didn't know you were going to hang around each other, did I? How the hell did that happen? She sought you out, that's how. It is possible she's just off her rocker. Really, Amanda, what the hell. Stay away from her."

There was a pause and sounds of both of us rustling.

"Eric, why did she tell me she had to try to pay you back? Why did she start hanging around me?"

"Guilt. Shame. But, pay me back? How?"

"Paying for me to live in Oxford for six months. Really Eric, she seems fine when I'm with her. Really. I think she does feel bad. I think that's the point."

"Great. She feels ashamed but she also wanted the money. Convenient shame since six months of paying for you in Oxford is what, a few thousand dollars?"

"Okay. Hmm, wow, you are angry. No, I do get that you feel betrayed. I'm not saying she didn't do something sleazy, but maybe she was desperate for money or something."

"Um. Okay. Look, you woke me up in the middle of the night. So she didn't know a trustee would buy the thing and then I would. And, by the way, I really did feel way more caught up in it then I had to feel. I'll tell you about it some other time, when I know why. Okay? But look. I don't know. Yeah, she must be very sorry some rich stranger didn't buy it. Isn't she rich or sort of rich?"

"No, not at all. Far from it."

"She went to Tufts, a fairly posh university. Maybe she went on a scholarship. I don't know. Does she have family in New York? She has a brother, who found the drawing or something."

"Yeah, she never talks about her family. They're somewhere around New York but I don't think she ever sees them. She did say her brother was going to university in Massachusetts. That's right. Yeah, it's strange. She's sort of a loner, isn't she?"

"So she stalks you."

"Right. You're really giving me the willies."

"Why did she seek you out? We still come around to that."

"No, I know. She seems to like it when I tell her stories about us, about our family. That's not normal. God, most people just want to talk about themselves and this girl never does and looks deeply rapt when I tell her about Mom and Dad or me or you. You think it's some sort of extreme vicarious thing? Like she's that crazy desperate?"

"No idea, Amanda. You know her much better than I do."

"Eric, you know, I really wouldn't mind spending some time in Oxford. Sorry. I really wouldn't. Can we just pat her on the head and move on? Maybe if she's just forgiven by you, she'll move on. Would it drive you nuts if I spent a few months with her there?"

I groaned and waited.

Amanda wanted to ignore me. "And she seemed so excited about the internship and Oxford and all that, and she's going there whether I go or not, isn't she? What if you just come to see me there and tell her all's well with the drawing? That'll end her self wrath or whatever. Can you swallow your pride for an hour?"

"Pride? Yeah, what pride?"

"What? Oh dear. Things not so good?"

"No, I'll be fine. I just have to find my way back to an actual career path. No, no. Forget I said that."

"Really? You're job's not good?"

"It's fine. Yeah, Amanda, okay. That's a plan, since you've already been hanging around this crazy person. If you want to come back and live in Oxford, I guess I could tell her all is forgiven. I'll pat her on the back and tell her it never happened, as long as I don't have to see her again. What about you, though? Is she driving you crazy?"

"The thing is, I could actually use the financial assistance. It might take me a while to find a job. But are you sure? I'll never see her the same way again. No, she doesn't drive me crazy, but I had no idea about the drawing, or I would have stayed clear of her, wouldn't I?"

"Yeah, I hate weaving tangled webs. And I'm tired right now, so maybe I'll regret it, but yeah. So, take her help getting you back home, if you want and I'll come and see you after a while and end this sorry angst."

"Okay. No, I won't stay with her any longer than I have to."

Book Five

⚘ Chapter 1 ⚘

Here I am in the here and now, marching along and marching along on top of the world. It's the northern corner, up here in Dublin, in January. I'll warm up after I walk for a while.

I don't think about my stupid job most of the time, or the money I no longer have, or Amanda being in London and Edith in Cirencester and me over here, hours away and a sea in between.

I'll just get rid of the drawing soon. I'll get past the loss of money. It wouldn't be on my mind now, if that sad Peggy Avakian hadn't just come over here to Dublin last week. Jesus. She seems to be everywhere chasing me, going on about the stupid drawing. Boston, San Francisco, New York, Oxford and then here last week. And I didn't tell her about the damned attribution because I didn't want her apologizing even more and more and more. If I told her about Margy getting fired, Peggy'd become apoplectic.

But that should be over, now that Amanda and I have put her in her place and Amanda's moved away to London.

It sure as hell is January. This air is biting, and I have to put the collar up in my long wool coat and button the top button.

I've never hated a job before.

Marching and marching. Dublin looks beautiful, even after months of it and even in winter.

I wanted all this cool, damp, sunny, plucky air around me and I've got that and nothing else.

I'm going left onto Heytesbury Street and stop and there they are. They're so familiar now, the low rows of terraced houses with the great old Dublin doors. The brightly painted doors look huge for the single-storey houses and the windows are huge too. I raise my shoulders and do a Natalie Ziegler electric shake all through my body.

God, I miss Natalie. I miss a lot of people and places. I miss not having that damned attribution and knowing I'm beaten.

I move on. I have to stop driving myself nuts looking at beautiful townhouses. They're a bit cheaper than Boston and I still can't afford them.

Lennox Street has a café, but I can't stop. There's no way I'm sitting alone in some nifty coffee shop with bunches of twenty-somethings doing their interpretation of nifty-something.

I'm starting to sweat a bit and open my coat to air out my body as I walk. I take off my knit hat. Where am I? Grove Park. I'm wandering, not marching anymore. The Canal's fairly far behind me and the neighborhoods are starting to look grim here and there. And bland in between.

I wander south. If I could ever afford to buy something, I've calculated, even before that damned attribution, I'd have to go farther out to even blander land.

I stop and turn back and look at my watch. It's twenty after three. I should go back to work. I've been walking for an hour. Beatrice knows I have a dental appointment, or knows I don't.

Beatrice and Beth and Drew and Emma all ignore me now, after months of me ignoring them in my big office with big doors closed.

I feel my chest. The letter's in my suit coat inner pocket and I paid five hundred pounds for the attribution, so I have to hold onto it, keep it safe and secure. My Christmas anti-present to myself. It's anonymous forever. The sun's on the left side of my face and I know I won't go back to work.

Mathew Andrews is such an arrogant bastard. Of course, if Loraine Fitch said it might be the hand of Vincenzo Caccianemici, he'd shrug that off.

And twitchy Loraine wouldn't sign her name to that and everyone's so afraid of being labeled a fraud, including me.

How is it no one, including me, found a painting or print that at least shared the same subject and the same composition as the drawing?

If I walk fast enough, I'll stop dwelling on all that.

It's starting to get dark. God, it's only four-thirty. I look for a street sign. Swifts Alley. Cute. I head north towards the river and onto Werburgh Street and, with more people leaving work, we all hustle over the bridge onto Capel Street, me absurdly hurrying nowhere.

I actually have something to do, something to plan, but still I'm walking and walking and know I need to see more beautiful townhouses in beautiful sections of town. I need it. It looks like Boston and not like Boston at all. I'm north of the river and turn around after wallowing in Smithfield for a while. I should be hungry or afraid of getting mugged. It's not like there's no crime in Dublin.

The Capel Street bridge is right there but I walk past it and head onto the smaller, narrower streets. Some of them have rows of townhouses and I look into windows as I pass, slowly. Some have curtains drawn, some don't. It's past dinner time and some people are walking around upstairs. That Georgian terraced row is there waiting for me. The gorgeous doors shine in the dark. A youngish woman and a little boy are in one, in their living room through a large rectangular Georgian window, beautiful antique table lamps glowing. They stop me. But I can't loiter and drool and get arrested.

I'm walking on because they're walking away, out of the room. There's a good looking, probably nineteenth century landscape painting in a beautiful old gold leaf frame over the mantle and some gorgeous antique furniture. A car door closing somewhere makes me walk on faster.

It's getting late and I have to get some food in me.

I walk over the bridge and on towards Fitzwilliam Square. It's after nine.

Chapter 2

If I get to London Heathrow by eight-thirty and Paddington by nine-thirty, I should be in Oxford before twelve. I don't know what time Peggy takes lunch, but the layout of the museum online indicated only one door going in and out of the Print Room, with Conservation using the same stairway to either go out through the galleries or down to a staff door on the ground floor. I should be able to watch from the gallery and see who comes and goes. I might be able to watch her, to see if there's anything there beyond crazy hypocrisy. I'll stalk the annoying damned girl who's been stalking us.

I'm not sure about staying in that expensive bed and breakfast on Woodstock Road, but it's just around the corner from Leckford Road where Peggy lives.

Abject apologies are nuts up against all the callous disregard for Margy and me at the Boston museum and Christa at the Met. I've never known anyone who conveniently promotes herself and then apologizes for it as extravagantly as Peggy Avakian.

Stupid to take a Friday off work, but I'm that bored now.

It's a schlep and by the time I get to the Lyon's Head Hotel in Oxford, it's almost four hours gone and I'm in a hurry. A middle-aged French man named Luc, sure enough, smiles and moves too slowly, but I tell him I have an appointment and we just leave my suitcase in a closet behind his counter.

It is raining, sleeting, but not hard. Oxford is stuck in a valley of clouds caught from high above and it is early February. Just as advertised, there are the students on bicycles winding through. There are twenty thousand of them according to Luc, who says these things to me as I say goodbye and hurry down the street towards the centre of town. Twenty-thousand students on bicycles? It appears, not all at once, as I can only see a dozen.

I'm in the Ashmolean and it's ten after twelve, so maybe all's okay as long as Peggy doesn't go to lunch at twelve. The main stairs head up to the right and then the gallery I'm looking for up there should be back at the end on the left. It's a stunning, potent, famous museum that should remind me of the Fitzwilliam Museum at Cambridge, but it doesn't really. I can barely remember the Fitzwilliam. But as I'm walking, I have to really keep an eye out for a sudden appearance of Peggy. I'll just say I'm being a tourist and leave it at that. No long-rehearsed lies. No lies at all. But I won't let her see me. I'll make sure that doesn't happen.

So, it's the last main gallery of Italian paintings. There's a bit of an alcove and then a door and stairs, just like the map says. If I get close to the wall, I should be able to see someone come down the stairs, but it'll be at an angle. I won't be able to make out who's there. If I stand closer, anyone coming out the door would see me straight on. Shit.

I go back through the galleries and down the stairway quickly, without looking too harried. The white-haired gent with the big mustache smiles at me steadily. So does the young woman next to him.

Since I'm hustling out and just arrived, they have to be thinking I'm an insane terrorist or idiot.

It's still drizzling out, so I put my knit hat on. Where am I going anyway? There's the Randolph Hotel. Looks like

I could sit in their bar and look back out at Beaumont Street. Or there's the Oxford Playhouse cafe. The rest are offices or something. I'm getting wet and just head for the Randolph. It's an expensive hotel and the food at the bar will be, so I'll have to skip eating.

Half a pint of real ale will do. I sit at the only table available, next to one of the tall, pointy-arched Gothic Revival windows that should please the hell out of me, but I just want to look out. The entrance to the statuesque nineteenth century classical Ashmolean is diagonally in view. It's fifteen minutes to one. If she's gone to lunch, I'll see her come back. If she hasn't, I'll see her come out.

The ale's good, probably not up to the level of some, but what do I know? I seldom drink ale. The rest of the patrons have the look of people impressed with where they are. One older couple at a table next to me have on traditional English country clothes. His green wooly suit probably cost an arm and a leg, and his shoes look like Peels, so they're special. She has on the classic quilted jacket with a blue blouse collar sticking above a thin crew neck sweater and pleated skirt, that I've seen in places like this all my adult life. Kind of a formula. Maybe they're from Cirencester or Cheltenham.

The group of five middle-aged people in the corner look like Americans, rustling, smiling broadly, all in skimpy khakis and jeans and sweatshirts.

Oh, they're speaking some other language. Polish or something.

Nothing yet out the window. People walk out. When they walk slowly, looking around, it's pretty sure they're not employees. We used to laugh about the *employee walk* in Boston. Head straight, eyes not seeing, face expecting to be seen, as they strut with their art museum employee badge prominently displayed. They're in the *important zone.* Jamie and I did imitations of it. I showed Barbara that time on an early date, but she didn't quite get the joke.

Actually, a few probable employees have come out. There she is. Sure enough, it's her, walking with an older woman. The older woman looks sort of distinguished, in a stylish tan trench coat, plain cut and open with her hands in both pockets. They both aim to their left after walking down the front steps towards where I'm sitting. Peggy has an umbrella, a small one, but unopened.

I head for the door but realize they might be heading right where I'm standing. So I look through the glass of the doors figuring I'll duck back in as soon as I see them. That would be hard to do without being seen, but they don't appear after half a minute and I have to chance it and go outside. The mist brushes my face softly as soon as I'm out. Down the narrow steps with Magdalen Street in front of me, I walk straight and stand behind a group of foreign tourists looking at maps. Feeling covered, I glance to my left and don't see Peggy, until suddenly they're walking quickly right towards me, only fifty feet away. I freeze. I'm taller than anyone near me.

They stop walking and face each other, talking before there's a wave from Peggy, a smile from the older woman as she walks away, and Peggy starts towards me. I step between two buses parked at the light. The driver in the second bus scowls at me wondering why I'd decide to sandwich myself to death that way. All I can do is turn my back to the sidewalk and lean down as though I've dropped something . . . and turn again and step back onto the crowded sidewalk . . . and see Peggy a few steps ahead. I walk slowly until I'm about twenty feet behind her. I'm out of breath from all this artificial self-constraint.

She walks quickly even though she's not very tall, maybe, five-six. She stops with the pedestrians at the

Cornmarket intersection and I duck in a doorway twenty feet back. Fortunately, it could look like I'm trying get out of the mist. Then the lights change, and we all head across, and she veers left across the swell of people around her and aims towards Ship Street. It's very narrow, very medieval, and very quiet. If I follow closely and she turns around, there I'll be. So I stop.

I go to the window of a jewelry store on the corner and I can see her form through the partial wall of glass as she goes into a doorway. A few minutes later I approach the same door. It's a small café called, *Pippins*. There's a queue, all young, with trays at a counter ordering food, but I don't see Peggy, fortunately. Looks like it's mostly salads and soups and coffee. I step back and to the side and glance around. There's a restaurant at the end of the street ahead and some sort of bicycle rental shop in the middle. On the other side is a tall stone college wall. I walk to the end. It's more of a formal sort of restaurant, but I'm hungry and I go in. There's a list of specials on a blackboard.

The sad looking young woman who seats me has acne.

"Can I just order the asparagus omelet and salad special? I have to be somewhere in twenty minutes. Sorry."

"To drink?"

"Uhm, an iced tea. Yeah, but thanks. I appreciate it." She looks annoyed, possibly perpetually, or possibly it's me asking for iced tea in the middle of winter.

Ten minutes exactly and my food arrives, and I ask for my bill. I don't even know if it tastes particularly good as I eat and drink everything in another five minutes. I was hungry. All I had was a banana muffin at the airport for breakfast and a blueberry muffin on the train. What Margy and I used to call, *gluttonous glutenous carbs*. I have to go to the loo, so I leave three pounds for the tip and wind my way down a hallway, somewhere behind the kitchen into a dimly lit room and urinate and urinate for the first time in many hours.

Out onto the meeting of Ship and Turl Street, I'm waiting. It's a day of continuous drizzle. It hasn't stopped or increased all day and I'm fairly wet after ten minutes of lurking. Sure enough, there she is leaving Pippins and she turns in my direction so, already halfway behind the wall of the restaurant, I step quickly to the side and in a dozen steps, I'm on Broad Street. I go into a Boots Pharmacy to the left of me, then stand near the window inside, waiting. Nothing happens. I lurk-on for a minute. She must have gone in some other direction. I go back out and see her across the wide street, walking into Blackwells Book Store. I wait a minute and then cross, feeling absurdly exposed.

Mindless, I wander slowly into the bookstore and look. I cover the ground floor and don't see her and always keep an eye on the stairs in case she appears. Me going up the stairs is too risky, so I decide to just wait. Something like ten minutes pass and, sure enough, she comes down the stairs and, sure enough, turns into the space I'm in. I'm behind a row of books and backtrack, head down. Nothing for a minute and then, she's there, ten feet away. My heart jamming, I turn the corner and can see through a space in the rows. I stare. Then, I glance around to see if I'm being watched by anyone and realize there are bound to be cameras on everyone. I look back at her. She's paging through a book. She has on a long dark blue herringbone coat, opened with a tan crew neck sweater and no shirt under it, so her neck looks long and bare.

I pick up a large book on the top shelf and, glancing around a bit, cover most of my face with it. That's absurd, so I lower the book. Her damp hair is gripping her damp polished face and neck, long Auburn downy filaments clinging to her. She seems intent on her book. It's in the same nonfiction section I'm in, and she puts the book back and picks up another. She puts that book back and looks around, distracted. She walks away and heads to the front of the store. After putting my book back and quickly glancing around to see again if I'm being watched, I go to the end of my aisle and turn to see her heading for the door. She leaves.

I wait, looking at a book or two, then head for front of the store. Two people, a man about my age and a young, blonde round-faced woman with a short ponytail watch me and as I make eye contact with him, then her, they look stern. It's clear they think I'm up to something, probably some sick older guy lurking after the pretty young woman.

Handing them a sale-priced classic work of fiction by Henry James, "Washington Square", and I nervously get out a ten-pound note which requires a bit back from the bald, eagle nosed guy. His mouth is taught, and his eyes pointed as he stares into mine. Trying to look nonplussed, I nod and thank him and walk out slowly. They must have been watching me watch Peggy, so I walk in the opposite direction she went. And, after a few steps, I walk as quickly as I can, so I can cross. I circle around and back to the Turl, then to Ship and then I run.

By the time I get near the Randolph Hotel I'm winded, my chest heaving a bit, and I'm twenty steps behind Peggy, but can only watch her round the corner onto Beaumont Street, and I can only assume she'll drift on back, up the steps to work. I stop a few feet from the corner, no longer following, no longer looking at Peggy Avakian, the girl from Tufts, the girl with the drawing.

I walk back to my hotel possessed by self-disgust.

The Lyon's Head Hotel on Woodstock Road, with a carved wooden sign of a lion's head in relief hanging over the front door, is just a nice-looking bed and breakfast with a funny name. Maybe it's French humor. The owners are from Lyon. But it faces Leckford, Peggy's Road. I shouldn't spend the money but I'm doing it. I'm hiding in my room, small as it is, with antique furniture, including an old white metal bed. What's there to hide from? Peggy? No idea, but it is how it feels, and I can barely move. Never in my life have I felt so insipid.

There's a pub downstairs where I'm going to eat dinner since I'm finally drying out and don't plan on going anywhere out there tonight. I guess my plan was to gape at Peggy Avakian some more tomorrow. Gape at her without her gaping at me. I don't think I will.

The bath is down the hall and the TV is downstairs in a room with half a dozen stuffed chairs and magazines. It's a classic old Bed and Breakfast, just better looking than most. I'm lying down now and staring at the white plastered ceiling with sanded tan beams. Eyes closed for twenty minutes, I'm up.

I creak down the rickety stairs for dinner at seven, ducking towards the last step so I don't hit my head. Mr. and Mrs. Zimmer, the French couple who own and operate the place, are still behind the small counter in what must have been the front sitting room. The write-up online said they came from Lyon where they operated a small hotel for nine years. Luc and Christine.

"Bonsoir." I get out, trying to be friendly, then duck away not actually in the mood to interact with anyone. He's a burly bald man in his forties, with a mustache and light blue eyes that look intense against his slightly unhealthy, red blotchy cheeks. Christine's as burly as Luc but has a classic hipster look with dyed maroon hair that sticks up, off her head a few inches all around. Classic hip, classic antique, classicness all around me.

"Yes, oui. Bon appetite?" This reaches me halfway down the hall to the pub. I'm in a weird, rude state of mind.

As I enter, leaning my head down a few inches, I'm startled to see a small, ancient, stunning room with a small bar at one end and a fire burning at the other. Maybe it rates being called an inn after all. There are eight tables, half of them filled. The bartender, a young guy named Henry, welcomes me, asking me where I'd like to sit. I'm worried it might be too expensive, but I thank him and point to the window bench with the small table. When I sit and open the menu, I see the prices are high. It's over twenty pounds for a couple of entrees and seven pounds for a glass of the house red. Sure enough, it says Christine is the chef. I'll avoid the expensive, rich food, but there's a Salad Nicoise that's fifteen pounds.

For some reason I hate sitting here and waiting.

I'm practically moaning through stifled irritation. I'm drinking a dry cider and the room sparkles with low lighting and no bric-a-brac anywhere. Other diners are quiet, eating, chatting. Lots of atmosphere without being over designed. It feels real. Just like Amanda droning on and on about trains, I go on about overly designed expensive restaurants. Why don't they either leave well enough alone, leave the buildings the way they found them or hire actual designers. Let us eat in peace. Christ, I'm a cranking freak.

I have to wait until the food comes, and it does and it is quiet here and it tastes good but I'm not comfortable for some reason and so I leave as soon as I can.

I wind and duck my way back to my small, antique room.

I think of Peggy walking here and there, in her jeans and thin tan crew necked sweater. It's an image of her walking and walking alone, across the globe and turning and walking on some more. If that's it, I don't know much after all this stupid effort. Only wanting to rest, I fall into sleep.

❧ Chapter 3 ❧

Breakfast is quick, just muesli and cantaloupe and excellent toast and marmalade and coffee. Creaking in the hallway and turning to the stairs to go up to my room, I see both Zimmers behind their counter, ten feet away.

"Excellent Salad Nicoise last night. Really excellent."

"Merci. Thank you." Her face looks pleased and expectant, like she'd like to hear more. I'm in the way of people heading down who are in a hurry to eat their free breakfast, so I have to negotiate my way through them to the counter.

"I'm afraid I have to leave a day early. I hope that's all right."

"Yes, of course," Christine says. "All is well, I hope."

I must be looking strained.

"Fine. I just have to get back to sort out some things."

"Yes." She's printing my paperwork and I sign it and shuffle away.

All I can think about is getting out of town.

Nothing in front of me but Sunday, after taking a damned taxi to the train station, so angry about spending so much money. I'm trudging and trudging and trudging around in my very own shithead boring circle. But eventually I'll get back to Dublin.

◆ Chapter 4 ◆

I hate thinking about how the gallery is even emptier these days. We do get students at times and it is free admission and we are right between Trinity College and University College. But visitors are down to a trickle compared with summer and the students have settled into their work, or whatever they do. So, it's okay. I really do have to have my meeting with the board, even if they will hate my plans.

The big conference room where we meet is a waste of space, but I have to direct my thoughts in a positive direction. I'm the first one there, at two o'clock exactly, but they all seem to file in quickly. I'm nervous.

I wait and smile and they mill for a few minutes but I'm sitting in my chair in the middle of the long oval table and they notice and start sitting down. Beth did ask me to take her spot at the end of the table, but I prefer not separating myself that much, at this point.

"So, okay. This meeting was scheduled for tonight at seven, but I wanted to do this during museum hours for a reason. First, I really want to thank you all for coming. Some of you had to make special arrangements. And I didn't mean to raise any alarms in my email. It's just that I do have a basic concern that I wanted to raise and, I think, a possible long-term solution. We'll see." I stop and look around, then stand and pass a short four-page proposal to Sol Gerwitz on my left and Dorothy Connors across from me and slide the rest across the table.

Sitting back down, I'm giving them a couple of minutes to read.

"Sorry, no glossy pictures."

"An addition? Where?" I knew Kevin Smith would be a problem.

"Not exactly an addition, but please let me get to that after I make a couple of basic points."

There's general paper crinkling and grumbling now. I'll wait another minute. Mary's looking furious. So is Kevin.

"Okay? Let me lay out my basic concern." I pause a few seconds to get their attention. "As I see it, the debt we owe the Cobery family is great. The mission of the museum should always centre on the content of his original museum and the manner in which Trevor Cobery put this museum together. But . . ."

I wait to grab their attention again as I glance around the table.

"It seems to me we're missing a great opportunity. We do have to remain loyal to the will and the original mission, but if that means a lack of access for the public then I think we aren't keeping to that mission."

Again, I'm waiting and sure enough Kevin's shaking his head. "The mission and the will are the mission and the will. We can't start building additions. That was the point of this museum, to show the collection the way Trevor Cobery put it together. Nothing more or less."

I nod, expressionless at Kevin. The Connors are whispering to each other and Beth's skin is lavender.

Mary raises her hand and blares, "I thought this was made clear in the hiring process."

I nod again and open my copy of the proposal.

"Well, on page two I have the graphs of attendance in the twentieth century, and up until now. I've included other museums that are similar around the world in the graph below." I pause. There are exclamations about the uniqueness of the Cobery.

"Okay. I knew I would anger some of you and I'm sorry. Let me explain my view." I wait one more time until the undertone subsides. "If any of us were to go into the galleries right now, we'd see very few visitors, even for February, and we'd see those visitors acting like tourists, even if they live in Dublin. Most I've seen walk along and only stop occasionally to gaze. It's our museum, not theirs. They walk through and it's a one-time visit, like we're a curiosity. I don't think I'm exaggerating."

Beth and both of the Connors lean over towards each other.

Then Beth says, "But I'm not sure what you're saying, unless you would actually propose we change the basic structure of the museum. We can't."

Meaning, you don't want to, I'm thinking.

"No, I don't want to change much at all. I'll get to the physical changes in a minute. No, what I want is more direct engagement for the public. I get the value of tourists, but we're in a major residential city. I know Drew, who works part time for you Beth, deals with community relations and attendance. I'd suggest he and I, and anyone else who can help, get together and work on that as our main goal in the next few years."

The mumbling and paper rustling is continuous. I'm not making any eye contact anymore.

I raise my voice a bit. "Here's why revisits matter, I think, and I'm not going to just spout the standard one-liners about the role museums have in educating people, especially children. That's fine stuff. It just seems to me the best art museums are the ones that open their doors every day and allow the greatest number of people to use the facilities, all of the facilities, from the galleries to the cafe, as their own. It is, in fact, theirs. Much of any presence of curators in that process breaks the bond, I think."

"That may be the view in America. Not here." Mary has her arms folded.

"We should consider what Eric is saying."

That came from Sol Gerwitz next to me. It slows down the rustling for a second.

Simon Cobery looks at me. "Eric, I do think what you're saying is all very good and interesting and I appreciate your perspective, but I am afraid we have to remain vigilant about the will. Let's encourage more repeat visits. The addition, though? That would mean a major break."

"Well, the addition, as you call it, would just be using space we already have, but for the public, not us. It would be where people could stop walking through rooms, period rooms, and get to concentrate on just the objects, one on one. I came up with two galleries on two floors, so just a total of four new galleries. It's on page three. The galleries would support the chronology of the floor they're on, with furniture and sculpture in some galleries and paintings, prints and drawings in others. This is obviously all up for discussion, but we have enough in storage for this and I think it would seriously enhance our museum."

"Where would this be? I'm not sure where . . ." Kevin has a way of grasping negativity like it's an exposed electric cable.

"Move Maintenance to the coach house building. I'll move somewhere and Maintenance will get its own building. Move Conservation to the fourth floor, by eliminating this Conference Room. We can use my luxurious office for conferences and well, the rest is up to some actual architects. But not much construction costs and the public galleries will flow completely around the courtyard. No more dead-ends."

"Where the heck do we have the money, even if we wanted to do it?" Mary says, not raising her hand anymore and Kevin never did and he's vehemently against it all and saying so to Mary and the Connors.

"Raising money for buildings and extensions is some of the easiest money to raise. It garners participation and enthusiasm and might get us some needed attention in the community. I want this to become a second home to people in Dublin."

Beth's face is still lavender and she's actually raising her hand. "It might be great to do this in a standard sort of museum. We have an ironclad, a very distinct will, and it is what makes the Cobery, the Cobery."

I cough. I'm going to lose here. "Right, well I think the mission of the will would remain the same. We'd be adding to it, not taking away."

"Um, sorry, but that sounds like what politicians tell us before they put a car park in our backyard."

Kevin gets a bunch of laughs for that.

"Trevor Cobery can either remain the founding inspiration for this museum or he can be the on-going head curator who says, it's my museum, not yours. Stand here, move along to there. Keep moving. The only time you should stop is when we curators decide to educate you."

Dennis Connors leans forward for the first time. "Yeah, sorry Eric but, well I don't really see your point with curating. Because, I mean, curators are the very people who teach people about collections, about history. We're proud to offer free lectures to school pupils and university students. Beth has brought in lecturers from Trinity and University College."

I have to hesitate. I don't want to attack these people. They're all glaring at me. I won't show them the depressed figures on school groups coming to the Cobery.

"That's great. It's great to do that too, just not as a primary function, I don't think. People can't come here on their own and make it their own experience, their own private experience? Come in again and again and stand or sit and stare at those objects they love for their own reasons?"

"But they can stop all they want and sit in the cafe as long as they want." Dorothy's face is red. She's quiet and shy.

I nod. I think I was biting my lip listening to her.

"I think if you go into the galleries right now, you'll see them mostly wandering through. They're interlopers in our museum."

❧ Chapter 5 ❧

I'm in the small lobby of the Lyon's Head Hotel. I'm itchy. Edith isn't here yet and she should be. And I shouldn't be spending this money as though I'm even close to solvent, just to show off to Edith that I'm still the brilliant star who shines light upon her. I just want Luc to hurry up. There are two people ahead of me and I've been standing for ten minutes at least. Luc's moving through boggy, viscous air. In fact, it is hot as all hell here because they have the wood stove pumping and that's still no excuse for this dull motion. Meanwhile, Edith doesn't have her phone on and can't be reached.

Finally, after saying I want two reservations for dinner for two nights, Luc smiles.

"Here is your key and I will ring you up when your mother arrives. Merci, thank you and welcome back."

He means well, a nice guy. Just slow and I was in East Coast America too long.

I have the same room, and Edith will be down the hall, if she gets here. Wrestling with my key, I finally get in and close the door. It looks fine. I flop down, exhausted from the schlep, with my dark green herringbone jacket over the back of the desk chair and my small midnight blue canvas suitcase standing against the wall. My arms are behind my head.

This space is standard old beautiful. The wallpaper's a matted dark blue stripe on white background and it flows over the bumpy plaster walls. It flows up to a ceiling of lots of plain, sanded unvarnished beams with thick white plaster between. The furniture's antique and plain and the wide plank floors are almost completely covered by a rug with a dark red and blue small checkered pattern.

So, formulaic or not, I'm only sneering because it's ten times more attractive than my Dublin flat. I'd love to bulldoze that tepid mess.

My phone hums and vibrates.

"Hi Edith. You here?"

"Hello. Yes. I have arrived downstairs and I have my key to my room. You are in your room?"

"I am. I'm coming down to help you with your bag."

"No. Luc is carrying my bag. I am walking already behind him."

"Okay. Room fourteen, right?"

"Qui. Yes. Sorry."

I grunt. "How did you get here? Your phone was off."

"Oh, yes. I wanted to save the battery. I took a bus and walked and got a bit lost. I should have taken a taxi, but I was not sure how far it was."

"Okay. You're here."

She's not listening. She's thanking Luc in French. I wait.

"Oh, Eric. It is very, very pretty."

"Good."

"Such a nice view to the back lawn with trees. And such beautiful furniture."

"Almost as nice as your house. Anyway, would you like to rest or clean up? Then we can meet-up and go for a walk?"

"Yes, yes. Just a few minutes. Then we can see the splendid town. Such a splendid town. Oh, I wish Amanda still is here. Maybe we can see the house where she lived. Is it near here?"

I'm shocked and wonder how I hadn't anticipated that.

"Uh, I don't think so. We'll see plenty of residential Oxford. It's the colleges that make it special, though, right?"

"Yes. That's right. Eric? I have not heard from Amanda for two weeks. She doesn't do that. She always texts me and once a week at least she calls. Even in school as a teenager, she did all this. Have you heard from her?"

"Uhh, no. But I think she's in limbo just now. Probably busy, a busy limbo. I'll text her."

"I texted her. Many times, and she didn't text back." Edith's voice is tense.

"Okay, well I'll try and maybe we can try her boyfriend, or ex-boyfriend."

"Good. Okay. I will wash and phone you in ten minutes or so."

I put my head back and close my eyes.

We'll wander. I barely know the town. I'll ask Edith what she wants, a walk through the University Parks and through some of the residential sections or the town center? We'd see a little bit of the town and some college buildings from outside, from the street. Up to Edith. She was the one who wanted to come here. Maybe we'll go to the Ashmolean tomorrow.

❧ Chapter 6 ❧

Lying in bed, restless and awake much too early, I can't help thinking Edith and I should skip going to the Ashmolean. Yesterday was enough walking around Oxford for me, so I don't want to do that again, but maybe I should talk Edith into seeing a movie or something.

Still lying in bed, looking out at the dawn's early winter scattered English light, this is Friday morning, the eleventh of February and it looks bitter. There are wind gusts that suddenly whip light grey and white cloud streams across the sky. It seems to be sleeting out there, almost snowing. I'll get up and have a shower.

Breakfast shouldn't be too long and festive. It's already after nine and we have a couple of projects for today. But Edith said, in French, she wanted an omelet. It'll be good to eat something substantial.

The staff must be on break because Christine managed to wait on our table and will cook and then bring us our omelets. The coffee tastes great and we're next to the window, watching the operatic clouds and wind.

"I didn't know you spoke that much French."

Edith blushes. "Oh, just a little."

"From classes in town?"

"No. I might. No, I just learn a little."

I look at her and she grows sheepishly uncomfortable, shifting in her seat and turning her head to the middle of the room. So I look away.

"There are some French people in Cirencester," she says.

"Oh. You know them? Neighbours?"

Now her eyes sink inward. "No, there is a man who is French who works at the library with me." It's as if she had a need to say that. I didn't ask her to. I say nothing for a flat, dull second or two. She has a manfriend? Why does that thought sort of disturb me? I'll try to be happy for her, but I'll be a lot happier to avoid any details.

She's stiff and saying nothing more. She's happier than I am to avoid details.

"So, today should be fun, but I think there's a limit to how much walking we can do again today, Edith. It's not really such a small city and the college grounds are extensive. And the weather's brisk."

"Well, we can take a bus into the museum you want to see, and I would like to see too." Her eyes seem less hidden.

"Okay, good." I feel caught in some drama I didn't choose. I try eating. I shouldn't have told her I wanted to go to the Ashmolean. That was a plan that made sense to me last week. "Then we can visit one of the colleges after lunch."

"That would be perfect."

I wonder if Amanda knows about some Frenchman in our mother's life.

I sit back and look out again. A couple of hours at the Ashmolean might be good. My goal was to bump into Peggy Avakian, get in her face to see how she'd reacts to us. Now I don't want to bother. The nasty, morbid feel to the last trip came from creeping around, trying to be invisible. But, since Edith's been asking to see Oxford, I thought I'd take Peggy's old stalking game up a notch. It was just another morbid idea, because I was still feeling vindictive.

The omelets come and Edith's is devoured but it seems too rich and heavy to me. And the heavy duty, whole grain toast tastes extra heavy duty. We thank Christine and go up to our rooms.

Edith's at my door at ten-thirty just as planned and out we go. She has on the camel hair coat I gave her years ago and a long tartan wool scarf wrapped around her neck and hanging down old collegiate style and her best leather walking shoes, beautiful things she bought in Cheltenham for an arm and a leg. It was her one foray into one of the snotty-horsey shops, but she landed the perfect English ladies walking shoes. And she saves them for special walks, and she thinks Oxford's even more special than Cirencester or Cheltenham. She never got to go to university.

The sleeting stopped and so we walk down St. Giles.

"I looked online and thought maybe Balliol College would be good. It's central and a great, old, prestigious college."

"How old, Eric?"

I pull out my phone and start tapping at it as we walk.

"It was founded in 1263."

"Good, good."

"Magdalen is supposed to be stunning, Edith. And New College was founded in 1379. Not old enough?"

She smirks, looking straight ahead. "You pick one. I'm happy with any."

We walk on.

Edith stops. "You look cold with only a sports jacket on and a sweater on. Take my scarf. Here. Please. I am too warm."

I'm too warm too but take her red tartan scarf and thank her.

The idea of wearing a long wooly tartan scarf like this makes me feel ridiculous, but who cares? I'm already out of control anyway.

I flinch when the same two people are at the reception counter of the Ashmolean. He welcomes us and smiles warmly at Edith and takes her coat. Clearly, like so many older men, he finds her appealing. I'm losing her to the world.

It's ten after eleven and we wander the galleries. The damned museum's perfect. This is a museum visitors can own, come back to again and again and I grit my teeth in envy.

It's almost twelve.

"Edith, uhm, look, why don't we see about their classical stuff downstairs, and then, you know, see what we want to see next."

"Yes. You go where you want."

Edith is too forgiving of other people's ridiculous foibles.

Once we're down the stairs, we poke around, staring at labels, and some people walk by looking along with us. Some staff walk by heading to the door for lunch. I notice they have the staff walk and then I turn and face Peggy twenty feet away walking towards me. There's a second of her not looking, not seeing, then a flicker of some recognition and then shock. Her eyes darken along with her face. I stare, flushed, but remember any awkwardness on my part can be explained, since Edith and I are tourists. She's alone and slows down, her eyes up at me, then down. I step out of the way a foot to give her room as she looks again, still red-faced and eyes dark, all open pupils. Her mouth's open a bit and tense. I nod. She stops two feet in front of me.

"Hi," I say, wondering if she'll regain her composure. She's almost looking afraid. "How are you?" I add, and it sounds ridiculously tinny.

"Hi."

"I came here with my mother, uh . . ." I turn and Edith's watching from ten feet away, half hidden behind a small Greek sculpture. And I turn back and see Peggy wave meekly at Edith.

"Um, I've heard about your mother," she says in a low, shaky voice. She coughs into her fist.

We stand speechless for a second and have to move out of the way for some of her fellow staff members to pass and go to lunch. One I recognize is Ian O'Connor. I saw his picture online and he's with two younger people and they all gaze at us, say hello to Peggy, and walk by.

I think of saying something, like, *don't let me stop you*, but I don't. I say nothing, wanting to see how she'll respond to the odd, empty gap between us. She turns to me.

"Um, you're in Oxford for the day?" Again, I notice some shaking in her voice and I'm fighting wanting to help her somehow.

"Yeah, actually we came yesterday, and we'll go tomorrow."

Edith's standing next to me and I didn't see her coming. "Oh, Edith, this is Peggy Avakian. Peggy was Amanda's roommate."

Edith perks right up. "Ah-yes. Oh, it is so nice to meet you! Do you work here? Or study?"

"Hi. Yes, well, just an internship."

"Oh, and I am trying to remember. You are from New York? Yes? With a very good Armenian name."

"Oh, yes." Peggy's eyes lighten finally, as she smiles a bit at Edith, and even begins to shuffle her feet, her smile growing. It's more warmth than anything I've ever seen from her, except in that picture online, when she was with the art conservation group in Boston as a young student. Edith's on a roll.

"Oh, I can tell by your face. That is how I can tell. My family was from Romania, not so far away."

Peggy rocks back and forth, still smiling broadly. "Um, my father's family was from Armenia and my mother's side's from Ireland."

"Oh, Ireland where Eric is. Such a beautiful place and such beautiful people. Good genes. You have such good genes."

I have to bit my lip to not laugh. Edith's complimenting a stranger on her genes. Everyone's at a loss for words.

I just say, "Uh, well Peggy was on her way to lunch."

"Oh, yes. Don't let us stop you." Edith's turning her head trying to step back without colliding with people or art.

"No, that's okay."

"Oh, please let us take you! You are Amanda's good friend. Her good friend in America."

Peggy stiffens. I anticipated this. I knew Edith would be warm and friendly and I can see Peggy's feeling conflicted and I'm curious how she'll be with us up close and in her face. And for the next minute Edith pleads until Peggy's bound to accept. It's enough to make me have to fight laughing.

So then it's some awkward banter between Edith and Peggy about what to do next. The issue becomes where to go, other than a pub, since it's cold and raining, Edith says, after Peggy just stands facing her.

Peggy offers, "We could go downstairs. The museum cafe's very good." She looks very blotchy and probably just wanted a nearby quick lunch away from us. She waits and gets a polite nod from me and an enthusiastic yes from Edith. We head to the stairs, Peggy leading, then Edith, then me. The cafe's very attractive and we gather our food, Edith chattering to Peggy and me standing back watching half the time, averting my eyes the other half.

The vaulted basement ceiling is supported by thick columns everywhere. I wane, standing back, looking at the heavy arches curving above our heads. Lost in the architecture, I'm letting Edith run the show as she pays, after she insists for a few minutes. We sit, tucked in between columns and I let Edith talk and I eat some sandwich and drink some water. So far, it's been Edith asking questions about Oxford and Tufts and Boston and New York and Peggy's family. Peggy answers stiffly, looking like she's in riot control.

I say, "We should let Peggy eat."

Edith exclaims upon that, apologizing. I haven't been out with Edith much lately, but I remember her being a little more sedate. Peggy looks unhappily at her sandwich of brie and red pepper, lettuce and sundried tomato and takes her third tiny bite.

"You knew Eric in Boston? You met there?"

Peggy turns red and half nods, her mouth with food in it. Her eyes are hanging open.

I have to step in, out of bare courtesy. "Actually, we met when Peggy brought in something. But Tufts is right nearby. Did you know that?"

Edith raises her eyebrows trying to grasp what I'm saying.

I continue, wandering around the sorest of subjects. "Uhm, Tufts is close enough to Boston, so the museum is there as a collection for them. There's an affiliation between them, the university and the museum. We got a lot of students."

"Ah, and now Eric is in Dublin. He is Director of an art museum there."

"Right," I say. "It's just a small museum." I'm pointed toward Peggy who looks intensely, straight into my face, trying to interpret any possible meaning.

"And you like it you say. I hope you do," Edith says.

"I do. Yes, uhm . . . I'm off . . . I'll just be right back." I have to get away. Edith is driving the conversation straight at personal subjects and will do that even more precisely without me. So I head for the loo, getting away from any desire to watch Peggy squirm.

Gone for five minutes and Edith could have said almost anything. When I sit back down, Peggy has shoved half of her sandwich to the side of her plate. I notice what clothes she has on. It's the same tan crew neck sweater and jeans and flats as that day I followed her. She has a dark blue herringbone coat that she was carrying, over the chair next to her. Peggy glances at me as I sit and wonder what Edith actually did say. We sit and chat, with me intermittently taking our trash to the bins.

Sitting down the last time, Edith says to me, "Peggy would like to stay in England. Isn't that wonderful?"

"Yes."

"No, it's that I'm getting dual citizenship. My Grandfather was Irish so I can get Irish citizenship that way and live in Europe. But my internship is up in just over a year and jobs are really scarce. I just meant I would stay in England if I could."

"Ah, well, maybe you can stay as a student? Or go to an Irish university?" Edith asks.

"Oh, right, well, that would be very nice, but I'd have to get in and have the money and I don't think that would happen." Peggy drifts through this and stammers a bit at the end.

Edith tells her she would get in and maybe get a scholarship. She should try. And Peggy looks pained and nods and smiles weakly and I'm wishing Edith hadn't said anything about Irish universities. But there's the drift. Peggy wants to go to Oxford. As I suspected, that's why she got herself over here. The drawing will pay her way, or some of it. I decide to probe a bit on my own.

"Actually, if they don't change the rules, I think after you live and work in England for three years, you pay much lower university fees, if you have Irish citizenship. I think." I'm leaning both elbows on the table, turning my head to the right towards her.

"Um." Something seems to frustrate her. "I know, I have to work out what I can do and want to do." She continues blushing deeply and casts her eyes away from me and down, clearly wanting the conversation to end or head somewhere else. Shame over the little drawing escapade, or cards close to her vest? I sit back in my chair and Edith asks more questions. What town did she grow up in? How long did her family live on Long Island? What sort of work does her father do? I jerk at this.

"Uhm, Peggy's answered a lot of questions." I arch backward, figuring this is where to end Peggy's ordeal.

Edith sits forward and pats Peggy's shoulder and starts apologizing and Peggy steps in. "No, that's okay. No, I don't mind at all. My father works for Nory's, the American furniture store? He's an assistant manager in one and my mother works for Macy's, another store in the same mall, as an assistant accountant."

Her face is open, and she says this in as straightforward a way as possible, all blushing gone. I'm surprised at first, but then remember she's American and Americans can be so good at plain-speak. Edith isn't American and she's blushing now and tongue-tied, finally and I'm trying to think of something to say and Peggy seems to pick up on the awkwardness and adds more salve.

"They're just about retired now. They're moving to Florida."

"Ah, it is so warm there. You can go and visit them and sunbathe." Edith's happy for this girl.

Peggy glows. The smooth, natural colour added to her cheeks sets off the distinct, fine bone structure of her face and it all contrasts with her large hazel eyes and very dark brown hair. So, no more backing up, looking forced to face Edith and me. Peggy likes Edith.

It's Edith who starts to gather herself and explain that we have to get to our next mission, viewing a college. We all stand and shake hands, add thank yous and Peggy says good-bye. Her small form fades away. Edith and I shuffle around, clearing the last of our dishes and follow far enough behind to give Peggy space. No more stalking I hope, for anyone.

Out through the galleries on the ground floor, we get Edith's coat and leave. My head's too full to sort out how I feel about the pushy damned girl with the damned drawing now and so I just walk next to Edith, mumbling things with her about the weather and the time. On Broad Street Edith takes my arm and says, "I'm sorry I was rude to Peggy. I shouldn't ask such personal questions."

"No, Edith. There's no reason at all to feel that way. In fact, I think she really liked talking to you." I can see, looking down at her drawn face that she's upset. I squeeze her arm with mine.

"Uh." She shakes her head. "Words just come out some-times. I think she was a very, very nice young woman."

I say nothing, not able or willing to pass on the crazy tribulations of my recent life, and she says nothing, but clucks her tongue a couple of times.

We just walk on and then walk through some of the buildings and grounds of Balliol College. And it's amazingly beautiful.

⚘ Chapter 7 ⚘

Back in Dublin waiting for my meeting with Beth Kelleher and Simon Cobery tomorrow and I'm wondering -- what's this flat like when the sun is strong and the air's hotter and drier? No way it could be less dingy. I don't read or watch movies or listen to music here, because what? It's temporary? How temporary? I have to put in at least a few years, or I'll have the resume of a manic, jackass malcontent. I can't even look out the window. It looks at a brick wall.

So I've steered myself into a stupid cul-de-sac and there's nothing I can actually do about it. What gives me the right to change things at the Cobery when I didn't even visit the museum before I took the job? It was all right here, and I would have known all I needed to know in half an hour. But no, I did my tiny bit of research online.

It's their museum and I work for them now, whether I like it or not.

I sit on my temporary crap sofa wondering how long I'll pay that storage company in South Boston to hold my things. I have all the lights on.

Why do I feel an urgent need to own-up? Why do I feel like I have to explain myself? To myself? To Margy? I'll probably never have that chance. Ustaad and Jean? Christa? No, she saw me as a curator, not a person. She wouldn't even care to understand. Natalie? I always had to be careful around her.

We definitely got along really, really well, Natalie and me. Her being married kept us from ruining that. I can't email her, not yet.

I could try Christa. I was always simply honest with her. She was carved out of The George School, then Swarthmore and then Harvard. She was a lifelong, hardcore academic who loved every top-notch school and university she ever attended, and I was all hybrid education and duct tape. I told her, years ago, about my mediocre high school in Berlin and my mediocre university in Kent and I told her it was then I decided to hang around Cambridge to see if I could learn through osmosis. Christa laughed. I told her I was a guard at the Cambridge University museum, the Fitzwilliam, while I took courses at the Cambridge University Institute of Continuing Education. It was night school and just about anyone could take those courses, but maybe Yale didn't know that. I was a contriver. Christa was no longer laughing. I didn't doubt my abilities in all areas. I just was never a hardcore academic. Christa was. She seemed to accept me for who I was though.

I want to email her.

> *Christa – Sorry to leave so suddenly. Contrary to what you might hear, I haven't joined a cult and I didn't suddenly decide I hated everyone in Boston and the museum. I had an opportunity to get closer to my family and took it. You may have heard, I'm director of the Trevor Cobery Museum in Dublin. I did tell you about my desire to do administrative work, so here I am. Dublin is beautiful so please, please come and visit. Hope all is well with you.*
> *Best wishes,*
> *Eric*

I click on *send,* turn off my computer, put it on the floor, walk around the flat turning off all the lights and head for bed.

The easy contentment of waking up slowly after seven hours of deep floating sleep ends when I remember that Beth and Simon asked to meet with me. I know they're really annoyed and disappointed with me. I have to do this.

After my morning victuals and rituals.

Up the elevator and into my facile fancy office and into my methods of killing time. There's not a lot to accomplish. It really seems I can get most things done in a couple of hours a day. The place around me putters along and runs itself. It's one reason I walk around the building so often, like a visitor.

Ten o'clock and Beatrice buzzes me.

I say, "Come in, please." Beth has that slightly rumpled look. Her clothes are sort of cheap and formal usually, just like now. The dress is some kind of heavy wrinkle-free combination of materials. It's dark blue again and her low heals are blue. Her hair is straight to her shoulders and neat and she is no Margy Zorn. And Simon looks like a shadow of someone's ancestors, in the same baggy suit as always, I think.

We sit around the coffee table, after I pour them some coffee and offer them oatmeal biscuits, which they politely refuse. I sit back, resigned. If I succeed at this job it will be from lack of trying.

"Simon and I were asked by the board to give you a response to your proposal. It's a preliminary response but the board was almost unanimous and wanted us to address your concerns this way before the next formal meeting." Her accent is modified Irish/British. I've noticed she controls her speech by slowing down when she's nervous, like now, with cotton in her mouth. After all, technically I'm her hire and her boss.

Simon steps in. "It's fair to say you did stir up some thoughts and emotions, Eric. We probably look stultified to you, especially after the Museum of Fine Arts in Boston, but in many ways that's the point. We're not the National Gallery of Ireland or the Tate Britain. We like to think we're an alternative to those slicker institutions. And we do have our loyal members and public. Do you see that?"

"Yes, I do. Sorry if I seemed negative. Please don't think I was presenting some sort of ultimatum. I wasn't at all."

Nothing is said for a few seconds. They hate this discussion even more than I do.

"But tell me what the board said. Clearly, they weren't crazy about the idea of the addition of four galleries." I want this meeting to end.

Beth uncrosses and recrosses her legs and tries to smile. Simon is politely waiting for her. She has some sort of odd position of authority in the museum, maybe especially now that the crazy guy from Slick City, USA isn't fitting in at all as Director.

She says, slowly, "No, well, I think everyone was very interested in your comments about offering more to members of the local public and more, you know . . ."

"Access. Is that the right word?" Simon's adding. I just nod. On-going access, I want to yell, but just smile, tight-lipped.

Beth straightens her back. "So it just seems to centre around actually an addition. And that was generally seen as contrary to the Trevor Cobery will, to the mission of the museum. Sorry. Almost everyone agreed. Sol said he would send you an email with his opinion, which was really the only one that supported an addition."

They insist on calling it an addition. "Okay. I saw that it wasn't going over when I made the proposal and so I think we should put it behind us. I hope I didn't irritate too many on the board. It was just an idea. My job is to direct the museum, now, just as it is. I'm happy to do that."

The acid bubbling in my stomach must be contorting my face. I can't smile. They see that and get up. The meeting's over and I'll have to figure out a way to just get along with these people. Just get along, thwarted.

❧ Chapter 8 ❧

As poor Edith keeps saying, she always gets one call a week at least from Amanda, but not in the last six weeks. No emails and no texts from Amanda to either of us. Here I am in London at nine at night.

The Annex2, in Holland Park is far enough out to offer deals and close enough to where I have to go. It's still too much money and I'm so sick of thinking about stupid money.

I'll look for Amanda tomorrow. I hope she'll be at her boyfriends or somewhere nearby. I'll try not to be too angry, but it'll be hard. Why the hell is she so out of touch? At the very least it's disrespectful and hurtful to her mother.

At some point I have to get rid of the drawing here in London. Right now, it's downstairs in the hotel safe, at five pounds a day.

The early April winds are sweeping low, somewhere past cars and buildings. I hear gusts as I fall asleep.

I wake at six to a dark room with humming voices and footsteps all around me. Some footsteps come from outside and sound sharp and get swallowed by rush hour traffic. Inside it's all contained, but I have to leave this room.

I eat oatmeal and toast downstairs in the conservatory, no longer contained. The glass walls and glass ceiling are about never-ending space and trying to read the Guardian while I chew and trying to avoid the existence of other break-fast chewers is not satisfying at all, for any of us.

That ends and I'm out of there. The Annex2 is on Bromfield Street, right off Holland Park Road where I'm out in the cold morning air walking to the Tube stop.

Londoners look so filled with direction, always. It's not even rush hour anymore. Only fools and foreigners wander, lost.

In fifteen minutes, I've reached the Tube entrance and face the maps on the walls. I can only feel heavy and lumber-ing as I try to walk with the pedestrians around me. I'm not sure if I should take the Holland Park Central Line to Bank Street, or to Liverpool Street where I can switch to the East London line. I'm going to get on and ask someone.

Friction can be avoided on a tight little island by peo-ple who contain themselves. I'm half amused, half annoyed by this little saying I've just made up, sitting on a bench seat rumbling along underground towards Liverpool Street. I decided to not ask.

I look at my phone to see if by some miracle Amanda's sent a text or email and I see an email's there from Christa. Not in the mood, I click on it anyway. The small print is hard to read.

Eric – Well, I hope you like the museum in Dublin. It did seem a bit drastic, the way you fled from here. Ann is not pleased and can't say I blame her, Eric. Your sudden departure made things difficult for her. She has just hired a replacement for you. Michael Chavez from Harvard. Natalie Ziegler recommended him. He worked for several years at the Harvard Art Museums, so he should fit in fairly readily.

Best of luck - Christa

Christ. That's that. Shit. Not only have I been replaced, I've been erased. So much for Christa and Ann. Natalie, well, she hasn't called or emailed, but neither have I. There's no way to digest this amount of rejection and I have more important things on my mind, Edith and Amanda.

The train's at my stop. Liverpool Station is a matter of wading through noise and following signs to the East London line. I have to button up my old herringbone jacket and even put my collar up.

We make our way to the southern side of the Thames and finally, at New Cross Station, I'm walking out. There are a few of us exiting, including the very attractive young female who smiles at me and I look down. I'm in no mood and haven't been since Boston. I should have just smiled, me who prides himself in being polite.

Too late now. She's in her own zone again. The rest of the small crowd wandering out onto the broad, busy New Cross Road looks like a mix of students and immigrants, unlike me. I'm a lost emigrant. Goldsmiths College is nearby, and I see signs for it, but I have to go back down Pepys Road to 74, whatever that is.

There's not a tree in sight and the street has a bit of a haggard, beaten down student feel. The brick and concrete buildings may have felt cold and institutional when families lived in them years ago, but now they just look insubstantial. The numbers don't make sense as I walk until I suddenly see it, 74. This is where Brendon Morton lives and I'm hoping it's where Amanda lives.

The nineteen eighties tan brick is soiled and stained here and there, and windows are cracked, with someone's pillowcase dripping out of one. It's a nondescript, cheaply built four storey residence of single rooms and bedsits most likely. Up several concrete steps, the buzzers line up next to names written in script or block letters on various bits of paper or cardboard.

Sure enough, Brendon's last name, Morton, is there, indicating the third floor. I push the plastic button. The electric buzzer seems to work but what do I know? I wait and push again, waiting to either get buzzed into the heavy glass front door or shout into the small aluminum speaker. Nothing. I push again, for a few seconds. Nothing. Shit. I step back down the steps and look up cupping my hand over my eyes. The building stares out past me with its glassy black rectangular gawps. So now what do I do? I look at my watch. It's almost eleven-thirty. I stand. I'll wait for a while. Twenty minutes max.

Nothing like having no actual plan. I seem to be doing this a lot these days.

I sit on the steps, my jacket buttoned again, my collar up. After about ten minutes, with a few cars parking on the street and people going into other buildings or walking away, to something, somewhere, a young guy comes out of 74. He has that sort of spiked dyed black hair that seems like the ubiquitous, timeless style of turbulent youth. What period does it even represent at this point?

"Hi." I speak to him as he blinks at me with at least as much alienation as I feel.

"Do you know Brendan Morton?"

"Uh, I know of him." He looks warily at me, while half turning to get away.

"You wouldn't know if he's in? Actually, it's my sister I'm looking for. Amanda Matheson?"

"Nope, nope, don't know her." He starts walking away.

"Never heard of her at all?" I say louder to his back.

"Nope."

Fuck, why do I want to brutalize that little thug?

I stand there wondering what I can do. Cars pass at regular intervals making gear and exhaust noises. I'm cold and the sun's not worth much now, not making up for the wind. I don't want to go to the college and ramble around trying to look him up and he doesn't seem to have a phone number I've been able to find. I have to walk and try to get warm. I go down the street until it intersects with something, but I don't see a name and don't care. I just go left, pass an actual sign, Norbert Road and wander straight on for ten minutes. Then I amble back, getting hungry as hell, figuring I'll get something to eat at the small deli I saw near Norbert Road.

It's forty-five minutes later, going on one o'clock when I'm heading up towards Pepys Road and see two guys standing on the steps there. I approach.

"Sorry. I'm looking for Brendan Morton."

They pause, one sheepishly grinning, the other one not. The grinning one has a mop of sandy coloured hair and speaks up.

"You a narc?"

"Not that I know of. I'm looking for my sister, Amanda."

"Matheson, yeah, you look like her. You, you're not her, what, father?" the grinning one says churlishly.

His friend speaks up, "Please shut up Fraxton. He said, sister. Amanda, yeah." He steps forward and offers his hand. "Hi, I'm Brendan."

"Hi, Eric."

"Oh, yeah, she said something about you."

"Is she around?"

"No, not here." His eyebrows are raised and form a hairy brown crescent above his wide brown eyes. He might be attractive to young females in some way, but his unformed, bushy brown hair and bumpy complexion don't win him any awards from me. Not to mention his skinny, and still, rumpled jeans and colourless, dark, dirty jumper.

"Okay. I'm just trying to get in touch. I haven't heard from her for a few weeks."

"Oh. That sucks. Well, I haven't seen Amanda for, let's see, yeah, about a month, I think."

His cohort is getting antsy and starts to walk up the steps. "B, I'll go in then. I'm going to let you prove you didn't sell Amanda into slavery. Just joshing. Bye, really, joshing."

I give Fraxton a hate look. But he's gone. His words eat at me.

Brendon sees this and seems concerned.

"Sorry about him. No, I just haven't heard a thing from her."

"Did Amanda live here at all?"

"Oh, yeah, for a couple of weeks. But that was back in early February, I think. Yeah, or the end of January. I haven't seen her since then. Sorry, are you worried about her?"

"Well, I think I am now. She gave us your address as her address. I have no idea where she is. Do you have any ideas at all?" I'm trying to stay calm in my tone, to not sound alarmist and scare him away.

"Not really. No, she didn't say where she was going." He pulls his phone out of his sweatshirt pocket and thumbs it, staring down.

I say, "Yeah, we've been leaving all types of messages for weeks. Nothing back."

"Really?" He puts the phone back in his pocket.

"But, sorry, were you two involved?"

"Oh. No. No, Amanda and I are friends. We always knock about together, like back at school in Cheltenham. I'm sort of living with a girl." He looks disturbed having to open that private door to a strange, older guy.

"So she just stayed here for a while. You put her up."

"Yeah. That's it. She took all her stuff. Look, I can ask around."

"But is she enrolled in any courses at Goldsmiths?"

"Not that I know of. I haven't seen her there. She was going to apply to places somewhere for next year."

That's all. What appeared to be evasion at first is just bouncy, rubbery adolescence. It's all I'm going to get out of him anyway. I thank him and write my private phone number down on a card from the Cobery Museum, which he doesn't look at and just pushes into a front jean pocket.

That's it for Monday. It'll take me forever to get back to my hotel, at the other end of London, but close enough to Paddington Station where I might be taking a train to Oxford tomorrow.

And the effort of walking, tube riding and then eating is irritating but somehow distracts me. Back in my hotel room, the effort of talking to Edith is excruciating. Edith knows the agony better than I do. She's a mother and a child and grand-child and wife and sister who has experienced so much more of life's serious threats than I have. The phone conversation with her is short and I'm sure it's because she wants to spare me any unnecessary fear. I just tell her Amanda might be in Oxford and I don't even half believe it.

Tuesday is another blustery sunny cold day as I head out of Paddington Station on the ten-twenty train to Oxford. It'll take about an hour and fifteen minutes, me looking out the window at a scene I've looked at quite a few times now, the flat midlands looking even flatter in the late winter heavy frost, where the tundra and sky look like one. I'm going to skip taking the drawing to Spiro's Gallery until tomorrow. I sent them an email from the hotel, and they didn't seem to remember my emails from last week so obviously they don't care if or when I take the thing to them.

I'll go to 129 Leckford Road and see if I stumble into Amanda hiding out in her old haunt there in Oxford. She doesn't have any money as far as I know. Maybe she does. Maybe she has a job somewhere. She is an adult and can live her own life, but why this disappearing act? She's either in serious trouble or so angry at us she won't use a phone or computer to say where she is? It's starting to really unnerve me.

Just as well there's nothing to look at. I don't know. We're all I have, my little family unit and this is something I've always worried about -- after Dad died, we'd fall apart.

But, hell, in fact I used his death and the life insurance as an opportunity. I was just a teenager and a bit of a wreck after he died, but I pushed for my agenda. I'd get to England like those fancy English kids did. Get a cool house. Get Edith tucked away. Get Amanda into a cool school. Get some status for myself somehow, somewhere.

Nothing I can do about it now. I can drink my water. My eyes search though, nonstop. Sitting here on the train, they look at any young female with sandy hair. There are spurts when I think of Christa or Natalie or Margy, all off in the past. I nod off.

I'm pretty sure that at two something in the afternoon on a Tuesday Peggy won't be in her bedsit. I'm walking down Leckford Road looking for 129. It's remained consistently cold but it's dry now and not too windy. I really don't want to bump into Peggy but hope like hell I'll bump into Amanda. It's pretty far down the road. There's a primary school. There's 129 and I remember it from that one night I saw it. It's a Victorian red brick house that's been converted for most of its life into a bunch of bedsits. It has that slightly ragged, neglected aura, but the row of large windows to the left of the door is a giveaway as Peggy and Amanda's room and it stirs me a bit to see it. My vague plan is to wait outside and ask someone who comes out if they know Amanda, then suss out any more I can. It's going to be tough in this cold, though, if I have to wait. I should have worn more.

And wait I do. It's over half an hour, almost three, before a girl on a bike glides past and turns into the walkway of the house. She looks very young but must be a graduate student or something. Oxford is also filled with sixth form colleges and secretarial colleges. I step forward from my spot across the street.

"Excuse me?" Nothing. She keeps moving down and around the side of the house. Then I see the white wire running up to her ear. I wave from ten feet away, not wanting to scare her and she looks over and pulls at her ear plug and fumbles with her phone while holding her bike up with one leg.

"Hi. Sorry. I'm looking for my sister, Amanda. Amanda Matheson? She used to live here." I point to the large windows.

"Yes?"

"Do you know her?"

"No. Sorry, don't think so."

She has some sort of northern accent.

"Yeah, it's just that we haven't heard from her and, uhm, she used to live right there. With Peggy Avakian." I point again.

"Yeah, I see the girl who lives there, but, you know, don't actually even know her to speak to."

"Has there been another girl with her? How long have you been here because my sister hasn't actually lived here for a few months?"

"Oh, I moved in January. Sorry," said in a shrinking tone, her backing away.

That would have been around the time Amanda moved out but this place is transient and who pays attention to strangers? I thank her and step away. She locks up her bike looking a bit nervous about me lurking, so I walk back across the road. Then, when she disappears inside the front door, I wait ten seconds and step across again, this time across the tiny front yard to the windows. I noticed before that one curtain was half open. It's one of the two windows on the side of the house. There are five of these big windows and I'm under an old tall evergreen, standing on pine needles and pretty well hidden from the street and totally hidden from the front door. I put my face up to the window, my heart pounding, feeling like I'm entirely out of control, doing something wildly intrusive and illegal. But I can see inside if I cup my eyes and press against the glass. There's a bed near the window I'm looking through. It looks like the kitchen area I remember at the other end. There's the other bed across from that and it has pillows propped against the wall and some things on it. The bed near me is just barely made. The one over there has a cover wrapped around it fairly tightly and a coffee table in front, like it's being used as a sofa, maybe?

No sign of Amanda. The bed near me is Peggy's bed. Jesus, I step back, then look around to see if anyone saw me. No one's around and the car that drove by a few seconds ago was going fast and when I looked the driver was faced forward. I walk across the street and then walk some more. I'm going in the wrong direction and have to turn back. What should I do? Wait for Peggy? Ask her? I can't do that. It would answer whether Amanda's here, but I think I know the answer. She's not.

At Woodstock Road I get on a city bus that just happens to be there with a short queue. Any bus will get me into the centre of town. I'm hungry. Then, off the bus, finally, I go to the Randolph Hotel. It's going on four and there's only one other couple sitting at a table. I sit near the window and look at the menu, starving but distracted. I order the fish and chips because it's cheap and filling, knowing that it's there for the tourists. It takes almost half an hour to come and it's dark outside now. I eat and drink some warm house red. Then, I wait.

At five I pay and stand at the end of the row of windows, not caring if the handful of people in the place wonder why I'm staring out the window. I was staring into a window before. Around ten after five, after a few people have left the Ashmolean, I see Peggy. She has on the herringbone coat and ankle boots. She must have on a skirt or dress. She's alone. She disappears around the corner.

❧ Chapter 9 ❧

Banging around Paddington Station, then walking for over an hour in the cold night air and I'm back in The Annex2 in my room with a bottle of wine and some vegetable crisps and not able to eat or drink, just tired and damned. I'm sitting on the edge of the bed. I'm so worried about Amanda I can't stand up. I keep wondering if I should phone the police. Edith would want me to and, Christ, I can't even think about Edith right now.

I click on Amanda's phone number. This will be at least twenty times now. "Amanda, please phone. Please, shit, Amanda, please let us know if you're all right."

Then I sit on the end of the bed hearing myself breathe, my hands over my ears. I'll wait for ten minutes. I manage to pace. It's a bit drastic to phone the police, but if she's in trouble, I'm just standing here wasting precious time. The BT phone directory book is hard to follow, maybe because my mind isn't working. I don't want to dial the emergency number, 999. There's a number for the Metropolitan precinct in Kensington and I just try it. A woman answers and I begin to describe my story of the lost sister. Yes, I am a UK citizen. Yes, my sister is. I get transferred to the desk of missing persons and after waiting a minute describe the situation to Constable Stevenson. I can hear him tapping at a computer for the few minutes of me speaking and him asking basic questions.

"Well, Mr. Matheson, what I can tell you at this stage is your sister is a legal adult and can live where she chooses and unfortunately, she can choose to not get in contact with family members. Now, you say you have no reason to believe she's distraught or being held against her will?"

"No. I just don't know." It's important to sound reasonable.

"Um, I understand. Sorry. Again, you stated she has no medical or psychological condition that could come to bear?"

"No."

"Right. I understand the distress that this sort of thing causes and I have registered this information in the computer bank of the London Metropolitan Police so if any information matching the description of your missing sister arises, we will know whom to contact. All I can add is that we get many, many enquiries like this every day and in most situations, really the great majority of the situations just right themselves. I hope your sister has just decided to remain out of reach for a time and that she will get in touch with you soon. We will certainly do what we can and inform you immediately if we do come up with anything. If you hear anything, please inform us."

"Yes, okay. Thanks." So there's nothing else for him to do at this point, but I have read about the police giving tacit support to sex slavers. I have no idea where I read that.

"Thank you." He clicks off. He's probably happy to hang up. He had that monotonous controlled sound to his voice and it's possible he says all that ten times an hour.

I start getting ready for bed, brushing my teeth, thinking about how I can avoid speaking with Edith for another day at least. She hasn't been calling me or texting in the last couple of days. She's waiting for me to call her with some news. There's no way I can sleep. That's clear enough ten minutes later. My coat's on and I'm out into the night. Ladbroke Road, pretty, pretty. Squares here and there, all perfect. Clarendon

Road. It's a good thing I put on an extra heavy jumper. Why the hell is Amanda not phoning back? Over six weeks and not a word. Her mobile phone is still working. It's not canceled. I don't give a damn about Beth or Simon or Natalie or Christa. I just want Edith and Amanda to be safe, and I know I can't control events or people. I just want them to be safe. That's all I want, their safety and their health. I'm getting exhausted and cold and all frayed around the edges and have to head back to the hotel.

⚓ Chapter 10 ⚓

It's Wednesday and I'm off to the Circle Line to get to South Kensington with my drawing to leave it with the people at Spiro's.

It turns out Spiro's is across from where Christie's used to be. Inside, a woman with short curly brown hair and lots of lustrous dark skin is sitting at a long, shiny antique table.

She greets me with genuine charm and what sounds like an American accent, in fact a bit of New York. But I won't ask, not today. Her teeth are bright, and her eyes are some sort of golden colour, apparently from tinted contact lenses. As I tell her who I am and why I'm here, she gets on her little phone and rings Alec Stebbins, the person I exchanged emails with. It's warm inside here, so she has the top two buttons of her white shirt unbuttoned emphasizing the long line between her wonderous breasts.

In my tortured state, I don't want to contemplate Sarah of the desk and I have to back up and wait and look around. There are some elegantly framed works, paintings mostly, on one wall with dollops of artificial light from the ceiling on each one. I go and stare at one and then another. The first one has a label that says it's by Gerald Talbot, 1870. Only vaguely know the name and it's a bit generic. Stacks of hay in a field and hardy yeoman and yeowomen shucking around. It's actually well painted, just a dull subject. My sheet of prices that I picked up from Sarah's desk lists it at, twenty thousand pounds. Not exactly expensive.

The next painting is by William Strang and that's certainly an artist I know. It's really well done and I'm staring at it. It's a portrait of a First World War soldier. The price, I find, is eighteen thousand pounds. These things are paintings, I'm thinking, and this is the most expensive gallery in London, and I paid twice that for my drawing.

Alec Stebbins is beside me and I turn to shake his hand. He's young, even nappy-faced, with big, circular blue eyes, in a black baggy heavy woolen jumper with a wooly tie and white shirt beneath, plus perfectly tapered dark grey trousers and plain, undoubtedly expensive black leather shoes. On top, he has shaggy longish sandy hair and chiseled features. We walk into the elevator as he asks me questions. I'm supposed to impress him so he'll want to sell my work of art.

"When did you work in Boston?"

"Until a few months ago."

"You must know Ann Vander then, in that department."

"Yes. I worked for her."

"Right, she's a regular."

I add nothing and he gives me the glance, for the fourth time at least. I don't think he's decided about me yet. He has an accent that's one-part fancy public school, trimmed phrasing and hard consonants, and one part hipster, with the lack of trying and the droopy eyes and mouth. It's a combo that I've seen before way too many times in London.

We make our way into a small version of a sort of Print Room that's about twenty by thirty feet. There's a large table in the middle with desks here and there wedged against walls and black archival boxes filled with prints and drawings on shelves along one wall and a handful of paintings leaning against the opposite wall. There's natural light coming in from a row of long horizontal windows on two sides high up above the shelves. I can see a hallway leading to other rooms with paintings on the walls and in storage bins. I take the drawing out of my briefcase and remove the bubble wrap as he watches, and one other staff member joins us. She's a middle-aged woman in a short, thin olive-green cotton cardigan and jeans. She's thin and curvy and showing it off very well. I get introduced with a distracted wave of Alec's hand and barely a wave back from Liz.

"Anonymous sixteenth century Italian," Alec mumbles as he leans over the drawing and then picks it up and moves his head around it. He hands it to her. "Mathew Andrews attribution," he says to her as she adjusts her glasses, then takes it and gazes. He looks at me.

"It looks quite good. No possible names? From the studio of Parmigianino? No? Matthew's so dogged. That sort of limits its panache, as you know. But it is a fine example and . . ." he strays and turns to the woman. "What do you think?"

"Yes, nice. Did Mathew like it? Maybe he'd like to buy it." She aims a weaning smile at me. She's very cool and attractive and knows it. Her pumpkin golden, sensual hair is almost shoulder length, streaming back easily, with the occasional tuck behind her ears, still with the perfect number of loose trills.

"Mathew was in here, what was it, four months ago?" Alec says to her.

"You bet. For someone's Degas charcoal that he heaped scorn on. He looked around a bit wanting to tell us what shit we sell." She says this to him and they both laugh, facing each other. They actually get a bit overcome by it. Maybe they're lovers, I'm thinking as they laugh and laugh and shake their heads at each other and then gaze around the room, loving that too.

"But we're not above inviting him to our openings, again and again," he says.

She bites her bottom lip, smiling at Alec. "Wouldn't it be amazing to have him at one of those with Gertrude Manning? Can you imagine?"

They laugh again. Hilarious ambivalence is more than I can take.

"Okay, I'm off. Sell the drawing for whatever you can."

"Oh, sorry." Alec turns to me.

I keep walking. "You have my email and phone number."

"Right."

I only catch a glimpse of them watching me leave. Maybe I was stupid and rude. I don't know.

I'm feeling way beyond desperate, walking to the South Kensington Tube stop knowing I have to phone Edith and I have to go back to my Dublin crapflat tomorrow.

Ann Vander goes there all the time. Jesus Christ, she does that instead of her Goddamned job!

Did I just say that out loud?

I can't do that. Meanwhile I have to phone Edith with no news as soon as I get back to the hotel.

My fuming on the Tube is one constant roar between my ears.

I get inside my room, spent.

And Edith's beside herself. "You must tell the police again. This is not right, not right. No, Eric, this is not right. More time and no contact."

I hear a sound after this and it sounds awful, like a muffled wail entering my ear. I wait to give her time, trying to not fall into the hell Edith's in. I have to try to hold onto her.

"Edith, I'm not just saying this, but there's no reason to suppose the worst. In Britain, even in London, the crime rate isn't that high for, you know, anything beyond robberies."

"Oh my God! I have never been so afraid for my child. You, you are older. I don't worry so much about you. But, oh my God, Amanda is such a young girl. Oh my God!" She's crying and it's making me want to smash my head on the wall.

"Edith. Please. No, it's all right. Please, you have to just hold on a bit. I'll phone the police again when I get back to Dublin tomorrow and I'll get in touch with the college administrators at Goldsmiths. I'll do more . . . but, Edith . . ."

I have to stop because my voice is shaking and tears are forming, some dripping, burning. I take a deep breath. "Edith?"

"Yes."

"I shouldn't say this, because it'll sound stupid. I just think she's being stupid. Off somewhere without her phone. Please, Edith. Okay?" I'm twisted a bit, bent over a little, my stomach one tight muscle, glad I'm not in the same room as Edith.

She murmurs and we both sink into a few words of comfort, shallow and frightened as hell, but it's all we have.

Off the phone I slouch onto the bed. After twisting into a fetal position and then getting up and pacing, I lie down again, flat on my back. I can feel a swell of exhaustion slowly take over and a heaviness seep into me and I can't keep my eyes open.

Chapter 11

Dublin is there for me when I fly in. My museum flat will be too as the taxi pulls in. I climb up the stairs and open my door after searching for five minutes for my key, forgetting I put it in my wallet. My brain isn't what it used to be. It's a clammy, cool, breezy April day and I'm sorting through the pile of mail hoping I'll have a letter from Amanda and Jesus Christ, there is one. I rip at it noting the foreign looking stamp.

> *Eric,*
>
> *I'm very sorry to have taken off this way. Please, I know I've caused a terrible amount of distress being out of touch for over a month, but I have written to Mom. It was just that I wanted to get away. It's so hard to explain to you and Mom. I love you both so much and I needed to get away from you suddenly. I couldn't think straight, and I had to be away, really away, for a bit. So I came here, to Berlin. I've heard all the stories about it for years and wanted to see it for myself. Don't worry, I got a job bussing tables. Berlin is so beautiful and exciting. I love it.*
>
> *No phone, no computer, no nothing. Not forever, but, for a couple of months, it's been bliss.*

I don't want you to have to worry about me Eric. You're my brother, not my father. God, I saw how anxious Peggy Avakian was about her brother all the time and it freaked me out when I finally found out why. I'm not sick and in trouble like Peggy's brother. I'm not in trouble at all. I'm an adult and I will be able to take care of myself.

I'll get a phone in a few days. Okay? You and Mom mean everything to me. And, by the way, could you and I stop calling her Edith? She's our mother, not your wife or my sister. I know you felt you were filling in for Dad when he died and I know you've been the best brother anyone's ever had, but I think it's time for us to all move on, together.

I'm so sorry that Mom must have worried, but I knew if one of you knew, you'd both know. I will ring as soon as I get a new phone here, very soon. I love you very much.

Amanda.

I'm standing in the middle of my small room with some paltry white light from my two small front windows, rereading it. Damn, I'm so incredibly relieved. I should be angry. I sit down, crumpling into the cheap blue cover on my small sofa. My fears and exhaustion are slowly converting to acknowledgment. I guess I might want to do the same thing in her place at her age.

What an amazing relief. The letter's dated March nineteenth. It took two weeks to get here for some damned reason. I was in London for part of that.

I walk in circles in my little living room. I have to phone my mother.

She hasn't received a letter yet and she's crying as I read most of what Amanda wrote to me.

"Anyway, she's safe," I say.

"Such a silly, silly thing to do. Young people can be so..."

"Self-assertive and self-absorbed?"

"Oh, and she is in Berlin. Why? It is not safe there. Terrorists attack big cities like that. It makes me so nervous. And the Russians are not to be trusted, Eric. You know that."

"No, the Russians aren't going to attack Germany, Mom. And terrorists, well, we can't expect Amanda to not have a life." My voice is shaking, and all my muscles are in knots.

She grumbles some things, in German, I think.

I say a few comforting things and confirm I'm visiting her over the next holiday, in a week.

⚜ Chapter 12 ⚜

It's Wednesday in my office and my mobile vibrates and buzzes in my jacket pocket. Fumbling only slows me down but I finally look and sure enough it's a weird number and I just assume it's Amanda.

It is.

"Don't yell at me, please."

"When the hell did I ever do that?"

"Never, because I was so perfect."

"Very funny. Perfect at skipping Chapel in school and getting drunk at uni."

"Right. I was perfect at those things."

"You do realize it can be a dangerous world?"

"Um. I realized that a long time ago and rarely even take risks. Not big ones, not anymore. I barely drink alcohol and usually get to sleep before midnight. I just had to get off the grid a bit, Eric. I did have to. I left my phone and laptop in a locker in London. But so please don't worry about me. I have a new phone and promise to stay in touch. I'm sorry."

"Okay. Just stay in touch with Mom. You're right. I'm your big brother. That's all. And you're not sixteen years old and I don't sit around worrying about you. By the way, when you said Peggy's brother was sick and she was anxious about him, what did you mean?"

"Nothing really. I didn't mean he was vomiting."

"Funny. No, it's just you always said she was mum about her family."

"Yeah she was. She just told me one night at the Kings Arms that her brother was diagnosed schizophrenic. She was a bit drunk when she divulged that, I think. But that was why she left San Francisco and got an apartment with her brother."

"Really?"

"Yeah."

I'm jolted by this.

"What?" Amanda asks.

"Uh, I don't know. Why didn't you tell me that?"

"I don't know. Why would I? You hated hearing things about her, and she made me promise to not say anything about that. God, she was always asking me to not tell you things. It's going to make me vomit right now."

I'm unable to process this information about Peggy.

"So, anyway. I love Berlin. I'm probably going to have to leave in a few months and I do still want to apply to Royal Holloway for next autumn."

"Good. That sounds great."

"Are you going to Cirencester anytime soon?"

"Yeah, I am, next week actually. Look, Amanda, sorry, but I'm kind of caught up in this stuff about Peggy's brother, because I think he was the one who took the drawing to the crap dealer and all that. Maybe he got the money for it."

"Yeah, I guess. Sure, she told me she was only getting five thousand dollars from him for the Oxford trip. He went off to some American university."

"Shit."

"What?"

"Why didn't you tell me that?"

"What? She made me promise. She really made me promise."

"Why?"

"What? Why what?"

"Why would she demand you not tell me about this, about her brother?"

"She said it was the most important thing to her. It's very private information and she loves her brother. God, I think he's the only person she does actually care about."

I stand up and walk around the centre of my huge office. Amanda's telling me about spectacular bars and restaurants and art museums and galleries in Berlin. Now I'm looking out at Fitzwilliam Square and drifting through the most verdant of verdant city park space. I barely hear what Amanda's saying. We say goodbye for now.

I'm stuck here, looking out at beautiful things out there, knowing the day will be very, very long. And that will just lead to tomorrow and the next day.

❧ Chapter 13 ❧

Cirencester is almost obscenely luscious in its end of winter damp earth funk. It's Mother Nature about to give birth. I'm so frustrated with myself for not just enjoying it, living in the moment the way Amanda seems to be. The way our mother seems to be. The town's absolutely gorgeous.

And I've just turned out to be a whiner and can't even hide it from my mother.

We're walking the stoney streets of her town like we always do. I just whined at her that I can't afford restaurants anymore. She, naturally, is fine with that, but worried about me. She probably thinks it's some sort of early, midlife crisis.

I've never said a word about the drawing to Mom and I'm not telling anyone about the news from Spiro's.

My walking out of their gallery in a huff might have added some joy for them emailing me they'd try to sell my drawing for twelve thousand pounds. Minus the twenty percent they'd get, I'd only get back a tiny portion of what I paid for the drawing. If they sell it. I hate thinking about all that.

We keep walking, but the Cirencester walls that I usually love are closing in on me. I love Mom but how many walks can we take? Old stone walls and shops everywhere hold nothing for me. I know Mom loves me, but I also know there's some guy out there in town wanting to spend time with her.

"Anyway, Mom, I'm sorry I'm so dull these days. I hope I'm not keeping you from anyone."

"No. What are you saying to me? No-no. I'm here with you." Her face hardens and her eyes are coals. Nothing in or out.

"There's no French man in town you have as a friend?"

"No, I have a friend who is French, yes, but where did you get such an idea?" Still reticent.

"Okay. Sorry. You can have friends, from work, from town. Amanda and I won't be jealous."

"I have such friends. Yes, but they are all with their families too."

She's almost angry and I drop it. We amble home and fix dinner, eat next to the wood stove and drink some wine to enhance our efforts at cheerfulness.

Now I'm up in the attic knowing I'm going to lose my mind if I can't get out of the spin I'm in. I was starting to sweat at dinner down there with Edith, and my chest started to heave, and I had to leave with the excuse I needed some air. And Edith looked alarmed and still did when I got back twenty minutes later and my half-eaten dinner was ready to be heated-up but I said no. And she left it alone. It's one in the morning and I don't know what to do with myself so I'm just standing, looking out the small attic window at the big house next door. The stone exterior is all dusty flat charcoal grey in the night and the moon lit windows are heavy white smears. The trees are just wavering shadows. For some reason, I'm breathing normally now, finally, and the sweating stopped. I took an aspirin an hour ago and that might have helped.

Sitting and standing and looking out the window, after an hour I'm tired and have to lie down.

I wake up after about two and a half hours. I know right away I'll just be awake to do what I want to do. I get up and put my clothes back on, including the thick new jumper Mom gave me for Christmas. I walk to the window. No lights and the sky's overcast, so no moon or stars. It's almost four in the morning. I stretch and look around the room. I think I have to deal with some self-loathing and shame of my own and I'll write to Peggy and seal a thing or two with an apology. She needs to know the drawing's gone and that it's all over and never was a problem for her to worry about. I'm not the fancy Darcy curator I must have looked like before, me all superior in my lofty place, insulated from her mooching kind. Jesus Christ. Scrapping around for paper and a pen, I have to slink downstairs very slowly, and finally, there's some printing paper next to the computer that Mom never uses. There's a pen in the kitchen drawer. I step slowly back up the broad wooden ladder. Mom's radio is on below, playing Brahms, I think. She's always gone to sleep with music or voices. She likes it, she says. I sit on the floor and lean over, with a magazine below the white paper. I don't want to dance around the point, not after all this time and space.

Dear Peggy,

Amanda just let it slip that your brother is ill in some way. I'm very sorry if you didn't want her to tell people something that's clearly private and I can promise you she will keep it to herself and so will I. I pried it out of her. It just suddenly showed me a very decent picture of you and what you were up to in Boston and New York and a couple of months ago in Dublin. I'm just really sorry Peggy. I was so damned rude. There you were going to so much trouble to discreetly say you were sorry to me and I wasn't listening at all. To answer you now -- you clearly have absolutely nothing to apologize for. Just the opposite. You behaved extremely well all along and all of what you did for your brother was amazing.

So why did I buy the drawing? Hubris is one reason. But I also wanted to prove to myself and other people around me that it was okay for me to leave my job. They were all going to tell me I was afraid of success or just plain inadequate if I walked away from so much prestige and responsibility. And money. The job I have now does not have much responsibility, prestige or money. It has a big title but it's boring. It was the price I had to pay, I guess Peggy, if I wanted to, eventually, find a more suitable job and get closer to my family. Remember, living well is the best revenge, and living well can often be in conflict with money and power. I think that was your point.

So other people could do the Boston job better than I could and I could do other jobs better than that one. Now I just have to figure out what's next.

And now, since it has been officially-temporarily attributed, I'm selling the beautiful drawing. Its attribution is an on-going process. Who knows what someone will say about it in fifty or a hundred years? I think it's time for you and me to let it go, though. Okay?

I wish you the very best and think you should apply to Oxford, or anywhere you want. I think you've earned something great.

Yours,
Eric Matheson

After reading it a couple of times, I'm satisfied it's the end of apologies. I slide it into the envelope, write her address on it and put it on the floor near the ladder. It feels strangely good to have it done with. The girl with the drawing is finally gone and I can move on.

❧ Chapter 14 ❧

The first day back from visiting Mom, and I'm remembering
something Dad used to say. I don't seem to remember much
about him, but I remember this. *Count your blessings*. He said
that a lot and somehow, I blocked it. Those sorts of words
would have been immediately rejected as boring and useless
by me as a twelve or fourteen-year-old, but they're ringing in
my ears now. I'm glad to be back in Dublin. It's a gorgeous,
vibrant place and if I don't stop whining, I might as well stop
living altogether.

The issues of the morning seem even more mild than
usual. Most people look bleary and rough-edged from waking up in the early April cool damp air and still somewhat
restrained sun.

At ten my phone rings. It's Casey at the front desk.

"Hi, Mr. Matheson, there's a Peggy Avakian here to see
you?"

The confusion enters me slowly and I mumble, "Okay."

"Will you be coming to the entrance then?"

"Yes." I'm muddled, lost in a time loop. Why is she here
again?

I get up and go out my door. I walk on. Did she get
my letter yet? Did I say the right things in it? I move along
and after a couple of minutes of unconsciously negotiating
stairs and corridors, I enter her space. She's standing there,

like before, like the distant image in my mind, with that herringbone coat and ankle boots. She stares at me. I stand five
feet from her.

"Hi." Her face is flushed, and her eyes swollen.

"Hi."

"Can we talk for a minute?" She looks upset and I'm
thinking I'll just apologize more. I hope she doesn't start
apologizing. I sort of nod and hold out my arm to point as
we head inward, down a corridor towards the same spot we
talked before. We say nothing as we struggle along.

We're standing alone.

"I got your letter." Her face is so serious and she's blushing so intensely, I'm seriously worried about her.

"Good. Sorry," I say.

"You don't have anything to be sorry for . . ." She holds
up her hand to stop me even though I don't think I was about
to say anything. "I have no idea what I've earned. Oxford's
great, obviously, but that wasn't why I came all this way."

"Oh."

"Um, I can't do this anymore. This is the last time I'll
bother you. But I got your letter and I came here to see you
this last time."

"Can't do this anymore?"

"Eric, I have to know if you have any interest in me, personal interest," she says.

I have to take it in. I think I'm in shock and frown and
swallow and my arms feel unplugged.

"Wow. Peggy."

"I'll just go if you say, no. I'm not crazy. Please believe
me." She looks teary.

"No! No, you don't understand." I'm suddenly in a huge
rush, trying to talk. "Things are sort of tangled-up."

"Tangled-up?"

"Yeah, you don't understand how things are now."

"I don't?"

I shake my head for a second, trying to make sense to her. "I'm not really who you think I am."

"You're not?"

She starts to smile. I smile tensely, biting my bottom lip and watch her but I'm speechless, standing very still. She's just looking at me. She's so amazingly gorgeous and I don't know if I can hold back all the urges.

She steps back a little. "Should I go?"

I look at the floor, sucking in air. "Maybe we could get something to eat later and I can tell you about it."

She doesn't respond.

So I look around and lower my voice. "It's just, this job's a lot more form than substance. I don't want to pretend with you."

"Oh." A moment passes and she's wide-eyed, mouth slightly open, seeming to analyze that, analyze me.

I'm standing at attention.

She steps forward, right up to me, up on her toes, and kisses me, and I kiss her back, numbly. I'm stunned. The sudden sensations are broken a little when she steps back a couple of feet.

She says, "It's not your titles I'm after."

And I'm just plain in love with her.

She whispers, "Please, tell me. If you want me to leave you alone, you have to tell me. I won't come back. I promise."

All I can do is grab her and she's on her toes again and for a minute I'm in heaven, in her hair and face and soft wet mouth. She slowly pushes away, kisses me again, smiles into my eyes and I'm gone in hers. She pushes her forehead against mine. Together, we look around. A guard's glancing at us from twenty feet away in a doorway to a gallery. I think his name is Jack. Phoebe's wiping tables and seeing us peripherally and smiling in some way and Peggy and I both just look away, then at each other again. I'm lost in her and she smiles, because she sees that. We're both all erratic grins and breathing.

"I didn't know if I came here again . . ." she says.

I just hold her arm and squeeze it and she looks at where I'm doing that.

I say, "I thought you were bothered about the drawing. That was all."

She's blinking, thinking and I can smell her and I'm ready to grab her again and she says, "Um, I was, and am, but well, things got too tangled-up for me too." She winces and I do and we shake our heads.

"Yeah, the scary drawing. Peggy?" I'm trying to think, to keep her here, to talk. We sit on the bench, but I have to get a grip on the right things. "Are you staying in town?"

"Um, the Jurys in Christchurch."

"Can we see each other for lunch and dinner and talk about whatever we want to talk about? Maybe the drawing can untangle itself that way?"

She just nods, smiling that way I love.

"Great." I gawk at her, grinning and look away to try to keep myself from walking out of the building with her right now.

We stand up. I make an effort to not look at her too intently and I squeeze her arm again, gently. She walks away. I have to go back to work.

And I know it'll be a very long, very dizzy day, but I'll see her at lunch and that's in an hour and a half. What I have to do is tell her how great she is. I didn't in words, and she was standing right here, coming all the way here, again. And she's still right here. I can't believe she's interested. And I guess she is. We'll see what I have to offer her . . . but we'll see.

Printed in Great Britain
by Amazon

87225157R10214